Trout Heaven
by Stephen Michael Berberich

∿∿

A Trail Guide to Landing a Big Corporate Fish
or
How I Found Love in Foster's Creek

This book is dedicated to The Gazette business editor Steve Monroe, who made me a better reporter.

Copyright © 2018 by Stephen Michael Berberich, All rights reserved.

Preface
Clear, moonless evening, June 22

Imagine that last, faint glow of daylight draping across a mountain range along the western horizon.

A green AMC pickup pulls off the interstate to a state highway. Its headlights flash across a farm produce stand.

The driver squints through the windshield for a moment and nods his head in approval upon seeing the stand. He pulls a black bandanna over his nose with his right hand and feels for the truck handle with his left. He tugs down his dark green baseball cap to meet his shades.

Stepping out silently, the driver deliberately leaves the truck door open, all the while watching the movements of a lone, slender figure working behind the produce stand. A single incandescent bulb dangles and sways over a counter by the cash register as the wind begins to pick up.

The old farmer tends to business as usual. He doesn't notice the customer from the green truck at first, any more than he would quickly notice anyone stopping for his fresh fruits and vegetables. It's closing time. The farmer is busy packing away piles of sweet corn and small baskets of tomatoes, peppers, yellow crook-neck squash, and strawberries—his daily final chores.

The masked 'customer' doesn't expect the old man to look up. Old men are slow. Besides, he knows the farmer's behavior. It's been the same every evening for the past two weeks. Each evening at the same time, the driver saw the farmer bending down, packing away produce. Sometimes the farmer was counting his take for the day from an ancient, metal cash register, mostly with his back to the darkened, lonely State Highway Route 7.

The masked man has planned well. He is sure he won't be seen or found out. He won't be nervous or hesitant.

His only concern is what Sassafras County Sheriff Roger Deeds will think of him.

The man closes in swiftly.

"Mister, stay on the other side of the counter, please," says the farmer, bending over a crate of green peppers, seeing only the customer's black sneakers next to him.

Instead of moving away, the masked man steps in closer. "I can't right now, Pops," he says.

Before the farmer can argue, a gloved hand pulls the farmer's head back roughly. The man slashes deeply into and across the farmer's throat with an 8-inch serrated fishing knife.

The killing is swift and neat, with just a muffled "augh" from the farmer gagging on blood in his throat.

The killer walks to the green pickup clutching $413, the farmer's daily take, wrapped around the bloody knife. He left the coins.

Behind the wheel again, the killer laughs maniacally. He reaches across the truck seat for a small object. It will be the perfect clue, a gift especially for Sherriff Deeds, he figures.

As he turns the ignition key, the killer reaches out the window and drops the sheriff's gift to the ground. It's a well-worn crack cocaine pipe. He figures that the sheriff will surely link a senseless killing on a rural road to a crazed druggy from the city.

He checks the road. No headlights are coming. No tail lights leaving. The killer drives off slowly, assured of his perfect killing and perfect getaway as he merges back onto the interstate.

A senseless murder? The killer thinks not.

BOOK ONE – Fool's Memoir Dashed
Tranquil morning, Appalachian woods, July 17

My name is Henry Clyde Ford. You've probably heard of me. I effectively hurt people; put people in jail; bankrupt them; expose them as frauds. I like my work, but I've grown tired.

Along those lines, I have quite a story to tell. I can promise you that.

Before I begin, it is only fair to say that the story I have in mind is not the one I intended to write at first. That was to be a memoir of my triumphs as the famous investigative reporter. That's what people think I am. Deservedly or not, it is my reputation. I've looked forward to writing that memoir for a long time.

But as I sat down at my cabin in the woods early one morning to begin, everything began to change because … well, it's complicated. You'll see.

Instead of keeping a steady line hooked onto my memoir writing, I became haunted by a place called Trout Heaven. It was the kind of place that didn't appear on any maps or in photographs, I'd seen. Yet, in planning to write my memoir, I had been there all along and didn't know it. This place without a place, Trout Heaven, would spawn that far better story I have promised for later on.

On the morning I was to begin my memoir, I was really psyched. *This is going to be my best book*, I thought. *Finally, I can sit down and write it.*

There I was, on the porch of my brand-new log cabin, my sanctuary in the woods pondering catchy titles. Hmm, maybe, *'Untold Truths, and Other Lies! by Henry Clyde Ford.'* Or simply, *'How to Expose Corporate Creeps Just for Kicks'*.

Another Pulitzer? Maybe. I was that confident. This was my best chance to do a memoir at last. All fun. I deserved it, deserved all of it—the log cabin, the solitude, the memoir writing. For 30 years, I'd worked my butt off, more than 25 years of that time as an investigative reporter at the Washington Inquirer in the Nation's Capital. And then, one day I had a brainstorm. I needed a cabin or something to escape from my demanding job. I needed some serenity for a change, maybe a few days a week...maybe a lot more...maybe retire? No, I couldn't yet. Needed the cash. But, I digress.

That morning of my memoir awakening in waiting, I was at peace, sipping my coffee on the porch of my new cabin, ready to begin writing my book, as I said. It was a beautiful July morning in Appalachia. I took a deep breath. I enjoyed the musty forest air. A sweet, moist breeze was drawing off the mature oak and beech trees and whistling through the scattering of pines around me. I admired folds of distant mountain crests plowing up behind each other, each further distant from the closer ones of darker shades of blueish gray.

Yes, I thought, *I would write this book, my third book, on the porch of my new cabin with my new best friend, the river.*

She was mine then, only mine, flowing steadily, whispering softly below me, her massive power muffled by the dense forest. I watched her unbroken movement 50 feet or so beyond a natural forest of huge tree trunks. For a moment, I imagined trout swimming, heads facing upstream, waiting for a mayfly or maybe an immature stonefly, or a midge.

I momentarily flashed back to dad and I, knee deep in waders, fly fishing the Nine Mile Creek in Onondaga County near our home in Syracuse.

Yet, this Sassafras River was much more conducive to the task at hand—mystic, quiet, secluded. Yes, indeed, romancing the Sassafras River was my new love, along with a magnificent view of the forested hills beyond her, beyond my laptop, beyond my work at the paper. The new book was half written in my head. My mind waited eagerly for my fingers to bring it to life.

I had carefully chosen that particular spot for my hideaway cabin.

And so, finally, there I was that morning. Alone. Relaxed. Focused. Ready. *Go Hank, go.* I thought to myself, nearly saying it aloud.

But something compelled me to look up from my laptop once again before starting to type.

Something was not quite right. The atmosphere had changed, seemed different. There was an eerie silence. The rush of the river was the only sound I heard. No chirping squirrels. No song birds. No piercing cries of circling hawks or eagles. No cicadas or even crickets.

I'm naturally a skeptic, being a newspaper man. I thought, *There's something else in these woods this morning.*

Chapter 2

I stood up, walked around the cabin and saw nothing. I decided to go on with the plan. *Well okay, so it's quiet; all the better. Here goes,* I thought. But, at that very moment, as I placed my fingers back onto the keyboard ... THEY appeared!

I put down my coffee on my log table and watched in horror. Completely out of place, yet they were out there, directly in my line of sight, just above my laptop screen, just over my log porch railing, out across my river, dead center-top on the opposite mountainside.

They were several roaring bulldozers. They crawled and growled across the far mountainside like freakish mechanical lions hungry for the kill.

I closed my eyes. I opened them again and squinted. They were still there.

In just a few minutes of hideous roaring and oily stench, the horrible machines were raping Mother Nature and spoiling my hard-earned view of the Appalachian hills, my ideal writing post.

I screamed, *Oh no,* or something. I just know I screamed.

My ideal setting was being brutalized by those freakish monster machines.

Okay, so you might be saying, 'Why was this so devastating? You can still write, can't you? Go ahead and write, fool; what are a few bulldozers to stop you now?'

Stop it! I've given you hints, for Lord Sake. Pay attention, will you!

Sorry for that.

Okay, here's why: At just 50, I was burned out. I had convinced myself that all the stress of my job had earned me some peace of mind. I said that already, I know. But, it is important.

There I sat watching. Before I could begin writing a glorious memoir of my best work—how I had exposed swindlers, wise guys and corporate frauds—I sat stunned as the first cancerous seed of urban sprawl germinated and took root right in MY view, MY woods, next to MY river!

Well, the remainder of the little tragedy of my memoir book may shock or amuse you. Take your pick. The bulldozers were just one thing. Deal with it, right? I am a big boy and, surely, I might have adjusted. But, as shocking as those rude, filthy mechanical beasts were, they were only a foreshadow of several life-altering tempests to come: the alluring chick—excuse me, alluring woman—the death threats, the delicious vacation resort fraud that fell right into my lap, the visitor from outer space, the monstrous lake creatures.

Really. I'm not kidding. And, there will be more.

But, I think all that can wait. Yes, I am sure. Do I have your full attention now?

Chapter 3

Before I get to the heart of the better story to come, let me indulge you with just how humiliated I felt on the day of the bulldozers.

I soon considered that some mighty sick minds sent those first bulldozers out to rape the mountainside. What they created made no sense. It was a 7-eleven store. I was likely the only resident within sight of it, yet there it was, a magnificently unsightly pimple on my landscape view.

Like hornets rapidly molding a paper nest, contractor trucks followed the buzzing bulldozers zipping back and forth in a cloud of dust, rat-tat-tating of nail guns and whining electric saws, leaving me with a convenience store singing softly with recorded soft rock tunes day and night. That construction dust cloud rose from cars and trucks on a dirt road the dozers gouged into the mountain forest to the store, a road I hadn't previously noticed.

Worse, I was also getting paranoid. Did they know me? Did they know I was looking at them? Oh yes. It was surely a deliberate act against me, I feared, to ruin my perfect venue for offering the public a book about my clever newspaper investigations. Was it vindication by one of the corporate victims of my vicious pen? No, I don't ever wield such a pen. Clever maybe, not vicious.

In some way, I would rather that vengeance be at the bottom of it.

But then, the scribe, that's me, my professional side, absolutely groaned when I learned the truth. It was not about me at all. The truth was that they came to that place just by my stupid luck. There were motives yet uncovered. As an investigative reporter, I would suffer dearly by my unforgivable negligence to learn of the plans behind the bulldozers, the 7-eleven, and much more to come.

Before the dozers arrived, I had considered myself lucky to find a 29-acre lot with a view of the Sassafras, though it was more than luck. Being on the staff of the big city newspaper helped. Each Friday for many months, my buddy Nils in the classified department two floors up on the 16th St. Washington Inquirer building, would e-mail ads to me in the newsroom on backwoods Appalachian properties that would be published the next Sunday. That gave me nearly two days of lead time to check out the properties before any readers or even the most slow-witted realtors saw them (Although I've never met a slow-witted realtor; have you?).

I thought I had done my due diligence on those tips. I could often be seen (if anyone noticed) on Saturday mornings driving up and down winding, sometimes dirt mountain roads and walking wooded paths to find a property.

Yes, I did study the properties well. But I failed to study the people, politics or culture of the region. You'd think a newspaper man would have been also reading the local newspapers for re-zonings at least. Dumb.

The only anomaly in the tranquility of my search in these hills, to my knowledge, had been a senseless, violent killing of an old farmer, Emmanuel Smythe, at his produce stand three weeks earlier quite near my cabin, in fact.

I was reading the Blue Hills Gazette on line one slow afternoon at the paper about a family from Ohio that drove by Manny's produce stand at midnight. They were on their way back from a vacation trip to Washington when they noticed that most of the fruits and vegetables at Manny's produce stand were still on display with a single light on. They stopped and found the old farmer in a pool of his own blood under an open cash register.

When I read the shocking story, I wondered if my expectations for pleasant days in Sassafras County were naïve and foolish. The police report said someone had slit Manny's throat for a day's cash intake. It couldn't have been much money because Manny took home the cash to his lakeside farm each day, the story said. County Sheriff Roger Deeds suspected that a drug addict killed Manny. That seemed unlikely to me and it tweaked my curiosity for a moment.

If you've ever spent some time near such an enchanting river as my Sassafras, you can imagine how I fell in love with the Appalachian hills.

I had begun planning my cabin retreat five years before the bulldozers arrived. It was a thoughtful plan by a resourceful newspaper man.

Yet, despite all my real estate searches, site planning and scrounging for extra cash through freelancing writing—don't tell the IRS or my ex-wife—I would be sickened by those bulldozers stealing away my serene writing spot.

I found myself instead watching something entirely different, something sinister, diabolical, and tragic, to disrupt my plans and dreams, right before my eyes. Nirvana turned to heartburn. Some investigative reporter, huh? I didn't see it coming and should have.

As a well-known, savvy journalist, I felt ashamed. I hadn't a clue that county planning officials for months had been mulling over plans for commercial real estate 'development' smack center in my personal serenity view.

The 7-eleven was merely the seed.

Well, before you feel too sorry for me, there's also an important historical context to my story. More than 60 years earlier, a meteorite crashed nearby. I knew about the event when I was searching for property. No big deal, I thought. I didn't worry. It added color. Can't happen twice, right? My beautiful cabin lot, my river view was unaffected. So, when I came upon the region, the fireball from space, though not entirely forgotten by old timers, was considered in these parts to be ancient history.

However, the story I'm about to tell centers on the bizarre link between the random meteorite event and the deliberate invasion of the bulldozers more than a half century later.

Chapter 4

I guess I could have suspected trouble. But, then again, who would have warned me? The only friend I made at the time in those mountains was Manny. Yes, the same old farmer killed at his fresh produce stand.

On my regular drive back to the city on Sunday nights or sometimes Mondays, I often stopped at his fruit and vegetable stand. I enjoyed speaking with that farmer. Manny was a very pleasant local fellow with a leathery wrinkled face. He always enjoyed chatting with me at his Route 7 stand. The tales Manny told were highlights of my weekend trips through the hills in my tiny sports car. He'd always carry the bag of produce I bought to my convertible and place it on the passenger seat with a comment like, "Some spiffy vehicle you got there, Mr. Ford. Can't haul much, eh?"

Old Manny's folksy stories of colorful mountain people would stay with me all the way back to D.C. He knew all the families in the region, their heritage, the distinguished citizens, as well as the unmentionable bastard cousins. "Mr. Ford, yer gonna enjoy folks up here, fer sure," he promised. He'd send me off with his bizarre and colorful tales laughing with a toothless smile full of the beautiful harvests of summer and a friendly handshake. "Yes sir, many a story fer yer newspaper in these parts, Mr. Ford."

I doubted that. But he was well worth the stop each trip.

I had looked forward to enjoying many more chats with Manny when I got settled in; perhaps he knew the trout streams too.

Don't misunderstand. I'm not patronizing the old guy. Oh no; Manny was a hillbilly, but not an ignorant hillbilly. He was up on current events. He even told me he'd read my expose' of the Mondani Seed Corporation scandal. The giant agribusiness made genetically engineered wheat and corn seed that requires twice as much herbicide to reach the high yields touted by its advertisements. "Just ain't natural, Mr. Ford.

Sure, to put growers like me outta biznis," he once said. Manny would be a great friend in my new home away from home, I thought.

As I said, Manny was murdered before my cabin was finished.

Chapter 5

Oh yes, in case you are still with me, waiting anxiously to hear about the meteorite, it was a whopper. The "Miracle Meteorite of Sassafras County" as chronicled by the old Blue Hills Gazette, once inspired a temporary flurry of sci-fi pulp fiction in literary magazines of the day, as well as a spike in astronomy studies by college students.

It caused massive property damage. Newspaper accounts of the day reported that a very large, fiery ball crashed into the mountain valley splashing solid earth up as if it were spackling putty. The violent blast carved a two-mile wide crater between Hope Mountain and Charity Mountains. Not a trace was ever found of 15 people and their homes near the impact. Scientists said they likely just vaporized.

The 'splash' dropped megatons of projectiles of molten earth into the Sassafras River flowing near the meteorite's crater. Soon, the debris had damned the river flow entirely.

Further clippings from the Washington Inquirer story files (morgue) revealed that the U.S. Army Corp of Engineers dynamited the blockage in the river and eventually freed the flow of the river again, but only after the second try.

After the first dynamiting failed to free the river, the Corp regrouped to think over strategy. But they took too long. The river swelled across the valley and spilled into the still-smoldering deep crater left by the meteorite. The water slipped through a new crevice in the raised lip of the crater.

Before the earthen lips of the crater cooled, the river water had filled the circular crater, leaving a 2-mile-wide lake of murky, milky liquid under a thick cloud of steam that stayed over the water and surrounding land for months, according to newspaper reports. The impact crater was estimated to be larger than the Barringer Crater created by a meteorite in Arizona 20,000 years ago. Because this rock hit a mountain valley the resulting body of water was twice the size of the Barringer Crater.

The feds designated a "state-of-emergency" around the crater rim, a sound precaution, because no one knew the mineral nature of the invader rock or even the particular physical matter in the earth there a half century ago, not to mention any manmade matter from dumps, warehouses, barns or small industry.

To this day, there are rusty, faded warning signs still ringing the lake circumference:

ATTENTION:
Due to the instability from
deadly toxins and hazardous
minerals uplifted from the space object
this land is condemned.
KEEP OUT!

That one frightening, federal edict struck more fear into the locals than all the dynamite blasting by the Corp. No one understood why the land was contaminated. Yet, everyone, according to newspaper accounts, obeyed and stayed away, that is, except for an initial rush of out-of-town tourists for a while.

Before the National Guard arrived to restore order, a steady assault of gawking travelers caravanned up Route 7 to see where the meteorite had hit the valley. The tourists were then disappointed to learn that the feds had fenced off all access to the crater. There was absolutely nothing to see by car. The tourists would then disperse to enjoy the beauty of the mountains and valleys. The state chamber of commerce reported that tourism spiked that summer without an explanation.

The forest regrew quickly around the lake.

* * *

When I bought my 29-acre lot, I came up often and simply admired the view of the river by myself, sitting on a fallen log or down on the riverside.

Manny tried to tell me where to go for local gossip, a one-pump gas station, a general store, modest public gathering places like that. But, I didn't.

And then, I unfortunately lost interest in local gossip, being freaked out by Manny's murder. I just wanted to be left alone to write my book, with one essential exception. Someone at those gossip mills may have tipped me off to what was coming, and soon.

I did find Bobby Macintyre, someone Manny recommended to me. Bobby called himself a farmer, but he was mostly very handy with a hammer and nails. His family had lost a majority of their farm to the meteorite crater long ago.

Bobby and his and sons and hired help built most of the barns, sheds and small homes in the area.

Bobby's Johnny and Jeb built my cabin from the rather tacky commercial log cabin 'kit' I'd purchased on line. The logs, roofing and hardware arrived early one Saturday morning on a flatbed truck.

Johnny and Jeb, just 18-years-old, were all country-- earnest, honest, likeable, with a slight streak of independence that even Aunt Bee Taylor on the old "Andy Griffith Show" couldn't have tamed. The Macintyre boys mocked my mail order cabin good-naturedly while they quietly fixed all its flaws and mistakes. Good boys.

As I watched the boys climb like monkeys all over my new structure, little did I know that when they were 15 years old, three years earlier, these very boys had unwittingly set in motion a sequence of events that would dash my plans for a serene nook for writing my memoirs.

Chapter 6

In essence, and in complete innocence, those same precocious 15-year-olds had already tripped the switch that would eventually send in the bulldozers, and more bulldozers, and more, and more.

On the day the boys began my cabin, I gave them a lunch of peanut butter and gooseberry sandwiches on rye. As we sat on the tailgate of their pickup, they told me why things around there were beginning to change and change rapidly.

They said one cloudy but warm Sunday morning three years earlier Jeb and Johnny snuck out of church and went down to the lake, now called Crater Lake. "It was about the fishing, was all, Mr. Ford," one of the boys told me. They said that they had had a sneaky scheme and it could not wait a day longer, he said.

The scheme was hatched inadvertently by their father Bobby Macintyre. The Saturday night at the family's small 15th birthday party gathering of the boys' friends, he took two long packages from his truck and presented them to Johnny and Jeb. They were delighted to unwrap brand new Simano fly fishing rods and reels. The boys love trout stream fishing more than anything else in their world.

Jeb said, "These were small fly-fishing rigs, Mr. Ford, but the slick, ball bearing works, strong drag and all were for catching trout say, up to five to seven pounds."

I was intrigued.

They told me the rigs were sturdy though and perfect for catching rainbows or browns so large with drys or nymphs you'd think the fish were steelheads or wild salmon. "Mr. Ford, we decided to spin them out at home first. You know, into that condemned lake. Why not?" said Jeb, "It was our property and right next to the church. But, I'm tellin' ya, Mr. Ford; those damn rainbow trout in that lake were bigger, much bigger … and strong! One took Johnny's bait, line and rig—reel and all, right outta his hands."

"I think you lost me. Nymphs must be immature bugs, right? But drys? Why use them on the static surface of a lake?" I asked the boys.

"Oh sorry, guess you aren't a fisherman," said Jeb. "Dry flies are usually fished on the surface of a stream, as you may know, sort of in and out, bobbing because they don't absorb water and look like adult insects.

"Yes," I just said, not to slow their story.

Johnny continued the story, "In two minutes of casting into that mysterious lake, the biggest rainbow trout we ever saw jumped one of the drys and commenced to run the hook deep, too deep to catch and pull back."

"Sounds exciting."

"Yeah, Mr. Ford," Johnny said with a grin, "you should go fly fishing with us, or maybe super trout hunting on the lake. That's what we call it; big-game safari in the deep."

"No thank you. I've got a book to write and I'm really anxious to start. Maybe later. How deep is the Crater hole anyway?" I asked for no reason.

They didn't know; no one does, they said.

And that was my introduction to giant trout living in that lake, but not my only invitation to go fishing. I'd be doing that soon, for a lot of reasons.

They continued to fill me in on what happened that fateful Sunday morning when they slipped out of the church.

Their church was near Crater Lake and close to the Macintyre home. The teenage boys schemed all night that they would sneak out during the service. They would cast those new poles a few times just to feel the action. Maybe they'd get lucky and reel in any kind of pathetic fish that might have slipped in from a little inlet to the river that opens in storm deluges. They didn't want to catch fish, just break in their birthday gifts.

At daybreak that Sunday, they hid their birthday gifts in the shoreline bushes at Crater Lake.

Rumors had circulated for years that, yes, there were fish in the lake, but that they were almost certain to be toxic and disfigured. That did not matter to the boys. The rumors just added to their excitement, they told me. Their plan included sneaking back into church after testing their gear. They would melt back into the congregation just as folks were walking out an hour and a half later.

As they planned, the boys snuck out of church unnoticed as services began. They ran around the building behind the windowless wall where the alter and choir stood inside. They climbed up the rim of the meteorite crater, and slid down the mud embankment of slippery reeds on their butts. At a pile of rocks at the lake's edge they retrieved their prized fishing poles.

They were not concerned about getting seen. Other than a government-prohibited 25-foot buffer around the toxic lake, Jeb and Johnny were on their own property, the small part of their farm left after the meteorite crash many years earlier, which had wiped out profitable farming for their grandparents and pushed their family into the home improvement business.

Most of the good citizens around the region still believed the government's original warnings that their meteorite-created lake contained high levels of radium and heavy metals. Do teenagers care? Not on your life. All they knew was that the lake was off limits to everyone else and that it was next to the church. Perfect. They wouldn't get caught! No one would be on the lake, except two precocious teenage boys with new fishing gear.

Their church, the Our Sacred Lady of Cosmic Heaven, was built years after the meteorite hit. The building materials were donated by the good intentions and contributions of folks respecting God's celestial hand in reworking the land, river, and lake with a mighty fist to terra firma. It was the ultimate confirmation of their fear of The Lord, it was said among the congregation.

And yes, the unwavering faith of the people for the power of the Lord was exactly what fast-talking Rev. Gideon

Sugarman counted on when he marketed a divinely inspired building fund more than four decades earlier.

The Sunday when the two devilish boys snuck out to "fish with Jesus Christ our Savior," as the reverend would later say, was a day when his flock would receive another astounding miracle, the miracle of the giant fish.

Down at the lake, only five minutes after the boys had cast their lines, they began to catch gigantic fish. In a bit more than an hour, Jeb and Johnny reeled in 36 gigantic rainbow trout. The biggest one was a state record, 35 inches, 23 pounds.

The boys ran to the church. They needed their father's help to carry all those fish to Bobby's pickup. When they ran back through the church doors out of breath, most of the congregation had departed, but Bobby was still standing there, as was Rev. Sugarman.

The very next Sunday Reverend Sugarman preached with all his heart and soul that "God, my beloved, is not finished with the good folks in these hills and valley." He knew before anyone, that a new miracle at Crater Lake was why the Macintyre boys were delayed in returning to church.

It took many months of public and closed-door discussions at the County Zoning Board sessions before officials fully grasped the awesome commercial promise of the Divine fish. They saw dollar signs swimming all over the suddenly not-so-toxic lake.

Chapter 7

The Macintyre boys further told me that word spread of the divine miracle of the giant fish. Local reporters showed up. All the fuss over big fish eventually got quiet soon, they said. The story faded in the local press.

I suggested to the boys that government regulators might have killed interest by playing up the quarantine. They said their dad thought so too.

But sure enough, the county planning and zoning board had become abuzz with activity, possibilities, visions of massive development money pouring into the remote area, with the multitude of giant fish the principle tourism currency.

Yes, I knew of the meteorite. I then knew of the giant fish—the Mac boys told me about—and then I knew of the 7-Eleven store on the opposite hillside. Still, I thought, *It's a forest. Why would there be more development? Why worry over a new traffic light, or a new barn, or a new convenience store? Maybe I can get my milk and eggs at the little store.*

But it would not stop there. Quietly, some say mostly secretly, the county was plotting new tax-reduction opportunities for any new businesses drawn there because of the record-size rainbow trout. I'll paraphrase Genesis: Fishing begets camping. Camping begets hiking. Hiking begets rafting, boating, dining, and star gazing. And, don't forget skiing. And on the umpteenth day, the greedy did not rest as God did on the seventh day.

The local bureaucrats must have been salivating over new tourists coming to the county. The pupils of every local official's eyes turned to tax dollar signs, even before I settled on my property purchase—all leading to those bulldozers' first appearance that fateful morning as I settled myself quietly into writing another Pulitzer Prize winning book.

The first stinking bulldozers and the little store were just the harbingers of far worse insults to my view. Boy, did I ever feel dumb. And thoroughly defeated ... for a long while, at least.

Chapter 8

The boys built my cabin in just a few days. They graciously received shipments of rustic furniture I had ordered from Mountain View Log Furniture and put the stuff together. I found it assembled inside when I arrived the next weekend. I could not thank them enough but I didn't' enjoy myself there. The bulldozers had been carving and clearing all around the 7-Eleven. It was depressing.

I could not write. I returned by Saturday afternoon to my Capitol Hill townhouse.

After a month I returned to the cabin on a Friday night late, still hoping for regaining my peace of mind. I woke to bad news.

On the mountainside more building was underway around the convenience store, a lot of it. My snooping instincts perked up. I called the Macs again to see what they knew. Bobby said he heard that the county officials were planning a shopping center and a hotel because of the "goldmine" in taxes they sniffed in Crater Lake. And then he laughed and said, "Bring it on, brother. We'll take 'em all fishing. We have the only access all the way down there to the stone walls of the lake."

I was floored.

Bobby asked if I'd thought over fly fishing, "The boys keep asking me," he said.

I decided to take up the Macintyre boys' fly-fishing invitation, just to get my mind off my disappointment.

Johnny and Jeb came by early that Sunday with enough gear for ten fly fishermen. It was a perfect diversion for me, since I was already contemplating selling my property and splitting before the giant fish build a city around me, something I laughed about at the time with the boys.

Instead of dwelling on big worries, or the stress of investigative reporting at my job, a day of fly fishing seemed perfect. Conversely, I could at least dwell on reminiscing about the days with my dad in Onondaga County.

Fly fishing done right is nothing short of a pure art form. It is all about the artificial 'flies' you wrap on the end of the line and how they bait the fish to bite them. Fooling fish with bits of chicken feathers and fur wrapped around a hook with a little tinsel is magical. A streamer fly, as it's called, weighs practically nothing. It takes a thicker line that the nylon on a spinning rod with much more weight to it for casting as far as 100 feet and usually about 35 feet. You assume the fish will not spot the thick, weighted line. Between it and the fly is a thin, leader line of nylon, virtually invisible in the stream, while the fly is left alone on the surface or just under, appearing to be alive in the whirling water current.

I rode with them in their pickup into the woods on a small country road to one of the Sassafras River's many feeder streams. A weather front on Saturday had passed, clearing the air and opening an azure blue sky with puffy white clouds. It felt good to get away and to be with a few friends in the region at last.

During the half-hour ride I tried but could not get them to talk about the rumors of developing the mountain side in my cabin view.

No time for that stuff, we are goin' fishing, was their attitude.

We found the stream of gorgeous clear water, rippling over random rocks and reflecting the green surroundings where the current was steady and smooth. The stream was running at a brisk but not too rapid rate for spotting any fish that may be foraging two to four feet below the surface. Small trees overhung much of the stream edges, an intriguing advantage to the fisherman, my dad would say. Some huge boulders interrupted flow periodically both up- and downstream. Another advantage to the fisherman. Pools downstream of a big rock can be deeper from the churning current and good hiding for trout, as are the cover of overhanging branches. Tangling your line in a branch is always a hazard however.

They handed me a 9-foot, 6-weight fly rod, one of Bobby's. "This one has really fast action," one of them said. The boys then stood side by side staring at me, waiting for a reaction.

I stopped playing dumb and admitted, "Okay, okay. Don't worry. I know what action means. It's flexible under stress, I guess. Isn't that right? Best with dry flies, right?"

The rod did feel good to the touch, if I recalled from my youth when I had a bamboo rod. This was made of graphite with cork on the narrow handle and, they were right, a lot more 'action' than a bamboo rod.

I couldn't remember if I still had that bamboo beauty. Oh yea, my ex, Janet, has the house and anything in it, likely the fishing rod too, that I once called mine. I cursed the thought of her new boyfriend using it.

Bobby's rod was light—maybe just a few ounces—and allowed quick strokes as I practiced. I was loving the day already. It is a sport of quiet solitude, just what I needed to get my anger under control over the bulldozers from hell.

The boys made sure I was comfortable and familiar with the technique, which I was.

I felt that they looked at me as a clown dressed in a fly-fishing costume of chest-high waders, a landing net clipped to my shoulder strap, Bobby's green camo wind breaker much too big for me with hood, and a black fishing belt holding a waist pack with a sheathed knife, small box of Bobby's dry flies from his big yellow tackle box, insect repellent, and a water bottle. Clunky, for sure. And, of course, they had put a goofy looking floppy hat on me to further camouflage me behind my oversized, Polarized driving sunglasses. All I needed was a big red nose that honked and a squirting flower on my suspenders. The devil in me let them heap all that on me, knowing they were playing me.

They seemed skeptical, even smirky as I got set to cast. They watched me with critical expressions as I tied one of Bobby's favorite flies to a leader and pulled about 12 feet of fly line out past my rod. Then I pulled a lot of line off the real and held it coiled in my left hand. I wristed back and forth in a flicking motion with my right arm and slung the rod tip up stream. I was lucky, though nervous. The fly line flew majestically through the air in a long casting arc parallel to the water but not yet hitting the water only rocks or branches. I repeated several times, and gained confidence as the boys' smiles broadened.

After more false casts than I needed (showing off then), I made the final cast, allowing the fly, leader and line to rest gently to the water some 50 feet away. Not a champion cast, by any means, but good enough to qualify as a fly fisherman in the eyes of my resident experts, now gawking with their mouths wide open.

"I'll be doggone, Mr. Ford. You were hustling us," said Johnny. "Come on, Jeb. We better start fishing before this city fellow shows us up."

Jeb told me to stand straighter for a more accurate cast. After that I was on my own.

Before they walked down stream and the three of us separated I anticipated for maybe hours, I asked them about what Bobby had told me about the county development plans, "Do you boys worry?" Maybe my voice was too loud over the running stream and echoes in the valley, I thought, as they seemed to cringe.

"About what?" asked Johnny.

I lowered my voice and took a step toward them. "About what I was talking about riding over here. I hate all that talk of the construction of a shopping center and hotel, whatever, just in my line of sight at the cabin."

When they seemed to grasp my serious tone suddenly, the boys slugged themselves back out of the stream in all their gear, holding their poles over their shoulders. They stood with me again, each replying grudgingly.

Johnny said, "Mr. Ford, you are a good guy and I'll tell you the truth. Even though we are in a good spot to benefit off charter fishing in Crater Lake, things are happening that may not be good for the people, especially landowners here abouts. You best sell now and find another place to write your book."

Jeb countered, "No. I don't think you need to leave. I like your spot. Keep it. Write your book. See what happens, I say."

Johnny looked disgusted and said, "We know there is going to be a lot of interest in the lake. A hotel is coming. Who would have ever? Things are out of whack, Mr. Ford."

I asked, "Do you know anything else that your dad may not know or is not willing to say about the people behind the development?"

They looked at me as if they saw the devious reporter emerging from my eyes as we stood in such an idyllic scene, loaded for fishing. They were reading me correctly.

Jeb said for both of them, while giving his brother a nod, "We heard crooks from up north are bribing county people to get that hotel sited. They are dead serious, people say. Several landowners around the lake have gotten calls from Boston and New York, asking if they would sell part or all of their property."

"Yeah, they want to get to the lake," Johnny added.

I held up my hand in a stop signal, "Hey, wait a minute. Crooks?"

"Well," Jeb said, "that's what people think."

"Any evidence they are doing things illegal? The crooks?"

"No. Well, we don't know," Johnny said. "People just say they don't seem to be the kind of people we want around here. Pushy and rude, some say."

"So, it is hearsay?"

"Not the hotel. That is definitely sliding right through red tape and bullshit, people say," Johnny shrugged and took steps back into the stream. And that was that.

They jumped rock to rock along the stream edges downstream and soon disappeared around a bend, still chattering. I had made my impression as a hack fly fisherman, but was lucky. I had not fly fished since my teen years back home with dad. I had also worried them. And I shouldn't have. I'll make it up to them someday, I decided. But, they had said enough for me to soon go on another kind of fishing expedition: into the county records ASAP.

Back to fishing, I tried to see the streamer sink slowly beneath the water surface. It pulled the near-invisible leader with it, I felt grateful for the moment. It was easy to see the wings of mayflies on the surface as well as any stirring of the trout because most of the meandering stream, say 20- to 25-feet wide at points, was shaded by overhanging trees and summer flowering viburnums and the dull brownish red berry clumps of climbing bittersweet. The stream was wide enough and slow enough that morning to spot an occasional trout surfacing. I made up my mind not to recast into the circles they left behind. Too much effort. Rather, I would soak in the environment around me.

Soon, I settled on Jeb's advice to stick it out on the mountain and write my memoirs, no matter what happens around my cabin and beyond. I'm not one to be scared off!

That day for convenience, the boys let me use their father's very full and diverse tackle box. We had left it hidden in reeds near the stream. I returned to it several times to try his different flies.

It occurred to me that any fishing through the county records won't be any more difficult than trying to comprehend Bobby's tackle. Thanks to the American Fishing Tackle Manufacturers Association's classification system, artificial flies range in a multitude of weights recommended to catch fish ranging from small stream trout to sailfish in the ocean. And no kidding, I think Bobby had them all, but I was sure in no particular order, and thus putting to shame the good intentions of the AFTMA. The association also classified line weights. Bobby had also stored many of them in that heavy yellow box.

I was warming up to Sassafras County again.

At times that day I simply waded in the shallow waters, ignoring my fishing line. I watched the squirrels and common grackles squawking over acorns and huge 'V's and 'W's of geese flying north, low over the high country. Their gaggling often muffled out all other sounds in the forest and surely froze the movements of any trout against rocks or under brush.

That I couldn't verify, but the fish soon returned to sniff my line once the gaggling stopped.

I chose an imitation mayfly called a Wetwing in Bobby's box because there were so many real bugs fluttering near the stream surface. He had frequently tied deer hair around a hook to simulate the mayfly fluttering. Within the tackle box he had arranged four smaller flip open aluminum fly cases with a dizzying assortment in each.

I tried imitation flies of bugs I hadn't seen in those parts—grasshopper, midge, caddisflies and others.

But the homemade flies worked best. Bobby made flies to look like no insect in particular. My dad always said there are no rules to fly selection and every rule you hear about can be broken. It was not unlike the government's Security and Exchange Commission's rules of reporting financial statements, which I often researched for my corporate crime investigations.

The boys had also reminded me what dad said about stream trout. They often like to stay in their spots where food is plentiful and easy to forage. The trick is to find those spots, sometimes called fishing 'holes'. We agreed to move further apart when we came into view of each other and, in that way, would keep a lookout for those feeding spots.

It was a strategy I embraced because not having fished there I could not read the water hydraulics and currents well. But I was in good hands with Johnny and Jeb.

Find the fish is the first step to catching them, they repeated. Curiously, Johnny also commented that finding the fish is not a problem with the Crater Lake trout. "They seem to find you," he said with a nearly inaudible snicker.

Yes, all my boyhood joy of fishing in the woods was revisiting me. There was more to my new hideaway than the cabin. There were wonderful countryside streams and woods around every hill slope.

Late that afternoon, the boys found me again with my three 14-inch rainbow trout fish in my basket; half the number they each had landed. They explained some of the flies I didn't recognize in Bobby's box that were famous. Dave's Hopper that looks like a grasshopper, they said (Could a fooled me!); Green Hair Frog for bass, and Salmon Fly for, well...

Chapter 9
Fast forward three years and to paradise lost

During the next three years after the first bulldozers arrived to scar my mountain view, an inconceivable sprawl of commercial "development" followed. The initial wound to the forest for the 7-Eleven festered into huge gashes of no particular pattern into the earth, which would then give birth to an excuse for a new, yet gaudy town. Yes, an entire town of tacky structures, oozing up from the hills week-after-week like grotesque mushroom heads twisting and distorting up through a soft bed of green puffs of pine and spruce from my viewpoint.

The tiny, perhaps tolerable, convenience store was eventually dwarfed by a motel on 35 acres. It was a franchise of Vacation Inns and Resorts, Corp., out of Massachusetts. The motel offered fishing guides and fishing lessons on a tiny pond they built, yet the Inn was a mile from the lake. The motel's only access to the lake was a partnership with the Garrett Family, which owned a small section of the lake's shore—a deal without any logical relation to the agricultural zoned Garrett lands.

The presence of a vacation-oriented franchise led to the commercial development cancer metastasizing in the forest across the river from my cabin. As a result, I didn't spend more than one or two weekends every couple of months there. My disappointment with my property was a big blow, but the beauty and serenity of Sassafras County drew me back from time to time. I fly fished with the Mac boys again in a different feeder stream, but then they got busy with their fishing pier construction on Crater Lake and I didn't fly fish again. I was too uncommitted to buy my own gear.

Instead, I'd sometimes drive past the lake and see a few boats going after the fat monster trout. I'd then continue to the streams Jeb and Johnny showed me. I'd sit on a rock and spot the rainbows in the water. They were the sporting trout, the migrating trout, the natural rainbows in the stream, not like those overgrown fat lake trout.

There's one, I'd say out loud in my solitude. *I see you there hiding all those lovely stripes of pinks, greens and grays.* I'd watch and pretend I was him. *Keep my head upstream. Look up. Stay steady.* Rainbow trout can see anything moving almost 100 degrees ahead. This one's bottom was way down in a pool of slower water. I imagined him saying, *I'm staying here where any bugs passing I'll see, and then munch.* And, bam! He jumped and slammed into one, nearly out of the water. He fell back, and then let the current roll him a bit downstream toward me. I saw his rainbow-like sides. A beauty. One gulp and he was back in his spot in the flat pool of slower water, same spot. Trout are very territorial.

This was almost as much fun as fishing. The riffling of the current just past a boulder created this fish's 'bugging' spot, deeper water to be camouflaged by the gray water and green plants reflecting from above.

However, a trout can see well up through the surface into the air to catch an insect or see a predator. So as not to spook him, I waited for him to snatch another bug, tumble about before I retreated to my car on the county road. Rainbow trout are nervous fish. Maybe that day was a poor way to make a new friend, but it beat looking at the scraping and scarring construction on the mountain side across from the cabin.

Those moments meditating by a trout stream also gave me ideas for my book, which I'd jot into the reporter's notebook I keep in my back pocket at all times.

Back into the dismal cabin though, those notes though did not translate into good copy in my computer at the cabin. It was no longer just my river, no longer my mountain. I no longer looked out my cabin windows. I didn't sit on my nice log porch because I couldn't look at the powerful river without anger. Yes, I did stay angry. I stayed in the cabin, as Jeb had counselled. But I was not doing very well writing.

Three years of a weekend here and there produced rough chapter drafts with no flare, according to my daughters who were in college then. Stefani and Sierra enjoyed proofing copy for dad, but their reviews of my memoirs were harsh, more like my ex-wife might have offered. I knew they were right. I should have forgotten it.

I was getting lonely at my getaway. Maybe I'd invite my daughters up for some fly fishing, like we did with my father, their grandad, when the girls were little. Maybe on spring break? No, what was I thinking. Pretty college girls passing up time at a resort with people their own age for me? Not likely. My ex had brainwashed them, I was certain, that I was the problem in our marriage.

Therefore, when I came up, I was always alone at the cabin. I couldn't even glance at the ugly clutter of modern fast retail development. For your entertainment only, a partial list:

Shoney's and Denny's restaurants, a liquor store, a clothing outlet for outdoor wear, a Mobil and an Exxon gas station, a Baskin-Robbins, three gift shops, a CVS pharmacy, an Ace Hardware and bait shop. And, smack dab in the middle of my then-blighted view, an all-night McDonalds with a 16-foot neon blinking yellow arrow flashing alternately with equally large twin golden arches. The prominent landscape feature I see as I drive down the lane on my side of the opposite hill to my cabin is a bright neon Big Mac with two all-beef patties, special sauce, lettuce, cheese, pickles, onion, on a sesame-seed bun. The most disgusting part is the special sauce oozing out like bloody snot from the bun.

That bit of Mickie D theater-of-tack is the first thing anyone would see from my bedroom window, not that there was anyone looking out of my bedroom window except me. Oh yes, I did tell you the obvious, I think: I'm a middle age guy addicted to newspaper work leading to divorce, as I said. Of course.

Chapter 10

My plan for the get-away cabin in the woods also involved, though I denied it, was clearing my head of that divorce. It had been ugly. She cheated on me first, I think, unless you count my 25-year love affair with the newspaper and near total neglect of my wife and daughters, according to her.

The her is 'Janet.' She got sick of my long hours at the paper and lack of passion at home. So, she told her feelings to her attorneys, who in turn told me.

I hadn't a clue, nothing we ever discussed.

Janet's indiscretion was hooking up with a loser she met at our daughter's middle school PTA meeting, which I missed. The football coach of all things. My dignity would bear a college or high school coach, but not a middle school coach, for God sakes. Janet, then with her new squeeze, hired a gum shoe to trail me. Surely, I was cheating, she must have thought. She needed some proof.

But I wasn't cheating. I'm a news addict and as such I leave quite a boring trail. I do 95 percent of my reporting from telephone interviews at my desk at the Inquirer, only going out to confront and expose some white-collar sleaze-ball criminal, usually about six of those a year. That's the great fun of it—the payoff—but I do all the set up for my stings in the newsroom.

Janet figured—I guess like most women do—that all men will slip up eventually.

I finally did, but only sort of, in my opinion—at our annual unofficial Washington Inquirer holiday party at the Dubliner Tavern on F St. NW. It was a forgivable mistake. I don't think it should have counted.

It was part Janet's fault because she refused to attend those holiday parties after she'd endured her first and only one with too many drunken, frustrated, overweight scribes sharing too many loud, filthy jokes and insider stories that the spouses didn't get anyway.

My slip up was after one of those parties. I was drunk, and stupidly went with one of our grad school interns to her home.

I must have felt like I was the 'seducee,' not the seducer. "I just love all your pieces," she said to me, at the party, over and over, as she pouted and posed in a flimsy thing that was almost a dress. Don't wonder about the color or anything because I only remember her shape within it.

The boys at the paper loved how all *her* 'pieces' were put together, though no one ever brought up the distraction of our smokin' hot intern into conversation in the newsroom. Nose to the grindstone at the office and all that.

Anyway, the girl and I were both foolish and I was sorry the next day, and glad at the same time to get by with it cleanly, I thought.

Then, I learned that I didn't get away with it at all. Janet's sleuth friend snapped photos of my hand on the pretty young thing's bottom as we were walking and laughing into her apartment building.

I finally limped home at 6:00 a.m. The girl had worn me out. When I woke on our living room couch, the sleuth's snapshots were in an envelope on my belly, even a few he had taken between slats of vertical blinds in the intern's bedroom. Nailed.

After the divorce, what little savings I managed on my salary, after alimony and child support—went into my cabin property. The one soon to be engulfed by sprawl, a 'country-roads-take-me-home' down scale version of the Vegas Strip.

It may be hard to believe that big fish spawned all the "development" of the town across the river. But, don't underestimate the promise of easy trout angling among fisherman. One day, from what I could see with my Nikon Travelite binoculars at least, the new resort inn on the far mountain was crawling with fisherman and fisherwomen, loaded with gear.

I learned from Bobby Mac that Rev. Sugarman had sold shoreline tickets to the church property, a sliver of land

Bobby Macintyre's father donated to the reverend for his church. Rev. Sugarman held a fishing fundraiser for a new pipe organ and billed it as an annual event. It was moderately attended, some 25 boats or so.

Bobby put an end to it after the inaugural event led to brawls and a half-acre of woods burned from campfires left burning by drunken participants. He met with Sugarman and mitigated the reverend's intent for an annual event by making a $10,000 donation for an organ.

Meanwhile, as angler tourists landed monstrous fish, the feds used the budding tourist trap as the excuse to widen the new town's highway. They called it "additional supplemental economic bonus stimulus funds" to the state, which the governor said, was always in need of more jobs, like it was a mantra of his government. That's how the Blue Hills Gazette reported it anyway.

Substantial federal muscle and tax breaks diminished the local, don't-tread-on-me resolve of county executives and mayors for environmental preservation. Most of those officials were voted out by the next election, replaced by pro-development candidates who promised and delivered with lower taxes, jobs, and better services.

At the time, the state Chamber of Commerce liked to brag that Trout Heaven—yeah, that's what they named it—was the fastest growing town in America. Lucky me; I was part of history. I suspected that Bobby Macintyre knew all along about hidden plans for the new town, much more than his hint of a "possible hotel."

He was waist deep into already creating a pier complex. When we first spoke three years earlier, he anticipated big business from the town, still on paper. So, he knew something. That was then. This is now. I've grown accustomed to resisting local intrigues, like what really happened to Manny, or who are those 'crooks' at the 'hotel,' as Jeb once referred to them. No not my business, not yet anyway.

Chapter 11

I stopped writing from my front porch, as you can well imagine. I wrote at my kitchen table, secluded inside my cabin nearly every weekend with a magnificent view of my mini-fridge.

Rationale? I could still write, just not outside—too depressing--even if I face away from the new resort town across the Sassafras River—my teaming, double-crossing former best friend.

I hid in the cabin. However, I still fought on to write the book. The new plan: get the memoir book done quickly, then dump all memory of the stupid cabin idea, sell the property and never come near this place again. Besides divorcing Janet, whom I still loved, it was the biggest disappointment of my life.

Now that the cabin was no longer my paradise, let me tell you what I did to punctuate that conclusion: I took down my original cotton curtains—colorful, yet ruggedly masculine ones, with images of ducks and antlers of some type of fabric art completely out of proportion, but funky. I replaced them with thick brown Army-surplus canvas. The canvas lets in not one-foot candle of light from the all-night McDonald's and lets me sleep. I nailed the canvas blinds tight on the window frames to keep anyone from seeing inside.

Remember that additional-supplemental-economic-extra stimulus-for-the-promotion-of-business-in-Appalachia money from Washington, D.C.? It provided money to construct a hideous red steel bridge over the river from Trout Heaven to the top of my little county lane, not 50 feet from my log porch, yeah, that one, yes—the one-time seed bed of my germinating Pulitzer-Prize-winning best seller.

Was I bitter?

I thought so for a while. But, not for long. One day, an angel from heaven crossed that bridge.

Chapter 12

I was sleeping in on a Saturday morning after 10 a.m., as usual. I'd been up writing late at night at the kitchen table, accompanied by my post-divorce buddy Johnny Walker Red whiskey. The two of us had been at the laptop writing all that Friday evening, after I had worked a full day at the paper. Johnny, me and the mini-frig wrote chapter three, "The Symmetrical Engineered Food Hype," in my memoir of exposés.

In the morning, with half-opened, watery eyelids, I looked forward to proofing what Johnny and I had written, anticipating major revisions to my drunken keyboard pecking during the final minutes before I dozed off at 3 a.m. or so.

The chapter was from a story I had reported as a young, brash newbie at the Inquirer. It was well known. Even Manny knew the story, remember?

Giant agribusiness Mondani Corp. of St. Linus, Kansas tricked a Green Peace splinter group, the Green Seed Movement, into filing a law suit over estimated yields of the certain crop seeds, which Mondani marketed. The crops were the company's miracle cultivars of pest-resistant genetically modified corn and wheat cultivars.

I learned through former employees near the company's experiment farm that Mondani deliberately released inflated data from test figures. The advocacy group publicized the figures as the basis of false advertisement.

But Mondani suckered the group into publicizing experimental yield figures that were not from field tests. Field tests would have simulated real farm conditions. Instead, the tests were highly controlled in greenhouses.

The Green Seed Movement took the bait. They were trapped by Mondani into believing the tests were done in fields, exposed to insects and the fungus and bacteria that cause plant diseases. But instead, the greenhouse tests were conducted by Mondani with heavy fertilizer applications, sterile soil, and of course, no bugs or fungi allowed. The greenhouse tests are a common phase of crop breeding and experimentation, roughly parallel to testing a cancer drug in mice before patients.

The controlled tests gave the company estimates of potential harvest limits without causing crop failures. Those test results were useless to farmers and not normally publicized by seed companies. The company allowed the figures to leak to the public, however.

Green Seed Movement sued, incorrectly assuming the data was from field tests. GSM in turn paid a public relations firm to imply fraudulent practices by the bully agribusiness.

Moreover, the giant corporation milked the law suit along until the complainant, Green Seed, was broke. My series exposed Mondani's deception and led to the resignation of the corporation's entire board and its CEO. Yes, Mr. Ford strikes again!

But hold on: I also exposed the Green Seed Movement as a fraud. It was being funded by competitive seed firms in California, which caved after they figured out Mondani's trap. The competitors cut off funding to the fake advocacy group and the legal battle.

I sat at the kitchen table gratified. In fact, despite being hung over nearly every Saturday, it felt good to have written down the back story on how I researched and wrote the series on Mondani and Green Seed and similar exposés. It was fun, to put the real skinny on paper of my experiences in sorting out the truth in such a story. "Boy, was I good in my prime back then," I said to the little running Johnny Walker on the empty whiskey bottle, as I stumbled back to the bed and fumbled about for my pants on the floor next to it.

I staggered into the kitchen with foggy vision and sparkles of the worst hangover I could ever remember before I was in my 50s. I sat staring at each drip in the coffee maker, begging it to hurry up with my caffeine fix.

Between thunderous drips, something else caught my ear coming from the next room. I called into the living room. I heard it again—a very faint knock at the front door of the cabin.

"Who the hell is that?" I said out loud to myself. No one knew the location of my hideaway, not ex-wife Janet, not my editors, not even my fondest people on earth, my daughters, Stef and Sierra.

As I approached the door I heard a woman ask, "Mr. Ford?"

The lady's voice seemed too passive to be a sales person or a Jehovah's Witness.

"Yes?" I said through the wooden door, curious as to who would want to come to this simple cabin on the weekend and know my name. I didn't have a peep hole in my door; never expected anyone. I was suspicious.

"Mr. Henry Ford?"

"Yes, that's me, but I'm not that one who ..." I opened the door and saw before my tired eyes a sight any red-blooded male would want as his dream come to life.

She looked like a living angel. I do not exaggerate.

I said with a stammer, "Ah, I mean, I'm not that Henry Ford, you see." My jaw was hanging to the floor. She was the most beautiful woman I'd ever seen.

I felt self-conscious to be at a distinct disadvantage wearing a scrubby T shirt I'd slept in and my worst jeans, unshaven, facing a beautiful business woman at my door holding a small briefcase.

She wore a light green suit, light yellow shirt and well-tailored jacket and a form-fitted skirt. She was perhaps 35 at most. Her jacket had an embroidered script with her name, Tina O'Leary, under 'Vacation Inns' in a funny, no a goofy looking, smiley face fish logo.

Maybe it's just my sleepy brain, I thought at the time, but she really did take my breath away. Her copper red hair fell curly around her shoulders. Her grayish-green eyes were full of both uplifting cheer and wonder and there was only a half-hearted formal smile to greet me. A lovely mouth with pouting lips hung half-open as if she had just seen a ghost or a creature from Mars. There was no apparent make up on her face, not even to take the shine off a perfect nose. I felt faint looking back at her expression of wonder.

Chapter 13

"The coffee is very good, Mr. Ford. Thank you for inviting me in. I didn't mean to interrupt your breakfast," the woman said.

I caught myself watching her luscious lips. "Don't mention it. I never eat breakfast. And call me Hank, please." I should have waited to make that friendly advance until I found out what the heck the woman wanted, and why she came to my door. I smiled broadly to cover any possible blushing on my pale, scruffy face. I also suddenly felt much older than 53.

"Have you lived here long, Mr. Ford?"

She didn't reciprocate my first name advance.

"I built this about three years ago, shortly after Bobby Macintyre's boys caught those radioactive fish that brought tourism to my doorstep."

I could not help being too open and maybe a little bitter, but I was stunned by her looks—long waves of curly hair over the shoulders of her green skirt suit, eyes almost matching the suit, but with a bit more grayish green, complexion of an 18-year-old, shapely legs exposed a bit too high for her comfort surely, I thought. I didn't mind.

As she began sitting, her Vacation Inn uniform tightened around her body. She sunk into my old stuffed arm chair which left her knees high above the seat. Must have been regretful, but again, I didn't mind. Did I say yet she had a face of an absolute angel? I tried to stay cool, but instinctively shifted in my only other chair in the main room I called the living room. It was a stiff wooden back chair.

"Who is Bobby Macintyre, Mr. Ford?"

Oh, new to the area. Or, she was delaying the point of her visit. Why was she here? I wondered.

Despite her good looks, I was becoming aware of her keen intelligence as well. (Molasses-slow old male response, distracted easily by feminine charm and mystique.) There was still no woman in my life, hadn't been for a good while after the divorce.

I said, "Nobody important, I guess. Macintyre's teenage twin boys played hooky from church one day and landed the first giant rainbow trout, first of zillions of those suckers. You might say Bobby Macintyre's boys built your hotel, Ms. O'Leary. Or is it Mrs.?"

"Oh yes, I'm sorry, Mr. Ford. I didn't say." She paused, still not revealing her marital status. "I'm from the hotel. It's a motel. It is an inn, actually. Oh God, it's right on my jacket."

I caught myself looking at her chest for too long.

"So stupid and rude of me. I'm sorry, Mr. Ford."

She was nervous. "It's Miss actually. And, that's what I want to talk with you about." she paused again and tried to get steady on course. "I want to talk with you about the Inn."

Wow, for a second I thought this gorgeous creature was eager to talk about being single! Down, big boy. "Ahem, what about the inn, Miss Actually?"

She gave me a look of apprehension, looked down, crossed her legs and adjusted herself in the cavernous chair. It was warm in the room. She opened the top button of her jacket unconsciously as I instinctively tried to detect her figure under her clothes. For a few seconds, I dismissed her stern expression and wanted to accept her visit as my good fortune.

"It's actually Miss O'Leary, Tina O'Leary, Mr. Ford," she began, not yet looking up.

"Again, call me Hank."

She took on a sheepish, guilty grin, which to me was just cute, still under her spell.

She said, "You may not want me to be on a first name basis after what I have to say. That is, you may choose to ask me to leave now. It wouldn't surprise me if you kicked me right out of this nice cabin you've built in our great state, on the great river, on...."

I stopped listening. So, she WAS local. Now I was suspicious. "Miss, just what do you want?"

"We want your property, Mr. Ford."

Zinger! I made a mental note to do some homework on her firm later.

We sipped coffee.

Miss O'Leary glowed with energy, yet seemed troubled.

Breathless, yet I tried and failed to breathe in. Boy, was I ever in a circumstantial ambush. All I knew yet was that an opportunistic resort inn had oozed up into my cherished mountain view and its beautiful hatchet lady was in my cabin looking stressed.

As I said, I'd been a newspaper man for 30 years. Why then didn't I know after years of weekending in those hills that the aggressive Vacation Inn guys were trying to buy up property all around me for the past two years? What an idiot! I must have left my brain in D.C.

Well, okay. First, perhaps my instincts were weakened by my passionate desire for a silly cabin in the woods and a burning need to flush away the pain of divorce. Then, I get enchanted by an alluring she-devil in a tight skirt who wants me gone! I had no chance.

But of course, when she knocked on my door and eased her gorgeous legs into my stuffed chair, I didn't know much about her company. I just sat there facing this great looking woman still puzzled over her friendly yet somewhat shy demeanor. *Why isn't she dealing tough? She's the one who is nervous*, I thought.

Her voice went in and out of my consciousness as she fumbled for words, speaking in phrases and unfinished sentences: "Mr. Ford, we help people get affordable getaways in a tough econ …. We set up vacations with our membersh....." "It is something we considered here with the river side...." "This is an opportunity for you to...."

She sounded insincere, her words were hollow. I assessed her as a very bright lady who was for some reason not eager to convince me of her pitch. But I clearly heard her last comment.

I replied, trying to sound humorously sarcastic without chasing her away, "Oh, I see, an opportunity," just to save her the trouble of more lies.

She also seemed like a nice person. As I tried to adjust my mind to concentrate on her designs on my property, the purpose of Ms. O'Leary's visit did not sadden me. It seemed to intrigue me that I was out maneuvered and put in a squeeze by her company. I saw humor in that, while it is my nature--no my job--to be inquisitive. I was delightfully trapped.

Actually, she was the one who seemed saddened by the visit. It sounds stupid, I know, but I became more concerned for her emotional state than mine. Her eyes showed the kind of worried sadness when told a close friend or relative is gravely ill and there's little you can do about it. Should they pull the plug? Or prolong the pain?

I took a deep breath and chanced taking a diversion, "Miss O'Leary, pardon me but you might just be the most beautiful woman I have ever seen. I'm not trying to flatter; I mean it. You walk right in here to a middle-aged man's secluded cabin, all alone. You are crazy bold enough to accept an invitation to coffee, again, enclosed in a stuffy cabin with a strange man. You never lose your cool and tell me directly and professionally that you are here to take my property from me. You are either cunning beautiful or foolish beautiful. Either way, I am glad you knocked on my door." I couldn't believe I said that so well.

"Mr. Ford, I....." her voice sounded quite empathetic. She allowed her lovely eyes to show concern for me. That was another mystery.

I continued, "Miss O'Leary, let me finish. I'm not upset. I'm impressed with your manner ... ah, that is, more than with your beauty, though I'm sure they picked you to come here partly because you're an attractive woman and....."

She stiffened, "No, no, Mr. Ford, and thank you for your kind words. But they didn't pick me to come here for this. It's not even a regular office day on Saturday. (She paused.) I volunteered. I wanted to meet you. I wanted it to be me explaining the situation to Mr. Henry Clyde Ford, not by some other employee."

"Why? It's a nice Saturday morning. You could be enjoying the weekend."

"The motel, ah, the inn wants all the land it can get on this side of the river and over to the lake to preserve the beautiful view for our guests, maybe add a ski chalet as well, on this very spot. The board discussed making an offer to the owner of 'that lonely little house over there,' as they put it; your cabin. I looked up the deed and found out that Henry Clyde Ford, the famous investigative reporter for the Washington Inquirer owns 'the little lonely house over there.' That's why I volunteered."

"Because an old newspaper hack owns the only blight on the hotel's view, I mean motel's view?"

"No sir. It was because I admire your work very much. I wouldn't miss any chance to meet you. They wanted me to come here possibly on Monday. They don't know I'm here today, that is, except for Donald who is in a van outside. He's a bellboy who brought me over. I have a beeper and he has a gun. So, I wasn't worried. Tough young man, that Donald." She nodded and seemed to enjoy her levity. I detected a slight smile. Her tone lightened a little as she tossed that chip into the game. Cute little smile too; I'd been alone way too long.

"Again, Miss O'Leary, you may not have good taste in journalists, but you have remarkable guts. Suppose I was nasty to you, and again, you are a lovely girl."

"I'm not a girl. I'm 34, and....."

"And, it's my birthday, right?" I quipped.

"Huh?"

"It's a Shirley Temple line from a '30's movie. It goes like this, 'I'm not a kid. I'm a girl, and today is my Birthday'."

"Missed that one, I guess."

We shared a brief laugh that cut through the tension.

I was still not the least concerned about Miss O'Leary's intentions. After all, my dream of writing my memoir at my cabin was already on life support. My drunken evenings with Johnny Walker Red were not going well. And now, my property is a stain on Vacation Inn's mountain view. What an ironic kick in the butt.

As I found myself pondering how I would compose a story lead from the irony of the situation, she surprised me again.

She volunteered a personal confession. "Mr. Ford, I wrote my master's thesis at Harvard Business School on your unique investigative reporting technique you once called the pen vs. corporate America in a column."

"How nice. I can't wait to find out who won. The pen I bet." I was getting overly charmed by her again, sounding giddy, I bet.

"I better not say more about it, it was just a business school paper, you know. But that is why I volunteered to come here. I came early before my bosses changed their minds, something they do all the time, that is, change everything on a dime with no rhyme or reason." She stopped talking and just looked at me blankly, likely expecting some support.

I just looked at her. I was melting again in the presence of her beauty. Poor boy.

She continued, "It's my lucky day to meet you, Mr. Ford. I mean that. I guess I'd better go."

Good God, I thought. I put my hands on my cheeks to stop my head shaking in disbelief. *How can I let this blissful vision vanish so easily?* I couldn't let her go, but I couldn't think of a response.

I reverted to being stupid Hank again, "Your boy out there, the one with the gun? Who's it? Donald? How long did you give him before he breaks down my door and comes in firing?" I said with a broad smile, hoping I was charming.

It worked. She leaned back and laughed heartily, looking toward my open log ceiling beams. It was a warm and genuine laugh.

Don't start falling for this woman; she wants my property, I cautioned myself. *But, maybe that's okay.*

"Well, I should be going. And, Donald is a nice boy, won't do anything rash," she said smiling, laughed again. She started to climb out of the stuffed chair while struggling to keep those pretty legs together. On the edge of the chair she reached to the floor for a small briefcase and began to remove a slim manila folder.

I scrambled, "Miss O'Leary, you don't have to show me that now. Is it an offer? This has been a good morning for me, best in many mornings. Why ruin it? How about discussing it over lunch? Does the Vacation Inn have a restaurant? That might be better. Say 12:30 over there?" I was so proud of myself for framing another chance to see her with some sense of class, not my usual clumsy approach to attractive women, like *Hey there, you busy for lunch or somethin'?*

She replied, "I don't think that would be a good idea Mr. Ford."

"Well, I don't need to meet you there," I countered.

She looked worried.

I was puzzled, had no next move. I was done. She'd be gone now.

And then, she surprised me, yet again, "Mr. Ford, meeting at my motel restaurant would not look good for me. Remember, I'm here on my own. I was not supposed to come here until Monday, that is, if they still plan to use me. But....."

My God, I thought, *she is thinking it over*. She was shifting again in the big chair, and not aware of how distracting it was for me to notice her body shifting. I felt pathetic, boyish.

"I'm originally from this area Mr. Ford. I know a nice, casual place we can eat. I doubt if anyone at the inn knows it. How about if I come back here at 1:30 this afternoon. Then, we can do it."

"Super," I couldn't hide my enthusiasm bubbling over; my mind 'giggled' over her phrasing of 'then we can do it'.

But that didn't faze her at all. Instead, she seemed to like my eagerness, and smiled broadly again.

That's how I met Tina O'Leary. It would be the best day of my life since the birth of my daughters. Please forgive me for such a giant leap. There is little suspense to how much my heart went out to this woman immediately. So, let me explain things from Tina's perspective.

She said that we could not go near the Inn that weekend because 'the brasses' are expected soon to host a corporate month-long national review of the Vacation Inns & Resorts, Corp. Many of its board of directors were expected from different parts of the country. They would be staying at the Trout Heaven Vacation Inn for meetings and R&R together, and then, maybe more time there for top execs to look over the operation and the management teams, she said.

It would indeed be foolish for Tina O'Leary to bring over an investigative reporter who owns "that lonely little house over there" for lunch.

She feared being seen by Vacation's CEO, a Bostonian named Trevor Goodbred and especially Goodbred's 'unofficial' chief financial officer, Simon Levine, from parts unknown.

I wondered why the mystery around Mr. Levine, but didn't ask.

She told me those top two executives were at that very time traveling in a 'garishly bright,' lime-green Vacation Inn limousine from the company headquarters on Cape Cod in Massachusetts. They could be expected at any time, she said.

To me, that seemed like a long drive in a limo, but I dismissed the thought.

Chapter 14

About Goodbred and Levine, I later learned by researching them at the Inquirer that they were widely regarded in the hospitality industry as a crafty pair of wheeler dealers who were tight-lipped about any inside information on the workings of Vacation Inns. Their clandestine reputations implied to me that their work may not be entirely legit.

From lifestyle articles, I also gleaned that when Levine and Goodbred played together, all bets were off on good behavior. They were buddies off campus, so to speak away from the company business in escapades in all manners impulsive and zany. The two mid-30's business men acted like a couple of spoiled rich kids at summer camp, at least until they needed to put back on their corporate masks.

They were the best of friends. And quite the odd couple. Trevor Goodbred was tall, perhaps 6' 3" and handsome in a boyish way. He gave an impression of pure innocence and yet was aloof and serene while 'minding the store.' His thick mane of black hair was cut conservatively at all times, parted on the left. He was fit and energetic. It was an overall appearance of trust that likely got him what he wanted.

Simon Levine was equally skilled at getting his way but, from a far different perspective than charming Trevor. Levine could not hide his conniving nature, neither in his lumpy, unkempt looks or his rough and rude manners. He was the indifferent and undermining assertive one of the two buddies. Levine was likely not much more than 5'3" but appeared taller in the nearly two-inch heels he hid under long trousers always, not unlike the dynamic, yet diminutive Claude Rains, star of Hollywood.

In fact, Levine would have been such an actor. He was good at deceiving and persuading business associates and employees of his intentions to control them without appearing mean or cruel. His complexion was pocked since early childhood in New York City and then Bethesda, Md. His brown untamed hair was balding rapidly at 38 years old, the same age as his buddy, the handsome and charming face of the corporation, Trevor. Si Levine's saving grace was his gentle and often charming personality when happy. People liked him outside of the firm.

The two executives planned the long limo ride from New England as a fun getaway, with stops on the way for pleasure and perhaps an eye to places for expanding Vacation Inns. Their driver was keen to follow their activities for their very generous tips, I'd eventually learn. On their merry way down along the hills of Appalachia, however, they would be exploring potential sites for new Vacation Inns along the Eastern seaboard and beyond. One story in the Boston Globe quoted Levine, "Why not play for a while? We have to spend at least a month in God knows where."

* * *

While Goodbred and Levine were still on their unscripted road trip, Tina O'Leary, their PR lady seemed to be nervous about visiting my cabin on Saturday on behalf of the corporation but unauthorized by the brass.

Before Miss O'Leary visited me in the morning she was under the impression that the top executive pair could be arriving at the inn that day. But after she left me and returned to the Inn, she got a call from Levine asking her to forward documents to their limousine. Levine and Goodbred were making a last-minute diversion to testify at the U.S. Congress.

She was delayed and didn't show at my cabin at 1:30 as planned. I was sure I had made a fool of myself. I thought that she would not return. I dug out another bottle of whiskey.

Despite her awkward handling of the situation, I think I did well to make friends with Tina. Before we met, I was still ignorant of Goodbred and Levine and their alleged sleazy management of the corporation. Her visit effectively gave me a nudge—perhaps unintentionally, yet perhaps intentionally—to eyeball the company. As to my strong attraction to Tina, it would pass. I foolishly still loved my wife who had flecced me.

Meanwhile, I called the weekend national news editor at the Inquirer and got the low down on Vacation Inns and Resorts, then searched for their business plan on my computer. Jim, the weekend editor said the company likely was run by an opportunistic, greedy management at best. He said its marketing scheme raised suspicions with federal regulators more than once. Get in touch with Devin Shay when you return, he suggested. Devin was the Inquirer's business editor and one of my best friends at the paper.

Meanwhile surfing the web from my cabin that afternoon revealed that they offered guests 'lifetime' memberships with any stay of three or more nights at any of its locations. The membership plan gave families heavily discounted vacation packages for return visits to any of their other nationwide locations.

The editor Jim had suggested that the affordability of its deals during the economic recession would hold fascinating promise in the eyes of first-time guests strapped for recreation funds.

If guests purchased the membership, their first stay was free. I couldn't fathom such generosity. Something was wrong.

Guests paid their bill for the first vacation by simply making a reservation and down payment on a second vacation package within six months of an equal or greater value. I figured that the delay might give Vacation Inns lots of leeway to postpone reservations or change availabilities later. It seemed more like a membership Ponzi scheme for investors or pyramid scheme to entice bookings rather than a family membership opportunity.

There were points for faithful guests. Single and 2-night stays allowed guests to accumulate points. The point system was the prime promotional carrot, as I saw it. Families would get points for every person in that family. The points would theoretically help cement a booking of a discounted vacation package in the future and a chance to qualify for a membership of a higher class. Further digging into SEC reports revealed that class I, class II, class III and executive class all carried identical benefits.

This made no sense to me. Had to be a scam.

Inquirer business reporters said that Vacation Inns & Resorts was the fastest growing lodging enterprise in the nation. The company kept a low profile, but grew "like a fungus on rotten garbage in the humid tropics," one reporter told me.

Something stunk about it, Jim concluded.

And, surprising to all was that, so far, Vacation Inns & Resorts, Corp. had escaped fines or charges from federal regulation investigations.

Chapter 15

At 1:55, there was another knock at my cabin door, this time a firm wrapping with purpose.

When I eagerly opened the door, the woman standing there was not the perfectly tailored, professional Miss O'Leary in the green Vacation Inn suit. Instead, Miss O'Leary wore designer jeans and some kind of high-end footwear, likely cowboy boots. But who was looking at her feet.

She was radiant, wearing a bright white silk blouse two buttons opened showing a sterling silver necklace with two finger rings hanging on her chest just above and between the tops of her breasts, which were not showing at all. She was dressed modestly. I liked the way she looked and was relieved that the motel uniform was gone.

"I am sorry I'm late Mr. Ford. My boss called and needed papers sent to Washington for a hearing on hospitality industry stuff. Ready?" she said before I even got the door fully open. She looked a bit afraid, even minus the uniform armor.

"Won't you come in Miss O'Leary? I didn't know if you'd come again. Maybe the motel people would have preferred you to come Monday after all," I was trying to lighten her mood, being humble and friendly.

"I can wait outside here, Mr. Ford. I'll be fine if you are ready to go."

"And enjoy my view of Trout Heaven, eh?" She didn't react at all to my joke, all business. "Miss O'Leary, I insist. Please step in for a minute while I turn off the coffee and lock up in the back. [I had no back door.] I don't want to leave you out here alone."

She came in cheerfully and asked, "Still drinking coffee?"

"Second pot, sometimes I drink it all day. Shouldn't, but it's a bad habit I can't shake."

"But, at least you don't smoke Mr. Ford."

"No, Miss O'Leary, I don't smoke," I said, wondering just how much this chick actually knew about me. *Maybe keeping names formal was best*, I thought. It started to appeal to me. It was cute from her because she obviously was already on a friendly basis with me anyway. *Keep it going, it's working,* I told myself.

She seemed more at ease inside the cabin, so I suggested, "Come into the kitchen, I have a gift for you for being so brave and direct, coming here by yourself to fleece me of my land, my cabin, my holdout. After all, I'm like old man Lionel Barrymore sitting tight in the last house on the block before the developer moves in."

Nothing on her face.

The flick, "You Can't Take It with You?" I offered. "Barrymore? James Stewart? Jean Arthur? The old black and white movie?"

"Guess I missed that one, too," she said with a chuckle, head tilted to see into the kitchen as she lagged behind me, walking cautiously, looking around at the barren log walls.

I had strategically placed a bottle of 2002 Chateau Francois merlot on the kitchen table as a gift to her, but was careful not to place two glasses there with the bottle, though I had considered such a suggestive move earlier.

"Oh, great Lord." she exclaimed. "I love this wine. Have you been there? To the one in Chantilly, or, for that matter, the one in Paris?" she asked. She was delighted.

I was thrilled and relieved, but tried not to show it, channeling my best Bruce Willis stoicism, tightening my lips into a small lopsided grin. "Yes, the one in Chantilly, Virginia," I said. "4-star gourmet restaurant, award-winning French chef, vineyard right there, next to a big junkyard. I stopped in to Chateau Francois's wine store when I covered a story in Chantilly. The juxtaposition of heavenly dining and the auto graveyard was weird, but fabulous copy."

"I didn't see the junkyard."

"You only notice it in daylight. They start dinner at nine. If loving couples arrived too early, all the romance of the place would get compromised if they saw mountains of rusty auto carcasses outside, or from their $400 guestroom in the morning light to the east."

"Yeah, I guess," she said. "But, they also make the wine right there in a new winery I'm told."

"Yeah, guests think they are in Parisian paradise. Then they wake up to a view of old junk hulks and leaky transmissions. Yet another spoiled romantic view in Appalachia, huh? I've seen that movie too," I said sarcastically and then regretted it. I was pushing my spoiled view thing too much. But she didn't seem to get the connection.

"Yes, I guess so, but I've never stayed there," she said instead. "I do love this merlot though. How did you know?"

"I didn't. Want a taste?"

"Well, no ... yes, sure," she corrected, possibly remembering her manners.

I produced two of my best glasses—pint Mason jars.

I quickly turned on impulse to reach for the bottle before she changed her mind again. She also reached for the bottle to read the label at the same time and my hand grasped over hers. We were suddenly very close. My cool demeanor crashed. I felt all the molecules in my body warming and spinning out of control. It was an involuntary, very warm attraction, more innocent and heartfelt than from say an initial sexual desire. We slowly looked up to each other, faces just inches apart. I no longer felt like a 53-year-old waste of a man.

She spoke first, without withdrawing her hand from mine, but easing her head away a little. "Mr. Ford, maybe we should get going, at least postpone, ah ... a taste."

She had a way with words.

She continued, "The cafe I have in mind for lunch is in the next town. It's called Patrick, about ten miles from here."

I nodded toward the front door and she took back her hand. I worked on recovering my cool. *Bruce, don't fail me now.*

Chapter 16

I drive a silver BMW Z3 sports convertible, the original model.

Tina smiled and giggled almost like a child, "Nice ride, Mr. Ford; had it long?"

"Want the top down?"

"Not especially," she said with a glance back at the Inn across the river from us.

I hoped she didn't know that my little motoring toy was my only crumb left of shared marital possessions after Janet got the whole cake, and custody of my two teenage kids whom I rarely saw until they checked into respective college dorms.

Miss O'Leary's question made me wonder if she knew about my ex Janet, her gum shoe, and my one-night stand with the hot grad student. But I got a grip, *Oops, bit too paranoid, Henry. Relax. Of course, she'd not know about that.*

My runaway mind regained some dignity. "I've had this little scooter for 10 years now. I bought it when we, ah I, first started coming up here, you know." *Oops,* I turned my head away from her.

"I see," she uttered knowingly.

Why do women do such things with that superior inflection? What DID she see? What did she know? Who cares; on with the journey, I thought. "Miss O'Leary, aren't you forgetting something?"

She frowned slightly; looked sort of trapped.

"Your offer. For my land? Didn't you bring it?"

"I must have forgotten, Mr. Ford. How stupid of me. Looks like it's Monday for that, like you suggested anyway. Maybe I inadvertently had the same thought. Sorry. Well, I guess you don't need me now, do you?"

Another female ploy if I ever detected one. I said, quick as a bunny, "I wouldn't miss lunch with you for all the land deals in the world, Miss O'Leary. You are not only bold, but unpredictable," I lied. "You say you studied my stories, my style. I didn't think I had a distinct investigative style."

I turned the key and zoomed off. *Always gets 'em. Women love sports cars.*

"Oh, wow," she reacted to the rapid acceleration.

"I do love this car. Fits me like a glove."

She seemed to drink in the speed and the wind. After a minute she shouted over the roar of the engine, "Yes, you have a distinct style for an investigative reporter, Mr. Ford. For example, I know that Chantilly story, the two-part story you did, and..."

I was shouting too, "I did more than one Chantilly story. Was it the story of the town as a hotbed of corporate crime?" I added tongue and cheek. "Seriously, which one? The defense contractor fraud story or the airline CEO embezzlement at Dulles Airport?"

"The airline CEO. Although the Pentagon story about the contractor in Chantilly was a dilly, it was not interesting to me."

I slowed the car around sharp turns in the mountain slopes and said, "Thanks, I guess."

Our conversation was easier with less motor noise.

She said, "Your style, I think, Mr. Ford, is to lead the reader to the defense of the corporate or government party who is accused of crime or scandal as if they are the victim of an unfair public accusation or insinuation. The reader doesn't suspect that you are setting them up. I think you know all the while the accused fat cat is guilty and unscrupulous. Then later, even in another story, you reverse your slant and expose them with their pants down."

I loved that. "That is what you think I do?" I said while down shifting to climb a steep incline.

She watched me shift and then while admiring the road's carved rock cliffs, said, "Most definitely. You have patience. You take your time. Maybe it's because you got your first Pulitzer at a very young age, 27. With that GMO story you became very self-assured, I'm thinking. And, Mr.

Ford, do you do that deliberately? Or change your slant as you go deeper?"

Damn. She knows my age, I thought and then covered with, "Do what deliberately? I didn't think I slanted that much."

"Well, it looked good in my thesis. You often seemed to be attacking the accuser, like the Justice Department in the airline CEO case, taking no prisoners, big brother harassment. Then you joined the position of the accuser, not until the third article sometimes, hammering the reader with company employee quotes about how Champagne Airline's CEO Lance Manson Lowe lied and cheated them out of stock and their jobs. Did you switch deliberately?"

"I'm flattered. But sometimes I end up going after the fat cat, right?"

"After first laying out the victim."

"Yes, the paper gave me more latitude, more time, on stories sometimes than reporters twice my age after I was honored with the prize. I first thought they favored me. My ego, I guess. But it wasn't that at all. They were using me, of course. My Pulitzer helped their marketing plans. But, what you surmised Miss O'Leary is just good journalism, reporting both sides. I try to do it in more detail rather than punch it all altogether at once for the readers' assurance. I don't care what the reader thinks at first. I take a while to finish my investigations."

She simply replied, "Oh, right ... okay, Patrick is at the bottom of this drop and around the bend in the valley."

I expected her to continue. But, my explanation seemed to put her into deep thought. Her face became placid and her mouth turned down at the edges. She looked sad. Had I insulted her; said something wrong? Was I dismissing her admiration of my work? I didn't mean too.

I re-ran the conversation in my mind to find a reason and could not. She noticed me studying her suddenly flat expression with several glances her way. She turned to her right to watch scenery.

We said nothing again until we reached the town of Patrick and she directed me to the Smokey Joe's Mountain Café. The faded, artsy sign read, *Best Darn Cookin' East of Tennessee.*

I was intrigued and looked closely at the beauty beside me.

She had brightened up.

I pulled into a crowded little parking area at the café at the east edge of a town, which I could only figure was very small. *The food must be good,* I thought.

It was west of my cabin in an area I had not explored much in my blundering real estate search.

Tina was glowing with pride as she said smiling, "It's my uncle's place. I grew up here in Patrick." She hopped out of the car like a teenager eager to meet up with friends at a local dive. "Come on, Mr. Ford. I told him you were coming. He knows about you too."

"And he still wants to meet me?" I kidded.

"Come on. Don't be silly, you."

Well, she said that rather affectionately, I noticed, encouraged.

Swinging her head to the side she flipped her red hair in the air, catching the sunlight like it caught fire. She was very pleasing; that was for sure. I felt comfortable now with Tina O'Leary from Vacation Inns, even though they wanted my property. And, here at Smokey Joe's, she was at home, letting her hair down, so to speak.

Inside, the cafe smelled delicious. It was full of customers. And, why not? It was an old-fashion eating place, well worn, but well-scrubbed, full of wonderful aromas.

There was a line of booths with red leather seats along front windows. A modest counter had eight stools, silver with red-leather button tops. Behind the counter was a pleated silver wall with a big window to a kitchen, plus a small grill was directly behind the center of the counter. Clear, glass-covered trays of cakes and pies drew my eyes to the counter top.

The friendly cafe had a 1960's look, but not in a deliberate commercial way. It had clearly not changed in a long time. Pictures of Elvis, the Beatles, Marilyn Monroe, and Bogart, all the usual ghosts of Hollywood that customers would want to meet in a diner. The booths even had jukebox players with the transparent red buttons, originals.

She slid into the only empty booth. The table was clear except for a handwritten folded sheet of paper on the green and white checkered table cloth. It read, "Reserved for Tee." Tina discarded it quickly into her purse with a little affectionate laugh under her breath. At that moment she looked as innocent as a child, obviously very happy in this place.

I felt old again.

A little waitress approached, of no more than 95 lbs., in her 70's, white-gray hair in a bun and a kindly face. "Hi Tee. Yer uncle know you here yet, kid? Who's handsome?"

"I don't think so, can you tell Uncle Joe please," Tina answered. "Eloise, this is Mr. Henry Ford who has a cabin near the Vacation Inn in Trout Heaven. Mr. Ford, this is Mrs. Eloise Winters. She's family, Mr. Ford. You've been here how long Eloise?"

"I ain't sayin' how long I been here, not to this handsome fella, Tee. But, long nuf to know what's what, I guess. I'll git him." She disappeared toward the kitchen, yelling louder than necessary, "Somebody out here tah see ya, Smoke. None of the customers looked up from their lunches when she yelled.

In a second it seemed Smokey Joe O'Leary was standing at our booth beaming at both of us, loving seeing Tina, checking me out. He wore a food-stained cooking bib and an actual chefs' hat, his trademark I learned later.

"So ... Tee, this the newspaper guy you were telling me about." he blurted in sort of a question, but not really. He was already nodding in agreement with himself. I detected a trace of an Irish lilt.

"Yes, Uncle Joe, Mr. Ford is that newspaper man I mentioned." She turned to me. "They call me Tee, for Tina, Mr. Ford."

I thought, *Okay, that's a privilege I may never enjoy. She wouldn't even let me call her Tina.*

Joe sat down next to his niece and kissed her on the cheek. "Tee says you investigate white collar crimes, Mr. Ford. Showed me some of your stories about government corruption and corporate fat cats."

I glanced around from habit to see if anyone heard that. All clear.

"She's been a great admirer of your work for a long time Mr. Ford," Joe said as he put his arm around her and tugged her so tight it must have hurt. She turned pink. "Says you are the best, sir. Oh yeah, Tee says ..."

"Shut up, Uncle Joe. For God sake, you're embarrassing me," she said, blushing more intensely now. She gave him a mock knock on his head with her knuckles several times. "He knows about my thesis, Mr. Ford, that's all."

"Tee knows some good stories 'bout bad folks round here too, Mr. Ford. Don't ya Tee?" Joe said, looking sheepishly to Tina for approval.

"Don't pay any attention to him, Mr. Ford. I told him how corrupt some businesses, none in particular, are out there that no one knows about, not the media, that is." She was nervous suddenly, as if she said too much while affected by Smokey Joe's lack of inhibition.

"Oh yeah?" I chimed in.

Joe started to talk again, but she cut him off. "We came here to eat, not to talk, Uncle Joe. I told Mr. Ford you have the best food in the area."

"Best east of Knoxville," he replied prying his rotund frame with some difficulty out of the booth. He patted his niece on her silky red head.

"I read the sign, Mr. Smokey. Can't wait," I tried to say politely, though my reporter's antenna had already been activated by her comment about how corrupt 'some businesses are around here.' *What corrupt businesses the media doesn't know about?* I wondered.

Tina saw my expression, and said, "Try the trout ..." she paused, smiling, for my reaction, "Don't worry. It's from here. We catch it right out back in Foster's Creek. Best trout fishing east of Tennessee, people say." She laughed and pointed at the Smoky Joe slogan over the counter.

I couldn't quite bring myself to ordering the trout, but the thought of Tina in a trout stream? That registered.

My burger and fries were the best I could remember. She ordered the local version of a Cobb salad, a tossed salad with local cheeses, watercress, snow pea pods and ginger on a bed of spring mix lettuce. We shared a bottle of Pinot Grigio from Italy. Yeah, that surprised me too. Very nice.

She drank her entire glass of wine in three big gulps, and then said, "This cafe was a big part of my childhood and adolescence. I worked here the year before college. If you have time Mr. Ford, may I show you more of my little hometown, Patrick?" Her smile was so beautiful and alluring I didn't taste my wine at all.

She was comfortable and relaxed enough to open up about whom Tina O'Leary the business woman really was. From my perspective, that business side of this woman was the side of her I had chosen to ignore from the second I saw her name and goofy company logo embroidered on her green suit. I listened closely anyway.

She told me she had followed her New Jersey-native, now-divorced husband into the hotel hospitality business. It was his career choice when they graduated from Harvard together, but not her career choice necessarily, she said.

Two years before, they met at a party for new grad students. This big-city husband of hers, whose name is of no consequence to our story (and slipped my mind immediately anyway), was fond of partying.

She said, "He was a gorgeous fellow, but also an archetypically bright, well-healed student who didn't have to try hard to make good grades and, at the same time, make it with girls, drugs, and full-time fun."

She said he must have viewed her as a challenge, "because I am not impressed by males like that."

But, by mirroring her class schedule with his, he was able to finally lay on the charm, she told me.

"I, on the other hand, the straight-laced, small town girl, must have seemed very stylish—well dressed, well-mannered and fine-tuned by my public relations education as an undergrad from the University of Maryland."

As she was telling me the story of her days at Harvard, I imagined she was the prettiest woman on campus, a challenge most conceited business students or faculty for that matter would want to know.

Her grad school lover promised he would quit drugs, but was secretly escalating his habit, Tina said. And he could afford it, being from a wealthy family-owned development company in Newark.

He vowed on one knee while proposing marriage to obey her only wish: never to do drugs again. She said that she naively vowed to reform him, counting only on her nurturing instincts to reform her man.

"How stupid is that Mr. Ford?" she seemed to ask and exclaim in the same breath.

I didn't answer, just listened. I was ashamed to be wondering instead if my whole experience with her was natural for her or contrived. Why was she telling me, of all people, about her past? Was it the wine? A few hours earlier she was ready to hand me a contract, likely an undervalued bid, for my land.

She said the hotel business turned out to be exactly the wrong profession for her husband. They each got corporate jobs, but at competing chains. She was based in Boston, and he in New York. She advanced quickly to a regional management position, which she still held with Vacation Inns Inc. of Boston: Mid-Atlantic assistant vice president for public relations. She had begged Goodbred to let her help open the Trout Heaven location and had been back in the state for a year during the planning and development phases and had managed to stay so far.

Her loser-boy hubby was fired from his New York firm after he was busted a third time within a year for heroin and cocaine possession with intent to distribute. Although he had no need to sell the stuff, it goes with the rap and the crowd he hung with, she said.

The divorce was quick, she told me, "and I've been sort of married to the job ever since, Mr. Ford. How about you? Married to the paper?"

(Pardon the diversion but I should say here that later on the Internet I learned more about the dynamic Miss Tina O'Leary: awards for salesmanship, public relations, top national presenter at conventions, the usual stellar stuff for an outstanding young executive.)

There was no current husband or boyfriend. I found my heart giving in, letting me fall in love with this sweet rose in the rough, so to speak.

Just the same, some rather sharp thorns were still poking at my little gray cells. They screamed out when I wasn't thinking right, trying to get my attention. They asked: *Why did she mention corrupt businesses that the media doesn't know about? Was that a slip? Deliberate? This is a smart woman. Did she just dismiss Uncle Joe from our table talk before he said more? Did she have a story for me? Pay attention, fool. What's the real reason why she didn't bring along the offer? There's no way that she simply forgot. What did she really want from me? Joe confirmed her admiration for my work; is that it? Can't be.*

"Are you still listening, Mr. Ford?"

I came out of it. "Oh, yes. I mean no. Not married. Divorced." I was skeptical. That's who I am. But, at the same time, I couldn't discount the notion that Miss O'Leary seemed to be thoroughly enjoying my company.

Uncle Joe came back out with a dessert tray of homemade pies and creampuffs in one hand and two mugs of coffee in the other expertly shoving them onto our table with a big laugh and not a drop spilled. He said he was so happy to see Tee because "Oh my, she is such the big shot executive now, traveling the country to make people happy."

She was certainly making me happy. *Maybe the offer for my land from the motel chain was so pathetic that she is smoothing me over. Don't be such a cynic,* I told myself.

The lunch tab was on Uncle Joe, no matter how much I pleaded. He and I hit it off well. It was the kind of friendship that needs no thought, no preparation or adjustment to your personality. Joe and I were instant buddies.

Tina would tell me later that, although as a café owner Smoky Joe O'Leary was an affable, lovable character, it was an acting role for Joe in large part. In reality, Joe was reserved and private and took life seriously, according to her.

After lunch Joe showed me around the building, with Tina trailing quietly—the kitchen, massive twin freezers that were his pride and joy "big enough to feed the whole town in a blizzard, or another meteorite invasion," he said, as if the freak meteorite hit was an alien offensive.

He told me that during the Vietnam War, Chief Petty Officer Joseph O'Leary ran the main galley aboard the USS John F. Kennedy carrier. In his two tours in the Navy, the son of a coal miner struck for galley duty due to his famous skills in pit barbeque cooking for family and high school parties. Promotions in rank came easy because of his skill and enthusiasm for learning special dishes recommended by the officers and later on for the carrier flyboys, Joe said.

"Me and my brother, Tina's daddy, signed a contract to buy this dumpy building for $1,000 on the very day I came home from the Navy. We were 27 and 29. He had the money, my older brother. Some fella down your way named Macintyre fixed it up on credit. I still give him and his family free lunch anytime they come this way."

"Bobby Macintyre one of them, Joe?" I asked.

"Yeah, how ja know that?"

"He and mostly his twin sons built my cabin when my front porch view was still the beautiful Sassafras River and the hills beyond. Now my view is of Vacation Inn and tourist trap town Trout Heaven. Right Tina?"

Being in a comfortable setting, I had forgotten about our deal to use formal names, but she was no longer standing behind us. She had drifted off when Joe mentioned the Macintyres. Maybe she knew Bobby after all. I wondered why she lied to me back at my cabin.

"Yeah, well maybe you will find another cabin with a view Mr. Ford," he glanced to where his niece stood a minute earlier and turned back when he didn't see her.

The café building was much larger than it needed to be for a small-town roadside eatery. There was another wing, a second floor and a root cellar. Joe showed me his cellar proudly, with wine racks and neatly stacked supplies of potatoes, onions and other perishables and canned goods on silver Metro shelving. He made no move to show me the second floor.

Tina caught up, her wooden heels clapping down the steps, "He never takes anybody down to the cellar here," she volunteered.

"The tour is for your friend Mr. Ford."

"Call me Hank, please."

"And, Joe to you, Hank. The tour is for your friend, Mr. Hank." the three of us laughed as Tina got another shoulder hug from her Uncle Joe. "I will show him anything."

Again, he didn't show me the second floor or offer to.

I should normally have been suspicious of such flattery and openness from someone I just met—my standard reporter attitude. But I wasn't. I felt comfortable and I wanted to trust the O'Leary's. What a strange day that was for me.

He walked us to my car and with a hearty handshake and a slap on my shoulder. "I wish you well on your work here, Hank." I thanked him, though he was a bit overly excited and probably meant my work at the newspaper. Maybe not.

Chapter 17

The moment Tina sat into my car again she got quiet, even pensive, and said, "Let's not go back yet, Mr. Ford. I'd like to show you my town. Okay?"

"I'm flattered," I said.

Patrick is a town of about 3,400, she said, including the delivery men and bus drivers passing through. It didn't look even that big. It was tiny, just one main street of homes, stores, and two churches, Catholic and Methodist. If you were Baptist, you attended in the next town in the valley to the southwest.

My immediate impression was that Patrick was authentic, like an American mountain town should look. It was a far cry from the cluttered, classless commercialism of the gaudy tourist trap Trout Heaven.

Driving along the up-and-down wavy hills of Patrick's Main Street, I noticed, as I'd expect, the residences and occasional stores were an eclectic mix of clapboard, brick, or stone two- or three-story buildings. But they fit into a humbling pattern. Most of the structures had small street-side porches, some even first and second floor porches.

They were probably all constructed at different times in the town's 160-year history. Stars and stripes of old glory or Patrick Town banners adorned small flagpoles on one of every four of the buildings, I'd say. Main Street had two lanes, plus well marked parking spaces on both sides, except in front of Town Hall and the Patrick Fire and Rescue Co. (No. 51) firehouse. The parked cars and pickup trucks were inexpensive American brands, older models mostly.

The most prominent American flag flew over the small Town Hall building atop the highest of the rolling hills of Main Street. The Town Hall was a utilitarian, one-story brick structure with a stair-stepped brick façade that said, 'excuse me mayor, we had left over bricks,' and was elevated an unnecessary, extra six feet above the plain, residential front door with aluminum storm door and screens.

Perfectly tended perennial border gardens adorned the front and sides of the building beckoning all to appreciate civic pride the town felt for its little epicenter of important events and activities.

With little conversation, Tina let me take in the sights and sounds slowly along the Main Street of modest establishments:

Chattering men in overalls just inside an old-time hardware store; a general store with kids swinging on a rusty davenport; a small attorney's office of two partners, closed; several tiny franchises: Pizza Hut, CVS Pharmacy, and even a Curves women's weight loss store.

Those stores I spotted were scattered among the row houses, as we drove by slowly. Zoning seemed haphazard, but somehow, they all fit together peacefully. Kids were playing on a porch while folks sat on their front steps chatting and laughing like there was no need to do anything else all day. I heard a Good Humor truck bell down a small alley. A teenager was halfway missing under the hood of an old jalopy while three girls waited alongside. It all seemed like time had passed by Patrick.

In the middle of the last block was a clapboard structure called The O'Leary House, circa 1878. The O'Leary House was a modest two-story brick travelers' inn, which caught my eye. I slowed. It was straddling an alleyway. The inn was painted all white with a small front porch with tasteful Victorian woodwork and a railing in front. Hanging plants and two green rockers filled the porch along with small hand-painted signs, 'The Cellar, in back' and 'Herbs, Cards. Coins'.

Tina said, "Yes, a family treasure. It was the home of my daddy's grandfather from Ireland who was a leader in building Patrick into a decent town. He and my great grandmother Kalie lived there. He worked the mine and helped out-of-town workers stay the nights. They ran the inn until they built two large rooming houses for miners, railroad workers, and other transients." She pointed ahead on a hill to the right. "There is one of them still standing and still in business as a hotel," she said proudly. "Up there. See?"

She pointed to a large four-story white brick architectural beauty, which appeared to be freshly painted. The style carried a distinct French flavor with a dormer at each room at the top with the roofing tiles cascading down around the dormers. Side alcoves bracketed a wrap-around expansive porch, which ended in side entrances.

"They lived down there in the bottom, below the porches," she said.

I thought, *No wonder Tina O'Leary has stayed in the travel lodge business.*

No longer quiet, she opened up as a fervent and proud hometown tour guide. Just outside town, she showed me the Robert Byrd Elementary School. "That's where I beat up Butch Townshend in front of the entire fifth grade in the cafeteria. He was a bully, and ... the principal's son." Tina laughed with a nod which I read as 'oh yeah; I did that.'

"He poured milk down the front of my shirt, and then pushed it into my chest for not loving it. I pounded on him without mercy until he ran crying to daddy down the hall. All the kids cheered. I loved it."

"Remind me to be careful with a glass of milk."

"Mr. Ford, you haven't drunk milk in years, I bet."

"So?"

"So, what? You like milk?"

"Yes, silly. So, what happened? Did you get in trouble or get a gold star on your locker?" I was feeling rather familiar with Tina now. *Take my cabin. Take my heart and soul. Who cares?*

She finished the story, "Principal Townshend made me finish sixth grade in the next town." She then showed me the town's haunted house where "a million" cats lived, she said, not far from the town dump.

And she showed me her parents' house. "I grew up there," she said flatly. It was a white Cape Cod with twin dormers on a steep dark gray roof. Impassively, she added that each dormer fronted a child's bedroom for two. One had been her two brothers' bedroom and the other dormer was a bedroom for her and her sister, though she had not "set foot" inside her bedroom for years. Tina's words came out sounding rigid.

When I asked the obvious question, she said, "Mother and Daddy died almost five years ago, at the hairpin Pine Gulch turn on Highway 14. Their car crashed down into the gulch and exploded. The sheriff picked up a drunk on the road about the same time that night; skid marks near the turn were similar to tires on the drunk's car.

"When they died, it was also about the time I gave up on that dope fiend from New Jersey I had foolishly married and tried to reform. [Her face tightened.] These are their wedding rings, Mr. Ford. [She held her necklace in front of her.] I keep them close to my heart always to remind me to be careful in picking friends."

She was crying and said, "I'm sorry, Mr. Ford. I'm ruining your day."

As I reached for her, she pulled a hankie out of her purse and let her head rest on my chest as I held her close. Again, she pleaded, "I'm really sorry, Mr. Ford. I didn't think I'd...."

I straightened her up and kept my hand on her shoulder for a moment, feeling my arm muscles wanting to pull her back to me. But I didn't. "It's my fault. I asked about them, so let's take a ride, okay?"

"Sure. I've been thinking of Daddy a lot today because he first showed me your stories when I was in high school. He ran the town paper, *The Patrick Weekly*. It wasn't much, just a local rag of gossip and sports mostly. Daddy wanted me to be a reporter for his paper when I was a kid. But by high school I knew I didn't have the gift. I took the PR path instead. I organized all the dances and stuff. Close but no cigar, though I did great ads for Smokey Joe's Diner."

"But you are obviously very good at that," I said, as I dabbed her tears with her hankie.

"I do okay, but Daddy didn't see that in time. Well, you know it's tough to think about them, Mr. Ford. You see, now there is just Uncle Joe, Eloise who is his common marriage woman for 40 years, me and my twin sister, Shannon, and our brothers Thomas and Colin. Okay, let's go back to my car, Mr. Ford. Thanks for putting up with me."

Again, it felt very right being close to Tina O'Leary, though the molecules in my blood were no longer spinning wildly like before. I wasn't feeling that kind of attraction after being physically close to her the second time. This new feeling was comfort more than yearning or sexual or anything like that. I had a very kind and caring new friend, I realized, and gave up worrying about her motives. I had seen her astounding beauty. Now, I had 'felt' her heart. She was very smart too. Then I remembered, *Did she say twin sister? Good God. What's she like? Identical? There couldn't be two this beautiful, could there be?*

I put the top down on my little toy car to drive back to my cabin, so we could retrieve her car. She untied her hair and let it fall past her shoulders.

I put on my favorite white Dogfish Beer baseball cap that I hoped made me look tanned—a fantasy of mine. At least, give the old man that much.

Trying to avoid another silent, or even melancholy ride, I made a bet. "I know more hotel jokes than you do. I'll start," I said without looking at her. "I stayed at a family owned hotel in Munich which handed me a brochure that read 'because of the impropriety of entertaining guests of the opposite sex in the guest rooms, please use the lobby for this'."

"That's not a joke, but it is kinda funny, Mr. Ford."

So far so good, I thought.

I got bolder, "Okay then how about a West Virginia hotel joke?"

"There is nothing funny about a West Virginia joke, Mr. Ford, to someone born in West Virginia. Go ahead, though, you're driving."

Ah oh, a dangerous curve, I thought. I proceeded with caution, "You know you are at a West Virginia hotel when you ring up the desk and complain 'I gotta leak in my sink,' and the desk clerk replies ..."

In sync with me, Tina chimed in, "Go ahead."

She stopped laughing to add, "Good one, but it's supposed to be Arkansas, a Bill Clinton era joke. So, I'll let you go on that one, Mr. Ford. Okay, I know one: A man checks into a hotel for the first time ever in his entire life and goes to his room. But five minutes later he calls the desk. He asks 'You've given me a room with no exit. How do I leave here?' The desk clerk says, 'Sir, that's absurd. Have you looked for the door?' Then the man says, 'Well yes, there's one door that leads to the bathroom. There's a second door that goes into the closet. And there is a door I can't try to open.' The clerk asks, "Why not." And the man says there is a sign on that door that says do not disturb."

"Pretty good," I lied. But the whole idea was to just build a friendship, not to be hilarious. I thought I'd slip in some sex in a joke. I asked, "Do you like Rodney Dangerfield?" I faked pulling a necktie from side to side and shook my head, "I tell ya, my wife always wants to talk with me during sex. Just the other night she called to talk with me from a hotel."

Nothing from Tina.

"Don't like Rodney? You must. Here's another: One time I checked into a hotel and asked the bellhop to handle my bag. He started to feel up my wife. I tell ya, no respect. No respect at all."

I lucked out. She loved it.

The jokes digressed into racy one-liners as we got up to the cabin and I said, "Wanna come in for a nightcap?"

"That's ridiculous. It is only 6:18. The sun's still out," she laughed again as if it was another joke. "But not inside, right?"

She was right. We stood together in bright daylight. But, I remembered that the wine and mason jars awaited us. Luckily, she was willing to take that nightcap.

I closed the cabin door behind us.

I could only focus on one thing at that moment as we entered the dim light of my cabin with its canvas-covered windows: I needed to touch her. I didn't know how. But, in some way, right then and no later, I needed to find out if she would respond. *She had to come to me,* I thought.

As if guiding her to the wine in the kitchen, I reached for her waist to push her along in the semi-darkness. She was only just two steps inside when she turned to face me. We were close. We pulled into one another.

We never made it to the kitchen. We didn't even make it to the bedroom that first time. We fell to the middle of my soft living room rug.

Still, it was so right.

Chapter 18

"Mr. Ford."

"Yes, Miss O'Leary?"

We woke in my bed at midnight. I laughed proudly with a love-filled heart. I felt wonderful, fulfilled, settled. She clutched the sheet to her chin and sat up.

"Do you think that merlot is still waiting for us in the kitchen?"

"Yeah. I'll get it, with my finest crystal. Hungry?"

"Nah."

"Me either. Now, about that offer for my precious property Miss assistant vice president for public relations ..."

"Get the damn wine, Mr. Ford."

"You know, Miss O'Leary, these formal titles are rather cute."

"I know. We sooo still have a contract to discuss, MISTER Ford!" She laughed the most beautiful laugh I ever heard. She seemed at ease with letting her emotions show. She trusted me, I thought.

I didn't have a robe, just slipped on my shorts, still being self-conscious about our age difference.

As I walked into the kitchen I practiced my stoic look, thinking again that I was like Bruce Willis, the look, which masks the thrill that I was feeling. *Boy, am I ever so insecure about my manhood*, I thought. *I've become a pathetic, desperate, insecure ... no, no, I'm not.*

Yet, this thing with the young woman from the motel, whatever was happening, was not something I felt egotistical about. To me, she was certainly not a conquest of a younger woman I might have heard about from a colleague at the paper. I was just hoping that she too felt the affair was right. I saw or heard no doubts from her, as I might have expected, until maybe later that morning.

Chapter 19

When I woke again, it was daylight.

She was not in the bed.

I could hear clanking dishes in the kitchen. The aroma of eggs and toast filled the cabin.

She was fully dressed, in different clothes, a skirt and green Vacation Inn sweat shirt. "You were still sleeping so I slipped over to the motel and stole some food stuff from the galley and changed. Here, you like eggs and bacon, Mr. Ford?

I couldn't think of something to say.

Awkwardly, she added, "So, I was wondering. How is the memoir coming along?"

She sounded a bit impersonal. I noticed with disbelief that she had changed her expression to a sort of phony vulnerability and an almost a theatrical, distant air. I told her it was coming along okay.

I think she caught herself with the impersonal tone because she lightened up and continued, with her hands to her cheeks and an open mouth, "Oh, good morning. I swear, where on earth did I leave ma mannehs, Mr. Ford," she said with a Louisiana draw, while moving the back of her hand to her forehead in a fainting posture, feigning to stagger back. She laughed.

I took a guess, "You do a wonderful Blanch Dubois, Miss O'Leary. And, good morning to you. Thank you for all this. You didn't have to." I was so pleased that she had not changed her humor and attitude as well as her clothes at the motel. She was still happy to be with me. *Miracle upon miracle,* I thought, still feeling old despite all my good fortune, so far.

She didn't have a lot to say while I ate, just fussed around with rinsing pans and washing dishes. Then, she sat down to the table to have coffee with me and took on a serious tone of voice. "I have something to say, Mr. Ford. I hope you don't think this is a confession or that I have deceived you in any way."

She paused for a long moment.

I lost my appetite.

And then, she said, "In no way did I expect what happened between us to happen, I swear. I was genuinely taken by you and hopefully you by me."

She was clearly holding back and became nervous. Was she ending it so soon? I was still feeling amorous and was not yet sensitive to her mood swing. I stood up and began trying to pull her up on her feet and hold her close. Instead, she moved her chair in further to the table away from my hands. I sat back down.

"I need to tell you that there is something very wrong with my company and I can't stand to know about it any longer without telling someone. I can't live with myself working there much more. It's so bad, even though the job took me home here. Sure, I admired your work. You are the best investigative reporter I found for whom to base my thesis. I continued to follow your work because my daddy loved it too … aah."

She took a breath and closed her eyes for just a second or two. And then, she looked right into my tired old bloodshot eyes and continued, "I didn't ask you to be the guy in the cabin that's blocking my company from its plans for a ski lodge, as absurd as that seems. And then yesterday, oh my … then, last night I thought I cared enough to sleep with you." She stopped talking and turned away and said, "I shouldn't have."

Oh boy, here it comes, I thought. Quickly, I ventured into the fray, "Wow, you're pretty mixed up right now. Drink your coffee and relax. I'm a man, Miss O'Leary. If I never see you again, yesterday was to me great because you are quite a woman, a far better woman than I ever deserved to find me interesting. Whatever your story is, that's okay, because I believe in you for some reason. I know it sounds crazy because we just met. Now listen, I don't think you made a mistake at all staying over. No, I don't think you made a mistake. I know you didn't. I absolutely can assure you that you made no mistake staying over." That was the best I had at the moment—pretty pathetic.

She got up from the kitchen table and paced about slowly, hands on hips.

I watched her with an open mind as we each collected our thoughts. I didn't care about her guilty conscience as much as getting her mind back to wanting to be with me for more than one day. Of course, I just got out of bed with the gorgeous woman and didn't care if I had been manipulated to get my land. I only cared if that might end it. I took from her difficult statement that she didn't intend to use sex for anything. I hoped she was sincere in that.

I began eating again, mostly to let her think. Glancing over a sip of my coffee I then noticed her watching me closely. Her face was stern. Her body had lost her pretty posture and she slouched, shoulders turned down, as if carrying a heavy load.

She circled the table, and only began to talk when she was behind me, "My company, you likely know, Mr. Ford, is a motel chain that is part of a large group, many of the brands are not as well known as ours. We are the fastest growing chain in the industry by far, the most profitable, on paper that is. In my job, I deal with only the positive, the sunnier side of the business.

"For the past several years, I've been very proud to represent such a fun and entertaining company. The public mission is to make people, that is, families happy. My bosses are whacky but I just assumed that was all part of the business. I've loved working for them. They have been charming and supportive of what I do.

"Here is my problem and it is more than what we just discussed; you know; sleeping here and all. I am up for a promotion, a position in the corporate office of the entire Vacation Inns Group, headquartered in Boston. When I learned I would be interviewed at corporate for that position, I embraced the idea and like everything I do, I wanted to do it right, the best I can. So, I asked friends in our accounting department if I could be allowed to study the finances of the corporate group before I had to face my interview in Boston next week. I needed to be able to answer all the questions and more. I needed to be totally informed. That's who I am."

She seemed scared to go on.

I encouraged her, "You did the right thing. Any career transition coach would teach that."

She continued with, "Thank you. Well, at the accounting department, there was something that changed my impression of the corporation. For the first time, and to my shock and dismay, I learned that those friends of mine in accounting, who had previously been cheery with me, seemed to be scared to death. I mean really damn scared. By taking a sudden interest in the books, the finances, of the company and the group, my visit intimidated the hell out of them almost instantly. Me, the nice PR lady they always liked. We had worked together for several years in different departments. Yet, when I asked to know more about their department, they treated me like I was a spy for an enemy nation.

"Something is rotten in there. Their faces were freaked out. I had specific questions, like 'can I see the revenue sheets for the past few years.'"

I stopped her and offered, "What's wrong with that? A good business reporter's first step: What are your revenues and expenses? Next, what are your projections?"

She agreed, "You would think, yes. But the bottom line—I'll get right to the point—is that I think my company has been cheating in its financial statements, Mr. Ford. Cheating big time. There is a deep recession in the country and the company on paper is still cleaning up financially. My accounting friends, maybe former accounting friends, one in particular, are afraid for their jobs."

"So, you are saying that you've had a change of heart about your job?" I asked.

"Right, with my promotion interview coming up fast, I don't know what to do."

She continued to pace in a small circle until she leaned back with her bottom resting for support on the mini-frig. She looked directly at me.

I folded my hands on the table in front of me, a little body language sign I figured would help steady her. It always works for me interviewing a nervous person.

"Here's the rub, Mr. Ford. I think all of them are cheating, maybe criminally—all the member hotels and motels, car rentals, and travel clubs in the group, are misrepresenting the business to the stockholders, the large investors, Wall Street, the public, the government. I suspect the huge membership numbers are fake too."

"How long have you known?" I asked.

"About a month. I have a mole inside accounting, a good friend who finally fessed up. She caved to my questioning over brandy at her house, lots of brandy. I slept over on her couch I was so drunk. She now considers me as someone she can share her terror with, you know, to get things off her chest. She is a great friend who is trustworthy, who has thoroughly convinced me that my employers are crooks.

"I have contemplated quitting. But there is a problem. With this promotion opportunity, I think it would look suspicious if I walked away now, after I've been probing around in accounting. I'm sure they know I've been in there. Maybe that is why they want to promote me away."

"Where would they send you to cool off? Boston?"

"Headquarters are near there, yeah. I'd go to their Cape Cod location. But, if I stay here, I would be still close to my family. It is perfect for me because they are thinking of making the Trout Heaven Inn the hub of a new corporate region. I would be a natural to stay. I just don't know, Mr. Ford."

I asked, "Have you told anyone else about this dilemma of yours and your suspicions about the company cheating?" At the same time, I was thinking fast. I began to feel pinched, in a quandary so to speak: Should I try to continue the affair and stay with her because I could love this woman? Or should I cut ties and jump into investigating this delicious corporate fraud story? The two are not compatible.

I dismissed the thought and hit a reset button in my mind, because Tina O'Leary had opened her heart in my kitchen. I had no choice but to help her and to hell with the consequences. To hell with any conflict of interests. She was worth the risk of a reprimand at my job or worse, getting fired if I get the story while I slept with my source.

I put up a stop sign with my right hand and said, "I don't have to ask if you're sure of all that, because you are here telling me, and you probably know more about me than anyone else in your company. So, did they really choose you to come here Monday, or didn't they? Was that a real contract on the piece of paper you started pulling out of your brief case yesterday?"

"Yes, it was a real contract. As I have said, they didn't know I was bringing it over here yesterday. I had volunteered earlier to do it and they were considering me to do the task on Monday, as I told you before we spent that lovely day yesterday together. But they didn't say for sure they'd have me do it. So, I couldn't let them not choose me. I decided to come on Saturday to make sure I met you. Donald, the Bellboy, told me he would not tell anyone; I think he has a crush on me.

"Still, before I came, I didn't know if I had the courage to share this situation with you, Mr. Ford. I needed to find out if I would offer the deal for your property or share what I just said. I just had to meet you and see for myself. If you were a complete bastard, which considering your aggressive reporting was a real possibility, or even someone not to be trusted, I would have turned right around and left your cabin, or just perhaps given you the contract Monday.

"In any case, the real issue is that I have to deal with the scandal brewing at the company as best I could. I'm pretty high profile over there, you know."

I said, "Yeah, what a tough spot you're in Miss O'Leary. Thank you for trusting me, if that is what you are doing."

"I guess so; I feel like I am. But, frankly after last night, I am pretty mixed up. For me, this sleeping with you on top of my dilemma doesn't add up right." She gestured toward the bedroom by tossing her arm in that direction and shook her head. "I've admitted that I have admired your work; I woke up worried that I was acting like some kind of groupie, bedding down my rock star."

Wow, that's heavy, I thought. *She really does trust me.* I tried to hide my chuckle. It was so damn flattering.

This time I put up two hands to stop her worrying, "Listen Miss O'Leary, you've dealt with two tragic and traumatic events in your young life already: your doping husband and your parents' death. And those are the only two that I know about. For you, this will pass. You are going to land on your feet if you stay clear of the trouble. I agree, as public relations, you will be on a high wire."

She was blushing, but shaking too, almost crying out of relief, "I think I care for you a lot Mr. Ford. I have surprised myself."

I changed gears to help us both clear the air, "I'll try this one more time. The names, Mr. Ford and Miss O'Leary have been really cute. But, we've already been lovers. Call me Hank, will you?"

"I don't know how cute it is. We still have business to do. Mr. Ford will do for now. That way I remain formal to my bosses if I refer to you. Sex is on a whole different level; I think you understand that. However, this, to me, is more troubling than marrying a drug addict when I knew that he was one all along. My parents' death was a freak accident I had no part in. But, I came here to show you an offer for your property and instead I slept with you. Well, okay, you're right, Mr. Ford." She managed a crooked smile.

"Right about what?"

"The names are cute. Okay Mr. Ford, let's keep it that way, okay? I'm too confused. It's comforting to know I'm not completely nuts. But maybe I am. Am I?" The smile was gone.

I laughed a little and walked over and hugged her. I pulled away for her sake before I got too comfortable. I took her hand and pulled her tenderly back to her chair at the table.

I poured coffee. "Let's get to work on this Miss O'Leary. By the way, I still want the contract. I won't be here Monday. Slip the contract under my door. Come over before your bosses arrive, and then tell them you volunteered to do that. I have to go to the paper tonight. Tell your boss you left it, take that chance, as if that is what you understood them to mean Friday. Act like you were anxious to please them. But then tell them you talked with me as I was leaving. Tell them that I told you I was heading back to Washington and will be traveling for three weeks. That's three weeks, get it?"

"Yes."

"Tell them you gave me your cell number. Tell them that I called from my work and that I read it and I'll have an answer for them in a few weeks. They won't know that the contract is still on the floor inside my door. Act optimistic. Tell them I sounded optimistic. That will give us time. I know you can spin positive."

"That I can do."

"Can you also fake a family emergency or something and get that interview postponed? You will need to focus on our investigation, Miss O'Leary."

"OUR investigation?" She had a happy smile look of a kid on her birthday.

"Yes, I'm going to help you. I have to help you out," I said sternly.

She jumped up a little and blurted, "Oh my God, Mr. Ford. I didn't really …"

I replied with a big loving smile, "Oh shut up. Now, the practicality of all this is that I can help you because we do this all the time at the paper, me and the business section, expose corporate fraud. But really, I can help you, Miss O'Leary because you are you. I want to very much help you, again, because you are you. Get it?"

Tina O'Leary took a deep breath, sighed and exhaled with an audible "ahhah," and didn't move, letting a broad, contented smile slowly fill her with relief. Her eyes, welling up with tears, gave me a loving look. It was the kind of moment when a woman might have embraced her lover. She didn't. And, I was content with seeing the fond look she gave me.

BOOK TWO - An Appalachian Summer to Remember

I still may one day write that memoir. For now, it is less important. After first introducing you to all the ins and outs of my dilemma, that is, of losing out to bulldozers from hell, scoundrels from Boston, and greedy local lawmakers, it should be obvious, why I chose to help Tina, rather than stroke my ego with memoirs.

As I promised then, the remainder of my words here will be another kind of story. I hope you agree that what follows is far better than memoirs from a newspaper reporter.

Chapter 20

Sunday morning after the day I met Tina, I gave up the memoir struggle. My lonely, darkened, often drunken, days shut away in the cabin, angry and frustrated, were finished.

In retrospect, it wasn't going to work out in such an environment, though so promising at first. When Tina showed up, I was tilting toward full-blown alcoholism.

Tina O'Leary ever so gently had tipped me off to a far better story. Her heart and integrity while facing her more impossible dilemma than mine had overtaken my first impression of her stunning looks.

So here goes. I will try to reconstruct tips, quotes, and pieces of the Vacation Inns puzzle provided to Tina and me from an eclectic bunch of unlikely sources.

'Puzzle pieces?' you may ask. Oh yes. That Sunday morning in my kitchen, when I vowed to help Tina, I didn't have any factual proof whether Vacation Inns & Resorts Corp. was criminal or just sloppy and careless. I would be simply casting into a fishing expedition without any bait or even knowing where to cast lines yet.

Was I doing it just for the woman? Sure.

Chapter 21
Washington, D.C., Tuesday morning

According to their driver Gordo Jones, Levine and Goodbred arrived on Capitol Hill in their bright lime green limo at 9:59 a.m. for a 10 a.m. hearing on The Hill.

Trevor Goodbred was to testify with other hospitality industry CEO's before U.S. Congressman Lem Handwerker's Ethics Committee hearing on activities of the Motel Advancement Foundation of America. The group had been lobbying against a bill to expand taxing of interstate hospitality chains.

Gordy Jones was a state native who enjoyed Tina's friendship since they were chums in high school. After she was hired to do PR at Vacation Inns, she recommended they hire Jones, whom she said owned and operated a prominent taxi cab firm back home. He owned the only taxi in Patrick and surroundings, prominent indeed locally.

Gordy Jones, forever grateful, often kept his old pal Tina informed on the whereabouts of the execs. They talked by cell constantly.

As for ol' U.S. Rep. Lem, I knew the man well, his reputation that is.

When Tina called me Monday saying her bosses were summoned on the road to an emergency hearing by a very irate Handwerker staffer, I told her not to worry that she hadn't known about the pop hearing.

The once popular 67-year-old, 12-term Congressman Lem Handwerker of South Florida was a bitter man. He had just survived his latest reelection by only seven votes. I take partial blame. The election followed an exposé by yours truly in the Inquirer.

My story revealed that he allegedly kept a high-priced call girl on public salary living in a luxury suite at public expense at the Excelsior Hotel near Union Station.

We then followed with a story on confessions by hotel management that they knew Handwerker was paying hotel restaurant workers and a concierge to cover up Miss X's considerable expenses for meals, hair salon and her membership to its fitness gym.

The good lawmaker then pleaded to constituents that he was a happily married man and the story was the work of his political opponent.

He also claimed that the hotel, a Florida-based chain, and Miss X had conspired to frame him. He vowed to expose the nation's hospitality industry's "outrageous widespread fraud and price fixing," he stated.

As it turned out, what I told Tina was correct, that he was on the war path and Vacation Inns was among the chains in his sights. CEO's from competing hotel/motel chains testified that Vacation Inns was the worst offender of bad practices and gave the industry a bad name. After their testimony became public, Levine's secretary in the Boston office forwarded the call from Handwerker's staffer to their limo heading south, somewhere in the Poconos.

While Goodbred and other hotel CEO's were busy dodging old Rep. Lem's questioning, Trevor's buddy Simon Levine partied in the limo the entire afternoon. Driver Jones bragged to drinking buddies later at the Inn that when Mr. Goodbred returned earlier than expected to the limo in the East Capitol Parking Garage, he stepped into a disgraceful scene of debauchery going on behind the limo's tinted windows.

Si Levine and Gordo Jones were entertaining three 'escorts' from the Excelsior. Trevor Goodbred found the ladies 'making busy,' said the driver, while losing their itsy-bitsy lingerie, sharing Martinis and gorging on platters of delicacies from Al's Lounge and Delicatessen on South Capitol Street.

Goodbred had been gone only three hours. Yet, the limo was trashed with food, clothing and spilled drinks.

He ordered the driver to motor to the parking garage roof and to let "these ladies" out at the elevator wearing their clothes and jackets please, Gordo reported saying.

Levine was known for his playful leisure life style. It amused straight-arrow Goodbred, who was too careful and ambitious to allow him to be caught in mischievous public displays like that. Goodbred always maintained a décor of false dignity. And his love, his vice, and his passion were making money—anyway he could get it by hook or crook. No tip to the hookers from Trevor, said the driver, but Si had cashed out on them already.

An hour later, Trevor and sidekick Si were riding out on Route 50 West in Virginia from Washington, D.C. to catch up on their trailblazing for new sites in the lovely and historic Appalachian Range.

Their driver laughed with "those two screwballs," he said to Tina, all the way up into the mountain range in Virginia in the green stretch limo, stopping only once to a full-service car wash in Fairfax, Va.

Chapter 22

Yes, money was the only game to Trevor Goodbred. According to a friend at the Boston Globe, Tina's boss Goodbred was a franchising genius with enormous charm and good looks who would cut any corner, forge any document, or skirt around any law or regulation to beat the competition, and get away with it.

His tall and slender frame with straight black hair and a neatly trimmed thin mustache always impressed in made-to-measure suits, ties, and shoes from Louis Men's Clothier in Boston and the best casual wear from Mr. Sid's in nearby Newton, Mass. He always paid in cash, according to Tina's accounting friend. Trevor never left a trail. He always wore a gold Pierre Cardin watch with a sapphire crystal glass cover.

My Globe source continued to track Goodbred's trail after he left Massachusetts to colleges in Florida and Maryland. The source told me that when Goodie was just 24, he cut his swindling teeth as an undergrad student at the Robert H. Smith Business School in Maryland. To get in, he borrowed from his mother who was then re-married to a corporate tycoon in New York. After securing his funding, he changed his name from his birth name of Phillip Pfeiffer to Trevor Goodbred as he entered Smith.

I was able to find two classmates who knew him. One confirmed the other that Goodbred, once established as a dashing and charming Northeasterner, conned his own professors into believing that his father, who was really a drunken vagabond on back streets around Boston Commons, owned a chain of Chummy Chowda Cafes. All it took was for Trevor to photo-shop his father's face into the legitimate chowder chain's photos and web pages.

One of my University of Maryland sources, a graphic artist, did the dirty work on Trevor's false identity cards.

I also learned that Trevor's father George Pfeiffer was never heard from or seen again.

With the phony family heritage as collateral, the budding young entrepreneur Trevor Goodbred rented dilapidated warehouses all over the Washington, D.C. suburbs near his college and promoted them as undeveloped apartment buildings. He convinced 22 of his classmates to start their business careers with 2-year leases for just $3,000 up front. He would arrange loans for improvements through his father's credit, he told them.

Ss demolition crews later razed the warehouses as he knew they would, young Goodbred hid in Europe, taking an extended summer vacation. He had been at Smith for only three semesters, but long enough to be trusted.

Young Trevor invested part of his $66,000 he raised from classmates into a rundown potential motel site way off Massachusetts Route 6 halfway out on the Cape Cod peninsula. The future Vacation Inns headquarters building (after a beginning in young Trevor's studio apartment in Boston) was a former high school built in the 1920s. Goodbred saw it as the first Vacation Inn and Resort for his firm. It was perfect—near, but not at the prime New England vacation spot of Provincetown, Cape Cod.

That became Vacation Inn Corporation's signature formula—being located not quite in the 'high rent' districts, saving overhead on deceptively lower budget locations and advertising them to be located at prime resorts.

Simon Levine was a classmate at the Smith School and was one of the student investors who sunk $3,000 into the scheme by that nice handsome fellow Trevor Goodbred everyone there knew and liked. The diminutive, plump and already balding Levine at 29 was envious of Goodbred's cunning and good looks, and yet, despite being swindled, he was still an admirer. It was the last time Levine would foolishly trust his own money to the dashing Goodbred and the two eventually formed a mutual admiration and co-dependency.

It took Levine a year to track down and confront Goodbred hiding out in France. Goodbred gave back the money to him but also invested in Levine by promising him a stake in his plan to build a motel empire if Levine agreed to reinvest the $3,000 or more into Vacation Inns once back in the states. The investment is a sure thing, Goodbred reportedly told Levine. It would be a unique resort/lodging combination that had never been tried before. Levine would have to promise never to breathe a word of it to anyone.

That fall, they downed a bottle of Beaujolais under the red awning of Fouquet's restaurant on the Champs-Elyeess to seal the bond on collaboration.

Once set up for business in the United States, devious Trevor Goodbred admired Levine's tenacity and identified with his new partner's sinister thirst for crooked dealing. He also saw the gentler Levine as the perfect fall guy to shield himself from criminal activity.

However, on their return to the states, Levine was arrested for a prior charge of corporate fraud. Goodbred needed to wait for his pal to be freed from prison to manage the finances of the corporation the way Goodbred envisioned.

One year later, when Levine was released, Goodbred brought him in as an unofficial comptroller to use his book-cooking genius to put a lid on a scandal that was boiling up in the media concerning competitors' claims of fraud in Vacation Inns' membership scheme.

The original Vacation Inn marketing pitch had been conceived by comptroller Max von Kindel another Goodbred investor at Smith. I would eventually learn that von Kindel maintained two sets of membership rolls—one for the U.S. Securities and Exchange Commission and one for the real books, kept allegedly only at the company's Boston headquarters. Wiry and cagy in movement and personality, Max von Kindel was known throughout the corporation as Max von Swindle. Only after one year of von Kindel's system, he and his CEO Trevor Goodbred posed as cover boys on the June 2010 Lodgings magazine, the official publication of the American Hotel and Lodging Association featuring the centerpiece article, "Reinventing the

Motel/Resort," a seductively engaging piece on the Vacation Inn's splashy amenities.

Von Kindel was the only other person on earth who knew of the deal Goodbred and Levine had cooked up in Paris. Goodie owed him, it was said.

Soon after that first taste of national fame, however, Goodbred was anxiously waiting for his buddy Levine to be released from prison. Von Kindel was not doing enough in Goodbred's eyes for the new corporation to profit from the tricky membership plan.

Trevor told his board of directors it was time to bring in the cavalry. Goodbred's trusted man Si Levine from their days at the Smith School was the best way to get U.S. Rep. Handwerker off their trail.

But Goodbred was wise not to risk hiring Levine publicly. His buddy Levine had just served time in federal prison for bilking member franchisers of Slash and Dash Discount Stores, which he'd taken part in strategically locating them in impoverished inner-city neighborhoods. Levine escaped with a minor sentence by framing the CEO as responsible for "a revelation of fraud in the company dealings," Levine told government regulators that he'd discovered through an "independent" investigation.

Rep. Handwerker's committee was suspicious of the mercurial rise of the motel chain because the Vacation Inns Corporation was a white-hot commodity both in Wall Street and Main Street, while raising eyebrows at the SEC.

Chapter 23

Meanwhile 'back at the ranch,' the corporation that is, Goodbred was using great media coverage and Vacation Inn's skyrocketing financial reports, to scout cheap new resort locations at a dizzying pace.

For instance, after the pop Congressional hearing in D.C., Goodbred and Levine would toy with an idea of buying another run-down motel near Virginia's Luray Caverns for their next Vacation Inn. It was on the way to Sassafras County and in an economically depressed area. They stopped at Luray, Virginia to find out why the spectacular caverns attracted so many tourists.

That was a very bad idea, driver Gordo Jones later reported to his gossip pal Tina.

Trevor Goodbred had been seriously claustrophobic since childhood. Maybe it slipped his mind, said his driver. It looked harmless, he said, as they entered a doorway from a gaily designed gift shop.

They followed a typical tour down narrow steps of stone to the towpath through the limestone formations. Levine complained about the cool damp air in the caves and dragged behind. The lowest level, said the guides, would be 152 feet below ground level.

Trevor Goodbred began to feel sick.

Once he was deep inside the third chamber of Luray Caverns, Goodbred was nauseous and began to stumble. Levine, Goodbred and their driver were mashed in tightly among 'the common people,' Trevor called them, while walking on slippery rocks and narrow boards during the public tour of about 22 people.

One of the two teenage girls presenting the tour told Gordo later that that man with you turned pale as a ghost and staggered as he walked. The driver explained that it was not up to him where his boss goes.

Goodbred tried to find the words to express his discomfort. But, he could only grunt and snort miserably as he tugged on the back of driver Jones trying to get his attention to leave the caverns. But his efforts failed.

He vomited violently as he stood over 5-year-old Marisa Chavawn Moore, an African-American child on a church trip to Luray with her mother. Goodbred's entire Denny's grand slam breakfast of over easy eggs, sausage, bacon, biscuits, coffee, a large orange juice and home fries, poured right over little Marisa's head.

The little girl's mother was livid.

It happened so quickly even the normally slick-mannered Goodbred was unnerved and horribly shaken by the incident, Gordo said. But standing on shaky legs and delirious in the cave after violating a child with his puke, Goodbred was speechless for once in his life. He tried again, but he could not speak! The damp enclosure of the limestone cave had made him dizzy and near unconscious.

The innocent little child had been wearing a lovely white dress and matching white leggings when she walked right into the hurling vomit stream, which covered and matted the $100 relaxed hair styled specially for her mother's vacation.

Her mother had planned the trip, a Christian fellowship tour, to broaden the child and help her overcome shyness and stuttering. Her mother felt that the child, too sheltered in private school, needed to see the world. The busy working mom signed up for St. Peter's Church annual bus retreat to the hills of Virginia entirely to benefit her little girl.

Witnesses said "the big throw-up man" straightened and turned to address the mom after the accident. But instead he hurled again into mom's cleavage, which weighted down her V-neck sweater with the liquid load, exposing much of her breasts as she bent to the aid of her daughter covered with bits of Trevor's breakfast and stomach bile.

Finally, Trevor Goodbred managed gurgle talk, according to Gordy the driver. He said something like, "Gowd lady, I am sooo sowrry." Goodbred told the lady, as best he could, that he didn't want to be in the cave, and then blamed "my business associate" Simon Levine who said he'd be fine. Goodbred half apologized and stumbled to his knees. Goodbred then yelled over top of a dozen other tourists to Simon Levine. "Si, we have a mess here. Get this lady's name and contact information. I want to repay her with our best vacation package and ..." He bent over and choked again, according to Jones.

Concerned only for his boss, Levine pushed hurriedly through the crowd of tourists, said Gordo. While looking up in fear of the stalagmites falling on him in the chilly cavern, Levine yelled something like "What the hell Trevor? Are you sick?" He helped his boss up.

Goodbred, more composed, told the lady they were there to scout a new location at Luray for the fastest growing travel motel chain in the country, Vacation Inns. He asked her to give Levine her contact information and offered her a free membership good at any of our 35 locations coast to coast.

She could only glare angrily at the big, pale man and said nothing.

He started to hurl again. Goodbred took off running toward the cave entrance, ignoring pleas from the girl tour guide's plea for them to stay with the group.

Simon Levine chased after Goodbred without speaking to the woman or even looking at her and her daughter. In Levine's haste, his shoulder accidently rammed into the mother and daughter. They fell and rolled under the guardrail toward Dream Lake, a reflecting pool. Only quick feet of the tour guide saved the mother from the open pool of ice cold water by jumping in first to catch her. But her child lost her balance clinging to mom and fell into the shallow water. Mom jumped in to save the child and was knee deep in the cold water splashing everywhere. Other guests got splashed.

Gordo said the group would then miss the chance to admire a perfect mirror effect of the still pond reflecting the above stalactites appearing as stalagmites on the surface, one of the tour highlights.

The tour group, including the guide and the enraged mother in the pool of ice water, turned to see the two men from Vacation Inns running away, with a man in a chauffeur's uniform running behind them.

The younger of the two girls guiding the tour walked little Marisa and her still silent, still seething and soaking mother to the cave entrance.

Had Simon Levine taken her name, he would have learned that Marisa's mom was Valarie Moore, Esq., a distinguished Columbia University corporate law professor.

Moore was acutely aware that her Christian fellowship vacation for her only child was off to a disastrous beginning because of those men in the caves from a company called Vacation resorts, or something.

Gordo Jones drove his executives to their next stop on flatter ground, The Inn at Little Washington, which is an historic and expensive hotel in a town in the Virginia hills. Little Washington was laid out by George Washington on the site of a trading post for frontier families and the Manohoac tribe. Goodbred recovered in luxury, but dashed hopes of establishing a competing Vacation Inn there or in nearby colonial Sperryville. Driver Jones said that Levine advised him the region was locked in history for tourists and "far too classy for a couple of outlaws like us, Trevor."

Goodbred regained his stomach and strength in luxury as the two brushed off the unfortunate incident in the nasty caves as a joke. Gordo Jones said his bosses concluded that the Luray Cavern resort management was obviously risking the safety of tourists, which could not be further from the truth at the responsible tourist attraction. He evidently brushed the incident aside and never gave another thought to Valarie Moore and her daughter.

Tina, their public relations point person, also never got Valarie Moore's name from Gordo Jones. If she had, Tina would have insisted that Levine try to compensate Moore with a free stay at one of their inns.

In fact, Tina had little knowledge yet of the odd bond between playful Levine and slick Goodbred and the worst kind of devilment and selfish behavior they brought out in each other outside of their official duties in managing the hospitality chain.

They were bad, but usually lucky together, Luray being an exception.

Chapter 24

As their luck would have it, on the next day after Luray Caverns the two men discovered an individual who might allow them to keep Levine in the shadows and still manipulate the corporation's finances. Goodbred still worried about how to shield Levine from any federal investigation. Another conviction and he would risk exposing the company for any shenanigans. Therefore, they were traveling incognito in the limo with tinted windows. And, Goodbred had not allowed Levine near the menacing glare of old Handwerker when he was being grilled in Congress.

Traveling through the ultra-conservative Lynchburg, Virginia area and their destination, Trout Heaven, they stumbled upon the solution to keeping Levine under wraps.

They discovered sugar-sweet, born-again Christian Anita Rapshire, a local civic icon of solid morals. She was the St. Parish Baptist Church membership director extraordinaire. Perfect.

Jones had spotted a highway sign for the church-sponsored bull roast.

Levine, napping, woke instantly and spouted, "Stop, stop. These are great. I do them all the time."

Mostly to take advantage of a good country cooked meal Goodbred and Levine attended.

Goodbred, amused, said, "Where better to feel the culture?" He hoped the food in the hick town would be delicious, and trusted Si.

The stop would be well worth it. Yet, the 'performance' by Rev. Rapshire was far better for them than was the delicious food.

This was the final day of Mrs. Rapshire's annual church membership drive. There were more than 100 people at the outdoor event on the sloped lawns of the church. Yet, she had no difficulty noticing three guys in snappy sport coats stepping out of the gaudy green limousine.

Si, Trevor and their driver "witnessed" that very day, just like everybody else on the church lawns. Unlike the other people there, the three from Vacation Inns didn't so much witness for Jesus Christ, but witnessed for pretty Anita as their savior and protector from any future investigations of Levine's financial management at Vacation.

At a settled point during the outside dinner, Anita Rapshire rose to a podium, which was not much more than a metal music stand.

Simon Levine was spellbound. She conjured up images somewhere between the staid and elegant beauty of Catherine Deneuve and sweet and shapely Dolly Parton, complete with a Tennessee twang. Her manner and kindness fully projected her loving wholesome heart and handsome looks.

Here is a selection from her church membership sales pitch from a video recorded that day and available on YouTube, including glimpses of Trevor Goodbred with a crooked, closed mouth smile while nodding approval, and Si Levine ogling at Rev. Rapshire between bites of his lunch.

She began, "Folks, I do indeed hope you like the roast beef. I hope you like the roast beef good enough to come back. We've got lots more from God's house on the hill here in Lynchburg. Yes, sir. Praise the Lord."

Banjo and mandolin musicians struck a few notes just slightly reminiscent of Amazing Grace, quietly.

Alternating her best preaching and sales voices, the daughter of a Baptist minister Anita Rapshire stepped back up to the microphone:

"Brothers and sisters, yes indeed, I want you to consider this roast beef, this potato salad, this corn-on-the-cob and apple cider today as God's gift of nourishment, a special kind of nourishment from his heart to yours as you join us in this outdoor chapel of faith. Consider this a free ticket to be faithful for the rest of your days. As Jesus said, 'and I will give thee the crown of life.' What gift could be better at this place at this time today, folks?

"The roast beef costs $9.50 a person, yes. But then, God's nourishment within is free. Hear Jesus today, brothers and sisters, and stay with us as members of this blessed church. He will guarantee that for what shall it profit a man, if he shall gain the whole world, and lose his own soul. Can I get an Amen, brothers?"

Goodbred stood and shouted, "Amen!" Even Si Levine, a boy raised Jewish in Bethesda, but of no known religious tendencies as an adult, shouted Amen in the intense fever of the moment.

"And can I get an Amen, sisters?" Anita led the joyful crowd and, with not a fork moving now, she continued to quote Jesus Christ, "Or what shall a man give in exchange for his soul? Let us pray and bless this meal brothers and sisters of Lynchburg and beyond."

The Vacation Inn men appeared to be in a trance, surprised and delighted.

After a short blessing, Anita continued to preach, as her words and tone subtly transformed into a pure sales pitch for church membership. She gestured wildly, danced about, and proselytized the public until in short order she had recruited dozens upon dozens of families into the fold of her church. They rushed to the podium to touch the hands of their reverend, as if she was God in residence.

It was all happening before Levine's envious eyes. He, Jones and Goodbred were chatting and nodding in approval.

Gordo Jones said Levine whispered to him, "I love this woman to death."

We learned through Gordo that Levine told Goodbred that "this luscious woman is perfection. Sign her up Trev." Levine was convinced Anita Rapshire would put a protective halo over the corporation. "Trev, I want her," their driver heard Simon Levine say while chewing his blessed roast beef and staring at what was left on his paper plate like it was a direct gift from God.

Spiritually, Simon Levine was enigmatic, a man of unknown beliefs. At heart, he was still known as more like the rather grubby, lonely child he once was, always looking for mischief and still resenting his parents dumping him off to summer camp by himself each year.

Later that afternoon, they met with dynamic Anita. Convinced by Levine's halo theory, Goodbred offered her a job as Levine's membership financial officer for the entire corporation. Seemingly a naive country bumpkin Anita was the perfect candidate, they thought. She would be easy to manipulate by the generosity of the company. They offered her the best stock options in the entire corporation, they said.

They said she could set up chapels in each new Vacation Inn. Gordo said that Levine and Goodbred privately discussed making said chapels accessible only through the resorts' gift shops, in which they would add a few crucifixes and pocket prayer books, Goodbred suggested.

The good church lady was impressed. She was stunned that two gentlemen from an important northeast corporation were attending that day and were willing to be saved by Jesus Christ, her Lord and Savior.

She told Goodbred she'd think about the job offer. Simon Levine hugged her tight, surprising his partner Trevor. No harm done though. Anita by then was taken by Simon's charm and seemingly enthusiastic worshiping.

As she watched them climb back into the gaudy green motor coach, Anita had a chance to speak with Gordy Jones. He said she told him that life gets so exciting when you are led by the Holy Spirit. "That Mr. Levine was so courteous and attendant to my preaching," she told Gordo. She said she certainly would look forward to helping Mr. Levine do the books. She called him that poor fellow who seems empty hearted and in need of God's fulfillment.

Goodbred had convinced her, Gordo said, that Simon Levine was desperate for help with the blessed finances. To that Anita said to Gordo Jones, "Tell them God speed."

Much later, I became friends with Anita's husband, Clarence Rapshire, mainly through fishing. Clarence would tell me that when Anita brought her story home that evening, he thought the two out-of-towners must have been just hitting on his attractive preacher wife with their fast talk and money. She then thought, yes, their offer was flattering, but too outlandish to be taken seriously.

But then, Clarence changed their minds though when he heard about the giant rainbow trout in Crater Lake, just over the next hill from the Trout Heaven Vacation Inn and Resort. He was an avid angler who missed fishing at Percy Priest Lake near their prior home in Nashville before she moved them to the church in Lynchburg.

Chapter 25

The next day, Anita and her unemployed husband assessed their future with their four children, still in grade schools in Lynchburg.

Anita then sent back a hand-written preliminary offer to the two kind gentlemen from Vacation Inns and Resorts Corp. and accepted their $78,000 a year salary with generous stock options, with no further negotiations. Tina said giggling that Anita was convinced that the stock options put husband Clarence over the top, by saying something like, "Sounds like a mighty sound investment. Can't go wrong with givin' folks affordable vacations, Sugar Babe."

Tina aimed to make Rev. Rapshire an ally at some point if possible.

Anita Rapshire was to be Vacation's front lady on finances, but concerning memberships only, a puppet chief financial officer reporting to Levine. She would realize once on location that she was not at all responsible for SEC reports, stock holder conferences, and annual reports. Those were Simon Levine's bailiwick responsibilities, which he would keep close to the vest and share with Anita through SEC reports prior to posting them for her initials.

Only three other people knew Levine's system, Trevor Goodbred, Levine's private secretary Pauline, and the chief accountant in Boston named Bertrand R. Smith, whom Tina or the Trout Heaven Inn accountants never saw or heard from. Former comptroller Max von Kindle had disappeared.

The system was so full of loopholes and trapdoors to hide the truth, accounting personnel in each Vacation Inn region could not decipher how their reports to headquarters translated into official public financial statements.

For example, his system accounted for new memberships only arbitrarily. When former guests cancelled their memberships, the system kept the account active, not canceled. Accounting reserves were reported in three straight SEC quarterly reports to cover new acquisitions. However, it became increasingly difficult to cover up mounting losses with Vacation Inns officially adding dozens of new properties in many states and the purchase of a supporting cast of so-called supply and service companies growing at a dizzying rate. Investors continued to pour in support.

I overslept Sunday night after spending most of the weekend with Tina. The excitement, the passionate lovemaking, and wine predestined me to crash like an elephant in my cabin bed without setting the alarm clock.

I called in late. Before I left, there was a manila envelope inside my door from Tina, as we had planned. I resisted opening it to read the offer. Clipped outside of it was a note: *Thank you Mr. Ford for understanding.* No signature.

Instead of driving all the way on Route 7 to I-81 North, I crossed the Sassafras and doubled back to take a closer look at our target for the investigation, the Trout Heaven Inn.

My sports car was distinctive and easily recognized, perhaps later as mine. Instead of driving right up to Trout Heaven Vacation Inn and Resort, I parked behind my dreaded 7-Eleven store where it could not be seen from the Inn. I purchased a knit Tennessee Titans cap and a big gulp Slurpee in a Titan's cup to hide my face below my shades and walked to the golf shop at the Inn.

As if on my cue, Goodbred's big green limousine soon pulled up to the Inn and onto a covered veranda of fake stone and a maroon tin roof. I realized for the first time that the picture postcards shown on the website of the Trout Heaven Vacation Inn were lies. They were evidently taken from the Inn's entrance road high atop the mountain. Judging by those pictures, the Inn appeared to be constructed of logs with a Yellowstone Lodge design with tiny guest windows three stories high, and the mighty green-gray waters of the Sassafras River beyond. Nice perspective. Clever.

However, with a closer look, it was apparent that the log construction was simply 3-dimensional aluminum siding made to look like logs. Covered walkways to the golf shed on the right and the outdoor Trout Flipping Café were constructed of temporary 2x4 framing covered with translucent plastic sheeting drawn tight. Signs to the golf shop, nature trail and more were duct taped up on the plastic.

The only activity around the Inn that Goodie and Si could have seen upon arrival, if they had noticed, was an elderly couple with golf clubs slung uncomfortably on their shoulders. They were fussing over which of the only two old green golf carts to choose, the deciding factor perhaps being which one had the least rust and dents.

The two corporate big shots ignored the struggling seniors, rather than try to help them.

From the limo, Simon Levine climbed out first, while still clutching the job offer to his new best friend (hopefully) Anita Rapshire in his thick hand.

The church lady would train for her new position there, at the future regional headquarters in Trout Heaven. They also promised a future promotion to headquarters in Boston. She preferred to keep her family near her native Tennessee. But Goodbred made the incentive offer anyway because Levine hoped she would one day join him in Boston.

While Si Levine chattered on about Anita on a tiny veranda, Goodbred had another woman on his mind. He asked bellboy Donald, "Is our PR lady O'Leary here yet?"

Donald responded, "Yes sir, Mr. President, sir. Miss O'Leary is probably waiting for you in the lobby."

"Very good. What's your name, son?"

"Donald Smythe, sir."

"Well Mr. Donald Smythe, I am the Chief Executive Officer of Vacation Inns Corporation, not its president, officially, that is. But, I am nevertheless flattered," said Goodbred handing the boy a $50 bill. "Can you remember that Donald?"

Without waiting for an answer to hear the boy's high pitched thank you, Goodbred charged into the motel entrance to greet Tina O'Leary, who had been watching them just inside the door and behind a potted Alberta spruce. Before he reached her, Tina told me later she heard him turn to ask Levine, "Smythe, Smythe, where do I know that name from, Si?"

"Manny Smythe," Levine said, closer to Goodbred's ear, "It was the farmer who had the produce stand, Trev, on Route 7. This kid might be a relative. All these hillbillies are related in some way. ... Oh, hello Miss O'Leary. How are you, dear?" Levine said, surprised to see her suddenly standing right next to them. She had heard everything. He extended his arms as if to welcome a hug. She politely declined and greeted her bosses with a firm handshake.

Bellboy Donald Smythe, only 19, remembered the $50 of course, but mostly he told us how terrified he was by encountering Goodbred and Levine.

Donald sensed trouble from the pair, he confessed to Tina. She and I would value Donald's perspective often in the coming weeks.

Chapter 26

When I drove back into the city and to my job at the Washington Inquirer, I felt a moment of shame that I didn't miss stopping for fresh vegetables at Manny's stand. Instead, Tina O'Leary was on my mind, my every other thought and breath, as I had driven back.

I continued to have no qualms about investigating her company. Yet my first thoughts were on love, and I admit, I knew it was not a smart thing to dwell on so quickly for a 53-year-old divorced man attracted to a woman in her mid-30's. I thought, *Sure it could work. Sure, I'm no schoolboy, but Henry Clyde, this is different.*

Okay, I know what you think: the male ego is difficult to keep down. To be frank, the sex was enough for me to dwell on. I never had a woman's sense stay inside my head like that. She stayed in my hands on the Beamer steering wheel, on my computer keyboard at the office, on the sheets and pillow on my bed in my home on Capitol Hill. I felt her hair on my cheeks, the smell and softness of her skin.

Even when I fell in love with my former wife Janet years ago, such complete fulfillment didn't stay with me like I was feeling. Not to knock my love for Janet. We had had an instant connection that felt right also because we had so much in common, so much fun and sure, sexual relations were great too. But it wasn't this intense, which also concerned me. What are the chances of someone like young Tina falling for someone like cynical old me? Zilch. I needed to have reasonable expectations. My soul still missed the loving companionship of Janet. But that didn't alter missing Tina day after day.

I didn't dare share these thoughts with friends and employees at the paper. Colleagues might dismiss me as a fool. After pondering my expectations for a day or two, I decided to rationalize my desire for Tina. It was my mission to help her. She was going to be facing some serious choices.

Vacation Inns and Resorts Corp. was at the very least bordering on the criminal and maybe a major corporate scandal. Right up my alley.

Because Tina was the company's public relations face, I worried about her safety. Small town roots might explain her naive view of life contrasted with her outstanding physical presence. City girls with Tina's looks would have hardened their public persona long before age 34.

After only two days back in D.C., I wanted to see her again. But, I couldn't bring myself to inventing an excuse to race my sports car back to the hills. I didn't know if she was still there after the corporate board convened. Maybe she was showing them around the location. I didn't want to know, I convinced myself. But I was very worried about her up there in the lion's den.

At my desk at the paper I decided it would be best to put my mind to filing creampuff easy stories so I could start investigating Vacation Inns Corp. on the sly. I filled my weekly story budget on the intranet with the easiest slugs I could invent.

My editors didn't need to know about a Vacation Inns story yet. I learned a long time ago it's not smart to tell your editor much until the story gels. Otherwise, you end up explaining over and over again why you dropped the story idea. They never forget screw ups, just your good stories.

By 5 p.m. Wednesday. I finished my creampuff story for the day, an award for a top Latino entrepreneur in D.C. for the metro section, and had some time left to poke around cyberspace for background on Vacation Inns.

I clicked on D&B Hoovers.com, the business research company. Very quickly, I confirmed that in the past decade, Vacation Inns grew faster than any motel or hotel chain in American history. Evidently, no one noticed. The company reported its most recent openings in Maui, Yellowstone, Charleston South Carolina, New Orleans, and Trout Heaven.

Company accountants reported all the mergers and acquisitions, land purchases, and loans to a parent entity in the group, Greater Ability Corp. I could find nothing in Hoovers on GAC. I was intrigued. I then opened the SEC filings for Vacation Inns to check the legitimacy of the Hoovers' summary, when my phone rang.

"Hi Mr. Ford, I'm sorry to bother you at work." It was Tina. "Something's come up and I have to tell you about it, but not on the phone. I've got to see you as soon as possible."

I felt my heart swell, and then I replied, "I can't come up until after...."

"I'm in D.C."

"Where?"

"Right now, still in my car. I have to drop off some papers at Congressman Handwerker's office on The Hill. Then I can see you."

I said, "I live up there on The Hill, near Congress. I'll put something together for us to eat and I'll meet you at home, 414 C St. It's right next to Union Station so if there is no parking on the street park over there. And ... Miss O'Leary. Whatever it is, we'll deal with it."

I didn't have to say it was good to hear from her. I am sure each of us heard that in our excited voices. After I hung up, I worried what could possibly have happened to her after just three working days at Vacation Inns.

Chapter 27

A redheaded woman soon showed up at the old writer man's house.

She was not the worried or distraught Miss O'Leary whom I expected. Instead, she was beaming, and well, how could I say this better, smoking red hot! When I opened the door, I was amazed to see her wearing a light pink and green floral mini skirt tight against her beautiful curves with a white cotton halter top tied around her neck revealing her shoulders and arms. Her complexion was glorious.

"Wow, come in, quickly," I said, laughing.

But, she stood there, posed one hand on an extended hip, smiling devilishly.

I asked, "You wore that to old Lem "The Letch" Handwerker's office? The old fart must have died of a heart attack; come in before you get a summer time chill."

"I changed in the lady's room at the Rayburn House Building and put on a raincoat. Like it, Mr. Ford?" she said giggling.

As I hugged her, I felt hidden tension in her shoulders and back. She kept me close longer than I expected. "I hope you don't mind me coming," she said in a familiar female leading question.

"Of course not," I said. I pulled myself free of her arms reluctantly. I was still concerned about the urgency of her surprise visit. "Come on in to the living room and talk to me. I have a glass of Chateau Francois already poured for you."

My narrow 3-story townhouse was sparsely decorated, but I'd made an effort since being banished from my marriage to hire a decorator for my functional living room. As a reporter, I often entertained people there, potential sources commonly.

On my coffee table by the couch I'd left the two wine glasses of merlot with brie and crackers I had hoped would make her feel comfortable in my living room. Obviously, she was comfortable with me anywhere, judging by that sexy outfit.

Soon, with a half glass of wine, it became clear to me that what came up was nothing, but a notion in her pretty head to see me. Nothing had happened to her. She told me she had been extremely insecure at work and kept second guessing our plan to expose the company.

I didn't try to further convince her. Instead I just said, "Miss O'Leary, I would like to show you the bedroom. It's the best room in the house, very luxurious."

Upstairs, my bedroom was just a bed and dresser I picked up at Value City furniture store. Empty walls, sheer curtains and no wall pictures. Stark and functional.

Soon I guessed correctly that getting close was the kind of reassurance we both needed. She thought the same.

Our love making convinced me that this was not just a brief affair. I was grateful that at my age and having spent an eternity between any sexual relations, I was still energetic. Tina seemed more than just happy with me in bed. I dismissed troubling thoughts that getting laid in my cabin had been a casual one-time event. For the past three days I had feared that Tina was but a passing bit of love-life gift for me, quite the miracle. One fabulous evening with Tina at my house convinced me otherwise. We were a couple and would remain tight. She even admitted feeling "amazing," such a comment I imagine is not easy for a woman to utter so soon.

We agreed not to discuss the gathering storm at Vacation Inn Corp. It was a silent pact to just enjoy our new-found love, get to know each other outside of sex, well, just a bit, I guess. We talked all night.

In the morning, I asked her to lock up when she left. I had to get to the paper. First, however, we agreed over coffee on certain ground rules on our plan to expose Vacation Inns for what they were doing to an unsuspecting public, and perhaps to unsuspecting investors. Both of us would be risking our careers in the process. We agreed:

- Not to be seen together any place where a Washington Inquirer colleague might see us. If they got a look at her, I would have to tell how, when, where, and what I did to meet her. I don't like lying to my friends. But if I told anyone she was my lover, I ethically could not write or research the Vacation Inns story. (I was willing to risk getting fired for the love of this woman. I felt I could still be objective; stupid me.)
- She was not to mention my name to anyone at Vacation Inns & Resorts, Corp. If we did share our investigation with someone, we would have to agree that such a person was trustworthy and useful.
- We would clear our sources with each other before getting useful information from them. That did not include my regular sources that were not necessarily associated with this story. Certain 'deep throats,' if you will, often help me wring creeps from high positions out of the dirty corporate laundry, my specialty. Tina respected that.
- We would keep the cute surname suffixes, which might help if we are seen together.
- I would let Tina proof my copy whenever possible before publishing.
- For her protection, Tina would like to know when my story or stories on Vacation were scheduled to appear. That could be tricky. The paper tries to cram political, crime, and society news into a shrinking news hole. I promised to do my best, so she could lay low in a hurry if necessary.

Chapter 28

Tina opened a new private email account on a server used by the O'Leary family and unknown to her employers at Vacation Inns. We began to share secure notes, as far as we knew. She told me she would start staying more frequently at her parent's home with her sister, who worked in Charlestown in Virginia, instead of staying at the Inn. "I can chill out with her whenever I need to, Mr. Ford," she said.

Tina's prior studies of marketing and accounting when at the Harvard Business School gave her an edge to learn why her friends in Vacation's accounting and finance departments were nervous. She had a sharp mind for figures and she saw that things were not right. Friendly attitudes became tones of suspicion when Tina would ask about quarterly SEC reports and revenue charts.

Meanwhile, after I cleared the idea with Tina, according to our rules of engagement, I informed our business editor Devin Shay at the Washington Inquirer that there may be a story at Vacation Inns. I ask him to help me in confidence to understand some of the latest tricks in corporate bookkeeping yet to keep the idea off the paper's intranet story budget for the time being.

"It's bullshit, Hank," Devin immediately said, surprising me, "Membership scams are a dime a dozen. The SEC can be tipped off by that, sure, but then go after more blatant corruption elsewhere. Memberships in service-oriented corporations are a category of accounting the SEC often miscalculates or maybe just ignores. If you want to nail these guys at Vacation Inns and Resorts, you need to look deeper than that suddenly not-so-toxic lake up there."

I said without thinking, "Not-so-toxic lake? Well, they lifted the quarantine on that lake when people caught big trout there and attracted these Vacation Inn guys. Do you know more about Crater Lake?"

"No; just guessing. Seems suspicious that's all." He picked up on the trout reference and told me that, as far as investigating for tricks in SEC reports, that I should start "fishing" for submerged assets in the stream of footnotes in the company periodic reports to the regulating agency.

When I returned to my desk, I emailed Tina about what Devin said. We agreed that each of us should only provide cold hard messages with little nuances about our investigations into Vacation and delve into further analysis in person. So many ideas! We agreed to meet soon to share our latest thoughts on the investigation in person.

Tina and I met the next Saturday evening at the Red Coat Inn in Middleburg, Virginia. It is in the affluent horse country where few Inquirer reporters would likely be grazing. She made the reservation in her previous married name, Tina Schlichter, because my name was well known and might be recognized.

I did pay for dinner. I also picked the place. An hour from D.C., in the foothills of the Blue Ridge Mountains, the 2-story stone Red Coat Inn, circa 1728, oozes romance. Candlelight dinner in the old Virginia style seemed perfect to me. The food is famously exquisite.

Over dinner, we only shared broad ideas in our conversation in case we'd be overheard in the intimate dining room.

She whispered, "They were cooking their books big time, for sure, for a long time. I have learned."

I whispered, "But I don't understand how this could happen these days, after all the tighter laws in financial regulations? Enron? Charles Keating's savings and loan thing? WorldCom?"

"Ssshh. Keep your voice down, Mr. ah ... you," Tina said. People had begun watching as my voice got louder with each mention of a high-profile financial scandal.

So much for the dinner talk. We saved the juicy stuff for talking in our guest room.

Over dessert of an old fashion apple cobbler to die for, I asked about her family. She asked me about my daughters in college. I spotted sadness in her lovely blue-green eyes as I talked about my pride and joys, Stefani and Sierra as children. I did say something nice, I don't remember what, about Janet, and hoped Tina didn't see me shifting in my chair.

After dinner, the maître de showed us around. The rooms at the Red Coat are decorated in colonial style, four poster canopy beds (They creep me out, but women love them, I think.), high ceilings, period dressers and desks, and walls papered in 18th century flowery patterns. The colonial sleeping experience runs about $300 to $500 a night depending on whether you want a view.

We thanked the guide politely and walked the 400 yards to the $120 a night Hampton Inn for a nice clean room and a good laugh: $500 a night in drafty dumps that our wise forefathers certainly would not have chosen given the choices we have today. We looked forward to the big free breakfast buffet instead of "feasting" on the George Washington's favorite at the Red Coat, which was advertised as a watercress and shad omelet for $23.75.

Oh yes, our Red Coat guide was sure we'd book, due to the tiny colonial window that overlooked courtyard gardens, though it was dark. Maybe it was also overlooking a junkyard, we joked.

My apologies to history buffs, but we both felt the best historic sites offer a bit more authenticity to commemorate, like Monticello, or Independence Hall. We respected our hosts' history. We just left and held our jokes for later about how they rip people off to experience a vague connection to real events.

The dinner cost me plenty, especially after the whiskey and wine. But Tina was worth a king's ransom to me, not to mention that she came with a fabulous new investigation I could somehow report, maybe a series, as long as I kept her name out of it. Life seemed good again.

If the Inquirer suits found out I was dating my primary source, they would surely force my early retirement. Could I really get away with it? Time will tell. The trick would be to keep my reporting separate from my love interest. Are you kidding? Impossible, but if I could keep her a secret, I could get away with that little, well not so little, break with journalistic ethics.

In the Hampton Inn guest room, she continued her report on Vacation's fraudulent accounting department as we sat on opposite edges of the bed. "At first, I didn't think this was possible after all the shit hit the fan with derivatives, Ponzi schemes, and even Fannie May. Mr. Ford, I hand-picked this company. The execs have been great to me, just great. I trusted them and they have been wonderful to me, though I guess my job was to make them look good. It figures that they'd be good to me too.

"But, as far as I can guess, this hotel/motel business is a sleeper for federal regulations, pun intended. Conglomerates may be all the same, that is, multi-industries. But this group is all clustered around hotels and motels. It's not like the fraud at WorldCom, Enron, or HealthSouth in the 90's."

"How so?" I asked.

"Well, Goodbred and Levine may have already put their escape plan in place. They would then activate the plan if they get caught with hands in the cookie jar. My mole in accounting says they have Swiss accounts that are growing fast. Levine's private secretary Pauline has flown to Mulhouse, France four times in the past six months."

"Right up the Rhine from Basil, Switzerland."

"Yeah, she stayed there and in Geneva each time."

"Carrying money?" I asked. "It is illegal in Switzerland for a bank to reveal an account holder's name."

Seemingly in the same breath, she continued, "Also, they fired their first comptroller, who ran a tricky membership formula for the firm when it was just getting started in Massachusetts. And then, Goodbred got Levine back from the penitentiary to put in place his signature style of even more fraudulent accounting for memberships."

"Who was that?" I asked, though I had read about von Kindle. I wanted to get her take.

"Who was what?"

"The one they fired. He could be valuable."

"Oh, he is former CFO Max von Kindel. The smartasses in accounting called him Max von Swindle. But you know, Mr. Ford, I don't think Max really thought he was scamming people. He seemed to be in total shock that they let him go."

"We might need him later. Can you find out where he is?"

"Might be tricky; he's foreign, German if I remember correctly. But I'll get right on it, Mr. Ford," she said.

My mind was mush with alcohol, *God, she is cute.* I was getting my thoughts mixed up with my desires. *How much longer can I sit here across the bed? No, Hank. This is why we rendezvoused here, ... I think. Main reason, I think. Forget it.*

I recovered my wits with, "Who … who is the new finance genius, Levine?" which I already had guessed.

"Thought you knew that?"

"Just remembering. Sorry. Is Levine difficult, that is, a hard ass like Goodbred?"

"No. Simon Levine is playful but shrewd. He is not a cut-throat arrogant ass like Trevor Goodbred. Accounting says Levine is too smart for such a high-profile position as CFO. But they are in denial. Goodbred keeps Levine hidden because he is a white-collar ex-con. They hired some church lady from Lynchburg to appear to run finances while Levine really runs finance." Tina hadn't told me yet about Gordy Jones' report on the Luray/Lynchburg capers.

"Now, you've got my attention. That's wacked," I said laughing.

"I don't know her or if she will stay at Trout Heaven for the region or go to Boston. Levine is unofficial comptroller and is smitten with her, according to the limousine driver. I don't even think Levine is registered as such with the SEC. Weird, huh?"

"What do you mean you hear they are planning an escape? I mean, what is the evidence? We have to be sure, Tina, ah, I mean Miss O'Leary."

"For example," she said, "this fraudulent scheming is not just about greed, it's diabolical."

"Wow, you must have really good inside sources," I said.

"No, I made my own deduction from the PR and marketing campaigns. To the public it is a chance to invest in fast profits in a rising company during tough economic times. But people don't know until it is too late that the scheme is parasitic."

"Parasitic to the lodging guests?" I asked.

"Yes. I'm sure now. The vacation deals for new members are accelerating."

"What about that church lady?"

"Her name is Rev. Anita Rapshire. Married, four kids from Tennessee by way of a Baptist church in Lynchburg, Virginia where she was drawing in members like there is no tomorrow."

"Jerry Falwell country."

"Different church. I suspect that the church lady has not discovered that the scheme appeals cleverly to any leftover coins left in the pockets of ordinary chumps. In this recession they might be desperate for a little affordable pleasure spending. No one is eager to spend on a lavish or even an ordinary vacation trip in a recession, when they are frantically playing catch up on bills, college tuitions, or even worse, unemployment and looming home foreclosures.

"So, I figure Vacation Inns Corporation is preying on the vulnerabilities of people already in big time debt."

"What do you mean?"

"The come-on is that the first vacation is free," she said.

"Yes, but that makes no sense to me; too generous," I said.

"That is where they get you. The first vacation is free only when you sign up for membership and book the next vacation in advance. In no time, the guests are billed for that."

"Of course. I knew it was too good to be true," I said.

She continued, "I figure only the sharpest vacation guests are going to understand that stipulation in the fine print of their agreement. Also, if the guests do understand, they are offered to delay paying for their first vacations by putting a $50 deposit on the next vacation of at least three nights.

"Another incentive pushes suckers into reserving entire weeks with just a verbal false promise from Vacation that they can shorten their next stay if necessary. These angles are new."

I asked, "How do you know that."

"Just several months ago, they didn't seem anywhere near this level of trickery, according to my accounting friend. She wants to quit but is afraid to. Has kids in school here. And Vacation pays her well."

"Yeah, to keep quiet, huh?"

She continued to tell me more; some of it was what I'd learned about the fraudulent membership scheme, but I let her talk.

Tina said, "Levine's system accounts for new memberships arbitrarily. Cancelled memberships were still counted in various forms as revenue. Each repeat vacation by a guest or family was counted as a new membership on the books. Such multiple layers of membership were listed as accounting reserves to cover the cost on the books for new acquisitions."

Tina said she learned that people signing up as members now automatically get three shares of the company. But the shares don't get activated until their third vacation, according to miniscule fine print in their contracts. Vulnerable folks see the stock value rise mercurially while the execs may be planning to parachute out. Nearly all members may be hooked into a failed venture, Tina believed.

"I knew some of the membership trickery at the paper and you've enlightened me further. But, is there no real proof that they are planning to scram?" I asked.

Again, she chose not to answer. But she added, "It makes me sick, Mr. Ford. I hate working there now."

"How are you learning all this? Are you protected?" I asked, reaching across the still-made bed for her hand. I fretted, *Was she getting over zealous?*

She told me what driver Jones reported to her about Rev. Anita Rapshire's hiring by a smitten Simon Levine and his pal Goodbred, as well as the story of Simon's hookers in the limo on Capitol Hill while Goodbred testified at Rep. Handwerker's hearing.

None of it surprised me. It was good to know anything about the exec's vulnerabilities.

She then swung back to talk more about her mole in finance. She went on with her information, interspersed with her fears, as we still remained on either side of the bed, still dressed in dinner attire. She said, "Vacation Inns' accountants want to keep their jobs. Jobs are tight. That is overriding their professional responsibility to be honest with the public. But I have that friend there who does not care and has good reason to get them. She believes someone at the company killed her best friend."

"What!!? Now, you are scaring me."

"Well, that's what she believes. That best friend of my mole had figured out the whole scheme and blabbed about it to friends. She died on the company retreat to National Harbor near D.C. and her body was found months later in the Zekiah Swamp, a huge tributary and swampland off the Potomac River. She was decomposed beyond recognition and identified only long after the retreat. There was a tipped over canoe and a wound on her head, but my friend blames the company because her friend knew too much. The woman who died in the swamp was known to be afraid of water; couldn't even swim. It fits."

"Wow, heavy. Tina, please be careful. And advise your friend in accounting not to quit. I can't protect her—it *is* a her, right?—but she is key to our investigation; don't you think?"

"Yes and yes. Yes, she is key. And, yes, she is …. Oh, brother, (Tina had detected my jealous bone. She came across the bed to kiss me gently on the nose holding my face in her soft hands, and then finish the sentence.) … a her."

Chapter 29

We woke late at night at the warm, clean, and modern Hampton Inn near the historic Red Coat Inn, and laughed again over whether sex would have been better in a $400 bed. Who cares? We were up for more talk.

It was my turn to shock Tina with a Securities and Exchange Commission report on funny business at her company, "My trusted friend Devin Shay on the business desk at the Inquirer is unearthing hidden treasures of fraud in the footnotes of Vacation Inn's SEC reports, Miss O'Leary. As I mentioned, he doesn't think just a membership scam can bring them down."

"Footnotes? You're kidding," she said.

"We know companies all over the world, not just in the U.S., that gain a lot of success while learning to avoid any hints they might be another Enron. They try to overwhelm regulators with detail now. They provide much more financial information than is necessary. In the case of Vacation Inns Corporation, it has worked to their advantage, Devin thinks."

Tina suggested, "Maybe that is why Vacation Inns are being investigated by the Handwerker committee."

"Yeah, that and more, I suspect. But, it is not a serious investigation. It's tertiary, certain locations only, Devin says. He doubts if the SEC folks care much about the membership mischief. Instead, suspicions have been raised over the corporation purchasing future "vacation" land at dirt cheap prices during the real estate bust. Devin suspects that sometimes, even before they build a structure resembling a motel at a new site they claim the expenses, depreciation, etc. of a full-fledged motel that doesn't yet exist. It is something to ask your friend about in accounting, if you can trust her.

"When companies act this way," I explained, "it is basic SEC deflection. Much of the additional data, that is, the lies and the cheating, is buried cleverly in annual 10K reports and quarterly 8K reports that companies are required to file with the SEC. Their hedging is most apparent, Devin says, in the graphics in footnotes and these guys are really good at it."

Tina asked, "If the federal regulators set the requirements for those financial reports, can't they use special software to detect fraud, that is, inconsistencies?"

"I'm sure they do; I'll ask Shay. Frankly, I hate those graphics and tiny footnotes; you go blind with the tiny print and I wouldn't be surprised that SEC analysts miss a lot of tricks and inconsistencies in them."

"I know something of accounting," she said eager to explain.

I laughed affectionately (I hoped), "I'm not surprised. I read your bio—stellar grades in business school right, accounting and all that?"

"Don't make fun of me."

"I'm not. I'm appreciating you."

"Whatever. Listen, Mr. Ford, I do know that in the SEC reports and in a company's financial records the MD&A's, you know, the Management's Discussion & Analysis, often includes the company's own declaration of risk factors. There are none with Vacation Inn's records, I'm told. Again, it is just weird."

"I will ask Devin. He is free next weekend to give me a full report on those kinds of technicalities in regard to Vacation Inns. He also mentioned GAAP is another tipoff."

"What's that?"

"<u>G</u>enerally <u>a</u>ccepted <u>a</u>ccounting <u>p</u>rinciples that companies put into their public financial reports to show, in a nutshell—the income statement, balance sheet, and the statement of cash flow, and so forth. Devin says companies can interpret the GAAP in different ways to their advantage. It is a science of deception apparently."

"Mr. Ford, this is getting too complicated. We cannot do all this detail ourselves. What can you do to get us some help fishing around through all these technicalities in SEC reports?" she said. "Pardon me staying on the fishing metaphor—we *are* talking Trout Heaven—but my instincts tell me that such bits of bait here and there is not enough to catch the big corporate fish. We will need to expose more serious criminal activity under the tip of that membership fraud iceberg. So far, the only glaring clue would be murder perhaps."

"There you go again with murder. Take it easy, Miss O'Leary. One thing at a time," I offered.

"I didn't say there was a murder. We don't know if that woman got whacked," she corrected me.

"Thank you, Miss Corleone. Anyway, we need more confirming evidence, or corroboration from moles inside the corporation, or associated with the corporation. Then, I hope the real work can begin."

"What do you mean," Tina asked.

"If we can confirm they are cheating and cheating big time, we start deep sea fishing on the execs themselves, what kind of people are they really? That's when you may need to step out of the way and hide. They could come after you Miss O'Leary, considering that you've said Levine is whacky and Goodbred is a scary super-passive aggressive."

"Okay then, maybe it is time for you to meet my best contact in accounting, Mr. Ford," she said with caution written in her tight smile.

"Are you sure you didn't study reporting instead of PR?" I asked.

She didn't miss a beat, "Daddy taught me some. But seriously, here is what you need to know from my friend in accounting, Mr. Ford, before meeting her, and soon, I hope. Vacation's attorneys have been spending a lot more time lately with the corporation's accounting executives, which together, they created a secret language for SEC about interconnected transactions among companies in the group and partnering firms that senior management wanted to keep quiet, but were required by the SEC. I don't get it fully, but that is what my friend said."

"Well done, Miss O'Leary. I don't get it either, but it sounds intriguing. However, keep in mind that a source inside the firm is not that convincing in the eyes of the law. We need to fish both sides of the shore to corroborate their tricks: using both your friend in accounting and my friend on the business desk, Devin, to find outside testimonials."

"Thank you, Mr. Ford," Tina said, shaking her head. "I mean, hey, membership tricks, M&A's, footnotes, GAAP, MD&A's, and now Vacation's so-called secret language for SEC deflections? This is daunting. We can drown in all this data stuff and waste valuable time. Anglers have to plan their strategies before they find the fish, right?" she said laughing at the obnoxious continuing fishing analogy to the Vacation books and crooks.

"This is some romantic getaway, huh?" I said while stroking her hair and smiling. "But, speaking of fishing, I did some fly fishing with the Macintyre boys," I said to wrap up things on a high note and split.

Tina lit up with excitement, actually jumped up and down, "You! Henry Clyde Ford, the hermit crab at the city paper? A fly fisherman? No way."

"Well, I wouldn't call myself a fly fisherman, like I'm Joe Brooks or Ted Williams. I'm obviously more like handsome young Brad Pitt in "A River Runs Through It," I'd say," again thinking that would wrap things up on a big laugh. Not!

Even more excited, she said, "You, Hank Ford, know about Joe Brooks? The famous fishing writer and baseball player? Well, of course, you do. How about Joan Wulff winning the National Fisherman's Distance Fly Championship with a cast of 136 feet against a field of all male competitors. She made the sport what it is, by golly. I can't cast past 50 or 60."

"Feet? You *are* fly fisherwoman. Wow, and besides, I'm not from the city, but from a town in New York State you said you never heard of. Thought I was putting you on, huh? Anyway, you fly fish. Wow."

"Teen state champion, that's all," Tina said, beaming with her hands on hips. You any good, Mr. Ford?"

"I'm better than you."

"You say."

"Yeah, I can out fly fish any teen champ. Got a favorite spot, Miss State Teen Champion?" I was nearly falling over with delight over the image of fishing with her one day, maybe our next date.

Hands on hips, she retorted with glee, "You're on, big shot."

I loved it. Just for spite, I teased her, "Ever fish Crater Lake?"

"Yuk. Nooooo way, Jose. I'd rather stick with a real sport, with real rainbows," she said, as she poked me in the chest affectionately."

Chapter 30

The following Saturday evening working at the cabin on my laptop, I turned my attention to the big question of just why Vacation was so aggressively building up its development near Crater Lake.

Meanwhile, Goodbred had sent Tina down to the state capital for the weekend to hobnob at the annual convention of county governments.

I woke Sunday morning with the phone call from Tina at her meetings.

"Mr. Ford, sorry to wake you."

She was right I was in bed after a long night of researching Vacation Inns and Resorts on the Internet as well as finding out as much as I could about the people living in the hills and valleys around Crater Lake.

"Miss O'Leary, your voice could wake me from the dead."

"Hope it doesn't come to that. Been sharing your evening with Johnny Walker again?"

"All through with that. I'm sober; just sleepy. What's up? Are you coming back early to give me company in my luxury suite overlooking the Sassafras?"

"No such luck. But, I thought as long as you are studying the territory, I might share what I've been hearing from the county folks. Vacation is actively working the zoning board members of all the counties near our least favorite town of Trout Heaven. Some delegates thought I was here to grease their palms with everything from memberships to trips to some of our resorts across the country. It seems that Goody has been on the phone with a lot of them hinting friendship, the quid pro quo type, if you get my drift."

I said, "Can you send a list of their names to the Inquirer from there? Not from your office back here, but from the convention? And, nothing personal. It is my work email."

"Sure, I've got to go find Anita, the new membership gal. She is a stitch."

"So, you said. The church lady, right?"

"I'm going to get her to take you to Rev. Sugarman's church," Tina said, mocking my fierce resistance to restraints on my freedom.

Some feelings are meant to keep to oneself, even in passionate love.

I replied, "Right. Keep her right there with you. I'm going fishing today with Bobby Macintyre. See ya."

"Again?" she asked.

She didn't finish sayin goodbye when I heard her greet Anita Rapshire with, "Hi Anita, sorry I couldn't make the prayer meeting this morning. Hungry?"

I hung up.

Chapter 31

What have the Macintyers known about Vacation's plans for Crater Lake development? And, when did they know it? Those questions were burning a hole in my brain.

I called Bobby and before I could start a conversation, he invited me to their home. "If you want to know more about the lake fish and why those fellows at the Inn are hot to dip their toes in it, come on over."

Bobby said the boys were talking about taking me to go fly fishing with them again.

I thanked him but said I was more intrigued about the big trout in the lake this time.

That Sunday evening about 4 p.m., I drove into their long, downhill gravel lane through a green tunnel of 60-year-old Pines and deciduous hardwoods, forest grown back after the burning rock cindered the land.

The lane ended at the lake about 300 feet from a large Alpine home off shore. The home was undoubtedly built after the meteorite leveled any structures many decades earlier.

In the few years since Johnny and Jeb's 'miracle' of the lake trout, the Macintyers had built a fine fishing pier, the only one on the lake of any consequence. It was a serious commercial venture. The family put their savings into a large, well-equipped boathouse. I thought they were smart to take full advantage of the lake edge, which they had acquired by shear cosmic luck.

On a floating dock, 20-foot square, the Mac's constructed a staging shed, complete with changing rooms for each gender and a simple "recovery" lounge with patio chairs, small tables, snacks and beverages—coffee, tea and soda. The staging shed was connected to the shore by just a narrow boardwalk with high railings. It was all approved by the state health and occupation safety agencies.

They didn't plan the unusual layout for a boating pier just for the comfort of fishing clients, but rather to prevent them from fishing off the pier. You had to take a boat out and, at the time, theirs was the only rent shop, not counting Vacation Inn guests taking out small jon boats off the Garrett property.

Just off the side door of the shed was a narrower wooden pier with tie hitches limited to only their eight fishing boats for rent—six johnboats with small outboards and two 15-foot crafts with canvas cover and 50 h.p. Evinrude motors.

On the opposite side of the shed was a fishing party boat for daily rents that could accommodate 15 guests, rod tubes, swiveled chairs of vinyl cushions and cup holders along its sides. "What is all this?" I opened conversation with Bobby as I walked from my car down to the pier.

"It is our new venture. Like it?" he said, extending his hand to greet me. "We can take one of the Evinrudes; they are the bigger two next to the jon boats, the flat ones."

"Great Bobby. I do know a jon boat, kind of basic, yes. What's the big bertha on the right?"

"Party boat. We call it the U.S.S. Sugarman after our pastor, Gideon Sugarman who built his following on faith of the meteorite. The old guy is a scream. Very devout, don't get me wrong. Just unique in this world," Bobby Macintyre said, as he led me into the surprisingly stylish boathouse on the edge of the lake shore. "Come in here. We put plumbing in for men and women's restrooms. My wife had a decorator do it up like Hemingway's house in Key West. We have wired it to keep bait cool and provide good lighting for weighing fish and cleaning them if people want 'steaks.' That's what we call the big chunks of trout. Like it, Mr. Ford?"

"Call me Hank, please?"

"Okay, call me Bobby. The boys though prefer to know you as Mr. Ford, okay?"

"Fine, should I pay you now for the outing or when we come back loaded with monster fish?"

Bobby laughed, "No charge for media."

I was taken back, "Oh, I'm not planning a story. I'm sorry, Bobby if you were expecting publicity. I just want to find out about the lake and the fish. It seems like I'm committed to being a resident in the neighborhood, despite all the distracting bulldozing on Charity Mountain that ruined my view from the cabin. I'll pay you."

"How about if I charge you half only. My boys invited you. They told me you might write a story. You know how presumptuous kids are today. I should not have imposed on you."

"Half it is. What do we do now? Pick out gear or something?"

"The boat is already loaded up with gear, soft drinks, bottled water—we discourage alcohol on the lake—and these here floppy hats like mine."

He was wearing one—sky blue with white lettering:

Macintyre's Pier
Trout Heaven

I put on my Washington Inquirer cap instead, giving me a chance to avoid taking one of those silly hats.

Bobby's son Jeb met us at the boat. The three of us took off with the roar of the big outboard.

I was fascinated by the Macs and their set up and didn't look out onto the beauty of Crater Lake until I was seated in the back of the boat and relegated to silence by the powerful outboard over my left shoulder.

I noticed the lake edges first. I didn't see much shoreline of sand or gravel as you might expect around an eastern mountain lake where eons of weathering would normally push sediment and stones downhill to the water's edge. Crater Lake's surface all around me jutted and lapped directly into rock cliffs five to six feet tall.

I looked back at the Macintyre's' shore of softer edges shrinking into the distance. Bobby noticed me looking back and gave Jeb the wheel. Holding on the boat railing, Bobby slid back to the only other seat at the stern. He hollered, "We brought that all in, the gravel, sand, after we blasted the lake wall into pieces. That rip rap behind that little sandy beach we made is from the old rock wall."

I hollered back, "Never seen a lake like this."

He said, "I don't think there are any like it. Water used to top the cliffs before the feds opened some of the lake back to the river over yonder."

"Army Corps of Engineers? When?" I asked.

"Ten years after."

"What?" I asked.

"They drained some when it all cooled, they say, ten years after the big rock from space made this big hole for us to play in. Before my time, though. They didn't want it to spill back into the river later, say in a 100-year storm. Lots of run off from these hills, Mr. Ford. I mean Hank."

"Or another million-year meteorite, huh?" I said, while trying to get the song "Goin' Home" by the rock group Ten Years After, out of my head. Lasted all that night. I hate when that happens.

Bobby said one theory on the fish was that they "swam upstream" as the water was drained out by the Corps and something in the aquatic environment has encouraged them to grow larger than their predecessors in the river. Another theory, he said, was that "God put them here. It's what Gideon likes to believe and it's good enough for us."

There were no other homes or piers in view. The only other structure visible was the tip of a modest steeple of Our Sacred Lady of Cosmic Heaven peeking above the pines. The cliffs were the most outstanding feature of the shores all around. Bobby told me that the farmers around the lake had long ago rebuilt their homes on high ground near their livelihood—crop fields and livestock grazing land—and to be as far away from the lake as possible, he said. "Until the county blessed our fish, the lake was thought to be toxic. It was bullshit."

I didn't see any other piers or boat slips cut out of the cliffs.

We knifed through smooth glassy water at high speed at first then into choppy, more like rippling waters, at mid-lake. Above the rocky cliffs was nothing but the deep green forests on mountains folding into and beyond each other. The scene was eerily primal. There was no trash or any other signs of human degradation. I imagined a sequel to Michael Crichton's book, 'Jurassic Park,' featuring temperate forest dinosaurs, not the tropical ones he created.

We crossed the center of the 'prehistoric' lake to the location of the original break, where long ago the Sassafras River breached the edge of the burning crater and filled it with water. "This is the best fishing, Mr. Ford," Jeb, said, as the boat slowed. He dropped anchor on a ridiculously long rope and continued, "Some say the rainbows come back to this spot with their migrating instinct, thinking to go up river to spawn."

Bobby added, "For whatever reason, they seem to migrate here and by our property and the church. Thank God, right?" He laughed and picked up a fishing rod. "Show Mr. Ford how to catch a monster, Jeb." He said.

I'll be fine," I replied. "This is standard action, no tricks to casting and reeling in?" remembering my dad fishing with me in the Ocean City, Maryland inlet on summer vacations, off the Rt. 50 bridge or the rocks at the southern-most end of the barrier spit facing the inlet blown open by the Hurricane of 1933, which pinched off Assateague Island from OC.

We baited our hooks when the boat settled. I slashed my trim casting rod as Bobby and Jeb did the same. They said the best retrieving of the fish will come from twitching the line stop and go, stop and go, etc. The light but steady line they used allowed a lazy sinking to keep the bait and lures slowly sinking if at all, they said. My cast didn't fling out far. No comments from the experts. I reeled in to try again and I pulled in my hook to bait it better.

"Look long enough you can see the fish swimming fairly deep right under us," Bobby said.

"There! I see one. Good grief," I shouted too loudly, as the fish scrammed. It was a Rainbow about three and a half feet long crossing the bow. The water was startlingly clear.

Jeb said, "Mr. Ford, this whole opportunity is nothing short of amazing. Just four years ago, this lake was off limits and had a reputation of being poisoned long ago by nature's doing."

Bobby added, "We knew there was something in the lake because there was movement across the surface, especially at night in moonlight. Something was happening. Could have been birds or otters. We didn't know and didn't even come down here much. We lived in our old house up in that valley and we respected the quarantine, rarely even looked."

Jeb said, "It was hard to get to the lake with all the cliffs and forest debris from neglect. Right Dad? He forbade it, because me and Johnny tried to come down here as kids, but we were all scared of the water being poisoned. Everybody was."

"The boys thought there would be fish, though," Bobby said, "even when they were little, we'd wonder. Even that day, when they carried a couple of those big boys up to the church in secret, I thought they were playing a joke."

Jeb laughed and said, "We showed Rev. Sugarman and Dad where we got to the lake and the pile of fish that we left there. Just to prove it was not a prank we pulled another one in in no time. They could not believe it."

"I made the boys release that one and buried the others with a front loader no less, because we thought they were contaminated for sure," Bobby remembered. "But the one we took over to the state recreation department, was clean of any toxins, according to state inspectors."

"Remember Rev. Sugarman when we told him they were good fish, Dad? He was funnier than all get out." Jeb said. "He started preaching right there at the recreation department offices."

"He went with you with the fish?" I asked. "This preacher knows an opportunity when he sees one."

Bobby was grinning from ear to ear. He said, "Yeah, Rev was off and preachin' He said something about God sent me here to save you. I am at your deliverance, great trout."

"He was loony," Jeb said. "He was preaching to the fish, Mr. Ford."

"Don't be disrespectful, son," his father disciplined. "The reverend is old and senile, but a sweet, God-fearing man who is good to all of us. Don't talk bad about Rev. Sugarman."

Jeb looked ashamed, "Sorry Dad. We love that guy, Mr. Ford." He is a good preacher too. So, anyway, that was the whole story."

Bobby continued to tell me the history of the fish, "The reverend got busy with his next sermon about our miracle fish. And we got busy developing our waterfront presence immediately after getting the okay on the fish inspection."

My cell phone buzzed. It was Tina. "Are you alone or on speaker phone?"

"I am on Crater Lake fishing."

"Anita Rapshire left just after breakfast and drove back. She said she and her husband have a fishing reservation with the Macintyers. Are you with them?"

"Affirmative. I'll get back to you Devin," I said, thinking fast and unable to scramble my thoughts.

She said confidently, "Oh, I see. Needed to tell you. Bye."

I told Bobby it was my editor at the paper.

"Keep you on a short leash, do they?" he said, sounding disappointed with the interruption.

If the Rapshire couple left the state capital in the morning to keep their fishing appointment, I figured, they would be on the lake or soon to be. I needed to ease Bobby into my concern over Vacation.

We kept catching the big ones. Again, the clarity of the water caught my eye. So primal. *What would this be like if the entire lake gets 'developed' by Vacation Inn's gang?* I wondered.

Five minutes and another whopper catch later, and my third 30-incher, I breached the subject, "Bobby, what do you think of the new Inn using the town name?"

"Have you seen the new causeway they got the state to build? I don't like that. Opens up fishing right off the bridge."

"I didn't know the Vacation Inn boys got that approved. Why?"

"With all due respect, Hank, come on, man, you REALLY didn't know they had something to do with a road over the lake edge with a low bridge."

"I saw the road myself, sure. But, ..." I let him explain it.

Jeb started the outboards without another word from his dad. Jeb said, "Want to see the new road and little bridge from down here on the lake, Mr. Ford?"

He steered about a thousand yards around a slight bend in the lake edge, which told me the meteorite or God's hand, didn't create a perfect circle hole as I read on the Internet.

It was almost like humans had carved a bubble in the shoreline, some 200 yards wide. And over that bubble of water was the causeway and the new county road. Fishing rods hung over it on both sides.

"It is a wonder they didn't makeshift a boat slip as well," I said, because there are people on the cliff too. See?"

Jeb cut the motors and said softly, "We just hate this."

Bobby said, "They can't have access to the lake under the road on the ground. Those folks under the bridge are trespassing on Smythe property. Sherriff Roger Deeds takes their names and shoos them off when he or his deputies can, but he is lenient. One of these big whoppers will feed a family for two maybe three days, Mr. Ford. And, there are lots of poor folks in these hills."

Jeb was not sympathetic, "We hate this," he said again, a little louder. (Some heads on shore looked up.) Then even louder, he said, "If the damn trespassers are caught three times, Sheriff Deeds throws them in jail."

"Shut it down, Jeb," Bobby cracked. "Let's leave these folks to their business."

"Dad, does Donnie know about all these people trespassing?

I spoke up and asked the obvious, "Donald Smythe, the bellboy at Vacation Inn?"

"Yes, he lives up there on the hill over the bridge," Jeb said. "You know him?"

"Just know of him," I said, thinking fast. "His name came up in conversations about Vacation with a friend. Say, you didn't mention if you like those folks or not, the Vacation Inn crowd coming into your beautiful countryside here."

We were cruising at a moderate speed toward center lake when Bobby leaned over to me and said, "No, we don't like them."

"Want to know something," I said, "neither do I. And it is not because they are an ugly scar on my scenic view. They are a sleazy bunch, Bobby."

Just as I fessed up my feelings on Vacation, Jeb yelled back from the wheel, "Hey there's Johnny with those people from the inn."

The Macintyre's other larger fishing boat was heading to the hot fishing spot where the Army Corps of Engineers had blocked off leakage to the river decades earlier, where we had caught our big ones. Jeb turned the boat toward the other boat.

I would soon have the pleasure, I guess, of getting my first look at the lady minister and new finance officer Anita Rapshire. I played dumb. "Looks like he has visitors also," I said.

Bobby said, "That would be Mr. and Mrs. Rapshire. She made a reservation last week."

I thought, *Funny, she hadn't told Tina about it and stayed over at the convention until the morning. And on Sunday, her day of worship, of all days.*

I asked Bobby not to reveal my name. I steadied myself on the side of the boat and walked to the front to ask Jeb to do the same.

"Ah, so you ARE doing a story. Undercover. Cool, Mr. Ford," he said, pleased to be part of it all, whatever IT was I was doing.

Johnny slowed his boat carrying the Rapshires. Jeb pulled our boat up to it. As water slapped against the boat sides from their wakes, I could hear Anita chattering to Johnny as she had likely continued since right off the pier, as we saw her gesturing and facing him closely in the front seat, shotgun to him steering.

Anita was, as advertised by Tina, a stitch. Responding to Johnny pointing at his father in our boat, she called out, "I've seen them, Mr. Macintyre, those big rainbow trout. Your son told me of your professional transition for your family. God has surely selected you to make a great difference in this world. God bless you, sir. Yes, it is his will for us to reevaluate our lives to God's purpose. I am so pleased to meet you."

She was very excited.

"You must be Rev. Rapshire and Mr. Rapshire," Bobby asked, as if there was any doubt.

"Indeed, I had some skepticism, Mr. Macintyre, when they told me of the divine trout. I am ashamed. Just as God selected Gideon Sugarman to preach, he has called on you and your fine sons to follow the occupation of those blessed fishermen on the shores of Galilee long ago."

"Thank you, ma'am," Bobby said, a bit overwhelmed, I think.

To say there was joy in this woman would be a gross understatement. She instantly lifted our collective mood to high altitude. We were suddenly within her flock, right there on the water's surface. We would have not been shocked at that moment if Jesus himself walked right over to us.

Bobby addressed his son Johnny in the other boat, "How's it going son. Did you show them around?"

"Yes sir," Johnny replied with a big smile, and with an appreciative nod to Rev. Rapshire. He offered, "Dad, she is the new financial officer for the Vacation Inn and this is her husband."

"I'm Clarence Rapshire, Mr. Macintyre. I love your set up and never have I seen rainbows quite like these," said Anita's husband, while continuing to bait his line attached to a small Sutton Silver with a worm on the hook. Clarence was cradling a fishing rod on his lap like a pro.

Bobby glanced at me, and then said, "Thanks for coming, folks. This here is my other son Jeb and Mr. ...."

"Henry," I cut in, "name's Henry. Hi folks."

They both said hello to Mr. Henry, leaving me still incognito for the time being.

Bobby then suggested to Johnny, "Son, take them to the east edge. We saw some nice ones over there." Bobby seemed eager to put distance between us and the Rapshires. "Keeping any or just catch 'n release?"

Anita responded, "We will keep them where God put them, Mr. Macintyre."

Clarence objected, "No, we will keep one. Mr. Levine said the inn's chef can prepare it for us tonight."

Anita cut in, "Simon Levine, the inn's nice executive who brought us here. It is lovely. Oh, life gets so exciting when you are led by the Holy Spirit. I guess we will be off now, Mr. Macintyre. You certainly are not one to watch other people have a good life. You are taking God's direction and making you and your family live the life that God gave you. Bless you. You too, Mr. Henrich."

Jeb gunned it and they were off.

Bobby's tanned face was drained of color, pale as a harvest moon. And, I took note that the usually very friendly man, for once, didn't insist on her calling him

Bobby. He managed to only say, "Well, what was that all about?"

Jeb said, "I think she is nice, Dad. Just got her job and all. And, she is not bad looking either."

"Yeah, handsome woman for sure and seems true to her faith. But what bothers me is that she is too nice for those Vacation creeps. That lady was duped," he said.

At that comment, I realized then that Bobby and his boys knew more about the sinister Vacation Inn and Resort Corp. than they were willing to admit to.

As the Macs predicted, we had no trouble pulling in about five big ones a piece within 30 minutes and release them. The boys each said they were sick of eating fish. Pretty funny, I thought. And, I didn't need smelly fish to ride home with me to D.C. later that night either.

I considered the trip a success by knowing the lake, the Macintyre's opinions—sort of—about the Vacation Inn guys and enjoying the encounter with the inn's new membership director extraordinaire, the Rev. Anita Rapshire.

In fishing terms, it was a bold reminder to keep the fisherman's open mind attitude, that there is nothing wrong with your tackle as long as you caught the fish. And that the pleasure is in playing the game.

As I walked back to my car, Jeb ran up to me with a fishing rod. "Mr. Ford, we want you to have this. Jeb and I thought you'd be wanting to do more fly fishing before you get too discouraged with what happened over at your property and beyond."

It was a new Simano fly fishing rod and new Asquity fly reel, all super lightweight and slick and compact reel.

"It's a trophy for landing the monster trout and an invitation to go fly fishing again with us, okay? But, I see you are a bit cramped in the Z3. We'll hold it for you."

"Deal," I said, and then shook his hand and thanked him for a great time on the lake. I felt better about my new 'neighborhood,' yet a bit creepy about the temperate zone Jurassic lake.

Chapter 32

Tina's 'mole' in accounting was a very nice but nervous middle-aged woman named Mary Marinaro, who insisted that Tina and I meet her only under certain conditions and only at her house in Sassafras County, one mountain distance and out of site from the Inn.

Tina called from Joe's, "Mary will meet you Monday evening if you promise to never publish her name. She wants us to come over late, after her 4-year-old daughter is in bed, about 9:30 p.m. The daughter is from Mary's broken marriage and means everything to her. She doesn't want her child to hear our conversation."

I said, "Okay; that means a late drive back to Washington. Got a spare bed we can share at the luxurious Trout Heaven Vacation Inn & Resort?"

"Very funny," Tina dismissed.

I asked to take off all day Monday after the next weekend. Tina sprung for dinner at Smokey Joe's and drove me to Mary Marinaro's home. She lived in a dated Victorian, two-story house with lots of character and excellent gingerbread craftsmanship around windows, doors and gables, which seemed, as far as I could tell in dim porch lighting, was all in serious disrepair.

Mary was a short woman of medium build with dark brown hair in what was likely a bob do when last cut a good while ago. She had on a white apron which she discarded revealing a pretty floral dress of multi-colored roses and drawn at the waist with a pink braided leather belt. Very smart.

She was delighted to see us. I shook Mary's hand quickly as she let us in through the back door, because I had one eye on a piece of her chocolate marble cheese cake on her modest kitchen table. The table and matching chairs had an old floral Formica pattern from the '60s. Unlike the exterior, Mary's home was immaculate and orderly inside.

I complimented her taste in décor and asked in jest if I smelled coffee.

"Yes, Mr. Ford," said Tina eagerly, "it is a lovely home. I've been here for dinner with Mary and her daughter several times. She keeps her home the same as her work at Vacation Inns, perfect."

"Don't listen to her Mr. Ford. I do okay," Mary said. "I hope you like the cheesecake. Yes, there is coffee. How do you like it?"

"Black. And please call me Hank. I don't know what's wrong with her (Tina), wanting to maintain formalities all the time. Don't you, Miss O'Leary," I said raising a blush and smile from my girl.

"It's a little funny thing we have going as friends," Tina said trying to hide her blushing.

"Cute," said Mary, chuckling. "Now what can I do for you, Hank?"

I jumped right in as we gathered around the table and the cheesecake Mary was dishing out on her best Royal Dalton rose patterned China. "Although Tina never uttered your name, as such, she has been sharing the concerns of a friend in accounting, which turns out to be you. And, before I go further let me thank you for meeting with us, and [the flavor just kicked in] this astounding cheesecake Mary!"

She said with a knowing slanted smile, "It's a lower fat recipe made with no fat sour cream and cottage cheese and low-fat cream cheese and yogurt. Which means it's not as filling. But, then you will end up eating two or three slices instead of one. You'll see." She laughed a bit nervously.

"She's tricky, Mr. Ford," said Tina as she got a nod from her best friend at the company.

I asked Mary, "Tina told me that you've only become concerned lately. Is that the case?"

"Yeah, Hank, I don't think there is a corporation in America that does not play tricks with its financial reports. Sometimes it is an accepted practice to get the company off the ground, to delay being fully honest and open."

"I do understand that part, Mary, but my business editor friend at the Inquirer ... he says ..."

"Let me finish Hank; please hear me out. Tina said you guys are looking at the footnotes and stuff. There is more. This is what's just killing me inside. I feel trapped and afraid of what I have found lately."

"Go on. I'm sorry."

"Did Tina mention the Swiss accounts?"

I looked at Tina, who nodded okay. I answered that she had.

"I found the routing codes to a Swiss account in the computer of one the executive's assistants when she was out sick. It is a CH code for Switzerland and numbers for IBAN there."

"What's that?"

International Bank Account Number. I believe I'm correct on that. I was suspicious that the bosses might be bailing on us. If the company folds, me and my little girl would be out of an income. Simon Levine and Trevor Goodbred are funneling money into accounts in Switzerland, separately, I guess. But of course, I can't trace which bank, or city, even how much. I just recognized the kind of coding I've seen before and I'm pretty sure of it."

"Whose assistant was that, Mary, if you can say?" I asked.

Mary hesitated, looked at Tina, who said, "Levine's I bet."

"Yeah, Tina. That's right," Mary admitted.

"Pauline Hahn," Tina said.

I asked Mary, "When were you first getting these suspicions?"

"Last year. It was screwy pension assets that sent up a red flag for me. They have been reporting a 10 percent return on employee pension asset investments for nearly two years now. It adds up to improper income for the company."

"Is that odd?" I asked.

Tina jumped in, "Unheard of for seven straight quarters. The 10 percent return on investment is impossible in today's economy, Mr. Ford. Right Mary?"

"That's what I found. I have never liked such aggressive accounting and I had never seen pension assets earn so much before and we have about 1,500 employees thinking they are earning time on pension. And, there are other red flags of inflated income."

"Such as?" I asked.

"Vacation Inns is reporting big-time inventory reserves, you know, supplies for its sites, everything from bed linens to hot dog buns to beach chairs, in order to show pumped up earnings. Yet, I can't find much of that inventory on the books. And receivable goods and inventories were growing faster than sales. As I said, Mr. Ford, I mean Hank, I'm getting damn nervous, in my position especially. They asked me to report purchases of $190 million in acquisition of allied companies and to allocate $1.2 million to goodwill …, I mean charity!"

"Allied companies? What are those?" I asked, despite already knowing.

"Companies that support our operations, you know, hospitality, publishing, furniture, ecotourism, telecommunications, training, interior design, gourmet coffee, you name it."

"Oh, I see."

"Hank, maybe some of these allied companies are not doing what our books say," Mary was getting excited, chasing her own voice faster and faster. She was fearfully nervous. Her hand holding her elegant coffee cup was shaking then. She looked a bit scared and glanced at Tina for support. Mary said to Tina mostly, "I honestly think they are pulling out all the stops before they get caught at something."

"They being Vacation Inns?" I asked.

"Yeah, Goodbred and Levine at least, maybe other top execs. I found out that the company has been using every accounting trick in the book to inflate Vacation's operating income. The public shares are zooming up as a result."

I took my turn then to show some financial knowhow, "Mary, I think what your instincts and your figures tell you are correct. My instincts tell me the door is closing fast. And the fraud will probably come to light soon, maybe with the next quarterly 10K, maybe by its year-end report in January. Hopefully, the paper can nail these guys before they get out of Dodge."

"Whatever happens, Miss O'Leary, we need to do something before January. [Tina nodded in affirmative.]"

I then asked Mary "Why don't you write down, in long hand please and one copy only, a list of the Allied companies I need to investigate and why. Give it to Tina who can get it to me. I'll show no one else."

"What! Why?" Mary looked puzzled.

"Because officers of allied companies may be surprised if they learn they are showing up in Vacation's SEC reports. I don't have to tell them how I know.

"Tell me if you think any of them might have known they were being used and whether, in your opinion, they might be willing to work with me confidentially. Maybe put a star by those names. Do you know any people at these companies?"

"I know some, yes," Mary said meekly. "But, to write all that down? I don't know."

"If any firms or one of their officials might have a grudge or a dislike of one of your officials, that might be most helpful," I said.

Mary looked worried.

I was going too fast. I was losing her.

I emphasized, "Can you do that? Is it possible? Just a few to start with, maybe."

Mary and Tina were then staring at each other.

I realized I was morphing into hardball mode. Mary was, after all, not a corrupted witness to corporate crime, but a trusted friend of my Tina. I toned it down, "I hope this is okay, Mary. Anything could help and your name will never come up in print or otherwise."

Mary said in a strange tone without still looking at me, "Yeah, I can scrape up some company names and you can get them maybe from Tina here? I can't give them to you, though.

I let her question hang in the air; and decided to end it there. I stood up resolutely and thanked her for the coffee and cheesecake, but hopefully in a respectful manner. I believed that this woman was indeed freaked out.

I moved quickly sensing that the two women, close friends, may be thinking of chatting more when they could. I needed to return to Washington, D.C. in the middle of the night for work on Tuesday to scratch out more creampuff stories. "Thanks again Mary. I've got a long drive. Okay Tina, is this a good time to stop?"

We drove off quietly. Tina was unusually quiet; even pensive I'd say.

Chapter 33

I drove Tina back to her car at my cabin. It was tough to say goodbye without getting to spend the night with her. She just pecked me on the cheek and said she was tired and wanted to go back to her room at the Inn. I was puzzled by her reticence to talk over our visit at Mary's house. *Wow, is she cooling on us as a couple already,* I thought.

Not the case. She had lied to me.

Tina was feeling a need to spend more time with Mary, perhaps to reinforce her partnership. She had doubled back that night to Mary's after I left for Washington. She later repeated their conversation to me. Here is how I remember what she said transpired.

Tina told me Mary was glad to take her late-night cell phone call and let her in the back door again.

Tina said, "I told Mary that I realized it's very late but that I thought something was missing. I told her I know her well enough to see she was holding back with Hank Ford. I was right."

An emotional Mary Marinaro took Tina's concerns seriously enough to put on a fresh pot of coffee. The two women sat in the living room for comfort at that late hour.

Tina continued to tell me, "Mary asked me if I know about the traditional retreat at Halloween weekend. I did but was never invited, I told Mary. I asked her what that had to do with Hank."

Mary then took a deep breath, Tina said, and she figured her return to Mary's was going to be fruitless.

"But then, she simply opened up like never before," Tina said.

Mary told her that for the past ten years during a long Halloween weekend, the corporation brass had taken selected finance personnel to a retreat at the National Harbor Vacation Inn & Resort at Washington, D.C. That inn is four miles downriver from National Harbor. Some accountants and finance officers from every location or at least every region are invited. It is supposed to be a great honor to be invited to this celebration of outstanding performances. The stated purpose is to reward the accounting departments as the 'real company stars.'

Tina asked Mary why only those people.

Mary explained that lucrative awards are given to finance department employees at the retreat for outstanding performance. The awards are stock options mostly, which these days could become worthless at any time if the company goes bankrupt and the execs leave the country. The official reason for the retreat, the so-called agenda, is to conduct a review of the books before year's end.

"Mary believes that is the reason Levine says only finance people are invited. Weird, huh?"

Mary then told Tina the bottom line: The real purpose of the retreat was to find and exploit any new opportunities to inflate the company's income and to define how much was needed from each pot to make a showing to shareholders.

"This is only known to a few insiders, senior execs," Tina said. "That explains why I was never included."

Mary in turn also has an informant, someone among those insiders at headquarters, who says there may be another, more sinister purpose for the retreats, Tina said. "This is Mary's greatest fear, Mr. Ford. "Her informant thinks the retreats are the exec's chance to investigate the accounting personnel themselves; to exploit those employees' fears and joys, their personal plans and hopes in their jobs, their families and vulnerabilities. The retreat agenda is set up to entice the financial people to party and get their guards down."

Tina said Mary was crying at that point and she tried in vain to lighten things up with, 'Geeks have to have fun too sometimes,' but she said Mary ignored the joke.

Tina believed that Levine simply didn't want her there even though such a retreat could be an ideal public relations opportunity.

Mary continued to say she had been at the retreats for the seven years since she'd been with the company. They hired her to work in Boston, but then after a few months she convinced them she could work out of D.C. and then to the new Trout Heaven location because computer technology has allowed her to work anywhere. Mary was content living in the former home of her deceased parents, where they raised her and near her daughter's school.

"Hank, she told me she is so scared, but too hard headed to quit. 'I have bills to pay and this is a good paying job,' Mary said."

But ary also told Tina she believed she was the only one at the retreats who really thought the corporation is just one huge fraud, a house of cards. Her colleagues were in denial.

Tina asked Mary why she did not want to tell me about the retreats and that Mary had replied, "I didn't trust Hank."

* * *

The next morning Tina was still at Mary's. She woke at 6 a.m. and rang me with more details, which I was in no mood to hear after only three hours sleep. I didn't recognize the number calling.

What she said woke me quickly, however. When Tina told me further on the phone, Mary's phone, that she had to resort to telling Mary about our relationship, to get Mary to trust me, I was not at all happy.

She had told Mary that night that she "was more involved with this man than I've let on. He is a good man and one hell of a reporter. If I tell him not to report something, he won't."

Dumb, dumb, dumb, how stupid of Tina, I thought to myself.

Lucky Tina could not see my face. I was livid. She even laughed about Mary's reaction. "Mary was excited for me. She said our affair 'was amazing, that you are 'so old'." Tina said, laughing.

Still, I said nothing. *How bad could this get*, I thought.

Tina perhaps sensed my displeasure and went on that she had defended me as energetic and not at all 'old.'

I was thinking, *What next, the details of our love making? What's wrong with women anyway?* I needed her to back off me. By not replying (while angry) I hoped that she would realize that I didn't consider the exchange as a game; that I'm not some game. I even considered forgetting the story and telling her to just quit right away and be done with it.

At least Tina said she swore Mary to secrecy. She said she told Mary how amazing it was to meet me by chance because her daddy and she used to read every word of my investigative reports in the Inquirer. Tina said she talked with Mary about my story that broke open the Countrywide real estate sham, the Pennsylvania Avenue madam story, and Congressman Sam Jenkins' ill-fated attempt to approve missile technology for prisoners in North Korea, which was a real shock because Jenkins still became vice president of the United States. Mary knew about those stories, Tina said excitedly.

Was this the same Tina O'Leary? Could I trust the blabbermouth I fell in love with? I kept quiet.

She continued still, "I was so pleased she knew your work, Hank. I told her that you, Henry Clyde Ford at the Inquirer, was a big reason why Daddy wanted me to work on the Patrick Weekly. PR was not Daddy's cup of tea."

I wanted to scream, *Stop!!!* But she did then and seemed to be holding back tears. That would be a real test for me, I thought.

I still kept quiet.

She managed to tell me then that she told Mary ours was a mutual attraction and the formal titles we keep shows she and I are committed to keeping cool on a relationship "until this mess with the company is finalized over one way or another," she said with her thoughts running into another in long breaths. Maybe she then sensed I was displeased, yet I said nothing still.

I heard Mary say something like "I thought I heard you talking."

"So, you are still at Mary's, Tina. What is wrong?" I asked, probing the shaky voice that could mean tears.

"Nothing is wrong. We just needed to talk more."

"Oh?"

I heard Mary say frantically, "No, no."

Tina ignored her and said to me, "Call the following number please in a half hour, okay. Mary, can we get coffee please?"

She gave me Mary's home number.

I sat staring at the kitchen wall forever, and then planned to have a talk with Tina. I hoped she had a good explanation for breaking our most basic rule not to talk to anyone about our affair.

Chapter 34

When I called, Mary and Tina were on extensions. She had evidently talked Mary into sharing the story with me about the weird retreats.

I was cautious, "Hello, this is HCF. What's up?" Maybe I sounded snippy, regrettably.

Mary spoked first. She filled me in on the official and perhaps unofficial purposes of the October retreats. She continued, with Tina listening in. "At each one of the retreats, the execs seem increasingly interested in learning personal details about the accounting members, including me. There is a pattern and it is becoming predictable. I don't like it. I'm not 'family' with them, as they put it. Here is what they now do with that 'family' angle: For the past two years, each employee has been given an opportunity to go on what they call one-on-ones with a vice president."

"Yuk. This is very disturbing," said Tina. "Tell Hank about the one-on-ones. Sounds weird."

Mary explained, "The one-on-ones are rewards or prizes. People are expected to be overjoyed to be exclusively selected to play golf, attend a spa and massage, or just get a private dinner one-on-one with top brass. It is called reversing roles. When paired for these opportunities, the lucky employee can make policy with the ear of an executive, with a presumed promotion in the works at one point. The executive role plays the employee's perspective as accountant, finance officer, or even financial assistant."

I felt like myself again, no longer edgy and I asked, "Did you ever win a one-on-one role reversal activity, Mary? This just does not sound realistic."

She said, "The invitations to the one-on-one activities with top brass were either provided by raffle drawings or by "random" cards under certain dinner plates at meals. I disposed of my card in a toilet in the lady's room both times I got one. The activities are all done quietly and made to look, I think, unplanned. But they are highly planned by the brass it turns out, I hear."

"The toilet, huh? How appropriate," I said.

"After each of the last few retreats when they started the one-on-ones, we peons, the employees involved, compared notes."

"Who?" Tina asked.

"Co-workers and me, those I consider friends—some who had gone on the one-on-ones. We'd compared notes at lunchtime outside of the building in a restaurant on the main retail strip down at National Harbor and far away from the Inn. You know they bill it as the National Harbor Vacation Inn and Resort, but it is really squeezed into Oxon Hill between two pathetically dirty creeks and they shuttle people to the beautiful National Harbor resort spots."

Tina jumped in, "I know the formula: promise luxury, make guests then settle for cheap. So? The suspense is killing me Mary? What did you learn from comparing notes with colleagues who had won the raffle to do one-on-ones?"

Mary replied, "Throughout the entire retreat of five days, nearly every member of the accounting team won a special activity with the brass, but no one won more than one. We think they were a setup and were tape recorded by the executive companions on the one-on-ones. They asked the same questions every time in different ways and seemed to know a lot of personal information on each of us."

"Sounds reckless," I said. "A lot of planning is needed to pull off something like that. To me it reveals the execs' paranoia. You say the retreats got progressively personal?"

Mary said, "Everything about this freak show seems reckless lately, maybe paranoid yes, increasingly in the past few years. But, why?"

"Haven't a clue," I said. "I do think that holding the retreats for only finance employees would be a critically important opportunity for them to filter out employees working close to the flames, that is, close enough to the numbers to suspect the books are getting cooked by the top brass. Monitoring you folks, if they are cheating, would be imperative. As far as them becoming more reckless lately in your words, I'll share the concept with my editor," I said, without thinking.

Tina, excited, "No! You can't do that. Mary is very upset. Don't talk about this. Do you have to?"

"I guess it is not germane. I'll not share this, even anonymously."

"Thank you, Mr. Ford," Mary said in a weak and shaky voice.

"Hank. Call me Hank. I'm on your side." The sound of Mary's concern was winning me over again.

Her voice then lilted cheerfully, as if she knew more about me than she should, "I know, Hank. Oh, yes, I know."

"To get back to the retreats," Tina said, "is there more?"

Mary said, "I think I can tell Hank about this too, don't you Tina? The confrontation with Levine?"

Without waiting for Tina to agree, Mary told us, "During the most recent retreat I had too many Margaritas at a late lunch. Several of us lingered at the table with Simon Levine and his bimbo administrative assistant Pauline Hahn. Bleached blonde, leggy, big tits, you know the type. She is actually nice, but he was laying on some real sloppy come-on stuff on her in front of us. We are used to Levine's off-color sloppy joking and insinuating sexual innuendos. And Pauline is the perfect pigeon. She has all the mannerisms, fake blonde curls, and curves of a 25-year-old Pamela Anderson."

Tina asked, "Is she the same admin assistant who left the Swiss account codes on her computer?"

"Innocently and unintentionally, I'm sure. She is a lovely girl, and like Pamela Anderson, Paula is, in reality, pretty damned intelligent. Plays the bimbo card to perfection. But Pauline is also naïve," Mary explained. "So, at our lunch table at the retreat, Levine was getting crude with her. He can be charming at times, but he was getting drunk. Some guys at Levine's table, whom I didn't know—they came from other

Vacation Inn regions—teased Pauline about her sexy looks. They were assuming she is promiscuous. It was ugly. I felt sorry for her. I tried to change the subject."

"Oh-no, you can't. Men like that when they are drunk? They can't be dissuaded," Tina said.

"She's right," I concurred reluctantly, knowing my opinion meant nothing.

"Yes, I found out, the hard way," Mary said, "To gain some civility at the table, I mentioned to Levine some problems I saw in the quarterly balances. Remember, we were all finance types. I asked him some stupid questions and got a killer look from Levine. I went on and on. I didn't think the others were–listening, but Levine got hot and told me off. I excused myself and took my drink to my room.

"Then Pauline came to my room that evening. I was deathly afraid that her knock at my door was Simon Levine. I saw Pauline in the peep hole. I let her in. Pauline shocked me with a somber warning. She told me she overheard Levine and Goodbred saying that that woman Marinaro "can't be trusted and needed to be eliminated. Eliminated! That is exactly what Pauline said was Levine's words. She was also drunk, so I don't think she was on some kind of diversionary mission from management to frighten me. And, maybe they meant fire me not kill me! Pauline heard what she heard, though, I think. Levine has been beside himself. He is not by nature a violent man, but he was also getting drunk with buddies and his personality turned ugly and I didn't recognize the change in time.

"They apparently never thought that Pauline has a brain inside that pretty head. They didn't bother to disguise or hide their displeasure with 'that disloyal bitch Marinaro' in Pauline's presence. That is what she said they called me. As I said, Hank, I'm really scared now."

"What did you do?" Tina asked.

"Nothing. I faked getting sick and went home in the morning. Pauline had also told me that Levine seemed threatened by my questions. Pauline didn't remember my questions, but she said her bosses were clearly disturbed enough to talk like they would hurt me. I was terrified and promised to look Pauline up when in Boston and buy her a new dress or perfume.

"For starters though, I ordered a bottle of wine from room service and bonded with Pauline. She has a lovely heart and is compelled by men I think to act the bimbo part. She sleeps with Levine sometimes to keep her job. We swapped tall tales of the smarmy underbelly of Vacation Inns, but I was careful not to criticize management with anything she might inadvertently spill back at the office, see?"

"I get it, Mary. This is really heavy stuff," I offered. "Can you tell me, what were your questions that set them off?"

"Levine is our comptroller, though I doubt if it's written anywhere. I just felt that he would, like, help me in my job if he knew more about imbalances I noticed. Before I left, taking my drink to my room, I had asked him if he could tell me in confidence if the company was practicing a heavy rollup to attract more investors."

"What's that Mary?" I asked.

"Rolling up acquisition of unprofitable allied companies is the trend of high growth new companies," Mary said. "Remember, there was heavy drinking and I wanted him off Pauline's ass when we were sitting at a table drinking together. So, I also said, 'Hey, Simon, we are no longer a new company. Our profits ordinarily should be flattening out, not growing exponentially like we recorded." Remember, we were all bean counters of some kind at the retreat. It seemed like a fair and safe question among 'friends.' I asked Levine, "Are we rolling up new allieds or something? I might need to know for our reports.'

"I thought Levine was going to faint. His chubby face filled with blood. His eyes flared up, and he punched the table so hard things fell off of it. He said, 'No, rolling up. No, Miss Marinaro. And you don't NEED to know nothing, got it?!' He had been calling me Mary before that.

"I had still thought he might appreciate my professional perspective. I foolishly continued because I was intoxicated, I think. No, just so stupid! I tried to explain from my accounting viewpoint and therefore maybe impress him, 'Simon, don't be upset. I'm just trying to help because I know obviously that investors pay big for fast-growing companies, right? A company can turbocharge growth, you know, with acquiring meaningless companies.' 'That's not us Marinaro,' he said, dropping the 'Miss.'

"Before that I really had thought he liked me because I am very good at my job, probably the best in the company. I was shocked and embarrassed. But, stupid me. I offered a solution anyway. Remember I'd been drinking. My mothering instincts kicked in. He often seems like a cuddly boy, you know. I said, 'To protect the corporation from scrutiny, I have an accounting program that can smooth out the skyrocketing profits over a longer number of years.'

"Well, he demanded to know which Vacation Inn allied companies I considered meaningless. I told him I needed to organize a list for him. He exploded, 'So you don't know any such companies. Why don't you just shut up, Marinaro? That's enough from you. You are ruining our party,' he demanded."

"Mary, have you seen or talked with Levine since?" Tina asked.

"No, and I don't want to either. I was hoping he forgot the conversation in the drinks. But when Pauline came to my room to warn me, I believed that I was on a hit list or a firing list. I am laying low until he returns to Boston after the board meetings here."

Chapter 35

A long night indeed. When I finally arrived at my desk at the Inquirer, I found a stack of fax pages waiting for me at 11:30 a.m.

The pages contained Mary's hand-written list of 23 company names and locations. A second list gave me addresses, telephone numbers, and executive officers and accountants at each company. The faxes included no personal notes; no further explanation.

Tina had faxed it from Smokey Joe's at 9 a.m.

I was surprised, because on the night in Mary's kitchen, I had watched Mary shrink away from my idea of a list of allied companies for my investigation.

I couldn't decipher anything in common on the list of company names. Most were predictable suppliers or distributors as far as I could see. I hoped business editor Devin Shay would be a more discriminating judge of whether any of the companies were suspicious and worth pursuing:

    Alto Technologies, Redmount, NC
    Amaoco Draperies & Blinds, Henson, CA
    American Ecotourism Design, Orlando, FL
    Beck & Forth Hotel Supplier, Williamsburg, VA
    Begin Carlson Hospitality, Englewood, CO
    Better Coat Hanger Co., Inc. Baltimore, MD.
    Bronson Fire & Security, Spokane, WA
    Charlestown Safety Products, Inc. Ingleside, CA
    Christian Worldwide Hotels, Minneapolis, MN
    Commercial Pool Supplies, Saint Louis, MO
    Continental Bayside Contractors, Fresno, CA
    Country Draperies Inc. Middletown, Pa.
    Educational Institute of Fun, East Lansing, MI
    Energy Future Service Systems Brighton, UK
    Federal Analytical Consulting, Inc. Portland, NE
    For Children's Playground Things, Medland, OR
    G&M Financial Consulting, Cincinnati, OH
    General Meats Services, Minneapolis, MN
    General Hotel Training Services, Arlington, VA
    Hollens Bed & Spring Mfg. Co., Commerce, AR
    Home Box Office, Atlanta, GA
    Hotel Reservation Agents, Cologne, FR

Hammelberg Amenities Intern'l, Branson, MO
Hunter Properties, Atlanta, GA
Internat'l Sports Hotels, Geneva, Switzerland
J & D Audio Visual, Inc., Houston, TX
J.D. Power & Associates, Westlake Village, CA
Jaguar Facilities, Inc. New Carrollton, MD
Jones Travel Research, Trinidad
Minibar Expansions, Rockville, MS
Miracle Bath & Kitchen, Colorado Springs, CO
National Medical Supply Corp., Nashville, TN
Maestro Public Address Solutions, Markley, WA
No Better Hotel Renovation, Clearwater, FL
O'Brien & Brook, Corp., Washington, DC
Philips Electric, Rosewell, GA
Pineapple Communications, Bonefish, FL
Primo Hospitality Group, Toronto, ON
Rockwell Architecture, New York, NY
Roof and Siding Connection, Santa Fe, NM
S&B Coffee, Inc. Concord, MA
Snyder and Snyder Lighting, Hollis, AL
Seaward Resort Brokerage, Burlington, VT
Seimans Building Technologies, Berlin, MD.
Sillar Hospitality Group, Atlanta, GA
Southern Mattress Discount Warehouse, TX
Smithy Travel, Huntsville, TN
Snap-on Curtains and Drapes, Inc., Savage, MD
Southern Aluminum, Dupont, DE
Sperry Van North, Tampa, FL
Springer-Mitchell Systems, Inc., Stormount, VT
Standard Textile Co. Inc., Cincinnati, OH
Stanky Service Solutions, Scottsdale, IN
Super Fitness, Las Vegas, NV
St. Michele Wine Estates, Winter Garden, FL
Swanson Audio Visuals, Freetown, W.Va.
Ting Toa Carpets, USA, Macon, GA
The Heartland Security Group, Reno, NV
The Bed Linen Factory, Inc. Mundelein, KY
Thomas Furniture, Spencer, SC
Top Fitness Works, Geneva, NY
UpperCrust. Lawns, West Lake, MD.
U & T Travel Protection Plans, Hanover, PA
United Investment Bank, New York, NY
Valor Home Security Services, N. Chicago, IL
Ventura Flooring, Inc. Savannah, GA
Virgin Linen Service, St. Petersburg, FL

  Warthin Hotel Investments, Leland, FL
  Watts Pipe and Plumbing Co., Independence, KN
  Whiteboards 4 U, Inc. Boston, MA
  Wholesale Interior Designs, Batesville, ID
  Wisconsin Lodging Association, Brookfield, WI
  Whitcomb Waterfront Properties, Deal, MD
  Zurich Trust Co. Los Angeles, CA

 I thought, *Good Lord, why do they need all these allieds? I could start a chain to rival Hampton Inns with such a list.* I was still scratching my head over why timid Mary was offering the long list after all saying she would not give me one. And then, an email marked 'URGENT' in red popped in. The sender was TOL, aka Tina O'Leary, using her new email address on her laptop:

To: HCF
From: TOL
Subject: Did you get the list?

 I'm worried. I asked Mary why she held back telling you her experience at the retreat last year at the Vacation Inn near National Harbor when we were both at her house. She didn't think you would believe it.

 I guess you changed her mind. Thank you very much. She was fine with it. When I asked whether she would make a list of suspect companies for you, she pulled out that list I faxed, BAMM BOOM. She had it ready before we even got to her house, she said. She said that any one of these allieds, maybe all, could have something on Vacation, but she can't tell which ones might.

 Mr. Ford, she is scared shitless. --TOL

  To: TOL
  From: HCF
  List surprised me too. --HCF

  To: HCF
  From: TOL
 You now know that scrapper [our email code name for Simon Levine] didn't like her finance questions

at a retreat luncheon. She'd been drinking. Well, she avoids him like the plague. It won't last. He's the finance guy. –TOL

> To: TOL
> From: HCF
> I didn't ask but did he harm her in any way? --HCF

> To: HCF
> From: TOL
> No. Scrapper himself is skilled at always staying out of the fray. Mary left the retreat early and even regrets that. Some accountants in Beantown treat her funny now, she says, and Charmer [our code name for Trevor Goodbred] wants to speak with her. She is on sick leave hoping he forgets. --TOL

> To: TOL
> From: HCF
> She is not at headquarters, right? Based at Trout Heaven? Why then do they even care about a bean counter at Trout bi-gosh Heaven? --HCF

> To: HCF
> From: TOL
> No. Remember I told you. Mary was in Boston for a while, but transferred to the D.C. region and is helping set up a possible new region. She is very important to this project because she is top drawer in her field and like me she is a native, plus she wants to stay here with her kid.
> She doesn't want to attend this year's retreat for finance officers. It is coming up on Halloween. She may fake breaking her leg in a skiing accident or something.
> Mary said those probes into private lives of financial officers have intensified at the retreats. AND, get this! Mary's colleague who was found dead canoeing without a paddle in the darkness of Zekiah Swamp was

not the only one who has disappeared. At each of the past three of four retreats, an employee has died, either at the retreat or immediately after. --TOL

> To: TOL
> From: HCF
> They ski there already in October? –HCF

> To: HCF
> From: TOL
> Hey! Stay with me. I said people are dying from, or at, those retreats!

> To: TOL
> From: HCF
> Sorry, I was stalling; needed to keep you on while I looked up National Harbor lodging and you had already told me about the one death. Yes, I knew that. Wow, I see that the Vacation Inn there looks lush; not like a motel. Beautiful rooms, pool, golf, saunas, even conference rooms at a motel. I'm impressed. Would it not be fun to somehow crash that party, find a way to spy on them?"-- HCF

> To: HCF
> From: TOL
> Pictures are deceiving. That location is tacky.
> And forget it. Too risky for me at least. With my big mouth, I'd lose my job. Seems they watch and learn a lot about loose-lipped employees at these retreats. And someone would recognize you. --TOL

> To: TOL
> From: HCF
> I hate to remind you. You lost your job the day you crossed the red metal bridge and knocked on my cabin door. It is predetermined now. Maybe we could spy on

them from afar. Or, I could take a disguise, beard or something. If it very near the National Harbor, Inquirer editors will love that expense report. –HCF

To: HCF
From: TOL
Boy, you need to hit the pavement, do some surface probing. Vacation Inns are NEVER in parks or resorts next to the big resort towns or even in prime spots, remember now? Those marvelous photos on line are fakes. Our place near National Harbor is on the other side of the Oxon Hill valley in a swamp. We offer kayaking, tennis and shuttling to a nearby golf course. I've learned that every choice is disgusting. Don't ask.
To answer your stupid question, yes, it may be some juvenile fun to crash or spy, but there is no sense in rushing it until you get to the bottom of this crapola. Deal? We can crash their meetings later, somehow. — TOL

To: TOL
From: HCF
You're right. Deal. Back to Mary Marinaro. Please tell her I will do everything I can to help and as quickly as possible. It sounds like the top brass is getting desperate to take flight soon. And thank her again for inviting me into her home. That was courageous. –HCF

To: HCF
From: TOL
Will do. --love, TOL

It took real restraint not to write back with, "I love you too." I was pleased enough that her fingers at least formed the words that her lips hadn't yet.

Chapter 36
Washington, D.C., The Inquirer

After Devin, our business editor, had studied Mary's list of allied companies and having already studied SEC reports, he asked to meet me again at our favorite Starbucks on K and 16th Streets. That Starbucks provides the daily caffeine fix for D.C. high rollers for corporate America. It is almost hidden under canyons of stone and mortar, six to eight stories high, which are stuffed full of nests of evasive, chattering registered lobbyists running the country under cover. We hear a lot in that particular Starbucks.

Devin has always said there are three kinds of companies that cheat. First, there are the companies that have set up weak oversight, where all or most of the board of directors are cronies or insiders. Second, there are the companies with management facing extreme competition. And third, there are companies whose managers are of questionable character.

I bought him a cappuccino and we sat way in the back of the place. I asked which category of cheating corporations Vacation Inns fell under.

"All three. How long do these guys expect to keep this up?"

"Well," I said, "I figure whatever kind of fraud is spinning up there like a tornado will implode the corporate walls within a year. If they are intent on first expanding their land holdings all the way to Crater Lake, for one example, it could be another year. Only a guess at this point, but my money says they bail before the year-end SEC reports in January. If they don't feel the heat, then they will continue expanding."

Devin said, "We know there is considerable financial incest going on there. I can see no outsiders on their board. Most chairs are connected with wings or subsidiaries of the company itself. But that's no biggy, same as the membership scheme. Very common. No biggy at all," Devin advised.

"Okay. What about the allied companies," I asked.

"Well, you say these are just those your source says are suspect?"

"My source says any of those on that list could be exploited or shortchanged by the gang of thieves at Vacation Inns, maybe some are not even real companies," I said.

I studied Devin's steel gray eyes and frown beneath a deeply furrowed brow and nearly bald head. His hair around a bald dome was cut close, his wire-rimmed glasses thick and scratchy.

He stared at some notes for several minutes, shuffling and reshuffling. Then replied, "You can say that we immediately found four that were not companies at all before they were acquired on paper by Vacation Inn Resorts. There are others that seem to be strategic partners."

"Which ones?" I asked, while taking notes because I would see Tina again before Shay finished his report.

He said in rapid order, "The key ones are Continental Contractors, Inc., GE Capital, G&M Financial and Tax Consulting, Hotel Reservation Service, Hunter Amenities International, Hunter Realty Associates, Nova Hotel Renovation & Construction, Simmons Hospitality Group, STR [Smith Travel Research], UBS Investment Bank, and Valor Security Services. Got them?"

"Yeah. Why are those significant to my story?"

Shay leaned back for emphasis, "They all had what we call two-way transactions either at acquisition times or on-going. Two-way transactions with strategic partners raise questions, as you probably know, Hank. Two-way means that you both buy from and sell to the same party, each other. The quality of the revenue recorded on such transactions is always suspected. We are still looking into that, but the signs point that way."

"For all of these?" I asked.

"No, these guys are too smart for that. The partners are all 59 flavors of Baskin-Robbins."

"It's 31 flavors, Devin. You need to get out more. I'll buy you an ice cream when this is over."

"Very funny, Hank. There's more. There is unethical, maybe illegal bartering. Many of these, what do you call them again?"

"Allied companies, my source calls them that," I replied.

Shay continued, "... many of them informally provided stock swaps. In two cases we know of so far, Super Fitness of Las Vegas, and St. Michele Wine Estates of Winter Garden Florida, and possibly Jones Travel Research of Trinidad, were offered stock warrants as an inducement to join Vacation.

"For example, Vacation Inns Corporation in 2009 purchased True Fitness, a national franchising firm, for a purchase price of $2.8 million, plus stock warrants on paper worth $8,000,000. After the purchase, Vacation recorded the acquisition as $10.8 million. More than that, a month before anyone sniffed the deal, one of Vacation's investment partners, G&M Financial and Tax Consulting Corp. consulted with Super Fitness. You can bet that the scintillating 10K in the next quarter from Super Fitness, projecting massive growth through an M&A was written by G&M. Super Fitness stock doubled in three days. Much of its stock and the stock warrants from vacation, you can also bet, are flawed or phony. That is probably why your source included G&M on your list because otherwise that finance consulting firm in Ohio seems clean to me."

I was more than impressed, "Great stuff Devin, these examples are swindles extraordinaire! Can we confirm these findings anywhere else?"

"I thought you'd want that, "The New York Times reported that for two months before its purchase by the Vacation Inns gang, Super Fitness gave customers unprecedented incentives including stock warrants for their business, driving up revenues sharply but not necessarily profits. Investors looked favorably at Super and its stock nearly doubled in value. What was not reported was if the incentive period was Vacation's idea. Negotiations were underway during that same period, according to the Times reporter Stan Monroe. The acquisition was announced and recorded with the SEC just before Super Fitness filed its quarterly report. That report showed drastically lower profits and the Super Fitness stock tumbled, but Vacation recorded the value."

"Thanks Devin. I know Monroe. Maybe he has seen this as a pattern at Vacation with some of its other allied partners."

Devin looked down, paused several seconds, and then predicted, "If he has seen a pattern, Hank, he is likely fishing in the same scandalous lake. He's on the same story you are. I wonder if his sources would be the same as yours."

I began laughing a little before suppressing it, "I don't think they are the same, that is, if Monroe is onto the story too. I don't know what to expect from him yet," I said a little worried I'd lose my scoop to The Times.

"Listen Hank," Devin said, "this story will likely be in my section or at least parts of it, don't you think?" He didn't really want my opinion. Devin looked off, and pushed ahead.

If I knew Devin, he hoped I understood that he wants something out of all of his help too.

He relaxed and offered, "So yes, we've got the space if that is what you are thinking, Hank, that is if you've got the steak dinner for me and my wife Charlotte with your new redheaded girlfriend."

I was shocked. "What? New girlfriend? Of course, steaks all around. But, what new girlfriend." I detected Devin watching me squirm.

He continued, "Our intern Betty from American University saw the redhead with you at your apartment while Betty was gathering background for our Capitol Hill crime story."

I was thinking fast, in denial that he may be on to my Miss O'Leary. He couldn't be. I felt trapped. Recovering much too slowly, I answered, "Oh, nice try Devin. I think that must have been my neighbor who needed a ride."

"Betty says you seemed more than chummy. Says your girlfriend was dressed in a skimpy sexy thing, as Betty put it. Are you sure she wasn't your lover? You can tell me. I don't think you'd be with a hooker. Come on, I've got to know, ol' buddy." He was actually kidding. Devin didn't care for gossip.

"PR."

"What?"

"Yeah, that's right. She works in PR and I remember that outfit was for some kind of presentation that day." *Yeah, I thought, best presentation ever ..., in my bedroom.* I couldn't look Devin in the eye. I couldn't keep lying. "Can we get on with this?" I was hoping my sweat wasn't showing. I could not let the Inquirer or anyone know Tina is an employee of the company I'm investigating. All would be lost. Under the cover of secrecy, I knew I could separate her in my life and keep her out of the story. That's still not clean ethically, but I thought I was in love with Tina. And, she would eventually need protection too from her criminal bosses, which maybe only I could give her.

"Sure, if you say so Hank," Devin chuckled, likely at my discomfort.

Sharp guy. I didn't like his tone, but my friend was, well, my friend. He dropped it.

Back to business, Devin said, "As you know, Hank, we use the same analysis as the finance pros use on the commercial databases to screen for companies exhibiting certain warning signs. Take the Compustat service, for example, part of Standard and Poor's and Lexis/Nexis. I can run the other allied partners through some software. And with the right algorithmic parameters they use at the stock exchanges, it will spit out data to show them shifting future expenses to the current period as special charges. Like throwing a seine or large fishing net around your Trout Heaven boys, Hank."

"Clever, but I cannot stand any more fishing metaphors." Oops; I shut up.

"I only said one. What's that about? Anyway Hemingway, some companies' bookkeeping managers take certain bookkeeping steps to ensure that the sun will also rise, shining bright tomorrow. They may shift future-period expenses into the current dismal period as a special charge thereby relieving tomorrow's earnings of those burdens. Can you learn anything from the bookkeepers at one of these Vacation Inns?"

"Maybe. Tell me, what good is that information," I asked.

"It's enormous; can put these guys in jail for a long while. They have been in a little trouble with the Securities and Exchange Commission before."

"I know."

"Let me know what Monroe says Hank, if you will, please. If he is on to the story too, it will limit our investigation and force us to go to press with it."

"Okay, sure," I said with fake enthusiasm.

I was thinking that the story can't be published until I know Tina is free of the scumbags. All we had was chum or bits of bait to land the big fish running Vacation, who, by all indications, are likely far more crafty and diabolical than we had yet known. We had data, hints of unethical deals, strategic ideas, yes, but no insider witnesses we could rely upon.

Nevertheless, I liked Devin's use of the words 'OUR investigation. It told me he was totally aboard.

He said, "If we do have the full load to unearth, my staff can turn the software onto any improperly inflating of amounts Vacation Inns is reporting in special charges—the amount included in a special charge. Let's call it fishing by explosives. There's one for you."

"Uhg. Please. Oh yeah, the corporate jokers got in trouble before." I resorted to the part I knew because he was losing me, but I didn't ask for further explanations. He was on a roll.

"Yeah, four years ago," he said. "The SEC charged that from the last quarter of that year through July two years later, Vacation Inns had created the illusion of a successful restructuring."

I added, "That's when they really began to take off with expanding the number of locations. They were picking up the tide toward something still unknown."

Devin smiled for the first time, appreciating my tiny bit of insight. He said, "Yes, seems too fast for the likes of the SEC boys. At Vacation, they wrote that ... wait I have it written down somewhere ... ah, here it is, 'To inflate its stock price and thus improve the firm's value as an acquisition target.' But they had no intention of selling out or merging with anyone. The commission found that management created $243 million in improper restructuring reserves and other "cookie jar" reserves, which were released into income the following year."

I asked, "Is that the only enforcement charge from the regulators, Devin?"

"You might ask Monroe if you get that far with him. I know you, Hank. You won't blow your cover. But beyond actual SEC enforcements there are other warning signs to watch out for."

"Such as?"

Devin said in rapid order, as if he had memorized them years ago: "Excessive write offs, receivables growing much faster than sales, excessive reserves released into income, and growth margins growing faster than seemed possible in this type of business. Watch for decline in reserves. Also, improperly writing off in-process R&D costs from an acquisition. Oh yeah, speeding up discretionary expenses into the current period."

"Is that all you've got to go on Devin?" I said sarcastically, hoping for a laugh.

We both enjoyed laughing for some time, and then continued talking political gossip, like everyone else in that city, over another coffee and Danish, my treat.

I knew we could not filter through all of the data ourselves, but at one point I thought we could boil down the clues and get it to the SEC, maybe for a review just before we publish the story.

Chapter 37

Stan Monroe at the Times was in no mood for levity when I called the next morning. Being in New York City was a pain that ached down to his very country soul.

"Hi Stan, this is Hank Ford at the Inquirer. How's the Big Apple treating you?" I teased.

"I think I know you are at the Inquirer, Hank. Unless you've quit and are holding up in that log retreat in the woods. You lucky dog."

Just to aggravate him, I asked, "How are you doing up there in the big city, Monroe?"

"Goddamn fine, but jealous as hell, man. You know, I'm fuckin' sick of city life," said Monroe, who was a business writer for the New York Times, a fine aim for most people, but he was a country boy at heart from Central Florida and stayed on for the good salary.

"Is there anyone who doesn't know about my hideaway?" I said. "I'm still here pounding my keyboard for some good copy, which is why I called. I'm doing a piece that involves stock swapping, deals between large companies to boost their value before merging. I searched the Times and found that Super Fitness story you did when they merged with some big motel outfit up north."

"Vacation Inns, wonderful corporation of slime balls. Just the kind of folks we can fall in love with. Are you …" Monroe said and stopped suddenly.

I was put back a bit.

Nothing was said for several uncomfortable seconds.

I said, "I was wondering if you noticed a trend, a lot of this going on. I mean in that sort of industry." That was stupid. Monroe knows the Inquirer business editors are every bit as savvy as his editors. If I wanted a trend, I'd ask my business guys.

"Hey Ford, are you after Vacation Inns?" Monroe said in a lilting tone of 'You'll-never-catch-up-with-me-sucka.'

"Well, my folks said the motel chain is part of the problem."

"What problem?" Monroe was having fun with me and I didn't like it.

I came partially clean, "Tell me this: are you looking into the motel chain. I think I may."

"Hank, I have so much on my desk now that I don't think I'll be able to get back into the Vacation Inn and Super Fitness thing any time soon. And, as far as a trend, yes, big time. But, I think you knew that, didn't you? Figured that's why you called; not to play buddies with me. Whatcha got, man?"

"Not sure, Stan. I'll let you know." *Goddamn I hate this cat and mouse crap,* I pondered. He was definitely onto my story, maybe ahead of me.

I was hanging up when I heard … "Hey Hank."

"Yeah?"

"They biting?"

"What?"

"The trout, man. The damn giant trout. I got to get there. Yes, your place is near the motel, the crater, the huge trout. Not a mystery. I read in *Trout & Stream* that all ya need is bait. The Inn there lends all the gear. So? Are they still biting or not?"

"Nawh. It's slowed down now. Shoreline's all private property, as far as I've heard. I've not been over there. I'm writing a book up there in the cabin. No time." Another stupid lie, Monroe would take as an affirmative—I'm covering the story.

Chapter 38

Meanwhile, Tina was attending a special meeting of the board of directors who were staying at the Trout Heaven Vacation Inn. She expected them to go on discussing how to check out the Crater Lake while they were in Trout Heaven by taking an executive fishing trip there. I expected to hear some juicy details from Tina and confirm a date for the adventure with the Macintyres, who owned the only dock with a party boat.

Tina was surprised to be invited to the board meeting. They didn't normally invite her and she was worried. Goodie wanted a presentation, perhaps a local rundown of the lake history, she thought.

We agreed that Tina would call me after the meeting.

I advised her, "Don't use any accounting numbers in your board of directors' presentation tomorrow."

We hoped it would not be necessary. After all, how could she separate the wheat from the chaff, the truthful from the fraudulent? "It is a bad time to be under the microscope," I had told her. "Be as brief as possible, please."

She didn't call. And, she didn't answer her cell phone all that evening.

Chapter 39

I worried the evening of the meeting and all night in fact.

It didn't make sense. When I didn't hear from her the next morning, I just knew something had gone wrong at the board meeting.

Tina still didn't answer her cell phone all day.

I called Mary Marinaro at 9:45 p.m., after her daughter's bedtime.

Mary told me that Tina had left the building with the corporate head of security, Mr. Mays, about 2 o'clock and no one still seemed to have seen her for the remainder of the day and she was not at work the next day. "Hank, do you think something is wrong?"

I began shaking and felt faint.

"Hank? Oh Hank, are you there?" I finally heard Mary ask.

I took a breath and told Mary not to worry. "Tina will be there tomorrow," I suggested.

Then she told me that the board that day had sent out a memo to employees stating that the Trout Heaven Motel and Vacation Inn Resort had generated so many reservations and a long waiting list, that the corporation has launched a study of possibly setting up a new regional headquarters sooner than expected. "Maybe Tina was called into late meetings on that," Mary said.

Having been kept in the dark for more than a day wondering what happened to her. I was set to drop everything and drive up there. As I grabbed my overnight bag at home in the late afternoon, it was heavy. I'd left my laptop in it before going to work in the morning.

I fired it up and immediately saw that Tina had sent a fax message. I fired up the printer, which after five minutes began shooting out one page after another at an agonizingly slow pace, making me a nervous wreck. I could not believe how long her fax was.

It confirmed my fear that there had been trouble at the board meeting, but not about planning the Crater Lake fishing trip for the corporation directors, as Tina had expected.

Nevertheless she was smart enough to anticipate an anxious meeting and had hidden her digital recorder in her bra. Her faxed letter to me included her hand-written transcription of discussions. She was afraid to type it into her computer at the Inn.

> Dear Hank,
>
> The board meeting was painful, to say the least. I am trapped here for the evening and figured my old office fax machine and writing it on a legal pad seemed more secure than Vacation's server. And I deleted the memory record of it in the machine.
>
> Bear with me:
>
> I dreaded the next board meeting, as you know.
>
> When I entered the conference room, they all looked different than I remembered them before. And the board directors all seemed to be watching me, sort of anticipating my arrival.
>
> Sure, I had made a friend with the owner of that lonely little house across the river. I wondered if they figured out that I switched my loyalties. I blew off the thought.
>
> I clearly saw suspicion in their faces. Six men in gray or blue suits and ties, one husky man in a polyester green Vacation Inn golf shirt, two women in tidy pant suits, and a skinny boy of about 19 next to the only empty chair, which was reserved with a paper tent on the table with my name printed on it. I had to sit next to this kid. I found out shortly that it was deliberate.
>
> It is a large conference room of stuffy air, adding to a sense of solemn formality, the way all our Vacation board meetings begin. They sat at an oblong, veneered oak table surrounded by gaily upholstered swivel chairs with high backs that were patterned in pine cones, deer, and, of course, huge trout with eyes of a goofy smiling clown at a circus. Pure Ugh, as in Uuuglee, Mr. Ford.
>
> A whiteboard was erected behind and between Goodbred at the head of the table and Levine to his immediate right. As I slid into my seat, I could not look directly at either of the two men for a long time.
>
> I was soon unnerved by the hefty man in the golf shirt. It was Jack Mays, directly across the table. He is corporate head of security, based in Boston. He was not a usual participant in board meetings. It disturbed me to see him. I wondered why he was there. I only knew that Mays was some kind of attack dog that I'm told Goodbred discovered while visiting Simon Levine in prison.

At the meeting, each time I caught a glimpse of him in the corner of my eye, Mays was smirking at me like he knew something about me that I was sure to soon find out.

From my digital recording:

"Ah, there you are Miss O'Leary. Nice of you to join us," said Trevor Goodbred sarcastically, even though I was on time, but last in. Maybe I had been the topic of conversation.

I fought off paranoia, "Thank you Trevor for inviting me, sir." I said, and immediately regretted saying 'sir.' I was showing my nerves.

"You're welcome Tina. May I call you Tina?" he said, performing for his lame directors.

"Yes sir. I mean yes, of course, Trevor."

Goodbred brought the meeting to order with, "Before we get started covering all the particulars of the set up here with the new region proposal, I want to recognize the Trout Heaven Vacation Inn manager, Mr., ah, Johnson is it sir?"

"Hancock, Mr. Goodbred. My name is John Hancock, like the fellow with the big signature on the Constitution."

"Oh yes, thank you Mr. Hancock. Thank you for your kind hospitality Mr. Hancock. But actually, that was the Declaration of Independence if I recall correctly, right Jenkins? You were there, weren't you?"

Simon Levine looked up and, after an uncomfortable pause, led boisterous laughter at the expense of former state Senator Jimmie B. Jenkins, 86, a board director whose only qualification was that he was the older brother of U.S. Vice President Samuel Jenkins of Massachusetts. You know, the guy who tried to sell missiles to North Korea?

Mr. Jimmie sneered at Goodbred. We call him Mr. Jimmie. He is senile, gentle and yet devious.

"First, let's deal with Miss O'Leary," offered Goodbred.

I felt a shiver down my spine. I didn't like his sudden harsher tone toward me. We've always worked well together. He got snarky.

"As we all know, our lovely Tina O'Leary is the public relations head for the Washington, D.C. region of Vacation Inns & Resorts and she happens to be a native. For that reason, I have asked her to give you a prospectus on the state and some possibilities for expanding this first marvelous Inn in her home region. And, let us not forget, especially around our future shoreline of the bountiful giant trout-filled Crater Lake."

I was so nervous by then, I was sure sweat would show on my skirt when I stood. Meanwhile, the senior board members were all nodding and muttering to affirm Goodbred's emphatic tone when he said 'around bountiful giant trout-filled Crater Lake.' Weren't they close enough already to the damn lake, I thought? Apparently not.

Goodbred was staring at me, saying, "Secondly, I have a suspicion that she may be bucking to head our public relations and communications at corporate soon. Isn't that right Tina?"

"Well, ... I, ya." Some eloquent PR professional, huh? That is all I uttered. I was getting more and more nervous.

"Don't be shy Tina. We all know you will interview for that post soon and we think there is a good opportunity for you to move up to a post in Boston. So, for that very reason, I would like to introduce you to a young man named Bradley Armstrong on your immediate right. Bradley is your new assistant. He is going to shadow your every move for the next three weeks on his internship from the University of West Virginia at Morgantown. The PR department. Is that right Brad?"

The boy was leaning close to me and said, "That's right, grad school, sir. I'll do anything to help you out, Tina."

I hated this kid and his boldness immediately. Why not be courteous and refer to me as 'Miss O'Leary?' And why all this now? It made no sense, unless this means the end of me. Why not wait for the retreat and make me disappear? I gave the kid the once over and concluded that he was not who Trevor said he was. Something was up and I didn't like it.

I then glanced back at beefy security chief Jack Mays across the table. He was picking something from his teeth with a business card while still watching me with a smirk.

Goodbred continued, "Tina, just show our man Bradley what you do and why. Can you do that for a few weeks for me? We all know you're the best, girl."

"Yeah, sure," I said, probably a bit flip, and then I thought I had slipped and shown my displeasure with his chauvinistic remark.

I felt my teeth in a clench. Golly, Mr. Ford, the timing is terrible. To be burdened with the kid while helping take down my company, and all the while putting on a corporate happy face? I glanced at the faces around the table. Some did show some displeasure after my flip remark. So, I smothered them with my best winning smile and added, "Yes sir, that would be fun. I'd be delighted, Trevor."

"Magnificent. Now, Tina, the floor is yours," said Goodbred. "Knock us dead. Why do we want to be here with a new regional office?"

Mays tilted his head back to catch a better view of me stretching out my skirt suit as I stood and walked around the table to the whiteboard. I felt sick. The others were more respectful if not bored senseless.

I began, still wearing a plastered Miss America smile, "First let me just draw a crude map of what happened to this portion of the Sassafras River valley nearly a century ago and the trout miracle that made building a motel/resort here smart business."

I had already drawn the lake to accurate scale many times before to illustrate ground zero of the meteorite, the resulting Crater Lake, the river winding nearby, even the tiny inlet that spills into the lake only in big storms, and the mountain range.

I continued, "This is a big steamy hot hole in the ground filled with water from Sassafras River, which you all crossed on highway 7 to get here. The crater's lake had always been off limits. It was controlled until recent years by the federal Army Corps of Engineers. Then ..."

"Federal Corps? You mean there is also a state Corps?" Mays interrupted with a disrespectful chuckle.

No one else laughed.

"Excuse me Mr. Mays. U.S. Corps of Army Engineers. The feds thought the water was contaminated by mine salts and some kind of stuff from the meteorite. No one questioned it, to my knowledge.

"It hit the earth right here, at a point downstream from the motel here where the river today gets a bit strange and unnatural, due to the impact of the meteorite and some rerouting of the river water by the Corps after the blast threw megatons of earth into it and stopped it up. That led to the lake and they then opened the river. And I'm sure the folks in North Carolina downstream were happy to get their portion of the flow back."

Again, Mays interjected, "Damn straight they were, girl. But we got all the fish. I'm going after some this evening, if anyone would like to come along. How 'bout you?"

What was that? I thought, and continued, ignoring the ignoramus.

"Tina, please excuse Jack," said Goodbred. He's about a civilized as a raccoon; highly intelligent, but always ready to fight and shake things up. That's what I like about him in some places. My, my, but please not here, Jack. Should I be sorry I invited you, perhaps? Please behave."

Mays became sheepish and shuffled papers in a notebook at his chair.

"Continue Tina," said Goodie.

I ran quickly through my familiar power point of photos and data. I showed those directors who were still awake the demographics of the region, winter and summer recreational activities, nearby towns, and farms.

And then I said, "Here is Crater Lake, ladies and gentlemen. It is packed with giant trout, thus the name of the town and our new inn, the Trout Heaven Vacation Inn and Resort."

I showed the Macintyre twins holding a giant rainbow trout. "The trout bred like rabbits and multiplied at a frightening rate, I think. There are no predators of fish this size, except a few lucky bears strong enough to lift one out of the water and people like these happy fishermen in this picture you see on the screen. We love fishermen, right ladies and gentlemen?"

Goodbred was gleeful, "Here, here."

I tried to laugh along with others to Goodbred's remark. It seemed I was charming them then and then I relaxed too much. I went too far, "As you know, there are mother veins of coal and natural gas in these ancient hills. When it is removed or disturbed, spoils of heavy toxic metals and sulfur can become a pollutant of some concern. It has been many years since there's been any scientific study of the lake and the state has yet to test these fish, as far as I know. It's a puzzle.

"My father ran a series of articles in his paper, the Patrick Weekly, on amateur tests of the water and fish in the lake. The tests were performed by students at your college, Mr. Armstrong.

"The results of these tests showed ..." I paused while a collective gasp from many board directors subsided, and decided to take another route, even though there were actually some possible contaminants in the fish that were tested. ..."The unusual chemical composition of the fish and actually the lake water itself cannot be attributed to either the spoils disturbed by the meteorite or contents of the meteorite itself. So gentlemen and ladies, don't worry about eating our trout. It is prime grade fish meat, according to the county department of agriculture."

I felt streams of sweat running from my armpits. I stood there exhausted, staring at the blank faces until one of the women laughed and blurted out, "I thought you were about to condemn the fish, lake and us too, my dear."

I laughed too, with one or two other board members.

Goodbred looked puzzled as I sat, so I just looked down on the board table. Perhaps he was expecting more promise of success from 'the talented and beautiful Tina O'Leary,' as he likes to refer to me. "Thank *you, Tina, for a most interesting and informative presentation."* He then turned to old man Jenkins and other gray heads at the end of the table and said in an apologetic tone, *"You'll have to excuse Miss O'Leary's little lesson in water quality. Her late father ran a good little newsletter in a nearby town and I think Tina has a bit of muckraker in her too."*

Ouch, I cringed and buried my eyes into the cheap veneer on the table. How dare he suggest Daddy was a muckraker, I said to myself in silence, gritting my teeth, while not daring to look at the obnoxious bastard.

Oh-so-clever Trevor, however, was not through with me. He said, *"Why don't you show Bradley around the Inn and the grounds, Tina O'deary. Thank you."*

I turned quickly with a smile, I hope, and no intention of saying goodbye or farewell to the crusty, hypocritical board. I rushed out of the room in a deep sigh of relief.

But, to my dismay, Jack Mays also left the room, following me, with intern Bradley Armstrong in tow.

Mays caught up with me at the Inn's coffee shop, *"Buy you a cappuccino, Miss O'Leary? We need to talk,"* he said.

Wow, I thought. *A fax? And, so long. She must have been worried sick. Why hadn't she called instead?*

My guess was that she was at Joe's for dinner.

Guessed correctly. "Miss O'Leary. I'm dying here. Why didn't you call me after the meeting," I asked without thinking straight."

"Oh my God; didn't you get my fax?"

"Just now saw it. Forgot my laptop today. I'm home now and read it. That was one terrible day for you. I'm sorry."

"I should be the one who is sorry for not checking to see if you got it. The meeting was just the beginning of a horrible day and evening, Mr. Ford. I sent you an audio file just now too. Listen, I am sorry, didn't mean to keep you in the dark. I was so exhausted after transcribing, living the meeting over again and faxing it to you that I left the Inn right away and stayed with my sister today. I was unable to face the company and called in sick. I didn't want to worry you."

"Why a fax? Nobody uses them much anymore. I would not be looking for it from you either."

"Again, sorry. Maybe I was not thinking. I needed to share what happened. Didn't think of an audio file, don't use them ever. I was getting paranoid and also wanted to make sure to add commentary for your eyes only," she explained. "Then, today I remembered that you may be left hanging after reading my fax.

"There was more. After the meeting, Mays actually reached out and grabbed my shoulder from behind at the café and things went downhill from there."

"Are you okay? Did he molest you?"

"No, just mental abuse. I'm fine today. Again, sorry I slept all evening and had meant to call earlier. As I said in my fax, I recorded the board meeting with the little digital in my bra."

"Yes, lucky little digital, but okay, sorry. I miss you."

"Thanks. Me too. Well, the point is that I still had the recorder going when Mays touched me." I figured out how to send audio files. Look for it."

The digital audio file popped up attached to an email from Tina on my laptop. It was a second recording from her bra—the tiny digital device she had kept there, starting with the board meeting. This one she didn't transcribe but dumped into the audio file from her parent's house.

The second recording was necessary, Tina said, because she could no longer ignore Mays stalking her. He was bearing down on her at the coffee bar. Before she could reach the women's room to turn off the little recorder, it had incidentally captured his intrusion.

"Got it," I said. "I'll call you after I listen to it."

She hung up.

The recording evidently starting as Mays touched her from behind:

"Oh, Mr. Mays. You startled me," Tina said. "What brings you to the Trout Inn?"

Mays replied, "Just wanted to meet you again, Miss O'Leary. It has been a while. Do you remember? We met in Boston. Call me Jack."

I paused the recorder to remember a story Tina shared with me about the first time she met Mays.

* * *

Mays had first gotten fresh with her when Tina was a new employee at her orientation at Boston headquarters, which is halfway out on Cape Cod. It was at the cocktail party following an annual meeting of stockholders. He was drunk. He pushed against her and in a predatory way looping his arm around her waist while spilling some VO on her new red dress. He pressed his luck with a kiss on the cheek after introducing himself with an invitation to 'Wanna go for a smoke?'

When she refused, and she couldn't release his grip, the then-comptroller Max von Kindel pulled Mays away forcefully and scolded him. He walked Mays out of the reception room. Von Kindel, whom Tina didn't yet know, gave Tina a look of exasperation, she said, gesturing in the direction of Mays exit, and then apologized to her on behalf of the entire company.

Tina was impressed with von Kindel in Boston, she said, whom she deduced was one of the top executives. She naively took his gallantry as a good sign for her new employer, Vacation Inn & Resorts, Corp. She thought she then had at least one friend in top management.

* * *

I pressed 'play' again on the computer's audio recording:

"Listen Tina, may I call you Tina?"

"No, please keep it Miss O'Leary, Mr. Mays. Do you know how much you embarrassed me in Boston?"

"I apologize. I was drinking too much and you are so very beautiful. Are you single Miss O'Leary?"

Tina later told me she ignored his audacious question and instead gestured toward Bradley Armstrong.

"Is he on payroll yet?" she asked. Then, "Mays, make it quick [sarcastically]. I have an intern to train and I don't want one."

Mays said, "Bradley is not so much an intern but a replacement for you, whether you get the Boston job or not; but looks like you will, maybe temporarily though."

"Very amusing," she said.

"O'Leary, before that decision, I need your help as a native of these hills. There are serious security matters that need to be cleared up. I need to talk with you. I apologize for being abrupt.

Seriously, can I share a coffee? I'm not offering to buy coffee or any other favors. This is business."

Evidently too hold him at bay, she said, "Security matters are not my concern, but if you insist, get a table there and I'll join you in a minute," she said.

As she passed by Bradley at the restroom doors, she later told me, he smiled broadly. Tina said she was annoyed to look back and see his eyes follow her through the swinging door of the women's restroom. She went into a stall and opened her blouse. As she thought, her digital recorder had just stopped when she heard a beep. She reset it on 'record' in a new 90-minute file and walked out after a minute, nearly bumping into the boy again who may have been listening at the door. She ignored him and quickly joined Mays, who indeed had bought her a coffee.

She said that she drank from a water fountain to give her a chance to look down her blouse to see the tiny red recording light on the digital recorder just under her blouse.

I know this woman. It was no surprise that she remembered every detail.

As she rejoined Mays, incredibly enough he said, "You probably know there are armed groups of hillbillies forming out here to protect their properties around the lake and surrounding hills from honest efforts by the corporation to buy their properties and expand its resort. I am here to tell you, despite what you heard or know about these people, they are nothing but misinformed hooligans. We are here to help their community."

No surprise that Tina was stunned into silence.

Mays continued, "The truth is Miss O'Leary, if we don't get that land, we cannot complete our plans for a world class resort and regional headquarters," as he tapped her hand and then rested his hand on hers.

It was obvious that he was out for more than advice. He clearly did not like her, except her looks, and, she later told me that he didn't seem to care that he reeked of fish smell.

On the recording again, Tina said to Mays in a defensive tone, "My heavens, where has that boy gotten to. Trevor told us in the meeting he was to stick like glue to me."

"He's gone to get my Jeep," Mays barked. "We are going to take a ride."

"You and the kid?"

"No, you and me. And, ... Bradley too, if you prefer. In fact, he can drive while we cuddle together in the back to look things over. Just kidding, Tina."

Mays had arranged for his Jeep Cherokee to be driven down to Trout Heaven from Boston to get in some R&R fishing the now-famous lake, he said. Mays' Cherokee was painted in red, white and blue, the colors of the New England Patriots with the wind-blown colonial patriot soldier logo of the team, three feet wide, across the hood and roof.

"Climb on in girl," he said. He put a hand on her waist she told me later.

"Let's just pretend you have respect for women; just this once, eh Mays?" she snapped while inflicting a sharp elbow into his ribs, she said.

"Ada girl. I mean lady," he said, loving it. He called to Armstrong, "Boy? Take us down to the river first by the Garrett property. Keep it on her side so I can keep my eye on O'Leary, here," he said chuckling in self-satisfaction.

Although the entry road to the resort was on the northwest side of Charity Mountain, the corporation had already purchased some property from the Garrett family from the crest of the mountain and down halfway to the river's edge on the southeast decline. Though still at a distance, it was the first view of the lake owned by the corporation, which had filed to rezone to commercial from rural agriculture.

While listening to the recording and having been there at that hour, I could imagine that most of the morning mist had burned off the lake. I imagined sunlight flickering off the surface through the road side pines. I also pictured myself slugging Mays.

Back on the recording, Mays asked Tina, "You got hold of that fellow over there, right? He's got that cabin across the river, where the corporation will put a ski slope and lift."

She said nothing, knowing, I'm sure, that the deal with the owner of that little cabin, me that is, had little to do with Mays' purview on security matters.

Tina later told me that the Armstrong kid drove fast out of the tacky Trout Heaven Inn and around the scenic mountain range to Route 7.

"See how close we are from the Resort to the Lake, Miss O'Leary?" Mays said. She later told me he tapped her on the bare knee below her tight suit skirt.

"There is no need to sit so close, Mr. Mays, please," she said.

"Marvelous view from here," he said. "Can you see the lake from the Ford cabin, Miss O'Leary?"

"I wouldn't know."

"I thought you hand delivered a contract to him for his property," Mays said in an accusing tone.

"That's right," she replied. And that was that. She said that was the first time anyone with the corporation had referred to the coveted cabin as 'the Ford cabin' and it made her nervous. She clammed up for a long while.

Bradley Armstrong drove Mays and Tina, back up Charity Mountain through the town of Trout Heaven, then to the south along state route 7 past the sign for Macintyre's Carpentry and Home Improvement shops and the Macintyre brothers' charter fishing business. He then sped past the Hancock family land between Crater Lake and Faith Mountain, along an overlook of Crater Lake from Route 6 across the Smythe property, past Manny Smythe's sadly abandoned produce stand at the crossroads of Route 7 and U.S. Interstate 65, east along Faith Mountain and by the properties on hillsides facing Crater Lake and then up stream of the Sassafras River, including federal lands half blasted away by the meteorite, as far as my cabin across from Trout Heaven and the Vacation Inn.

Tina said it was sad to pass a prominent iron plaque that read 'In loving memory.' It lists the 15 names of those who were missing, presumed pulverized, after the meteorite impact. Mays didn't mention it, but Tina knew that 12 of the 15 were Smythes.

Only two public roads presented a lake view in addition to private property driveways into the Macintyre's, Smythe's, Garrett's, and Hancock's.

As Mays grilled her for information on the land owners, she talked about the scenery of intermittent forests of conifers and hardwoods, some cattle pastures, and a few fields of corn and soybeans, she told me later.

I listened to more than an hour of the recording and began to worry that the 90-minute digital recording file would end sending a beep off her bust.

I called her back.

When I told her of my concern she laughed and said she had stopped the recorder when Mays and Bradley had to pee all that coffee they drank at the Inn and disappeared briefly behind a tree. She also said that instead of being intimidated by the advances and aggressive questions of Jack Mays, the tough-minded mountain woman focused on her love of those hills and the people living there.

Tina said Mays asked when she expected to hear from the guy in the cabin.

She said, "Despite my protests, I was in for a four-hour drive by Bradley Armstrong and insinuating questioning by Jack Mays into all the properties on lovely wooded hillsides facing Crater Lake and up stream of the Sassafras River, only as far as Ford's cabin, as he called it repeatedly, directly across from the Trout Heaven Vacation Inn and blocking its expansion. I repeated that the deal for the cabin property was not my job but that the inn manager would handle it."

I asked if she had recovered from such a traumatic experience.

She told me, "Yes. But I also vowed at that moment, Mr. Ford, when it was apparent I was not in any real danger on Mays junket, to help you more than ever to expose the greedy out-of-town parasites."

Chapter 40

Tina then continued to tell me about another audio recording file she just then sent. "Call me back after you listen, okay?"

It seemed that back at the Inn, Bradley Armstrong turned the Cherokee keys back to Jack Mays who would park it in the VIP garage (the only garage) with his personal punch code. She said, "I resented that I did not have such a privilege."

She slipped onto the shadows of the Inn's portico to reset 'record' on the digital device. She wanted to ask Armstrong some questions and have his answers on it.

She walked back to the inn with Armstrong, though he lingered a half step behind. As he scampered to hold the door, she stopped in the doorframe and asked, "Bradley, who are you really working for, me or your Uncle Trevor? I emailed someone I know in Admissions at Morgantown from my Blackberry while you and Mays were pissing in the woods. They emailed back and said you are not a student at the University of West Virginia, young man. Come clean."

"Oh yes I am, Tina. I'm skipping a semester to work with you. It's you I work for, according to Trevor Goodbred, whom I guess you know now, is my uncle. Unc wants me to learn from you."

"Look you little liar, I also know that University of West Virginia PR department at Morgantown. I emailed faculty I know. No one there has ever heard of you. You can quit pretending. I am going to go to Goodbred myself and get rid of you on this so-called internship. You can stay working here as far as I'm concerned. But I don't want you shadowing me, because you are not who they say you are. I will tell 'Unc' immediately. Here?"

She said she then walked into the woman's restroom again.

The kid followed her.

She screamed, "Hey, what's the idea. Do you know this is…"?

Tina said the kid then pointed at her and said she was the 'one who is through here' not him. He said Mr. Levine said so.

Then he said, "They want you out of here."

Tina said he came very close to her and threatened her.

"I know you are a lock for the promotion to get you the hell out of here and relocate to Boston." He said, "They don't trust you here, so I'm learning your job, see?"

She pushed him back calling him an obstinate twit I think she said on the muffled recording. And then, she pulled her cell phone to call security.

When Bradley stepped forward again and said her call will go directly to Jack Mays while he is in town, she was able to fumble through her purse, found her large Blackberry smart phone, and put it into her clenched left fist.

"You can't touch me," Bradley said. "You are just a hysterical PR flack lady with a pretty face and smokin' hot bod." He was staring at her breasts and pressing closer as she backed into the wall.

She gripped the phone tight. Tina smashed Armstrong across the face with it as hard as she could. Tina was in excellent shape and the phone in fist must have packed a wallop. It was clearly a direct hit from the sound on the recording. I then heard him scream and something hard hitting the floor.

Armstrong had tumbled down. His head hit a marble counter top on a wash basin behind him. He then tumbled to the marble floor face down, injuring his face further.

Tina was at first scared, then happy. She said she then began kicking him toward the women's restroom door with her wooden heels each time he tried to get up.

As he finally crawled out, she screamed at the top of her lungs, "Stop coming in here Mr. Armstrong, you pervert." He looked up and was dumbfounded by Miss O'Leary's rage as she continued to yell at him.

I learned that several guests then walked over from the lobby. Tina yelled, "No wonder you fell. Don't you know now to stop coming into the girl's room. Shame on you, trying to molest another woman again. We know what you are Mr. Bradley Armstrong, nephew of Trevor Goodbred. I'm reporting this to him immediately."

She said that after he took a short crawl past the door and cocky Armstrong Bradley used a water fountain to regain his feet, he ducked immediately into the men's restroom to clean up his bloody head.

Chapter 41

We agreed to talk again the next day and take a time out to digest the ugly turn in Tina's dilemma. Now threats and intimidation were personal. After another agonizing night of worry over my Tina, my phone rang again at 7 a.m., an ungodly hour for a newspaper man.

"Good morning Mr. Ford." Without hesitation Tina told me that she stayed over at the inn to be on call to greet more executive officers coming in for meetings over the new regional expansion. Back in her room at the inn, her dreams were horrible. She feared that her job and her life were in serious jeopardy. For the first time, the tough-minded mountain woman was really scared.

"Tina! Where are you now? Not still at the inn I hope," I asked.

"I'm at Joe's for comfort food and his special coffee."

I said, "My home phone may not be totally secure. Can you call me at the paper in an hour? Are you alright?"

"Fine. Just fine. Oh, my salad is up. Thanks Uncle Joe. Mr. Ford, I need to talk with you. Miss you. ... Joe says hi."

She was faking. She wasn't alright.

At 8:35 a.m.—Tina called again, on my desk phone at the Inquirer. She said, "Jack Mays is an ex-marine drill sergeant, ex-con up for manslaughter years ago, and now, as I said, the corporation's chief of security. He's creepy. I am trying to figure out what he is after. And ..." She was panting.

"Take a breath. What makes you think he's after something? Is he there for the board meeting?"

She was clearly disturbed by Mays. She said, "But to answer your first question, he is snooping into property owners around the lake and river valley. He is making absurd statements about them. The land owners are paranoid and dangerous, he is saying. You heard the recording. I spent about four hours captive with this nut, Mr. Ford. He's slimy too; thinks I'd go for him if he persists. I'd kill the bastard first. Oh ... sorry."

"What!?" I said. I didn't think Tina ever talked like that.

"I shouldn't have said such a thing normally," she said as if she regretted her urgent tone. She paused, and then in a more sensible voice, "Don't worry; I can handle the creep. But because of our mutual interest in this company, I needed to tell you something."

"Tell me what? That a murderer has the hots for my girl." I couldn't believe I said that. We hadn't talked about our relationship being permanent. It just felt that way to me at least.

But she went with it, ""For the murder years ago, he got off easily, convicted of third degree murder. He killed the boyfriend of his wife at the boyfriend's beach house after tracking her there. He caught them in the act. The Boston Globe said police found the murder weapon right there in bed, a bloody butcher's knife. A real classic. You can look it up. It was eight years ago."

"And you say you can handle the creep. So then, it is okay for him to hang around with you for, what? Four hours in the countryside you say?"

"Let me explain, Mr. Ford. Again, Mays knows I'm from the region. Mays also says locals are forming gangs and holding their meetings in barns to plan their fight with our corporation. That is just crazy. We don't do stuff like that in these parts. Mays also implied that the Macintyre family has for many generations been feuding with the Smythes. This man actually said the Macintyres could be behind the killing of Manny Smythe at his produce stand. Remember that? Did you ever stop there?"

"Yes, I knew the stand and met Manny. But, how did he know about that? Newspaper reports, I guess. Go on then; you say there is a Smythe clan? And that Manny wasn't killed by a random nut, but from a deliberate hit by the Macs!!? You've got to be kidding? Why?" I asked.

She said, "I don't really believe that. But you probably don't know that old man Emmanuel Smythe was the great grandfather and head of the family that owned the entire side of Charity Mountain on about 45 percent of the sunny southern edge of Crater Lake. Many of those 15 people who died in the meteorite impact were Smythes, benefactors younger than Manny and two were his sons."

"Wow. And Mays talked about this?"

"He is trying to spread rumors and whip people up around here, I think. I'm not sure of his strategy, but his motivation is to divide and conquer to get their land, I guess. "He said we cannot fully trust our manager John Hancock to be loyal either. Hancock is a local land owner too on the river, around the mountain, nearer to your cabin, but has a limited lake view."

"Is Hancock handling the offer for my place?" I asked.

"He is the appropriate contact for that, yes. But, because he is a land owner near Crater Lake too, I suspect that the decision and the offer were made higher up in Boston."

"You know, Miss O'Leary, I really should unload this property before things get ugly, that is, if we are right, that they are planning to bail before the feds busts them," I said.

"Wow this is so weird. I didn't really want you to sell. But, it would also give you cover that you are going along and not fighting the sale," Tina wisely deduced.

"I'm going to pay Mr. Hancock a visit. Can you set up an appointment?"

"Maybe in a couple of days. I'd like to see you sooner than the weekend too," she said sweetly.

"Me too. Now about this creepo ..."

"Which one?" she laughed. "You mean Jack Mays?"

"Yea, do you actually NOT know what he is doing there?"

"No one seems to know, but people are edgy with him around. He seems criminal in the worst way. And one other thing that really made my skin crawl. He pretended to have a courting interest in me by asking questions about my background, my family and especially my father's newspaper. That stuck. I don't know what his real interest is in me now. It was also ill timed. Goodbred, during our meeting of the board, also said something rather nasty about my daddy, while pretending to compliment him. Said I had a bit of the muckraker in me too!"

"That's awful. Did Mays ask anything about the newspaper, the coverage, what kind of stories, etc.?" I asked.

"Why?" she asked.

"Just a hunch. Tina, ah Miss O'Leary—we still doing that?"

"Yeah"

"Okay then. Miss O'Leary, what happened to the newspaper? I mean, are there old copies from the time of your father's death?"

"Why do you ask? I don't see how that is important, Mr. Ford. I avoid thinking about all that."

"Trust me, and you have so far. Are there back pages, a morgue?"

"Daddy didn't maintain a story morgue as such. Who had the time? He also sold real estate, you know."

"You told me. I remember," I said gingerly. I was on tender ground.

She offered, "He did keep old copies in chronological order at the paper's office. I wish I could have taken it up and kept publishing it after ... well, you know." Her voice was shaky.

"Where was the paper's office? Where was the printing press?"

"Same place for both; collecting cobwebs. The newsroom, if you can call it that was in the attic over Uncle Joe's café in Patrick on the second floor he didn't show you. Bet you noticed. Daddy ran the press in Joe's back wing. We both have trouble even looking at the door to that wing. Daddy was part owner of the diner you know."

I said, "You might not have heard Joe tell me that at the café. Of course, that was before I knew your father was gone."

"Daddy kept the copies in a big walk-in closet. Probably still up there. I'll ask Uncle Joe, but I don't think even he's gone in there yet."

"Ask him in person please. Don't call him on a land line from the inn or on your cell. This is important. Nobody should know we are snooping into the Patrick Weekly's old newspapers. Let Joe know you will come over for a meal. Drive over there tonight and let me know, okay? And hey, where are you calling from now, down the street in D.C. again, I hope?"

"I'm in the old pay phone for the Amish on a road in Carpentersville. But, Mr. Ford, I don't see where looking up old newspapers would be interesting to anyone listening to my cell calls."

"It's a hunch. If the closet of papers is still there, meet me at Smokey Joe's Friday night. Can you do that?"

"Certainly, but I still don't see ..."

"I'll leave D.C. around 2 p.m. and meet you at the café at say 8 p.m. Meanwhile, today and tomorrow I'll keep checking out Mary's list of suspect allied companies. Are you good with that?"

"It's a date," said Tina, I detected a happy lilt in her lovely voice.

I let it go as 'a date' and really looked forward to another Smokey Joe burger, or whatever he calls it, with the works. But, I was really burning to get into the back issues of the O'Leary's Patrick Weekly, while I disciplined myself to remember to curb my enthusiasm when I would be with their still-grieving daughter Tina.

Chapter 42

Before the weekend and my trip to Joe's to thumb through the old Patrick Weekly's, I needed to meet with Devin again to share the bad news about Monroe, the business reporter in New York, and of course get my share of more sarcastic advice.

As I walked into his office, his desk phone rang. He held up a finger for me to wait and pointed me to a chair. He took the call on speaker so he could continue to edit copy on his screen. The call was from Ida, our receptionist.

"Mr. Shay, you have a call on line 47. She specifically asked for you."

"We are on deadline Ida; don't you know? Ask who it is?" said Devin.

"Yes, I know it's close to deadline, but this lady says she is an attorney from New York and she has to reach you today."

Devin accepted the call and held his hand on the phone, "Hank, come back will you? This is a complaint, or worse, a libel suit."

An hour later I checked in with Devin again. This time I got a lot more than advice about Stan Monroe. Devin wanted to meet me off site at Starbucks where he steered me to an empty table at the far end, away from other customers.

"Monroe is definitely onto it Dev," I said reluctantly. "The guy played dumb and actually coaxed me right into a corner. So, I think he knows I'm onto Vacation Inns too."

Devin razzed me, without a trace of a smile or any emotion, "Way to go, Ford. Hey, you know Mike Wallace retired. Maybe you can put those interviewing skills to good use on 60 Minutes," he said. He was disappointed in me.

"Kill the crap, Devin. This guy's on my story and what do I have?"

"It's all in the game, bro. First of all, Monroe is not the only one besides you on Vacation Inn's tail now. The so called urgent call was from a certain Valarie Moore, an attorney in New York. She brings you a gift from heaven. Mrs. Moore is suing Goodbred and the corporation for $4 million. If her suit drags out in court, you won't see Goodie bolting to the Swiss Alps any time soon, as you thought. This could be the perfect delay you need."

"Must be the going number these days," I mumbled.

"What? Somebody else sues them?" he asked.

"Never mind. Please go on about Miss Moore. Who is she again?"

Devin broke into a boyish smile I rarely saw on him at the paper and he said with glee, "Mrs. Moore is the big legal fish we could never catch ourselves. No? I see you are skeptical Hank. Tell me then, what do we have?" he asked sarcastically, "Statements from an insider at the firm who won't be quoted? Vague old SEC reports? And your lady source?"

"Go on," I said, "What the hell does that mean; big fish and all? And stop the fishing stuff, Dev. Are you mocking me?"

Devin got serious, "Wait 'til you hear this. She was on a church trip to Luray Caverns and Goodbred and Levine were in the tour group down in the caves. Here is the good part. Goodbred, it turns out, is manically claustrophobic and he freaked out down in the closed-in chilly limestone caverns. He threw up all over Valarie Moore's little girl and without another word spoken, Levine knocked the mother and kid into a freezing pool of cave water, accidentally I must assume. And that's not the worst of it for Moore, their vacation was ruined, the kid almost died of pneumonia, and Moore has never gotten an apology or the free vacation that they promised her."

"Wow. Why did she call you?

"She did not."

"She did. I was there. Remember?"

"Oh no, she didn't. She said she tried to call you, the great newspaper investigator. She was looking for dirt on Vacation's dynamic duo. When you were not at your desk, she asked for the business editor."

"My God."

"Here is the best part. She is a corporate lawyer. That's the big fish part. And Hank, I think it is truly a coincidence. I didn't hear her indicate she knew anything about the story you are investigating—nothing about membership schemes, faulty filings—nothing. Even though that is her specialty, I think."

"How could she know about my story? Unless she talked with Levine and Goodbred at some point, that is if they already know what I'm doing. I'm sure they do not. Maybe the offer for my property was to draw me out. Well, they certainly did that, didn't they? And now, this attorney is calling me about it."

"Calm down, Hank. I emphatically doubt all that crap. Don't have an anxiety attack on me now. This could help you. I just have a feeling."

"What should I do with Mrs. Moore? Why don't you call her back, Dev?" I said.

"No, you should call her back. You are the famous investigator she wanted to share her incident with. She will be suspicious if you don't maybe."

Devin quickly got impatient, and then admonished me, "You better get something on newsprint on Vacation fast or you will lose this thing to the Times. I think this attorney may be our confirming source on the data we are pathetically trying to fish out of the Vacation cesspool."

I agreed and told Devin I'd call the woman. But first I got to my desk and looked her up on line. I'm glad I did. Big fish indeed. Valarie Smith Moore was a senior partner in the venerable New York office of Braunstein, Gibson & Crockett.

When I read the next paragraph from her law firm bio, I think I yelped, "Yes! drawing looks from around the newsroom. The bio read:

Moore is chair of our firm's Mergers and Acquisitions Practice and as such is a highly distinguished corporate lawyer with broad experience in the legal areas of mergers and acquisitions, corporate governance and capital markets of conglomerates, with special emphasis in service and consumer protection cases.

Her bio continued to interest me. Prior to joining the firm, she independently represented major Wall Street firms as an M&A banking legal authority. It read:

Mrs. Moore is regarded as one of the top M&A lawyers in the United States and has been ranked as a leading M&A lawyer by Judges Chambers, *The Best Lawyers in America*, *The International Who's Who of Merger & Acquisition Attorneys* and *New York Magazine's* list of Best Lawyers in New York for the past five years.

It went on to say that she has excelled at the firm in advising clients on board governance issues, conflicts of interest, restructurings and recapitalizations, even the ethics of executive investment activities. She was a frequent speaker at legal seminars in the U.S. and abroad. And, she has authored more than 40 publications on SEC rules and corporate law issues. She was a member of the Board of Advisors of the School of Law, University of Virginia, where she earned her Juris Doctorate in 1985 and is an adjunct professor of corporate law at Columbia University in New York.

I couldn't have been more impressed. Yes, I could. I think I said "Yes!" out loud again, starting to sound like sports voice Marv Albert, when I then read the names of the 102 corporations she had represented while at the firm, starting with Apple, AT&T, Safeway International, Hilton Hotels, Direct TV, Transworld Holdings, United Healthcare, and GEICO.

Goodbred certainly threw up on the wrong mother's kid.

I took a breath before calling Valarie Moore. Maybe she would be of assistance to my story and help us. Or maybe she'll do it for us. Hope not. I wanted the kill for myself.

I decided to be modest, but rambled nervously, "Hello Miss Moore, this is Henry Ford. I work at the Washington Inquirer and cover corporate issues, not the law. I understand you asked for me, though. There must be some kind of mistake, I ..."

"Let me stop you right there, Henry; may I call you Henry," she said confidently. "I feel like I know you, been following your corruption stories for years. It is a real honor, sir. I didn't really expect you to call me back."

I slowed down; still humble, I hoped, "Maybe if you can tell me what my work has to do with your law suit of a motel executive ... is there a story for me Miss Moore?"

"Yes, yes there is, if you want to talk about it. I am in Washington right now. I am a corporate law professor at Columbia University. Did your colleague Mr. Shay explain my law suit?"

"He told me about the accident. Is that all there was to it?" I shouldn't have gone slightly negative so soon. It's a habit to draw people out.

"It wasn't exactly an accident. True, he was sick at his stomach, Mr. Goodbred that is. Heck of a name, huh? Didn't seem all that well bred to me. Oh, I'm sorry; just a little nervous. I don't often call a newspaper to complain."

"Go on Mrs. Moore," I said.

"That man stood there over my daughter in a crowd. It could have been anyone he hovered over. And, he made no attempt to try to turn or deflect his vomit or at anyone else. He threw up his breakfast all over my poor daughter and I have witnesses who say he actually aimed at her. We were with a group of parishioners that I know. It was awful Henry, just aw …"

I cut in, "I am sorry. Is this Trevor Goodbred we are talking about, CEO of Vacation Inns & Resorts Corp.? I'm sure you have read about his Inns, which seem to be popping up all over tarnation?"

"I've heard of Vacation Inns. Never stayed at one. We have pretty limited expense accounts, can't stay at fancy places,"

She was smart. Of course, her firm would allow fancy expenses. I felt I was back on track with this woman. She was not aware of my investigation. I kept drawing her out. It got more delicious with every word she spoke.

"Mrs. Moore …"

"Call me Val, Henry. I insist," she said, still excited to talk with me, I guessed.

"Val, from what I've heard you are fortunate," I teased.

"Why is that Henry?"

"Because fortunately you have not stayed at a Vacation Inn and Resort anytime, anywhere."

"My word, Henry Ford. You certainly are the cunning Washington Inquirer inquisitor extraordinaire. You *do* know these guys," Valarie replied, then burst into funhouse-like laughter for a good half minute.

Amazing, free-form laughter so early in our conversation. I liked her already. Well, that was also long enough for me to know she was intent on extracting serious revenge for Goodbred and Levine's rude treatment of she and her daughter.

She finally regained her voice, "Yes, I do understand that they are not fancy, Henry." And with that, she let out more of the same kind of laughter and it sounded like she took the phone from her ear to compose herself.

"Valarie? Ah, Val … Are you there?" I thought she was hanging up. She stopped laughing and we agreed to meet at the Inquirer's 'annex,' Starbucks. Valarie Moore was not going to be satisfied with a financial settlement it seemed. She wanted blood and she had the legal marbles to put a dagger into slick Goodie, sly Si, and their flimflam resort chain.

Chapter 43

Devin and I thought we had gotten to Starbucks first. We faced the door. I'd forgotten to ask Valarie Moore how we could identify her. No need. She came up behind us; had been scouting us out since we walked in.

"Hank? How do you do. I'm Val." She extended her hand as we stood. "And you must be Mr. Shay. Delighted. Please sit."

She was African American with fairly dark complexion and at a small to medium height, features of perhaps central Africa, broad smile of gleaming white teeth, and pure black hair of waves to her shoulders. The handsome attorney was far more feminine than I expected, considering all the home runs she'd hit, according to her firm's online scorecard. She wore a navy-blue dress drawn at her waist and a woven rattan necklace and nickel-size, round matching earrings.

She immediately asked what we knew about Vacation Inns and Mr. Goodbred. Valarie seemed genuinely delighted after Devin gave her an abridged version of his findings so far from studying the corporation's SEC filings, the footnotes, the stock swaps, and the possible fake allied companies. Valarie Moore did not touch her coffee throughout Devin's speech, did not move a facial muscle. Her grave demeanor showed no sign of any reaction or response.

I worried. She might not be who she said she was, though I recalled she flashed an identification card of some kind after handshakes with each of us. She carried no purse.

I felt myself exhaling when she leaned back in her chair and smiled broadly again for the first time after Devin finished talking about his findings.

She said, "Gentlemen, if you are going after these guys ... if you are going to use all this evidence against them in an expose, I can withdraw my lawsuit and step aside. It sounds like you guys can do more harm to them than I can by shaking a little coin out of their butts."

Well said. Okay, the lady was who she claimed to be. I spoke first, "No, please, no. Don't do that." I think your law suit can help us." I turned to Devin. "Don't you think?"

He nodded.

I said. "Now, if we do pursue this story, and, Miss Moore …"

"Please, Val to you both."

"Okay Val, we are still planning. We don't know how the story will run on Vacation, if we do it at all yet. Meanwhile, we have to ask you: can you keep all this confidential? We can do the same with your dirt on Vacation. Deal?"

She stood up and offered her right hand, first to me. "Deal!" she said quietly, but with strong resolve. Her handshake was now firm and resolute.

Chapter 44

Valarie Moore's complaint was a golden opportunity.

And then, in rapid order, another opportunity, which promised to be a platinum one, fell into our growing stream of evidence. It was a complaint by disgruntled vacationer Robert McGarrell.

Mr. McGarrell's complaint came directly through Miss Tina O'Leary. She said the McGarrell family's much-anticipated fun experience at Trout Heaven Vacation Inn went something like this, paraphrasing McGarrell's own words as we talked later in the story:

He had been trumpeting the promise of the Trout Heaven Vacation Inn and Resort to his family, with its promise of luxurious accommodations, dining, golf, nature trail, spa and, of course, lake trout fishing.

He said one of his daughters was very excited and asked continually as he drove, "Are we there yet, Daddy, are we?"

"Almost. Now for the last time, calm down, Lindsey," Bob McGarrell might have hushed his daughter.

The McGarrell kids, Lindsey, 4, Albert, 6, Alicia, 3, and baby Robbie, 4 months, had never had a vacation.

After Bob lost his good job at G&M Financial, he and wife Alice McGarrell of Cincinnati, couldn't see spending money on a vacation. They were two months behind on payments on their 3-year old Chrysler Town & Country minivan. They also had to foreclose on the 4-bedroom, 2½ bath rancher in the suburbs they'd mortgaged with an adjustable interest rate.

Cramped apartment life was getting to them. Bob's tax return service hit the skids with the growth of TurboTax and copycat services and Alice's waitressing didn't cover the monthly bills.

There was only one chance to enjoy a late summer vacation and forget their troubles for a while. G&M was one of Vacation's allied companies. Therefore, McGarrell knew Vacation well. He told his wife Alice that his former association with Vacation Inns and Resorts seemed sent to them by Providence. He even confirmed his notion with a travel agent that it would cost them not a red cent, at least for a while, long enough for Bob to get the family solvent.

As he drove around the final bend of Charity Mountain, Bob McGarrell was first to spot the Inn, nestled on the side of Charity Mountain overlooking the powerful Sassafras River. He told Tina he shouted to the kids, "There it is kids, over the valley on the other side of the mountain there: Trout Heaven Vacation Inn and Resort! Looks fantastic." His kids cheered as baby Robbie wailed in fright.

Lindsey demanded to ride the ponies. Precocious Albert wanted to catch a giant trout. And little Alicia just wanted what mommy wanted: to spread out in a soft bed and watch cable TV for once. They could no longer afford cable. He was eager, he said, to 'hit the links for the first time in many years.' He was excited by Vacation's ad, which promised no greens fees.

He also remembered that the vacation began to stink immediately as baby Robbie needed a diaper change before they even got to the place and out of the car and into mountain air. He said his other son, Albert, chimed in with, "Yeah Dad, good thinking. Don't want to stink the place up."

* * *

Chapter 45

Tina said that in those two and a half miserable days later, Mrs. McGarrell had had it. The experience ended something like this, Tina relayed:

The wife told Bob she wanted to go home that the Inn was 'creepy.' She reminded that nothing was finished and the people working there were 'sneaky and deceptive.' Alice McGarrell made her ultimatum while still waiting for her drink at the riverside bar after 25 minutes as she was frantically smacking mosquitoes on her arms every few seconds.

Robert McGarrell was not so willing to give up on their Vacation Inn stay after just two days, and four to go. He said 'things will work out; that the resort was just recently opened. While the two smacked giant mosquitoes, he rationalized.

Everything here is new he told his wife—the inn, the restaurant, the golf course, the pool, all of it. He was convinced though after he insisted there must have been something at Trout Heaven Vacation Inn that she and the kids liked. He tried one more time, suggesting another morning hike on Enchanted Nature Trail to assess how they felt about the vacation.

Alice evidently blew her top. She explained the trail was but 300 feet long and didn't go anywhere. It stopped in a swamp. They all got horrible poison ivy and she had to quarantine the infant Robbie from the burning, itching kids. Calamine lotion cost $9 a bottle at the Trout Heaven 7-Eleven and they were on their fourth bottle.

Bob admitted disappointment in the 8-hole golf course with browns instead of greens during a summer drought—no sprinkler system to water the greens and rough fairways. The ninth hole was a repeat of the first hole. There was no room in the forest for adding a ninth. After the eighth green, a duffer has to walk or ride a cart back half the mountain to return to the first; that is, the ninth hole. The holes didn't loop back to the tin roof shed the inn's staff called a club house.

Alice convinced Bob 'this place stinks more than Robbie's diapers.' She didn't finish dinner; just stalked off after she swatted a bug on her bare leg as its blood squirted onto her white evening dress. She jerked back and stood, accidentally knocking her daughter seated next to her to the ground. Daughter Lindsey had begged her way onto her parents' romantic dinner date, while their oldest son stayed with the others watching cable TV in their room.

Bob tried once more to smooth things over, saying all along that 'it's free this time'. There is no next time, concluded his wife. She took her daughter and stalked back into their room. Bob McGarrell meanwhile made a reservation for he and his son for a fishing trip to Crater Lake in the morning, before Alice would wake up, he hoped.

Donnie Smythe was waiting for them at 6:30 a.m. at the front entrance in one of the Inn's big green SUVs. Bob McGarrell and his son would only be gone for an hour and a half before he was back at the inn thoroughly disgusted with his fishing outing and encouraging the family to pack up.

The inn's promise to McGarrell of a "fabulous trout fishing day" consisted of casting off the causeway bridge, 12 feet above the lake. For fishing the lake on the Garrett property, the inn enforced a five person rule, leaving the causeway the only option for the McGarrell dad and son.

When the dad asked young Smythe why he and his son could not fish off the cliff like the others below, Donnie, with a cell phone to his ear, politely said no, because the few people fishing below were trespassing.

Ten minutes later Sheriff Deeds arrived to shoo away the freeloaders below the bridge, much to the dismay of Bob McGarrell, who thought the scene was rude and unnecessary. He had not yet gotten a single bite while the shoreline people had been reeling them in.

Chapter 46

As we had planned, I met Tina at Smokey's to look over back issues of the Patrick Weekly. I was hoping to unearth some tidbits on the origins of the Trout Heaven Inn.

I parked behind Smokey Joe's so our cars would not be seen together. I walked around to the cafe and detected a distinct aroma of onion rings. My open right hand rubbed my middle-age pot belly, as if to tell it, 'maybe next time big boy.' I'd become aware of my expanding waistline. Wonder why?

I pushed open the door and there she was, the reason I felt so happy while concerned about my waistline.

Tina was sitting in the same booth as before wearing a loose white cardigan sweater and a blue blazer. She looked harried. There was no lovely smile to greet her admiring Mr. Ford wearing his sports coat and tie he wore at the paper that afternoon. Maybe she thought I looked bad.

The place was quiet, just an hour before closing. Most of the supper crowd, full of Joe's heavy food, had long fallen asleep on their couches to catch Law and Order, or Survivor, I suspected. Didn't think the locals likely snuggled into Masterpiece Theater, but I could have been wrong. Joe did serve fine wines, after all. As a city boy, I didn't consider the locals as stupid hillbillies, as Goodbred's gang did. They had class and humility.

I intended to ask Tina if she knew something about Ms. Moore's lawsuit on Goodbred, but she beat me to the punch.

"I'm quitting," she said, as I sat opposite her glum expression. Her tone of voice was demoralizing as she searched my face for a reaction.

Also without a greeting, I replied, "If you need to, Miss O'Leary; I won't be the one to hold you back. You must be miserable working there now. But if you are serious, why encourage me to meet you here to investigate what's in those papers."

"Maybe that's it."

"What?"

"The papers," she said. "This is all getting way too personal. I feel like we are opening up their graves by intruding into their last days as they were putting out the last editions of the newspaper, which daddy and mother were so passionate about."

"Your mother too?"

"She wrote all the op-eds; had an opinion on everything and everybody in the county and sometimes beyond."

"With all due respect, I don't think your father would look at this in that manner. My intention is not in any way to disturb their memory. I want to look into anything on how Vacation Inns got here. Evidently, your dad was an outstanding journalist and publisher, even if it was a small-town rag, as you affectionately called it. He may have wanted us to find out if anything about Vacation Inns and especially its not-so-illustrious board were sniffing around up here and why. His daughter was an employee after all. He had a vested interest."

"Well, maybe I won't quit just yet," she said talking to her hands folded on the green and white checkered table cloth.

I asked why she changed her mind.

"I've got a lot of stock options in my job. They have accumulated to a handsome sum. It would look funny to cash out with no logical reason. I have to interview for the promotion still."

"Excellent, Miss O'Leary." I sensed she was returning to the chase. "I see where you are going," I continued. "If you dump your shares in total while they are riding high you may become part of the story. In the Inquirer piece on Vacation, we will need to report financial compensations, such as, who got rich, who benefited after such a bankruptcy. It would have to include your name as an executive officer with stock options along with the dirty rotten scoundrels you work for."

"Yes, that's it. I've been thinking about how you could run with this," she said in all seriousness. And then, she smiled devilishly and teased me, "Gonna be a challenge of your career, Mr. Ford" She was laughing with me now, not at me, I thought.

My heart swelled. I loved when she switched gears after thinking things through. "Are we going to eat, or what?" I said.

"I already ordered, Mountain Cobb Salad and a cheeseburger with the works. Now, which one tickles your fancy Mr. Ford?"

"I think I'll regret saying this, but you do Miss O'Leary, you tickle my fancy. Say, let's eat quickly. Are you up for cracking open that closet of Patrick Weeklies?"

"I guess. Oh, here's dinner," she looked up at Joe O'Leary with a food tray. She smiled and seemed to relax. "He made it back, Uncle Joe," she said to him. "Say hello again to my favorite reporter friend in the whole wide world, Henry Clyde Ford."

Joe put down the tray of food and greeted me, then asked her, "How many reporter friends do you have anyway?"

"I added quickly, "Yeah, that's what I want to know."

"You two will never know. Now scram, you," she said to Joe. "I told you we have work to do. Thank you, Uncle Joe. I love you very much."

Chapter 47

After Joe walked away from our table to clean up and closed the cafe, I felt the need to get serious. I asked Tina, "Do you think the fraud and deception by Vacation Inns' management started at its very founding?"

"That's what Mary Marinaro thinks. She said her trusted colleagues in Boston said headquarters reeked with a foul odor starting right away, with Trevor Goodbred naming himself as CEO, COO and President all at once. We now know he is the father of all control freaks. He had a checkered past in Maryland with a wholesale junk food distribution service. He even scammed his classmates and professors at Smith Business School. Then, he skipped to Europe and had a brief stint as a project manager with British Petroleum."

"I heard about that," I said, "but, not any details."

"Yeah, it was reported in the New York Times that he was implicated in an alleged scheme of BP construction managers bribing building inspectors on oil riggings. But, he beat that wrap. He met Levine at Smith and formed their collaboration when Levine tracked him down in Paris, but then Sly Si went to jail for a previous violation, way before Vacation Inns and Goodbred."

I chimed in, "We also learned, at the Inquirer, from corporate filings in Delaware that Goodbred's motel startup was called PGA Vacations. Then it was changed to Vacation Inns. In the same SEC report, von Kindel was hired as CFO."

"Yeah, that's right, Mr. Ford. Max was a marketing genius, as I understand it, as well as a competent finance man," Tina said. "Mary says it is thought that the PGA name was Goodbred's idea, and not at all as dumb as it appeared."

I suggested, "Wouldn't you think that would be a red flag marking his character? He probably thought it was bold and clever to piggyback his marketing on the solid foundation of the Professional Golf Association."

"Yes, well it worked. The real PGA sued immediately, but Vacation Inns, under the new name, managed to get $140 million in a reverse suit settlement because it was officially PGA Vacations, which in the incorporation papers filed in Delaware stood for Public Get-away Vacations. A real blunder by the duffers group, eh Mr. Ford?"

"Maybe he knew just what he was doing," I said.

"That's what I mean. He's slick, I've been telling you. The publicity over the suit gave Vacation Inn Corporation a great start," said Tina.

"How many Inns did his company have by then?

"Mary said records show there were just the six motels in the new company. The settlement from PGA allowed them to purchase what was left of the defunct Makeover Motels. Get that. God, what an industry. Unfortunate name eh?" said Tina.

I said, "What marketing idiot came up with that? Who were they targeting?"

"Attractive professional women in their mid-life crises. The wife of a marketing executive, who was better at chasing skirts than marketing, came up with it. At the divorce settlement, she got her lawyer to add a position for her in the husband's motel chain, sort of a gotcha clause, I would think," Tina said, shaking her head.

I guessed, "Marketing executive position, right?"

"Right."

I guessed again, "Was her gift position exactly the position her ex-husband had before he trashed his marriage?"

Laughing, she answered, "How'd you know? Yeah, well of course, never mind. It was made to look like his old job. People, I assume her husband's friends, hooked her up with a phony expert who convinced her that she must have been a ravishing beauty in her time. He had one of the nation's top makeover artist transform the woman. Then the phony expert kicked back and waited a week for the woman's ego to swell."

I took one more educated guess. "Then the phony guy popped the idea of Makeover Motels, right?

"How'd you know? Oh yes. You are Henry Clyde Ford. You didn't get that name by covering high school football, right?

"You learn fast Miss O'Leary. But, actually I think I read it somewhere."

She said, "Maybe you did. I read it in the Baltimore Sun years ago. What a dumb broad, eh Mr. Ford?"

"Well there's a literary side of my dear Miss O'Leary. 'Dumb broad, huh?' Fits though, you should write novels. What happened next in this prehistoric tale?"

"Don't you know?"

I shook my head. She scrunched her face.

I insisted, "No, really I don't."

Then, she insisted, "Go ahead. I don't mind."

I speculated, "Okay. Here's what I would expect: The chain went bankrupt and they were rid of her, just as they planned all along."

"Bingo, my boy. Am I ever glad I knocked on your door. What a news hawk you are. Genius!" she straightened her back and shook my hand across the table quickly, laughing.

Jeez, she'll call the old guy 'boy' but still not Hank, I pondered. Well, as I said before with every incremental tie that may bind, I loved it just the same.

I said, "But I don't know how long it took for that group to fold before Goodbred swooped down and grabbed the company up with his killer talons."

"Only one year. The former wife—as the new marketing director, mind you—also didn't know that the accountants cooked Makeover's books to show more losses than it really had. Some middle-aged ladies went for it and were coming back again and again."

I asked, "Does that make sense? Was this woman that stupid?"

"Stupid enough that the scam was likely already on young Goodbred's radar, his hooks sharpening for the kill. Meanwhile, the word is that she was content with the $3 million she got in the divorce and was just f-ing with her ex by hanging on to the job, his old job, so she could rub it in his face. She probably didn't really expect to top his performance. One thing I do know though, Mr. Ford."

"What's that? They gave a good shampoo?"

She soured, "Thanks for the glowing endorsement of my judgment. Of course not. What I know is that those accountants at her firm are still with Vacation Inns Corporation in Boston, the top finance guys, Mary says. Her bosses, actually. They are the main reason she is being very, very careful in helping us, Mr. Ford. They are the senior account execs and she says they are still blindly faithful to Goodbred."

"Wow. Poor Mary," I said. "Finished eating Miss O'Leary? Let's get started on those back pages, shall we?"

Chapter 48

We learned that in the dim evening light of the lobby at Trout Heaven Vacation Inn and Resort, Bellboy Donald Smythe was the first to see Bradley Armstrong's bloody face as he emerged from the men's restroom. He was woozy; trying to recover from Tina's left cross.

A small crowd of guests and employees gathered around Armstrong's prostrate body.

Donald located a tiny first aid kit of small band aids and gauze at the front desk. He ripped up his own T shirt and wrapped Bradley's wounds to stop the bleeding. He didn't know that the injuries had occurred in the women's restroom, not the men's, where Bradley had tried to wash himself of the blood.

Donald drove the young man all the way to James Madison Hospital 65 miles away. Donald waited all night as Armstrong was doctored up with 18 stitches to his head and face in the ER. He also didn't know Bradley claimed to be Trevor Goodbred's nephew. He'd done this for anyone, he later said.

Chapter 49

For the next two days, Armstrong stayed in his room at the Inn. On the third morning, he overslept and was late for another board meeting.

Still in pain, he managed to walk into the conference room 20 minutes late. It was Uncle Trev's special meeting of the corporation's secret mini-board. Members of this group were the most trusted directors, all the good 'ol boys, which Goodbred convened in emergencies. No females.

Bradley Armstrong had told Donald that Uncle Trevor would be counting on Bradley to give a report on the suspicious activities going on with accounting and the PR lady. Donald tipped off Tina.

Due to quick thinking by Inn Manager Hancock, Tina and I would know everything transpiring in the small meeting. John Hancock video recorded the room in secret and had captured it all.

Inn manager John Hancock, who was also a temporary board member during the Trout Heaven meetings, was not invited. He had become suspicious of the secret session, when he read the conference room log and noticed the reservation made by Goodbred's assistant just before the meeting.

At the scheduled appointed time, Hancock closed and locked his office door. He unlocked the bottom drawer of his desk. There he kept a secret video control panel. He punched the red 'record' button.

Hancock's system was sweet: pin-size cameras at each corner of the board room inside the AV speakers, and four-track recording capability. He paid for it himself. Few besides his wife knew Hancock was an electrical engineer who was once a video producer shortly after graduating from Georgia Tech University with a degree in film and media studies, minoring in technical communications.

On the video, we first saw Goodbred spotting his nephew sneaking into the conference room. "You're late Brad. Hey, what the hell happened to you? Get hit by a truck or something?" Goodbred asked. Bradley's head was full of bandages except for around his left ear. He had stitches across his forehead and his jaw was wired partially shut.

"Sho sorry I'm late. I fell down. Hit my head. Men's room floor wet. Needed shtitches. The bellboy was nice to take me all the way to the hospital and back. Shorry."

It was apparent to everyone at the table from his slurring that Bradley's front two or three teeth were missing too.

Armstrong looked humiliated. Likely, he could not tell the truth, that a woman beat him up so horribly in the women's restroom. He had had nearly three days to think about her and likely didn't want any more to do with the PR lady beast.

"Stop saying you're sorry. My God," Goodbred snapped. "The bellboy helped you? We need to talk about that Smythe kid, gentleman. I don't like having him snooping around here. We need to get busy with the Smythe property. Si, please fire that kid soon. Sit down Bradley. You look awful."

"Shorry."

"Stop saying you're sorry. Okay gentlemen, since my nephew here insists on being the center of attention, we will start with his observations of the increasingly odd behavior of our own Miss Tina O'Leary inquiring into financial records in accounting."

At the head of the table sat Goodbred with just five others: Simon Levine, Armstrong, Jack Mays, Jimmy Jenkins, and attorney James Whitfield Turner, the chief operations officer for the corporation. Turner was a disgraced former state legislator found guilty in 1992 for embezzling public education funds.

Hancock's recording captured Goodbred confronting his nephew Armstrong about his expected report on Tina "that pretty little sneak," he said. "So, let's have it. What has she been up too poking into the accounting department?"

"Nothing, sir."

"How can you say nothing? You've been telling me about the clerks and assistants seeing O'Leary there a lot. Seems she is buddies with Mary Marinaro. If she is interested in what Marinaro is doing, I'm interested. Mr. Levine tells me we should no longer trust O'Leary, right Si? Now tell us what you heard," demanded Goodbred.

"I'm told that Marinaro is helping O'Leary prepare for her interview for corporate vice president for public relations; that'sh all," Armstrong looked down at his hands, afraid to say more.

"Surely you must know more than that, boy. What about Hancock allowing O'Leary to contact that fellow in the cabin across the river. Are we getting that property or what? It is strategic, right Si? We need to show shareholders we are planning our ski lodge site over there before winter. It is worth a fortune, you fools. Does anybody here know that? Does anyone here know anything!?"

Levine stopped Trevor Goodbred's venting, "I know, Trevor. She took the contract to the man, a Mr. Henry, I think. Hancock will handle it because if we don't get that property, I told him we will want his property instead. Hancock's land gets us past the lake, and then we can close the loop, buying out these ignorant hillbillies. They are desperate for cash and probably never had to deal with New York lawyers, right Turner?"

Attorney Turner said, "Seems like these people are a bit backward, yes. I've run offers by Garrett's grandson who is near the lake for more of his land. And I sent offers to the Macintyre's and the Smythe's address. Do they have a phone? I can't find a listing for the Smythe family home."

Mays piped up, "May not. What's left of the Smythe family does not have a registered will from the old farmer Emmanuel Smythe anywhere. Now he is out of the way."

Levine said with some sympathy, "That poor man was killed right at his great little produce stand. I liked him. I bought his corn once."

Mays said, "And as far as I know your bellboy Donald is the only descendant. Smythe's wife and family were killed by the meteorite when he was just 18 and he never remarried. Just cousins and friends live on the land, what's left of it. The old man is out of our way now." Mays was holding back a half smile.

"You said that, Jack," said Goodbred pensively, and he then exploded with excitement, "The Smythe property wraps around a third of the lake all the way to Macintyre's pier and along Routes 7 and 65. We all read about the poor soul getting his throat cut, sure. But don't you gentlemen understand? Holy fucking glory, we'll buy out the kid. No, don't fire him. We need to look into this. The kid, then, is likely the benefactor. Jim, can you double check on that last-will situation?"

Jim Turner said, "Sure. If there is no will, the kid is our target, wide open. What's he like Bradley?"

Armstrong, still reticent, said, "He'sh okay."

Unc Trev screamed, "What the fuck is that kind of answer, boy. What the hell is with you? You get your balls cut off or something!!"

Perhaps Armstrong thought he'd better respond or have to explain his condition himself, "Donnie is a niesh kid, but a little slow. He likes helping people, sheems fitting into his bellboy chores. He likeshhis job. I told you he took me to the hospital and all. Very kind person; talked all the way about fishing on Crater Lake with the Macintyre boysh when they were teenagersh and schtill goes out from their pier. He invited me to fish. I was thinking of taking him up on it, but I guess that wouldn't be too shmart, huh?"

Goodbred, "I think it is an excellent idea, my boy. You can talk with him about the virtues of joining forces with the Vacation Inns team." He made a note, folded it and handed it to Jack Mays.

Mays read the note, holding it in his lap slightly under the table. He then looked up with a menacing smile, tore up the note and pocketed it. He left the room, as Trevor Goodbred removed a pocket mirror and hair brush from his coat pocket and dabbed his coiffure hair style that needed no comb, but was impeccably neat from all angles.

I wondered if that was a rug? Too perfect.

Meanwhile not 25 feet from the conference room, Hancock's heart was pounding, he said, after he was shocked by the gleeful and insensitive exchange on his video monitor between Mays and Goodbred over the Manny Smythe killing. His hand shook, distorting the video imagery on a hand-held monitor imaging the conference room where all pretenses of legitimacy were stripped and being held up for ridicule and mockery. Hancock thought the men in the picture were far too confident to reap unjust rewards from their diabolical plans.

(Hancock told Tina later that he became very paranoid from listening with headsets plugged the small monitor wired through his desk drawer and crouching with the tiny equipment behind his desk.He said he reached for a Post-it and scribbled a note to tell Donald Smythe to be careful around Armstrong and pasted the yellow square inside his wallet secure in his front pant pocket.)

Levine spoke next on the recording:

"Okay, so the Smythe boy is sitting on a fortune and maybe blocking our takeover of Crater Lake to complete the Trout Heaven Vacation Inn and Resort. The bellboy. Pretty funny. The bellboy is our ticket to success. Pretty funny, yes, yes. …," Levine paused, looked around at the blank faces watching and waiting for his assessment.

Levine then shifted gears and dismissed the notion, "Well that's pretty dumb. Get serious folks. Here is how we now project to shareholders: We are sitting on Fort Knox and will lose it if we don't get our annual report adjusted right now. I've got to get back to Boston to fix things in central accounting."

Armstrong, Turner, and Jenkins seemed puzzled by Levine's illogical wrap-up. What was the rush?

Goodbred asked, "Tell us Si, what have you heard from the group in Europe?"

"All good," said Levine. "The annual report will project our expansion plans to Europe. With the expected boost in investments, I'd say we can top the $1.3 billion price from the PRSE group in Europe when they buy Vacation Inns. They are chomping at the bit, Trev," he said.

Hancock was shocked, he told us. More than just eavesdropping on plans to fire people, to fool shareholders or to confuse the feds, the men in the conference room revealed their top-secret plans to polish up the façade of the nasty corporation and sell it to the very PRSE group that Vacation had already projected in Tina's newsletter to acquire.

The group was the Princess Resorts and Spas (PRSE) of Europe, based in Zurich, Switzerland. The die had been cast. Levine told the mini-board that Vacation's next SEC annual report should hook the Princess group and that its execs are ready to purchase the Vacation Inn chain.

The revelation was also a stunning setback to Hancock's personal plans with the company. He had been expecting good job security for a long time because of the recent expansion of the corporation would place himself right at Vacation's new regional headquarters at Trout Heaven.

Tina had already pitched the plans for the new region in the press, with an additional site planned near Luray and other new Vacation Inns already operating near Smokey Mountains National Park and the Outer Banks bay side in North Carolina; Opryland, Barton Springs, and Graceland in Tennessee; and a mountaintop site, 10 miles from Jefferson's Monticello in Virginia.

Hancock was about to lose his cushy job.

He said his whole body grew tense.

He couldn't use any muscles, not even to turn off the recording devices and lock them back into his clandestine little desk drawer, he said, which he'd previously considered little more than boyish amusement. He watched, still shaken, as everyone else left the room except Goodbred.

Hancock stared at the little monitor, still in shock, never considering someone might come to his office after the meeting. Oh well, it is locked, he said he had rationalized. But staring brought more clarification. Within a minute, Jack Mays returned and closed the conference door behind him.

Mays asked Goodie, "What about the PR girl, boss? I don't trust her."

"Jack, just between me and you, I'm going to ask you to make sure she doesn't come back after her interview in Boston."

Hancock, already leaning over the little desk drawer, said he fell out of his chair with a loud thump onto the floor as someone was pounding on his locked office door.

Chapter 50

Any good mystery needs an unexplainable spiritual element. None other than the Reverend Gideon Sugarman had provided that and much more—the church on Crater Lake, the giant fish, the gawdy resort Inn, the Macintyre boys, Goodbred, Levine and of course my Tina. If it weren't for Rev. Gideon, perhaps daylight on Trout Heaven might never have dawned.

That's why I wanted to know him for added perspective.

Local gossip columns provided background. From what I could presume, some naysayers ridiculed the Reverend Gideon Sugarman because he founded his house of God on a random, though spectacular, meteorite crash. He heard the ridicule from folks who chose instead to attend more conventional churches in Sassafras County.

Random? Not the case. He'd counter any doubters that the rock from the heavens was God sent and a deliberate message to "Get your selves in line with Jesus, brethren."

Other people, maybe the same ones, said Gideon was not really a reverend, that he made the claim so long ago that people just accept it. The reverend was well into his 80's. Again, such talk never bothered the little, stout reverend.

Gideon Sugarman was filled with the spirit of the Lord for more than six decades and felt he did not need to validate himself. His sparsely adorned church with very little idolatry was validation enough for him and his modest flock. He founded the house of worship in reverence to a big rock from God. And, no one had questioned it in recent years; people loved him so much.

He got the spirit when as a boy of 12.

Little pudgy Giddy announced to everyone in school that a visitor from outer space was coming soon. The boy's prediction was not totally dismissed as adolescent dreaming because his friends all knew Giddy watched the night sky each evening with his Buck Rogers Technoglass Telescope he won at the county fair for hitting the exact point of the stacked milk bottles to topple them three times straight. His eyes were that sharp. His mom told Giddy, he had the keenest eyes on Earth and he likely did. I found local sport's columns that reported that opposing little league batters who faced pitcher Sugarman of the Sassafras Pirates feared him. He could put his curve ball right on any corner of home plate with hawk-like accuracy.

One evening, as if divinely ordered, young Giddy was the first human anyone knew who saw the meteorite, that big rock in the sky. He was first to witness God's light coming to Earth from heaven, a Baptist minister wrote.

To this day, Gideon could prove to any man, woman or child that he was first to see it, tell anyone visiting his parish study that God meant him to see it first. His undeniable proof was a 20x24 blowup of a snapshot of the fiery meteorite about to smash into Sassafras County. The framed, spectacular photo, hung over his anointed sermon-writing desk. It is likely the only picture of its kind documenting the life-altering event sent to enlighten Man and inspire a new faith, as the reverend was wont to say. And he took the photograph.

As the countryside around the meteorite hit began to stabilize around the new lake with extremely heavy and rapid growth of new forest, the horror of death and destruction remained. The accelerated growth was itself almost a miracle, yet the freak thing was the worse tragedy of a generation. Residents were eager to put the event behind them.

Meanwhile, Rev. Gideon, who was a polite and civil man yet rather flamboyant single-handedly created Our Sacred Lady of the Cosmic Heavens Church on the lip of Crater Lake some 15 years after the direct hit from God.

The Reverend Sugarman was still a young man and newly ordained—no one really knew from where. But he was a talker and known far and wide. Gideon Sugarman convinced the Macintyre family of carpenters to donate a small strip of their land off Rt. 65 with access to Crater Lake. It gave the Macintyres a tax credit, I learned.

For the Reverend, the deal included labor to build the modest house of God on the property with building materials Sugarman got from heaven, he said, plus a long-term home improvement loan.

For several decades, while the good people near and around the hills worshiped at the lakeside church, they heard various versions of the story of Rev. Sugarman's remarkable prognosis "in the beginning," he would say, of his Our Sacred Lady of Cosmic Heaven. A local columnist wrote, "Ask him who the lady was and he would eventually admit, it just fit the mystery of its genesis. The Lady is the Earth."

More recently, and most unfortunately, Rev. Gideon Sugarman's life would invariably become entangled in the sticky web of the nasty lodging corporation, Vacation, as it affected everyone else near Trout Heaven. Vacation Inns and Resorts also, one could argue, consistent with the above, seemed to also descend from outer space. It is not beyond reason that publicity about the reverend's popularity and blessing the giant fish as God-sent may have caught the notice of clever charlatan Trevor Goodbred in the first place.

Continuing in irony, the sucky tentacles of Vacation Inn first wrapped around the good reverend when Rev. Anita Rapshire and husband Clarence arrived in Trout Heaven to take her new job with cynical Simon Levine. Lo and behold, she took no time at all to find a local church.

* * *

"Mr. Ford, call me if you want to know about Rev. Sugarman," was the message from Tina on my desk phone as I arrived at the paper one morning around 10 a.m.

I texted her private cell and she promptly called me again.

"I'm at my parent's house still this morning. Needed a breather. I called in late to tell John Hancock I'd be late and he had Anita Rapshire in his office just saying goodbye. Tina told me Hancock recommended she visit Our Sacred Lady of Cosmic Heaven Church to meet Rev. Sugarman and see if she'd like to join the congregation."

"When? Will she get the Vacation people involved with the church? Is that important? Do you think I could stumble in as a new resident just before she arrives?" I asked.

"Yes, yes, yes, yes. Damn, you are a smart one, Mr. Ford. She is going there tomorrow at noon. You can make it, right? You don't even need to reveal your identity. Best yet, the church is located on Crater Lake, as you know.

Tina added that Hancock didn't tell Anita, as far as she knew, that the rocky shores of the lake represented Vacation Inn and Resort Corp.'s most coveted real estate prize. Hancock of course knew it. She said he instead spoke kindly of Gideon Sugarman and, as a man of faith, Hancock encouraged her to meet the reverend.

"Well," I said coyly, "I suppose I can mosey on up there in them hills tonight. Know anyone who might want to bring a dinner for two to my cabin, do ya? Do ya?"

"Two carry outs from Smokey' Joes. Done. I'll be there at 8 p.m., okay?"

"Fantastic."

"And, Mr. Ford?"

"Yes, Miss darling O'Leary."

"Before we get distracted by our rendezvous, please don't be thrown off by his idiosyncratic methods. Gideon Sugarman is a genuine, God-fearing preacher of a bye-gone era."

"Just my kind of guy," I said.

Chapter 51

The new membership finance director Rapshire from Vacation Inn and Resort Corp. thought she had found Rev. Sugarman wandering around his chapel the next day at noon. It was me.

"Rev. Sugarman, is that you. I'm Anita Raps…"

"No ma'am. I'm looking for the minister myself," I falsely confessed. I'm Henry. He is expecting me. I am new to the area, you see." I tried not to laugh. Maybe Hancock didn't tell her Sugarman was in his 80's. Then again, maybe he did and I look the part. I thought it was funny.

"I beg your pardon, Mr. Henry. Yes, you were on Mr. Macintyre's fishing boat. Nice to see you again. Rev. Sugarman is also expecting me. Remember me? I'm Anita Rapshire, a new executive at the new Inn on Charity Mountain. Know it? No? Well anyway, perhaps he confused his appointment times, huh? Let's find him, shall we?"

She was every bit as attractive as advertised. Solidly build, busty, natural blonde (I think) with the face of a movie star, just as Tina and Goodie's chauffeur said.

More importantly, Tina had told me that Anita Rapshire's pure heart seemed to bring the best out of people. Reverend Sugarman was no exception. Indeed, he was easy. They bonded instantly.

We found Rev. Sugarman leaning back, asleep in the $568 office chair, ergonomically built especially for his aching back and paid for by his parishioners.

"There he is. He is surely a sweet man. Look at him," Anita said.

Anita noticed the big framed photo of the flashing streak of light as she walked through the open door to the Reverend's office. It was hung over his sleepy head and must more impressive than in newspaper clippings.

Unable to wake him with her greeting, Anita gently shook Gideon's big toe on his bare feet crossed up on his desk.

"Excuse me Reverend, ... Reverend? It's me Anita Rapshire from Lynchburg. I called? Were you sleeping, Reverend; I am so sorry. I came in because you said I could visit with you at four. It's 4:10 p.m. now sir and I thought ... oh, pardon me, this is Mr. Henry."

"We talked this morning," I said gambling that the old man would not question my lie. He couldn't have cared less. So, I added the perfect invite, "I'm looking for a local church, sir, being new to the area."

He was delighted with the pleasant church lady. "Miss Rapture, yes. How nice to see you? I must have dozed off. Yes, and you, Mr. Henry. Welcome to you both." He used elbows, hands and creaking knees to push himself up slowly to his feet. He placed a hand to the desk to regain balance, while extending his other hand.

"It's Mrs. Rapshire. I wanted to visit your church. My husband and our daughters want to find a church near the Trout Heaven Inn Motel and Resort. I just took a job there. Wow, look at that."

She admired the photograph.

I sensed I was catching a break by being with the charming and pretty Anita Rapshire. He was immediately taken by her and took little interest in me. Perfect.

Rev. Sugarman smiled and admitted, "That is part of the dream I was just having. It re-occurs often."

She showed interest by nodding encouragement as we sat before his desk.

He trusted her with the dream story, "It was a fateful evening long ago. Night time in fact, dark skies except glare from strings of bare incandescent bulbs outlining Discount Dan's Used Car lot. I was only 12 years old."

She asked, "Oh, so this is a dream of some truth, then."

"Yes. It was my first job. I was a kid, so Mr. Dan only paid me 50 cents an hour for odd jobs there." He told the nice reverend lady and me the whole, unabridged story, without any dreamy embellishments, I sensed.

I imagined little Giddy, as he was known as a child, was about to make his first big sale.

He said it was a pink and tan Cadillac convertible. The customer asked to see the convertible top down. Little Giddy reached up into the luxury chariot to unlock the rag top. As the convertible top unfurled Giddy saw what no one else in town saw coming: the biggest shooting star ever, in the night sky.

"I grabbed my Kodak," he told us, "which I always kept nearby to photograph automobiles for advertisement. It's the only reason they let a kid like me sell cars," he said. "I had that keen eyesight, you know."

In this case though, there was no time for focus, aperture settings "and all," he said. "I aimed at the bright light. And, by golly, the force of that projectile cutting through the air and hitting the ground, bounced me clear right out of the car. Every single person in that lot was knocked to the ground."

I think he was more than lucky, as if spirits visited him that day. That light from the heavens was dead center in the photo film frame of Gideon's camera. He had ability.

"How was it? As thunderous as I read about?" she asked.

"Marvelous, Mrs. Rhapsody," he said.

"Wow," I played it up.

Anita gave him a business card and repeated her name again.

"Oh, I see there, it is Rev. Rapshire! Please beg my pardon."

She listened intently then to the charming old preacher telling of "the dream," the same story he had told people he had about the day of God's cosmic visit for his eyes alone. He proceeded to tell more of the tale of the photo dominating the room.

"I envisioned it again just before you arrived. Happens all the time. Changed my life, it did. God wanted me to create all this."

He waved his arms majestically as if his church was St. Peter's Basilica.

"Amazing. I did not know that, Reverend," I said.

She offered to bring the conversation back to the moment, "Inspiration, indeed, Rev. Sugarman. Is that when you came to the Lord, if I maybe so bold, at just 12 years old?"

He paused, took a breath and uttered reverently, "Not immediately, but I knew something or somebody had chosen me for something. I was saved, yes, that day, but didn't know it until Jesus

Christ inspired me to share his glory and salvation right here. And as long as I am living in the flesh. Now, of course, I have been crucified with Christ, and I no longer live alone, but Christ lives in me. The life I live in the body, I live by faith in the Son of God, who loved me and gave Himself up for me. Gal...."

"Galatians 2: 20, "Anita finished his sentence with him. You and me both, reverend."

"Call me Gideon, my sister." He became very excited and then a bit embarrassed after the story, he chastised himself, "No, no. I'm not being polite. Enough about me. Mr. Henry, Rev. Rapshire, you would like a tour, not to hear my silly dreams, yes?"

She said, "Yes, you are very observant Reverend Sugarman. The dream is wonderful. Really happened that way, I'm sure."

She told him of her life in Lynchburg and before that in Nashville. "We didn't want to move again, but the kind executives in a bright green limousine, a dreadful lime shade, drove all the way to Lynchburg to my church to hear me, they said. Well, I was overwhelmed, of course, but my husband then heard of the fishing here, and the job was appealing to say the least, and ..."

"Fishing? You say your man fishes? Look here, my dear." He opened a room filled with fishing and camping gear and outdoor clothing, boots and hats. "Our church members are wild about fishing, most of them. We have an exclusive spot behind the alter where we can reach the lake. Only members can fish it; off the cliff. It works and we have regular fishing days."

"Only members you say?" I asked.

"Some boys christened the spot, you might say, one day when Jesus led them out of the service and into one of his miracles on the .... There, I said too much again. You fish, Mr. Henry?"

"Of course."

As Rev. Gideon Sugarman escorted us into the chapel, Anita inquired, "I suppose being close to the inn, many of the employees are members of your church Reverend?"

He said, "I always believe honesty is the best policy. We only have about 67 parishioners now and I don't think any are in the employ of the Vacation Inn. When we started the church many years ago, we had nearly 200 in the flock, but I think folks may not go to church as much these days, especially to hear an old codger like me. Yes, that's right, I believe you are the first Vacation Inn employee member, that is if ..."

Anita decided on the spot that the good reverend needed a membership drive and perhaps no one does it better than the ever-dynamic and trustworthy Rev. Anita Rapshire of Lynchburg, if indeed driver Gordo Jones' wacky tale was true of that day Simon Levine discovered her.

"Oh yes. Of course, I will join," she told him immediately. "One look at this marvelous chapel convinces me."

There was nothing marvelous or in any way classy about the décor of the Our Sacred Lady of the Cosmic Heaven chapel. A huge rugged cross dominated the back wall of purple drapes behind the alter hiding the unfinished organ pit. There was a nice upright piano instead, in front of benches for a choir. Red carpeting and white pews with no backs filled the space with the appropriate candle holders and pulpits, all of which Rev. Sugarman had shipped in second hand from relief efforts after an earthquake destroyed a church in Venezuela.

Anita, nonetheless, laid it on thick, "According to the Baptist World Press, I am the best preacher in Virginia, bar none. I carry the clipping in my purse, see. I take no credit, though, as you would appreciate. Few do. Even with my experience and my Bible study and ability to reach out to people, reverend, it is not enough. I tell people, they do not have enough of what it takes to fulfill your calling in Jesus Christ. He alone can fulfill your calling." and he does it by way of his Holy Spirit through you."

"Yes, he alone does so through his Holy Spirit through you," said Rev. Sugarman in whole hearted agreement.

Anita extended her arms and hugged the old man in a bonding embrace. "I have found a true partner in Trout Heaven, sir."

He was surprised by the remark.

Sugarman then injected, "Me too. But, I don't like the name of the new town they forced on these mountains. Too artificial and commercial. Our church deacons came to me about the name in fact; thought it disrespectful, ungodly and one even said blasphemous. Well, I cooled their heals, made a joke about a special heaven for trout. And they went away. I see the sloppy set up. Yes, I've been over there. And have thought there is fire and destruction ahead."

"Never you mind," she comforted him and wished him a pleasant rest of the day, and then left.

My mission was fulfilled. It was clear to me that Sugarman was not a fan of the Inn or the horse that brong it to his beloved Sassafras County: Trout Heaven.

Only two weeks later, Rev. Gideon delivered an honest, soulful sermon on how just a few words from Jesus moved the hearts of those non-believing Samarians on the road to Jordan. It captured the hearts of nearly 100 attending service, including 28 employees of Vacation Inn Resort at Trout Heaven including a very curious Tina O'Leary. They were all new church members recruited by Rev. Rapshire, their membership finance director at the inn.

Anita's favorite recruit was Mary Marinaro, who was Tina O'Leary's best friend, and who would soon also become Anita's best friend in Trout Heaven as well and begin to suspect trouble in paradise.

Chapter 52

"How was your burger, Hank?" Smokey Joe asked. Without waiting for an answer, he waved to us to follow him from our booth and through the darkened cafe, by that time in the evening closed to the public.

Tina's phone rang. She took it leaning on a counter stool.

I also stopped walking with Joe when I saw her surprised look.

Her eyes bugged out. She gave me a look of disbelief. "Ah huh. ... Ah huh. ... That's right. ... You have? ... What? ... She did? ... Okay, I'll be there. Thanks Max. I do still appreciate that, yes. Goodbye Max."

She then said to me, "Jesus!! That was none other than Max von Swindle, the guy who dreamed up membership scheme number one himself."

"What? Jesus, you are surprised, or Max is the return of the son of God?" I asked, completely at a loss.

"Actually, I guess I mean THE Jesus, in a way. He said he found Jesus Christ as his personal savior, he said."

"He called to tell you? Okay, sure. But how did he find you? Share cell numbers? He was kinda sweet on you, wasn't he?" I regretted asking.

"I am aware of that. And, no, he didn't call to tell me he got religion. The point I'm making is that people can change and he seems to have.

"Please listen with your brain, will you. Anita Rapshire needed some guidance she wasn't getting from Simon Levine. My guess is that Anita is too smart to mention problems she may be uncovering. So, she found Max's number and rang him up last month. He was living in Minnesota and teaching at Concordia College, Lutheran isn't it? Good place for a German, I guess. I think he is far more of a decent person than the creeps I now work for, Mr. Ford.

"In fact, Max just said he has been advising Anita on managing her job, which is a mere shadow of his old position at

Vacation before Goodie replaced him with that ex-con Levine to shield the bookkeeping shenanigans."

"Yeah, you said."

"Mary says Goodbred had fired him because he and Max had argued about the method he was using to keep the membership books. It was too transparent. Mary suspected that is what Levine told Goodie."

"Well, so what? What's that got to do with calling you?"

"He said Anita called him for some advice. She was becoming confused by how the memberships were recorded. He flew in and stayed at the Rapshire's house where she laid out the bookkeeping she knew about and compared that with Vacation's latest 10-Q reports to the SEC and a recent 13-K."

"Okay, quarterly 10-Q's and the investment form 13-K. Why would he do that?" I asked.

"I'll get to that. While Max was in town Anita and her husband introduced Max to Rev. Sugarman's Our Sacred Lady of Cosmic Heaven, your new friend."

"That's all very sweet of Anita and God and Jesus and the good Rev. Gideon Sugarman. Don't be so glib, please. I met Sugarman with Anita, remember? Not my new friend. But again, why did Max call you, Miss O'Leary? This is upsetting. It is unplanned and too weird."

"He called to warn me. He has remained at odds with Goodbred for firing him 'for no good reason,' he said. So, Max has been following the company's financial reports because he wants to help Anita survive the madness, he said. They are close now. He's been here for more than two weeks with the Rapshires. The 13-K is all bologna with no mention of Levine and where he is really investing.

"Max just told me he and Anita are both convinced the end is near for the company. She is upset, he said. She knows they played her, I think."

"Again, please, where is this going and why confide in this former insider?" I was getting upset.

"The point, Mr. Ford, if you've been listening, is that Anita has soured on the company, I think. Anita told Max of my interview coming up next week. I agreed to have coffee with Max at the church this coming Sunday. You can come if you are jealous." She laughed a little then covered her mouth and said, "Sorry."

"Very funny. You know I can't do that. Sugarman knows me only as Mr. Henry. And, please be careful not to tell Max too much about our investigation." I just shook my head and finished eating my last French fry. Never miss the last fry. It's the crunchiest.

Chapter 53

Joe led us upstairs to what they called just 'the door,' as referred to by Tina and Joe all week over the phone and in emails.

Joe said, "It's only been opened once, by me, two days ago to check for the papers. It had been closed since the day we buried my brother, Tina's father."

The door creaked, of course. The room that once served as a small town heady newsroom of deadlines and commotion was full of cobwebs and dust. Except for the dust, everything appeared ready for the next day's edition: two desks full of loose paper, two computers still plugged in, a 13-inch television on a file cabinet, and a dog bed next to one of the desks.

"It was mother's dog. She is a black lab, we named Mencken," said Tina, as quietly as she could, as if someone was sleeping or still present in quiet spirit.

I started to ask, but she added, "My twin sister Shannon, who is a nurse at Charlestown Children's Hospital, as I said, still lives in mother and daddy's house in Patrick and now has Mencken."

I didn't have to ask if the dog was named for the famous Baltimore Sun icon H.L. Mencken. I did want to ask about her sister, but didn't. We had work to do.

Rather than intrude further on the family's honored space, we decided to carry a couple of bundles of the papers, three months' issues, back down to the kitchen where we could spread them out on the large stainless-steel prep table while sitting on metal stools. "It's far neater than staying in the dusty newspaper office," I said, keeping an eye to Tina's emotional demeanor. She was slouching and breathing heavily.

She ignored my rationalizing and said, "I would like to start with the last issue Daddy put out before he was killed. Call me sentimental." She clutched the issue to her chest and then took it as far away from me as possible, to a booth.

Joe and I sat on stools in the kitchen.

I noted that Tina said 'before they were killed' not before they died. Tina's choice of the word 'killed' was the first time I heard it attributed to her parents' deaths. She and other people had always said 'died' in the crash when telling about the tragedy, not 'killed.' *Was that a slip or did she mean 'killed' in the accident?* I asked myself. *No, people do say folks were killed in a car crash too.* She appeared to be nothing less than spooked by the trip back in time. Tina needed space.

I said, "How about if I start scanning issues just after Johnny Macintyre caught that world record rainbow trout in the quarantined lake? Might be something about the lake and the group in Boston, or something." I nervously rambled, not wanting to upset her. "That didn't last, did it? The quarantine? Once the lake had value? And, world record? That was dumb because rainbows are only found in the U.S., right? And ...., oh." She wasn't listening, didn't look up.

After a while, she yelled toward the kitchen, "I want to keep this one after I check for any news about Vacation Inns, Hank." Since the tragedy, Tina or her siblings had not been able to bring themselves to find and read the last issue, Friday, Nov. 4.

I started with the issue on Johnny's latest catch. Main story, right column:

Giant Creatures of the Lake
Mystery Yields World Record Trout
by Lane O'Leary, Patrick Weekly staff reporter

PATRICK—The taboo waters of Crater Lake has yielded a world record rainbow trout.

Last Sunday, Johnny McIntyre, 15, reeled in a 36-pounder from the shadowy depths of the murky lake.

Young Macintyre said he has no secret bait or angling style that landed the monster trout. "You just toss in a line and bam, there's a beast of a rainbow trout coming up to get it," said Macintyre's twin brother Jeb.

The brothers six months ago were first to discover the giant trout in the lake, which has a shoreline onto their property. They were testing new fly-fishing rods from the shore. The lake was under a federal quarantine at the time, but the boys simply wished to try out the rods, which were birthday gifts from their parents.

More than a half century ago, the meteorite smashed into Sassafras County very close to the west shore of the Sassafras River, creating the mile-wide crater. River water filled the cavity which the U.S. Corp. of Engineers estimates to be about 1,100 feet deep.

On May 1, County Executive Morris Bradshaw appointed a blue-ribbon committee of biologists and environmental scientists to investigate the mysterious creatures in Crater Lake. But after five and a half months with no official report on the investigation, federal officials, who had originally put the lake under quarantine, lifted the restrictions this summer for no apparent reason except perhaps tourism. At the same time, the state tourism office reported that the lake was cleared of containing any "hazardous toxins." The state offered no official environmental report or reference for its claim.

Officials at the U.S. Environmental Protection Agency did not return repeated calls and emails from the Patrick Weekly.

The Macintyre twins and hundreds, perhaps thousands, of anglers have been catching unusually large trout since July 5, when federal officials lifted the quarantine of the lake waters.

"The boys and my wife and I eat fish nearly every day, which we catch from our side of the lake," said the twins' father Bobby Macintyre.

There have been no illnesses or deaths from eating the fish, according to county health records and no adverse health reports associated with the lake, they said.

Also of note, state health commissioner Morris T. Guthrie and his wife Giggles, the former Ringling Bros. circus clown, own a large piece of property on Blake Mountain overlooking the southwest side of Crater Lake ...

I stopped reading at that point. I could see where that was going. I could not believe the blatant insinuations underlying the news copy. I called over to Tina who was still reading every page of the last issue of her parents' newspaper, "Hey Tina, your dad's reporting on Crater Lake is pretty bold and provocative, I think. You want to see this?"

Walking into the kitchen, she said with a wry smile, "He always reported things like that. No stone unturned. Pretty good I bet, huh?"

"Yeah, and tough."

"That's what you get from a coal miner," she said. "Every male and some women in our family got tough real fast dealing with the coal companies. Some were actual miners themselves with all the dangers, filthy conditions and long hours. Lousy or no health care coverage and low wages, all things considered."

"You say he was a coal miner too?"

"Tried it one summer. Then, when he was 18, he enlisted. The Army made him a military journalist because he wrote so well. He reported news from Vietnam and got disillusioned because he had to also keep up with the news in the states, the protests, draft card burning and all. You know the picture."

I said, "Slightly before my time, believe it or not my child, [she laughed], but I know the history."

"Daddy was always a fighter, even won metals for prize fighting in the service. But Vietnam was one fight he eventually turned his back on and never got over it. Said it was a waste of good men and a stupid war with no upside for the United States. He began to include some comments from soldiers in Navy Times columns that were critical of the war, for balance, he told me, not to be unpatriotic."

"Don't tell me they brought charges that he was favoring the enemy!"

"Yes, that was the general reaction. Joe says daddy was mad all the time back then. Finally, he asked to be relieved of newspaper editing. The accusations went away. He has or did remain a battler for justice ever since that crazy stupid incident. My father and mother were the best of patriots, Mr. Ford."

"Of course." I hugged her, as she appeared shaken by her own words and memories. "Okay, back to work. Find anything in your paper?"

"I'm afraid so, Mr. Ford. I think they were already onto our Vacation Inn fraud story. Look at this."

I sat next to her in the booth as she pointed to a headline: *Resort Development Flawed, Records Show.* Tina's father Lane O'Leary reported negative comments about the Vacation Inn proposal from legislative analysts. The state was considering a bill to spend $12.5 million on roads in and around the new town Trout Heaven to accommodate the arrival of a large lodging and resort chain, which had already purchased the center section of Charity Mountain, from Route 7 to the Sassafras River.

The Washington Inquirer reported months later that savvy analysts in both the state house of delegates and state senate recommended rejection of the funding, based on documented reports of Trevor Goodbred's and Max von Kindel's past bait and switch ventures. The record clearly showed shoddy concern for local interests, concluded the analysts.

Tina surmised, "This is right-on, Mr. Ford. Those chairmen of the state senate and house finance committees, who received those damning reports from their analysts, are both now members of Goodbred's board, old Mr. Jenkins and Horace Borage. And the state comptroller, who holds the key vote of the Governor's 3-member Public Review Board, was Chester Holmes who owns property on Charity north of the Garrett land."

"And the Garretts?" I asked.

"Louis Garrett is the state legislator for district 6, which includes his land. He was also a snake charmer."

Vacation purchased its first plots from a Garrett family. Same?"

"Same. Lou owned most of it, but sold it to Cousin Hezekiah Garrett a year earlier. I know that because it is mentioned in the pathetic little Trout Heaven museum."

"They have a museum?"

"It is actually just a poster board in the Inn's lobby with a sign promising that a full museum is under construction. A lie. Mary said there is no appropriation for it yet." Tina said.

She pushed the paper to me for further inspection. She picked up another paper, the edition her parents published a week earlier. Her eyes flared open as she said to me, "Yikes ikes, Mr.

Ford! Look at this. Here is a pic of Mays on the Garrett land five years ago. He was here, Mr. Ford. Oh, my God."

I read the headline in the Weekly's business news, page 8, *Vacation Inn Security Chief Ex-Con*, then the story:

Chief Security Officer for the chain of Vacation Inns and Resorts, exploring a location in Sassafras County, has served time in prison, according to Massachusetts state records.

John P. Mays, of Falmouth, Mass., was convicted in 1999 of killing his wife's lover, Sammy Blake of Provincetown, Mass. Under Massachusetts law, Mays received the court's special consideration of domestic violence and served just five years, and won parole in three. Falmouth police records say Mays surprised the lovers at Blake's beach front home at the well-known resort at the tip of Cape Cod.

Tina stopped reading and said, her voice quivering in fear, "I guess killing his wife's lover outside of their home qualifies as a crime of passion in this case, right?"

"Yes, I guess. Not sure of Massachusetts law, but sounds right. Are you alright," I asked.

"No, not at all. The caption says Mays was walking the Garrett property. How'd they get that photo do you think, Mr. Ford?"

"Says here 'Photo by Shirley Fox'."

"That's mother. Oh, my lord, Mr. Ford, she was there," Tina said.

She stood up and paced, fists wailing over her head. She looked at me. Tina's eyes were so full of tears she probably couldn't have seen the fine printing of the photo credit buttressed up against the menacing image of Jack Mays five years ago in camouflage hunting pants, wielding a shot gun, and displaying a smug smile right into Shirley's camera lens.

"Get Uncle Joe. He's still cleaning up the back," she said.

A minute later, Smokey Joe hovered over the canopy of newsprint. Tina asked him, "Uncle Joe, did you ever see this man before?"

Joe studied the photograph. "Oh yes, he was here a couple of times. Last time I remember oh so well, Tee. It was early morning one day. Weekend, I think. He ordered breakfast at the counter. But then Lane, your Dad I mean, was down here getting coffee for the newsroom ... He and her Mom, they ran the paper you see, and ..."

Tina, nearly shouting, "Uncle Joe, this is important. What did Daddy say to this man? Can you remember?"

"It was not so much what he said; it was what he didn't say."

Tina, now really shouting, "So, what, ... what, wha ... Oh, my God. I can't believe Mays was here."

"Mays, yeah Mays. That's right. His name was Mays," said Joe.

"What Tina is trying to ask is 'what did the two discuss?" I offered.

"At first, yes, Lane didn't say anything right to the man, but he was angry, Joe said. "My brother grabbed me by my arm and said, 'This man is not welcomed here. Don't ever serve him, as a favor to me and Shirley.' And with that, the man stood up and accused your father of libel for smearing the man's name in the paper. They shouted at each other until I had to get them outside, where I saw them scuffle and one of them fell down. I remember this because this man was someone your father hated. Normally, my brother Lane didn't hate anybody, Hank. That's why I remember this man."

"What happened then, Joe?" I asked.

"I thought Lane was hurt so I ran outside real quick like, and he was okay, you know? The other man was running to this green pick up and then drove away. I asked Lane about this man, but he wouldn't say. Just took his coffee, still mad as hell, and went up to the newsroom where he led Shirley back into the room. She had been on the top step the whole time watching."

Tina, composed, asked, "Did they argue about the new resort coming to Trout Heaven, Uncle Joe?"

"No; as far as I know your daddy never mentioned that to the man."

I turned to Tina, "What do you think?"

"I think my parents were dead seven days later, Mr. Ford."

Her face was like stone, much past crying, past anger, just motionless and foreboding. Her eyes narrowed. She looked up toward the newsroom door, and then out to the parking lot. I could only surmise revenge was consuming her. But, who could say if Mays had anything to do with her parents' death, I thought. I let it go and said nothing else.

Tina got up and walked with Joe to the back of the kitchen and into the storage rooms for a private chat while I found several more articles over a six-week period, which reported that there were serious problems with the new resort development. Some sources commented on Goodbred's past shady dealings. There also were positive comments from local officials about the exciting new resort and the jobs it would generate and the tourist dollars it promised to the local economy. All and all the reporting by Lane and Shirley was objective in covering pro and con opinions on Vacation's plans for a resort.

Also, there were op-eds that came down hard on the prospects of Vacation Inns & Resorts moving to town, probably ghost written by Shirley Fox, as 'editorial staff.' Tina soon confirmed they were in her mother's words.

The op-eds were directed at the county and state. Shirley's opinion was that the government officials should not trust investing in a company whose executive officers ran a previous company with accounting and SEC 'reporting inconsistencies.'

"Miss O'Leary, your folks were already casting lines into the SEC issues way past local issues at the Trout Heaven site, maybe the same kind as those unearthed by Devin at the Inquirer and Mary Marinaro at the company, maybe by Mrs. Moore by now too. Your parents were about to bust them."

She surprised me with her sudden focus and tearless resolve, "Mr. Ford, if I don't come back from my interview in Boston, promise me you will nail these bastards. They will all be there at a corporate meeting. That meeting includes my interview. It also includes an awards banquet, entertainment, and corporate meetings to plan the next year's strategy. I need to shake some rotten fruit from their sick trees while I'm there."

This was one of those times when she had me at a loss for words, "Okay, sure," I said. *What a woman!* I thought, once again.

After just a moment of reflection, I insisted though, "But, I'm going with you. I don't know what you are capable of doing."

"Me neither. But, one thing I do know is that they wanted me to take that job, despite what they knew about my parents' investigations. Makes you think, doesn't it, Mr. Ford?"

Chapter 54

The Trout Heaven Inn's manager John Hancock and his family owned land adjacent to Crater Lake. It was west of the new town Trout Heaven, which was not visible from the Hancock's 2,200 acres of farm and primal forest. The family traditionally farmed, timbered, and worked jobs in nearby towns.

Hiring John Hancock was a strategic move by Goodbred and Levine to eventually purchase his property and expand the value or potential of the "resort." Hancock never in his life had had such a grand salary. He was behind on property taxes and medical bills.

Perhaps if the company gained his friendship, it would soften Hancock into selling, Levine figured. Tina said he allowed the local man to set up full control management of the Trout Heaven location but no authority beyond that location into the rest of the corporation. But, in his job description at the local level, allowed Hancock to order any facilities, furniture and equipment he wished that would please visitors from that part of the country, as Simon Levine relayed to his PR Director Tina O'Leary. She thought it odd that she was not afforded as much, but she didn't think it would "be neighborly" to ask Mary any questions about Hancock's alleged huge expense account.

Tina told me she thought of Hancock as a puppet of upper management, that he was extremely grateful for his job accommodations and never questioned management. He was a wimp, she said, but a nice wimp.

"John Hancock is in no way kin in fortitude to the famous revolutionary namesake," Tina advised. "This Hancock is meek and quiet, partly because he was happy for his salary to cover medical expenses and nursing care for his wife June, who has advanced Parkinson's disease. Play along with him Mr. Ford. Respect his position. Act it out as if he is in full charge of the decision, even though he isn't. He will appreciate that. He is a nice man basically, in a difficult spot. Be sensitive; don't hardball him. Make your pitch and get out before they start to know you."

For once, Tina's advice was not good for me, my reporter side that is. She had good maternal intentions for protecting me.

However, I can't afford to trust someone in a position like Mr. Hancock's. I intended to go after him.

* * *

I made myself late deliberately. John Hancock was not in his office.

His secretary let me in any way to his bizarre office. I sat waiting for 10 minutes while I wondered who in an insane world ordered all four office walls painted in a floor-to-ceiling pine forest mural. It was dark and spooky in there. Aside from a few odd papers collecting dust, there was nothing on his desk or credenza. His waste paper basket was empty. Was I in the correct office? I wondered.

Finally, I heard someone arrive and a high-pitched man's voice from behind me simply and quietly asked, "Coffee, Mr. Ford?"

Hancock came in with about a 24-ounce caffeinated drink with whip cream and a cherry on top. "We can walk over to the café and chat there, okay?"

"If you like, Mr. Hancock. Or, we could chat here and do some birding in the forest. Interesting decorating. Your idea?"

"I hate it. The corporation thought the manager of this location should work in the rural mountainous environment 24/7, I guess. Want to join me?" He gestured casually with his free hand out to the cafe. "Coffee's excellent there. We can find privacy there too."

"Good," I said. *Maybe this fellow is okay*, I thought.

It turned out that Inn Manager John Hancock and his expansive expense allowance had made himself a private glassed-in room in the coffee café, sort of like one of those unrealistic city editor's offices you see in recent movies. This glasshouse was full of papers and file folders on his desk and a bookshelf. Hancock said he mostly worked there where he could see the lobby, the front desk, concierge, door men, and all check-ins. Any problems? He's up and on it, he said.

He seemed to be a man with very much his own mind and spirit. Not a puppet or a wimp.

I ordered the most expensive cappuccino they made, with the most expensive Danish, the walnut maple bear claw. I don't even like walnuts. Just wanted some small way to stick it to Vacation Inns on my first visit, my first incursion behind enemy lines.

Ignoring Tina's advice, I came right to the point. I said without hesitation, "Your offer of $239,000 is pathetic and you know it." I lied. The offer was actually more than generous.

A smile creased his face as his thin lips vanished and his asymmetric rows of teeth appeared with multiple gaps and crooked incisors.

I tried not to show my impatient confusion when facing his stupid smile. I continued, "Mr. Hancock, I already know by your choice of a work environment that you are a discriminating man. Who could work in that wilderness dungeon they gave you. So, I think you likely know the offer was not at all what my land is worth."

"Certainly not, now with the town close by. I totally agree. What did you have in mind?"

"You know my situation Mr. Hancock …"

"Call me John, nobody else does." He paused, stared at me seriously, and then burst out with a quick but loud laugh. "Just a joke. May I call you Henry? Things are a bit stuffy in this mausoleum of an enterprise they call a corporation."

This guy is a gas, I thought. *He doesn't care at all about this negotiation. Perfect!* Although I ignored Tina's advice to that point, I respected her request that I remain sensitive. "May I be bold, John?"

"By all means. Please, be bold. Should be fun."

"I want to be bold, take a chance on a man I just met, because I have learned something about your situation too, your personal situation. Are you offended? If so, I won't continue."

"No please. Nothing offends me, Henry. But don't ya dare talk 'bout ma Mama, boy." Again, the ridiculous pause, stare and strange little laugh, bearing his ugly teeth. And then, his face in a flash became solemn.

With me in a silent state of wondering what kind of nut I'd met, Hancock continued, "I know who you are Mr. Henry Clyde Ford, where you work, what you do, so you don't need to be coy. My bosses don't know. I haven't told them they are dealing with a reporter; they don't need to know, do they Henry?" He paused and stared at me. (I didn't think of a response.) "Well, do they?"

I said, "Guess not. It's your call, John. And you can call me Hank. Listen. I want $1.4 million."

Nothing. Not a muscle moved on Hancock's face or body. He just stared blankly into my eyes, searching for something I supposed.

I stumped him? I continued, "John, I'm guessing that my spot on the mountain, in the prime view from the Inn from here, is very strategic to the fun-loving playboys who run this sorry firm. And because you, Mr. John Hancock, have wonderful mountain view property that does not face at any point the ugly town of Trout Heaven or its Vacation Inn, I am willing to return over to you personally the full $1.4 million you will surely give me from your management to pay me for buying my property and eliminating any change I'd block that ski lodge or whatever you guys plan for my side of the river. All that $1.4 million I will give back to you personally, John, if ..."

Hancock chuckled, "If, in exchange for what?"

"In exchange for a chunk of your spread, where this hackneyed, burned-out journalist can finally get some peace of mind, write his memoir and build a brand-new cabin retreat. Please stay with me, John. My wonderful view of the river and the mountains were devastated several years ago when this apology for the phrase 'resort town' spawned." I waited. Perhaps I'd get another of those silly laughs from Hancock.

But, nothing, not a twitch. The man had turned to granite. I was likely done.

I pressed on, "And, if you like the idea, perhaps you might offer me $2 mil. Your company gets my 29 acres, a fine log cabin almost new, and the greatest view back over here of the ugliest development ever to hatch out of paradise for only $2 million to do whatever the company wants with its prime motel view. Maybe the cabin could be a Ratskeller beer garden at the ski lodge site. And you get your shitty company's $2 mil to keep for yourself, minus a dollar for some acres you sell to me. But, it must face the Sassafras River. You still keep the $1,999,999 for pleasure, boats, sports cars, any measure of mid-life toys, or [I paused for emphasis.] medical expenses for your wife and you for many years to come. You will not cover healthcare with the cheap medical plan Vacation offers. Interested?"

Chapter 55

Tina was waiting for me at Smokey Joe's for dinner. I couldn't wait to tell her Hancock was not the man I had been expecting to meet; certainly not the frightened puppet of management.

She was sitting in our booth wearing a loose pink sweater with her parent's rings on the necklace outside of the sweater hanging on her chest. I timidly let her ask her about my meeting, "How'd it go?" she asked. "Did you sign the offer? Well, say something. How was Hancock? Didn't his awful office just bum you out, Mr. Ford?"

"Well, … it went well. And, no, fine, and no."

"Come on, I'm dying here. I've been sitting here waiting so long, I don't remember the order of my questions I just asked. So, did you sell, or not?"

"Not. I asked for $1.4 million, maybe $2 million."

"You did what?" she tried standing up, banging her thighs on the table in the booth and fell back to the soft vinyl seat again.

"I proposed a virtual trade for part of the Hancock mountain property. And I said he should ask the company, which he hates by the way, for more than $1.4 mil because that money will be his anyway. I'd sign for a piece of his land in advance he'd sell me for one dollar, no strings. That way, he can pay his wife's medical bills for the rest of her life."

"Holy Cow, you didn't? What did he say?"

"He'd consider my offer."

She stared at my eyes with glee.

"His very words. I swear, Miss O'Leary. Let's drive around that side of the lake. This was a blind offer. I've never seen Hancock's property. Might be nice to see my future retreat."

"I'll drive," she said like a schoolgirl. "He's got a trout stream. Let's ask for that too?"

"Let's? I thought it was just me buying it."

"Oh, stop. Let's order," she said red faced and yelled out, "Oh Joe, same as before. Okay?"

After dinner, we took that drive.

Chapter 56

Tina called me the next day with a weird coincidence. Hancock was desperate to talk to her. She said when she answered her office phone at the Inn in the regular manner, something like, "Tina O'Leary, public relations director for mid-Atlantic Vacation Inns and …" Hancock interrupted with "Cut the formality, Tina. I need to see you right away."

She said she didn't recognize his tone; certainly not the wimpy guy she'd expect from Hancock. He demanded that Tina come across the hall to his office and close the door. He said, "I don't want people seeing us meeting."

Her first thought was that it was too soon for him to react to my proposal. He might have been upset by my visit, or that he knew who I was. Or, my offer? She said she considered those and a dozen other reasons for his demanding urgency. Tina slipped over to Hancock's office not 20 feet from hers and closed the door behind.

She found him behind his desk in the goofy forest decorated office and asked why he didn't call her on the intercom.

He just said for her to lock the door. That she refused.

He apologized for his manner and delicately slid a sheet of blank paper with two hands across his empty desk top to Tina. He needed her advice and asked Tina to turn over the paper. He told her it was a letter 'from a fellow knows much about what he writes.' It was from Robert McGarrell.

As she read, she said he got up and locked the door himself and returned to his seat to wait for a reaction.

> Mr. Hancock,
> I want you to consider the humiliation and outrage my wife and I experienced at Trout Heaven Vacation Inn two weeks ago. First explain, if you can sir, the following note on the bill I received this morning from your company. It is billing us for our summer vacation at your resort, our first vacation during our oldest child's six years.

Instead of indicating that the first stay was free as advertised, I got this note: *Offer does not apply to VI&R Corp. employees, former employees, or employees of VI&R Corp. corporate partners.*

Yes, I am privileged to your latest advertisements as a former employee of G&M Financial Consulting, which is associated with your corporation. Full disclosure? I am a financial professional. I know finance law. G&M is not legally a partner of Vacation Inns & Resorts Corporation but is listed as such in your SEC reports.

Further, the clause, though in your membership contract, is COMPLETELY AND UTTERLY ILLEGAL, according to several precedents from U.S. Appeals Court decisions, says an attorney I've consulted. It is also HIGHLY UNETHICAL, according to the bylaws and directives of the Motel Advancement Foundation, of which your firm is a current member.

I must also say my wife and I were outraged by the conditions of the resort. There was nothing gourmet about your restaurant. My family resorted to ordering just cheeseburgers by the second and final day before we left in disgust. The golf course was a joke, the pool was dirty, the trails full of poison ivy. Shall I continue? You must know what a rip off you are offering, sir.

Let me be clear. This is not a threat, Mr. Hancock, just a reminder to be nice, as I am nice, as my wife and children are nice. Your latest ad says that by becoming a member, the first vacation is all expenses paid, as long as you book two more within three years. I did that, though I don't know where I will get the money to pay for two more week long vacations at your lousy Inns. Our bill for that "free" first vacation was $4,455.02.

I happen to know your firm preys on nice people like us, but I thought I could avoid Vacation's pitfalls because I know your books and your lies. I now know that I was not that smart. Again, I am a nice person. And so, I am going to pay you for a trip. I will pay for your all-expenses-paid trip into your accounting department to void my bill! Enclosed is the two cents to cover your trip there.

It will be a cold day in hell before I pay the other $4,455 for a free vacation.

Have a nice walk into accounting, sir. If not, you will hear from an attorney in 10 days.

Sincerely yours,
Robert S. McGarrell, MBA, CPA.

cc: J.R. Katzenbaum, attorney at law, Cincinnati, OH

Chapter 57

By age 20, Jeb and Johnny Macintyre had both married and had taken responsibility for their own business ventures in carpentry and chartered fishing.

They also took full advantage of their fame as teenagers, known for casting with Jesus, as Rev. Sugarman liked to call the boy's naughty excursion from his church service.

Their brides wanted them to abandon the high safety risks of hammers and saws and instead embrace their lucky new reputation with lake fishing, which promised to be more lucrative.

The twins and their wives founded the charter fishing business from the Macintyre family pier, the only substantial private pier on Crater Lake. Their dad, Bobby Mac, was their backer and COO. There seemed to be no end to the oversized rainbow trout yanked out of the depths of the old meteorite crater. A constant flow of eager anglers and curious tourists booked the boys' 12-person fishing boat, or rented flatboats and outboard by the hour from the Macintyre's.

Unlike the sleek bodies of normal rainbow trout that migrate hundreds of miles in rivers and streams, Crater Lake trout were portly, meatier around the middle. They were not as tasty, by all accounts, but great fun to catch.

I have wondered for a long time why no one knew or said why the trout were spawning without the benefit of a normal trout migrating cycle, or why they looked so portly. The Macintyers hushed my questions, saying that all the good that came with the giant fish overrode any thoughts of scientific study. Bobby said he prayed there would be no such study.

Why spoil a good thing with the facts—good or bad. And that was just fine for the Crater Lake fishing gurus, the Macintyre twins. They were reeling in a fortune. Plus, they had vision.

The lake had become a tourism magnet again. As the Trout Heaven Vacation Inn on Charity Mountain expanded closer to Crater Lake with more access through parcels of Garrett family land, Johnny and Jeb took a risk to cash in despite Vacation's shady rep.

The boys offered 25 percent off charters of 10 or more visitors from the inn.

When they brought a poster for their promotion into the lobby of the inn, manager Hancock put it on an easel, then had 200 miniature posters printed and distributed to every guest room and venue of the new and still unpainted plywood golf club house, the sparse Trout Heaven Natural History Museum, on each Home Depot picnic pavilion, a gravel playground, cottages, even the outdoor restrooms.

Hancock then took it upon himself to organize the first Trout Heaven Vacation Inn discount fishing trip of VIP's on Macintyre's second party craft, *The Shore Thing*.

It was an unusually hot and humid morning at the lake side with the chance of afternoon thunder storms in the forecast. The air was heavy but with no wind.

Trevor Goodbred, Jack Mays, old man Jenkins, Anita Rapshire and her husband Clarence and three other men and two women arrived in a Vacation Inn van driven by bellboy Donald Smythe at 8:45 a.m. with a photographer for stills and a video of the adventure on the lake. There were three other officers from other Vacation Inns and a few current inn guests who happened to book at the time Hancock tacked up the posters. Goodbred also ordered his beautiful public relation "gal" Tina O'Leary to go along to write a publicity piece for the media.

"Mr. Smythe?" Goodie rang out, "Come back for us at 5 p.m. or whenever I call. You got a cell phone, buddy?" Trevor Goodbred bellowed his orders as he walked down a gravel entry path to the Macintyre pier.

Tina said that Donald was terrified of Goodbred and for good reason. It was logical that he wanted the Smythe land on Crater Lake. It was the only property that extended to a wide swath of the lake on the side of the Vacation Inn, the west shore, and under U.S. Interstate 65 where it crossed over State Route 7, the very spot of Donald Smythe's grandfather Manny's long-abandoned produce stand. The narrow strip of the Garrett property, used by the inn up that time was inconveniently located on the far side of the lake from the Inn. Getting the Smythe property or part of it was Goodie's top priority.

After the mini-board meeting when Mays said he thought Donald was likely the sole benefactor of the Smythe land, Goodbred began paying special attention to Donald. He was keenly aware that further research through the county records, ordered by Levine, in fact revealed that long ago the young Manny Smythe lost his wife and three of four children to the meteorite crash. He had never remarried. The child who survived was little baby Elsie because she was with Manny at a doctor appointment on the day of the meteorite. Manny's daughter Elsie gave birth to Donald at an advanced age of 45 but died of cancer.

Goodbred was then convinced that Donald was indeed likely to be the sole heir to the land. Si was skeptical and paid no more attention to the bellboy's situation, Tina believed, while Trevor would be consumed with it, according to the grapevine.

At the Macintyre's pier, Tina arrived early and was checking out the pristine condition of their party boat. When Goodbred and his select executives arrived in a van, she soon heard him mocking the driver, Donald Smythe. He shouted back to him, "Sure you don't want to join us before you go Mr. Bellboy Smythe? You look like you need a little fun."

"No sir, I'm booked Friday for a boat alrea … dy," Donald knew he'd made a mistake.

(And sure enough, upon returning to shore hours later, Goodbred would be first to get off the boat eager to ask Jeb to see and review the Macintyre's weekly schedule; his ploy to learn of Donald's sign up date and time for Friday.)

Chapter 58

When I heard about the inn's booking for a fishing party at Macintyre's pier, I asked Tina on her new email account if she could get dups of any snapshots for me.

She wrote, "Way, way ahead of you reporter guy. I hired a photographer to shoot it and video record the whole damn junket. I'm going too."

She did better yet. She wrote a photography contract with a clause naming her as final editor. She would get two copies of all shots and video recordings within one day after the fishing trip. And, she asked him to leave the video with her for a day to review it for "company confidentiality." The real reason was so that she and Hancock could review the 'footage' for the best (perhaps damning) sections from the playback mode time clock.

It was all digital and those selected clips would be arriving on my laptop "in no time at all," she said.

The first clip opened with Johnny Mac standing on the bow of the boat with his beige Sperry Top Sider shoes wide apart, khaki pants, plain brown cap and a George Strait T-shirt facing his guests. His most motley crew of Vacation employees were all white people in loose fitting shorts, jeans and light tops on a myriad of colors.

Tina had said she planned to dress covered head to toe in sweats. I didn't see her on the video immediately, but everyone else seemed to be sweltering in the morning heat already.

That's where any semblance of normalcy stopped. I learned that Goodbred had required everyone to wear lime-green Trout Heaven Vacation Inn floppy hats, including himself. His hat was white, however, with green lettering. Everyone would see him as the boss, he likely thought, by choosing to pass on the green hat for a white one.

His outfit was strictly GQ: Navy blue Tommy Hilfiger blazer with gold anchor buttons and a gold paisley handkerchief in the pocket to match. His shirt was a baby-blue Brunello Cucinilli button down. He had on J. Crew chinos slacks. And on his feet were brown Jack Erwin leather boat shoes with no socks—very preppy Annapolis, I thought. Each movement, each breath he took spoke style and elegance. He was there to fish for admiration. He had no intention of fishing, just scheming, Tina observed later.

Johnny announced, "We have 14. Is that everybody Mr. Goodbred?"

Goodie saluted him with, "Oh Captain, my captain, let our trepid voyage begin." He looked for reactions from anyone to admire his paraphrase of Walt Whitman from his poem "Leaves of Grass."

Nothing from the fishing party. He shrugged.

Johnny continued announcements, "Ladies and gentleman, our lake is full of rainbow trout. We know that. But do you think there are secret spots for catching the big ones?"

He was teasing them, I was sure.

Once everyone and their gear, plus bags of food and coolers were aboard, Johnny asked a show of hands for guests who are familiar with lake fishing, He then asked for their names and assigned the others to team Clarence Rapshire, team Jack Mays and team Jimmie Jenkins. Johnny then said, "You will find that this kind of recreational fishing is a great social opportunity to make friends and exercise friendly competition among you. Is everyone ready for those secret fishing spots?"

Some cheered as the boat started moving off the pier.

"Okay then," said Johnny, "there are no secret spots. Don't need them." He started laughing compassionately.

Johnny stopped laughing when Mays grumbled, "Turn on the radar, man, and get on with it."

Johnny acted like he didn't hear and showed Goodbred into the boat cabin, where Tina had told me said there were drinks locked up exclusively for Goodie.

Johnny had already told me on our angling trip they do not allow detecting electronics or any kind of sweeping nets to catch fish on their charter boats.

Johnny returned to say, "You'll see, we don't need gimmicks. More important is that fishing can cure whatever ails ya. It lowers the blood pressure, relaxes the mind and enriches the spirit. At least that's what we think."

Mays lit a Lucky Strike and said puffing smoke in the face of the young man next to him, "Let's get on with it will ya. We want to catch some fish, not get a physical."

Johnny said, "I get it, sir. And for you Mr. Goodbred, angling adds lots of jobs and boosts the economy."

Goodie responded, "Now you are talking Mr. Macintyre. Don't let Jack unnerve you, son. He is harmless."

Johnny continued without looking at Goodie, "We believe that it is time worthwhile to tout the virtues of fishing, sir. Try to show respect for our catch, folks. For example, we participate in Rivers of Recovery and Project Healing Waters Fly Fishing on the river streams. Those are programs that specialize in the rehabilitation of combat veterans suffering with post traumatic stress disorder, minor traumatic brain Injury, stress, anxiety and depression. Any veterans here today?"

A smattering of hands.

"Let her rip, Jeb. [The boat picked up speed.] As we move out into the lake I want to say or perhaps remind you that fish are unique creatures and unique works of nature; not just skin, two bug eyes and meat. They anchor the aquatic environment. They limit reproduction of smaller creatures like mayflies and even mosquito larvae. Their excrement fertilizes aquatic plants, which grandfather said had no chance in the boiling waters after the meteorite hit. So, please admire these special trout for their beauty and grace, the adaptation to this weird environment and their clever means of avoiding predators, including you and me."

With the video camera microphone nearer to Mays than to Johnny's enthusiastic welcoming speech, I could clearly hear Mays grumble to other guests, "What a bunch of bull. All we want is to catch more fish than the next guy. Fuck that guy." This time Goodie couldn't hear him, or chose not to reprimand him.

Johnny persisted, "Just one more technical note, folks, please. All 15 rods are equipped with the kind of reels that rarely fail or get the line tangled, double-handled Fuego 100s. They are lightweight aluminum and have this kind of sweeping handle and easy bearings for maximum spin." Johnny continued to explain the gear as the boat slowed for fish by trolling and explained that by dragging a baited line through water with a spin lure on it, the fish follow and bite, "if you are lucky," he said, "and on this lake, you will be lucky."

"We'll be lucky if he stops yapping," whispered Mays.

In fact, I didn't see anyone still listening to their host except Anita who sat on the sideboard smiling from ear to ear. I bet she memorized every word from Johnny Macintyre. It was pure admiration to be sure. A civilized lady.

Johnny told his guests that the trout have spent their entire lives there like their private ocean with no river for migrating and spawning up stream like their cousins in the Sassafras River. They mill around doing nothing but eating and growing to whatever size the lake allows, which is considerably bigger than stream trout.

I was glued to the video watching Johnny go from person to person helping and providing advice it seemed.

Soon they started bringing in the big trout.

Although the Mac's prohibit alcoholic beverages on their boats, cans of beer appeared somehow and people began celebratory toasts after each catch. A lot of fish were coming into the boat.

I looked closer and spotted the source of the beer in a cooler that previously had only soft drinks.

After a while, Jeb looked disgusted as the guests became an unruly, argumentative crowd that then became a rowdy bunch. Jeb had walked to the back and sat on a stool in disgust watching.

While Johnny was reassuring the Rapshires and others on the starboard rail that trolling many lines at once is still smart, even with several tangled lines adding to the confusion aboard, "They might tangle sometimes but the reward is that it tends to call in schools of the trout by the sound and vibration of the gang trolls." Everyone was using small spinners or hootchies about an inch long. Johnny said they may trick the fish into thinking they saw reflections on small silver fish.

Meanwhile on the port side, Mays was whipping up an argument, which filled the background audio. The video turned to Mays struggling with a younger man, whose line had crossed Mays line. Not much older than a boy, the man had his hand on Mays rod wanting to switch and disentangle.

Mays shouted, "I can take care of my own rod. Thank you for losing my trout, bud." The fish had broken the line after bending Mays' rod over. He evidently brought his own gear.

The Macintyers carry only very light weight, flexible rods that can bend nearly double over to resist the pull and weight of a heavy trout. But the big trout are so strong they often spit out the hook, making the challenge greater than with more familiar smaller trout in streams.

That may have happened to Jack Mays as he blamed the young man.

Jeb looked at the rod tried to mediate, "Mr. Mays, would you like to try one of our set ups. Your rod is not going to handle the rainbows in the lake and might give you trouble all day."

"It is not the damn rod. My Betsy is my good luck charm and I'm not about to shame her by putting her down to use one of your flimsy sticks," Mays barked, with a little push on Jeb's shoulder. He then turned and shoved the young fishing companion next to him to gain some space for himself.

The young man spoke quietly. I think he said, "All right old fellow. I just tried to help you with the big fish. It was going to break the line and it did." He backed off and reeled in his line. After another obscene insult from Mays, he joined the others on the starboard side.

Mays told him, "Who asked you; numb skull? And, who goes fishing in a bathing suit? Where are your flip flops? Maybe you'd like to join the fish down there. No, they might bite off your pecker. Get out of my way, dickhead. He chugged another beer as the young man looked down at his Navy-blue boxer swimming trunks half covered with a wet white T-shirt. He mumbled to Jeb, "These were all I had clean. And it is hot."

Goodbred came into the frame with Mays, while waving off the camera. He said to the camera, "Thank you but that is enough here, Tina. Please catch me on camera with Mr. Johnny Macintyre up front next."

For the first time on the recording, I caught a glimpse of Tina as the camera turned and briefly captured her back side moving forward in the boat. Next was a zoom shot back to her full body that

I thought was hilarious. She was unrecognizable with huge sunglasses and a wide-brim straw hat, the kind old ladies wear gardening in the heat of summer. She had the sewn-in scarf of the hat tied under her chin completely hiding her hair and most of her chin and neck. Yet, I knew instantly the concealed video director was my girl Tina in baggy dark green sweat shirt and pants. I felt her sweating just seeing the image, but understood her outfit choice based on her fear of Jack Mays and growing distrust of Goodie.

The next clip was Trevor Goodbred reading from notes, a chest shot, "Hi everybody. Can I have your attention?" He started several times over ruckus cheering and arguing. One guy was already laid out, drunk I had to assume, on a bench at the stern. Goodie said to the camera, "Tell them to be quiet for a minute, please."

Tina did so.

Goodie proceeded, "Friends of our lovely and charming Trout Heaven Inn in these lovely hills, we are blessed with plentiful trout, companionship, team building and all with a positively grand summer day."

Behind him a line of very dark storm clouds approached from the west.

"Mr. Goodbred," Johnny said, tugging on Goodie's elbow. "We need to get back to the pier before the rain."

"Nonsense. It won't rain on our fishing party, Mr. Mac...," Goodbred said as a lightning bolt struck nearby on shore, following instantly by a deafening crack of thunder.

Most of the guests hit the deck. Trees fell on shore. Heavy rain pelted the boat. Several of the guests let go of their rods in fright. Johnny and Jeb scrambled to retrieve them first with their hands, then nets and life rafts on ropes. Some of the rods were lost.

The next video shot revealed 13 of the 14 "fishermen" huddled under the mid-boat canopy. The lone unconscious man remained asleep and exposed to the rain.

Goodbred's pep talk was history with everyone pressing against his fashionable duds. Before the camera turned off, Tina whispered to the cameraman, "Stay with him but hold it down to pick up him talking with Mr. Macintyre. Let's move closer as if we are getting B footage of the lake environment."

The boat was speeding to shore in the rain.

I turned up the volume on the recording and heard Goodbred talking with a voice I recognized as Johnny Macintyre. Goodie asked, "Can we see all the shorelines from this position and in what direction is the Inn, sir?"

"Yes, it is not but a couple of miles wide and almost a perfect circle. Your motel is over that ridge, can't be seen from here"

Goodie said, "It is not a motel. It is a resort. When we heard of these giant fish, we looked into locating on the shoreline, but there was not enough acreage for getting us in quickly and comfortably with a nice hospitality set up with the golf course and at least a water access. We had to choose the river instead."

"I've been there, yes, to your inn" Johnny said.

"We do have a slice of the Garrett property and paid an exorbitant price but we cannot build on it yet?"

"We know."

Goodie said, "We are prepared to do whatever it takes to own the entire lake, or at least a good part of the shoreline. Zoning issues are always easy to win if you've got the right dough."

"They are?" Johnny seemed to be playing Goodie.

"Do you know them? The zoning board members?"

"Nawh." Johnny lied. The Mac's knew all of them well.

"Tell me Mr. Macint…"

"Johnny, call me Johnny."

"Yes, Johnny. And please call me Trev. Tell me, Johnny, could you point out the other owners around the lake for me, please?"

"You'd have to ask my dad, if you want information on our neighbors. Kind of noisy fishing crowd you brought with you, ain't it?"

With that, the camera panned up to the two men. Goodbred stared at Johnny Macintyre for a minute or two and finally said, "Thank you very much, Mr. Macintyre."

Johnny was grinning and said, "Remember, Trev, call me Johnny."

The boys slowed the boat to trolling speed when the rain subsided.

In the next frames, Tina's hand—with new her nail polish—pushed the camera away before Goodie saw it pointing at him. It whipped around to capture Clarence Rapshire teaching several people the proper way to unhook the biggest rainbow trout I'd ever seen.

Jeb declared the Clarence's prize trout the champion of the day so far and a fight nearly broke out near Mays again. Someone turned on a Rock 'n Roll oldie channel at high volume. Soon people were dancing with beers in hand to Credence Clearwater Revival "Green River" and then "Rocky Top (Tennessee)," which even got Anita Rapshire up, minus a beer, though.

The only other action I noticed in the background was Goodie bear hugging the back of Mays to pull him away from angry men and throwing him under the boat canopy, finger pointing into Mays face and flaying his arms about.

Chapter 59

Once back on shore, Trevor Goodbred, still spotless and dry, began addressing Jeb at the dock, as I mentioned earlier.

Faintly I heard him say, "Quite a fine lake you got here Mr. Macintyre."

Tina evidently passed by with the video guy. I heard her whisper, "Just leave it here and load the rest of your gear. I'll turn it off."

Louder volume now, Jeb said, "Tain't mine. But I guess you could say it sort of is in a way, huh?" Jeb said, sharing a laugh with his guest, Mr. Goodbred.

"Say, Jeb, can I call you Jeb, or Mr. Macintyre?"

"No, sir. Call me Jeb. That's mah name."

"Okay, Jeb. We are going to make it big here in Trout Heaven. We are putting Sassafras County on the map. We want to purchase another part of Charity Mountain from the Garrett family to finish the resort golf course as you likely know. But we are going to buy up all the land around here, control the lake, except for your piece here."

Jeb laughed quietly, gave Goodbred a sly smile and replied, "Them's fightin' words round here, mister." Perhaps he was showing his annoyance with all the disrespect the boys endured on the boat. Jeb stared at Goodbred but got no reaction from him on the joke. "Ah, just kidding. I guess you have a notion to try mister, but folks been here long time and ..."

"They'll sell. Mark my words, for the money we'll pay," Goodbred said, still without expression. "How about $25 million for just this slip and pier?"

"You serious?" Jeb said in the best fake oafish accent he could manage. He didn't have the faintest interest in such a deal and decided to mock the Bostonian's superior tone. "Well, I'll be. Sir, that is mighty generous there. I swear, if that ain't mighty generous."

Instead of replying to Goodbred's offer, Jeb said to him, "Here, sign yer selves in this book for the next outing Mr. Goodbred, while I help the ladies with their things and weigh the fish they brong in. Why do the girls always get so lucky fishin' anyway, Mr. Goodbred?"

Access to the booking log is exactly what Goodbred was after. He answered, "Because we let 'em, Mr. Mac." Goodbred said, still belly laughing, "Lemme see here. Yeah, I can see you are almost booked for this week. But next week?" I could hear him mumble, "Oh look here. Boy Smythe is booked for Friday 4:45 p.m., huh? Flatbed and outboard, huh?

Jeb returned.

Goodbred said to him, "Seems our bellboy's up for some casting. Is that right?"

"Yeah, looks like Donald is going fishing with my brother Friday. Want to come? That why you are fixin' to come back soon?" Jeb said, still putting on the yokum act.

Goodbred kept mumbling and fidgeting while walking to the Vacation Inn van where none other than 'that boy Smythe' was waiting dutifully at the wheel for his party.

Goodbred smiled and climbed aboard the van. He waited for the others without talking with his driver, perhaps still scheming, contemplating ways to get a pier like Macintyre's on the other side of the lake, closer to the inn. It would be a safe bet that he was wondering how they could put Jeb and Johnny out of business. He finally said, "Ah, here they come. Smythe, my boy, help them put those coolers in the back. Loaded with trout. My heavens what a gold mine in a lake."

Donald was already out of the van and didn't hear most of Goodbred's salivating comments, Tina said later. After hearing Goodbred disrespecting Donald, Tina had yet another worry, for her friend the bellboy.

Chapter 60

Late afternoon on Friday the clouds parted after a morning of heavy rain.

According to Bobby Macintyre, his son Jeb expected fishing to be good that evening with Donald. He said he and Johnny helped Jeb load fishing gear, coolers and life jackets into Donald's rental, a small flatbed boat with an outboard.

Donald Smythe was a childhood friend with the twins. They knew each other's favorite baits, lay of the land and the lake, even agreed on favorite beverages and snacks for their evening of fishing.

The last piece of equipment Johnny passed to his brother was Jeb's Remington 750 semi-automatic. The deer rifle was Jeb's favorite firearm.

Bobby said Donald had laughed nervously as he asked what they needed the rifle for, to shoot the fish?

Johnny cautioned and simply said for Jeb to hide it because "funny things" had been happening around there lately. Donald agreed and told the Macintyres that he was nervous at the inn too and was thinking of quitting his job. "Si," he said, looked at him "funny."

When Bobby asked, Donald explained that Si is Simon Levine who was like an opossum who is stays in the shadows and nobody knows what he does, but that "he seems to be running things."

After Johnny shoved off Jeb and Donnie's jon boat for an evening of fishing on Crater Lake, Bobby said he peered through high-powered binoculars hung around his neck. There had been some rustling in the woods about a half mile away to the north. There were two figures and a vehicle there on the Macintyre property where an old farm lane met the lake shore.

Later that evening, just after dark, three loud rifle shots echoed off the mountains. It then rained heavily until dawn.

* * *

First thing Saturday morning Sassafras County Sheriff Deeds paid a visit to the Macintyre boys. They took the sheriff's cruiser to the old farm path where Johnny said there was a commotion the previous evening. Johnny suggested that the gunshots could have been deer hunting out of season, though he knew that was not the case.

At the bottom of the path, nearly in the lake water, they discovered an abandoned red, white and blue Jeep Cherokee dotted with New England Patriot logos on its doors and hood and Massachusetts plates. Its tires were hopelessly stuck in the mud up past the axles. The Jeep had backed a large boat trailer down to the shore. But there was no boat. The trailer ramp runners were down indicating that a boat had been launched. Deeds asked the boys if they recognized the vehicle.

Both quickly said 'no' at the same time. They said that the sheriff's eyebrows furrowed. He looked warily at them and asked them to level with him. He asked for "the whole story," they told me later. The sheriff told them it was pretty weird to find a vehicle with out-of-state tags so close to their pier and Jeb and Johnny knew nothing about it. Deeds knew them better than that. Perhaps he recognized that they had something they were hiding.

Johnny said he nudged his brother, and then replied, "Honest, we're at a loss too, Sheriff."

Deeds pushed his hat back on his head and reached for his walkie-talkie on a pull cord from the waist. He called for an impound truck and asked one of the boys to stay with the mystery vehicle until it arrives. He said to call him if the owner showed up.

Deeds told them he already knows that somebody was out on the lake last night.

Johnny asked who.

The boys told me that the Sheriff said with an angry face "Donnie, that's who. You think you can out smart me?" With that, the sheriff walked up the shoreline to his cruiser without another word. He radioed to dispatch to send a tow.

He then tracked two sets of men's bare foot prints that walked up from the water to and around the Jeep doors, and then continued up the hill toward the highway. Evidently the person abandoned hope of recovering the Jeep. Deeds kept muttering, they said, as he drove the Macintyre boys back to their pier. They asked if the sheriff wanted to see the log of renters for yesterday.

But, the sheriff declined to see the log.

Deeds was always intense, focused and always cool under pressure. The big muscular sheriff didn't even holster a gun. Didn't have to.

Back in the Sheriff's Office, Deeds was likely puzzled by a fax coming in from the Massachusetts Motor Vehicle Administration. It was a copy of the Jeep's title. It said that the owner was Jack Mays, security chief for Vacation Inns and Resorts Corp. the same Jack Mays, whom the sheriff had driven Friday morning along with Simon Levine to the airport to return to Boston. Coincidentally, Deeds had cruised by the inn on his normal rounds. Bellboy Donald Smythe arranged the ride for Levine and Mays with the sheriff.

Deeds made a couple of calls to confirm that the two Vacation Inn officials had indeed returned to Boston. Yet, Mays' vehicle had been at the lake at the same time.

Soon, Mays returned a call from Deeds. He told the sheriff that his Jeep was supposed to be locked in the Inn's VIP garage. He said he was planning to return to his Jeep to take some R&R in the Blue Ridge range after the corporation's annual meeting at its Boston headquarters. True to form, Jack Mays didn't know when to stop yapping. He asked the sheriff to "help" him catch some trout when he comes back Trout Heaven.

The next day, Deeds got a related call. A large white object had been spotted in the bright sunlight Sunday morning bobbing near the shore of Crater Lake. The capsized speedboat had three gaping holes in its hull. It got Deed's full attention. The boat was registered to a security guard at the Trout Heaven Vacation Inn, Claude 'Bo' Madison, a savory fellow with a rap sheet for domestic violence, narcotics possession, reckless driving, and burglary of neighbors' homes for prescription pain medicines.

Deeds notified the Macintyers. Bobby Macintyre had Bo arrested for trespassing and destruction of private property.

In jail Bo admitted 'borrowing' Mays' Jeep but would not name his accomplice. However, his feet matched one of the sets of mud prints. He said he had lost his shoes in the mud. Bo said he was only just fishing.

Deputy Sheriff Luke Brady, a frequent customer at Smoky Joe's, told Joe that the Sheriff smacked Bo across the face with the back of his hand hard and demanded that Bo confess that Mays had him tailing young Smythe. "Admit it, boy. Why?" he screamed.

Bo admitted that Mays asked him to scare Donald.

Deeds only then asked his clerk to come into his office to take notes, after he smacked him, according to Deputy Brady.

The notes later revealed Deeds asking, "Did you fire at him at close range?"

"No sheriff, he or somebody in his boat shot at us. I swear."

Deeds said, "Oh, sure they did. Do you realize Donald Smythe's grandfather was killed and word is out that he is the heir to his land? The motel wants it. Don't they? ... Well, don't they!?"

"Everybody knows Manny Smythe got killed by some crazed druggie. Don't know nothin' 'bout no motel."

"Everybody knows, huh? Boy, you are dumber than a tree stump. No druggie killed Manny, boy. It was a professional hit, God forbid; well timed, quick kill and no trace."

Deeds, for some reason, then offered the local hood a bit of advice, "If I were you I'd stop working for those outsiders at the Vacation Inn. They'll hurt you, boy."

When I learned of this interrogation, I was frankly not surprised by the sheriff's assessment of Manny's murder, though it was another disturbing criminal development.

In my mind, at least, all the ugliness around Mays, plus Levine's drunken threats to Mary, plus employees disappearing, their new suspicion of Tina on Hancock's tapes, Armstrong's confrontation in the women's restroom, and perhaps more, were adding up to be potentially stronger criminal indictments than all of our accumulated evidence of the financial shenanigans of Vacation Inns and Resorts, Corp. And, now Deed's assessment of Manny's murder! Does it tie in somehow--the first murder in Sassafras County since the '50's?

I wondered more about Deeds. *What does he know about such crimes and when or if he knew about more?* I vowed to keep plugging along on the book cooking side until anything breaks on the side of wrongful human dealings by Goodie's mop.

* * *

On Monday, Donald Smythe failed to return to his job as bellboy at the Inn. He had gone missing.

Chapter 61

"So, Miss O'Leary, you are awfully quiet. Not enough fish biting or something?" I asked as I settled into our booth at Joe's.

She was worried, "Actually, the fish were flying into that boat, Mr. Ford, most assuredly," she answered. "You saw the video clips, right? It was even more gross, not at all the elegance of fly fishing. And, with that imbecile ... well, never mind. More serious fraud fishing is going on inside the inn. Here, read this," Tina handed me a copy of Bob McGarrell's complaint letter to Hancock.

After I read it, I asked, "Did you contact this fellow?"

"Yes. And ... don't scold me, but I recorded the conversation. The man is serious. He knows Vacation well, very well. He knows a lot."

"Did you inform him that the conversation would be recorded?"

"Get real Ford. Of course, I did. I'm no amateur. Remember my father and mother were journalists, just like you, mister know it all," she said in an unusual sharp tone for Tina. "And I used my cell phone."

I just said, "Sorry."

"I should say I'm sorry for biting your head off. I'm a bit out of sorts. But, hey, this audio conversation; get this!" Tina handed me a tiny recorder.

We listened:

"Hello, McGarrell residence," a woman said.

Tina asked, "Is this the Robert McGarrell residence in Cincinnati?"

"I'm Mrs. McGarrell, his wife. Can I help you?"

"Mrs. McGarrell, this is Tina O'Leary, public relation director at Vacation Inns. You visited our resort in early September?"

The phone then gave a sharp banging sound, like it hit the floor hard. The woman screamed, "Bob, it's those Vacation Inn people. Can you take it?"

There were sounds of quick footsteps approaching, maybe into a kitchen. Then, mumbling what I thought sounded like, "Bastards want money." Or, "That's what (something) honey."

The wife, mumbled, "It's a lady."

Then a man's voice, "Hello, this is Robert McGarrell. If this is about my bill ma'am, there is no way that I'm ..."

Tina's voice, "No sir. I'm calling about your letter. I am concerned that your vacation was less than satisfactory."

The man burst into sarcastic laughter, then said coldly, "Sorry."

"I am calling to help, sir. Please. It's about your letter. I think it should be taken with the utmost seriousness. Not because you are a dissatisfied customer, which lays bad PR on the corporation. But, because we care."

"What is your name lady?"

"I am in public relations for the Vacation Inns corporation sir. My name is Tina O'Leary. Plus, I live in the area and take this sort of thing personally."

"I appreciate that you sound so pleasant. But, but if you read my letter, you should realize that I know my legal and financial p's and q's. I am not paying that bill, Miss Tina O'something or other."

"O'Leary, Mr. McGarrell. I think you made some good points and so does the manager here. Now, if you don't accept the following offer, I will instead be willing to drive to your home to personally apologize. It is not really that far sir. Did you drive to Trout Heaven?"

"Yes, we did. What are you offering?" asked McGarrell.

"Mostly, in order for me to void your bill, and yes, that is what I want to do ... to void your bill, then I need you to meet with us in person. Now, this is the part you may not go for: We will pay for your family to stay another weekend this month for free, really free at any of our inns nationwide. I understand you like to play golf."

I stopped the recorder, "Are you authorized to do that?" I asked.

"No, I'm not, Mr. Ford. I'll pay for him if necessary. Don't you see where I was going on this?" she asked.

"No," I said.

"He knows something about Vacation's finances. I think he knows stuff that we could use to nail these bastards," she said. I'm hoping to get him to help us confirm what we are already on to."

"This sounds too risky," I said, as I pressed the play button and we resumed listening:

McGarrell said, "Yes, yes, I like golf. Look, Miss O'Leary, I ..."

"Mr. McGarrell, if I may be bold, are their irregularities in our accounting reports that you are hinting about in your letter? If so, I want to know what they are and I don't want to know over the phone. And, Mr. McGarrell?"

"Yes," he said, far more timidly.

"I believe you. I don't want to be a responsible officer of the firm if what you say is true. And I have no reason to think it is not."

"Well, you sound okay. But forget another 'free' vacation. My wife hated it there. Nothing is up to standards for a pleasant time vacationing. Do you hear me, Miss O'Leary?" he was steamed up again.

"Yes. Again, I would like to know more about the accusations you are making. May I drive up there? You can have your attorney's present," Tina said.

"No, it has to be down there. I don't want my wife to be further stressed by you folks. I'll come to you. But I'm not going to back off my position on that outrageous bill."

"Mr. McGarrell, if you come, the bill will disappear. Please take note of what I am saying. You have made my day, sir. I want to clear this up."

I stopped the recording and said, "You didn't have to say he made your day Tina, eh, Miss O'Leary," I said.

"I got carried away. It was for you Mr. Ford, as well as me. I may not be here too much longer if McGarrell is right."

She said she arranged to meet with McGarrell at Smokey Joe's the next day. She'd be wearing a red carnation.

"Give me your hand," I said.

I felt tension in her and massaged her hands. "Let's take a break from all this, okay? You must be stressed with the bizarre fishing trip, Mays, suspicions at accounting, and all. I want you to take a break and relax with me."

"Not tonight, Mr. Ford. I'm …

"No, I don't care what your schedule is. You don't know what I have in mind my. Frankly, I don't believe you can fly fish at all. Show me your stream."

"Okay, but not yet. I'm not ready to relax, Mr. Ford. I want these bastards' heads."

Chapter 62

We each watched with great anticipation as McGarrell walked cautiously into Joe's. He was a slight man with a pale complexion, no hat and close-cut gray speckled black hair. He had on a tie, white shirt, gray slacks and a blue blazer.

He spotted Tina wearing the red carnation in the last booth and facing him. Then he saw there was a man in the booth opposite her and my presence seemed to concern him.

"Thanks for driving all the way down, Mr. McGarrell," she said, as we slid out for a handshake greeting at the booth. "This is my associate, Mr. Ford. We have a settlement for you."

"A settlement? That sounds legal. I didn't bring my attorney Miss O'Leary."

"Call me Tina."

My stupid mind flashed on, *That was easy. I sleep with the woman and can't use her first name yet.*

I slid in with Tina and McGarrell sat facing us. I wasn't sure of her strategy, she insisted on doing this her way. I only knew that she wanted to gain McGarrell's trust; maybe find out what he knew. She was always good at gaining trust.

McGarrell said, "I don't understand why you brought me here instead of the Trout Heaven Vacation Inn. Do you have identifications?"

Tina produced her corporate badge while I showed my driver's license and explained that I was a consultant. She continued with a lovely smile and pulled an envelope out of her purse. "We are offering you a settlement, not a court thing, just an apology in cash, of $20,000, Mr. McGarrell."

I hoped McGarrell was too busy with his shock to notice I was shocked too. I held my tongue as Tina finished her pitch.

She said, "This is a lot more than just voiding your bill. I actually had that paid. This is an offer for you to help us. We know Vacation Inns is a scam. I was a fool to take my job with them a few years ago. Mr. Ford was the first person I confessed my concerns to. After your letter, I decided you would be the second and hopefully last person I tell this to before I leave the corporation. With me so far?"

"Yes ma'am," said Robert McGarrell as he opened the envelope and read the figure on the check signed by John Hancock, authorized by Mary Marinaro. I took it that Tina had secured their full cooperation, but worried that she may have told that wise cracking Hancock too much.

"Mr. Ford, do you want to tell Mr. McGarrell anything else about yourself?"

Somewhat flushed, I offered, "I am a reporter from the Washington Inquirer, but I am mostly involved with the situation as a friend of Miss O'Leary and her Uncle Joe, who owns this establishment."

McGarrell gave us a quirky smile and said, "Wow, you are Henry Clyde Ford. I follow your reports religiously. Boy, if this is about telling you what I know about a story you are writing on that slimy Vacation company, pardon me Miss O'Leary, then I'm in. Is that the deal? I mean Tina?

I said, "Thank you, Robert. Always glad to meet an avid reader. Yes, we are working on a story. It is in strict confidence that you know I'm working with Tina as an inside source. Is that understood?"

"You betcha. Boy, wait until I tell Alice I'm helping Henry Clyde Ford."

"Ah, could you hold off on that for a while Robert?" I asked.

Tina added, "Yes Robert, the deal is off if you share this.

"You guys can call me Bob."

She said, "Okay, Bob. What Mr. Ford means is that we would like you to help us with anything you know from your former finance job about the corporation cooking the books, falsifying records and reports. If you don't want to, I will reimburse all your expenses for the lousy vacation and the drive here. If you accept our offer to help us, you can keep the $20 K if you keep all this strictly confidential until it is published, including even your nice wife. Okay?"

Bob shook her hand and nodded affirmative, while zipping his left hand across his mouth to seal his lips.

I said, as proof of our sincerity, "Bob, we think Vacation Inns instructed its accountants to record revenue on memberships before new members are obligated to pay. They recorded it at the member's first visit, not later as the deal is advertised by them. The SEC boys may not catch this as bogus. You are aware, as you wrote in your letter, that new guests sign an agreement for future stays to apply as membership discounts. That's a very broad description of the first layer of the onion, the corruption that we suspect."

"I think that may be true, Mr. Ford."

"Call me Hank."

He continued, "Yes, I think they do that. Two years ago, again in the fourth quarter presumably, Vacation sold memberships wholesale in quantity to several vendors, one of which is owned by Levine's brother Sal Levine, who is serving a three-year sentence for extortion. Then Vacation boosted revenues when it sold a strategic partner, a travel agency, to one of those vendors and continued to record revenues from the sold entity for six months. We used to talk about it at G&M, but no one would dare say anything about it.

"Also, I just checked with former colleagues at G&M. Since I left that company, the Vacation Inns group has been failing to record liabilities saying as little as possible about impending lawsuits, long-term purchase commitments, etc.

"The most glaring sign of trouble, in my opinion though, is that I know the time-tested trend in this category of business is when companies get older its income slows. Tina, your corporation's revenue is still growing almost exponentially. But, the cash flow from its operations lagged behind its net income by 20 percent for the past three years. That didn't make sense and the regulators are sure to start noticing"

Tina clapped and said, "Bingo! We know something about these things. See Mr. Ford, my friend in accounting was right on!"

"I knew it too," I said. "Instead of securing an expert like you Bob, we have been trolling the data in a vacuum, keeping it going by playing on the Trout Heaven name, that is, using fishing metaphors in our investigation, fishing around here and there for evidence, all the while hoping to catch onto some better data, or at least data that will confirm our suspicions."

"Well said," Tina offered pleasantly, "Mr. Ford is a metaphor freak, but I concur. Please, go on, Bob."

McGarrell continued, "Vacation's long-term receivables, those of more than a year ahead, ballooned last quarter. That's a neon sign of aggressive or fraudulent accounting methods."

Tina was floored, "Wow, Bob please cash that check. What you told us already is worth it to me. I'm wondering if you have an interest in teaming up with us on this further. You are a gifted financial officer, no? [I shot a look at Tina, surprised, while she assured me with a tap on the wrist.] This is okay, Mr. Ford. Follow me here for once."

She rolled her eyes and laughed looking at McGarrell. "Mr. McGarrell, I mean Bob, could you report back to us what you find on these clowns? Do you still have friends at your old job at G&M who can give you access to what they know?"

"Love to ask them, yes."

Tina excused herself and returned to her office at the Trout Heaven Inn.

I stayed and had lunch with McGarrell. When I was sure no one could hear my question, especially Joe O'Leary or Eloise, I asked him, "Did you know all of what you said about Vacation Inns before you risked a vacation there with your wife and kids?" It had been on my mind the whole time.

"No and yes," he said, and then paused, thinking. "I learned most of the sordid details after our experience at Trout Heaven Vacation Inn, but I hated myself for taking a lark on that free vacation offer."

"Why?"

"I should have known better. As a G&M client, Vacation was always somewhat of a favorite of ours because of its mercurial success on paper. Remember, we supported their financial officers with data and by publishing the numbers. I never knew Goodbred, Levine or any of the execs. I was a low-level employee at G&M.

But, I knew one of my bosses had vacationed at one of their resorts near Myrtle Beach, S.C."

"And?" I asked.

"I can't involve him. I know of your reach, Hank. Let me just tell this: I didn't know that at that time that man who recommended the vacation for me and Alice had a lot of shares in Vacation Inns Corp. You can imagine for yourself why he recommended that I take the vacation. I feel very foolish, plus I literally endangered Alice and the kids. Dumb. Please don't ask me to reveal his name."

"I won't."

Chapter 63

A week after we met with our newest investigative partner, Mr. McGarrell, I was in Boston sitting by the huge windows of Massport Terminal A at Logan Airport. I wore a fake beard and golf hat with jeans and a Red Sox sweat shirt, gazing outside, feeling helpless and anxious.

Tina, several seats away, wore a long brown wig and black scarf across her shoulders and neck, atop a simple brown dress of a suburban housewife, I thought. At least her disguise looked authentic; mine felt fake all the way.

After a long wait, Tina spotted the arriving passenger she was waiting for, her sister Shannon. I could not help staring. Shannon was Tina's double as she even had Tina's stride walking toward us through a tunnel from an arriving flight. Tina quickly walked over to meet her.

"Is that you?" I heard Shannon say to Tina. She was a redhead with the same do as Tina wore those days.

"Yeah, yeah," Tina said quietly with a quick sshhh. The sisters meandered into the women's restroom one at a time. The plan was to occupy separate but adjoining stalls.

Once latched into her stall, Tina passed her wig and black scarf under the divider. They each passed her dress to the other also under the divider as quickly as possible without a sound.

They exited separately and met up at a magazine stand.

They spoke out of ear shot of others except me. I was planted in the designated spot near the paperbacks as we had planned.

Tina, now the redhead, said to her twin sister Shannon wearing the dark wig and scarf, "God, what took you so long?"

"Mechanical problems in Baltimore and I had to take the later flight," Shannon said, adding, "Tina, is all this really necessary for your job interview. I don't know why I'm here."

"It is absolutely necessary," Tina said resolutely.

Tina and I had already spent many hours at my cabin arguing about a secret plan she had to burglarize the headquarters of Vacation Inns Corporation in Boston during her trip for her promotion interview. She was thinking recklessly, I thought. She would not share the how's and wherefor's. But there was no way to stop her.

Her safety was my only concern. My only hope was to go with her. "Just tell me what to look for and where," I remember pleading to her just before she agreed.

She knew what she wanted. But, she would not tell me what she wanted to find and take away from corporate headquarter offices. Files, she said flatly several times. That's all I knew. She was in a private fit and was even afraid to let me in.

At Logan then, Tina and Shannon each booked a rental car, at separate car-renting agencies. I drove a third rental car. We rendezvoused two hours later at adjoining guest rooms at the Marriott Hotel in Falmouth, Massachusetts, on Route 6, a short mile south of the Vacation Inn and Resort at Sandy Neck, their corporate headquarters.

I checked in first and made coffee for them in my hotel room next to Shannon's.

I heard them arrive soon and took a tray of cups and the coffee pot over to them next door. I overheard Shannon O'Leary Henderson (Shannon's married name she retained after a divorce.) break the ice as she tossed off the wig, "You are right Tina, this thing is horrible. Where did you get the wig, a novelty shop?"

"Never mind that. Too late. My interview is tomorrow and we need to talk. We need to school you on who these guys are and how to act at the reception tomorrow night. By the way Shannon, I am so grateful you want to help me without knowing how. This will not be easy; although you will be perfectly safe.

"Your role at this reception will be acting as me, Tina O'Leary, PR lady for Vacation Inns. You will hear me in your ear bud hidden behind your hair as I will walk you through the hallway from the lobby and into the banquet room. You will be also wearing this tiny camera I got from John Hancock. Once you are in, Hank will be communicating with you while I will have other business in their corporate offices.

"Who is Hancock, an insurance rep?" Shannon quipped referring to the John Hancock tower in downtown Boston.

"Be serious. Hancock is a friend. I told you about him, remember? He now hates them too because they plan to dump him. He is the manager at the inn at Trout Heaven."

She handed Shannon a stupid looking Trout Heaven Inn pin, which I thought looked like a curled up fish about to vomit.

"Hancock put the teensy camera in the fish pin here. See? They give these away at the Trout Heaven Museum. If they see me, that is, see you, wearing it to the reception, it will show loyalty and team spirit. These guys are knuckleheads when they drink and party."

"I don't know about this, Tina. They will know I'm not you," said Shannon.

I was again astounded by their duplicity. I spoke up to try to reassure Tina's twin sister, "I really don't think so. I can't tell by looking, only by your voices a little because I know Tina so well."

Tina smiled and added, "We have the same hair do to our shoulders, same color, same everything. Hey girl, by the way, you have stayed in shape. Way to go," Tina said, selling her sister on the plan.

I had noticed Shannon's pretty figure too and wisely kept it to myself.

Shannon knew I was an investigative reporter. I tried to stay out of their way since Tina and I had already gone over the plan repeatedly. I jumped in only when necessary, such as, "Yes, they may be knuckleheads, but they can be dangerous knuckleheads, especially Mays and Levine."

Shannon still looked at me with uncertainty. She said, "I don't want to do this Tina. It makes no sense."

Tina took a deep breath and exhaled audibly. She could wait no longer to tell her sister the truth, "Shannon, sit down on the bed there. You will have a whole night to digest this and I'm sorry. If you want me to stay here tonight instead of in my room at Vacation headquarters at Shady Neck, I will."

"Damn it sis, what the hell are you talking about. You are scaring me."

"I think they killed Mother and Daddy. And I think they killed them because the Weekly stories were damaging their plans for opening an inn at Trout Heaven."

The next half minute they stared into each other's eyes without a word or any movement, the twins facing each other sitting on the edges of twin beds, mirrored images. They hugged and cried.

I returned to my room without a word, already knowing my assignments for the next evening's events.

Chapter 64

Tina stayed with her sister until 5 a.m. And then, she drove north across mid-Cape Cod to her reserved guest room at the Vacation Inn at Shady Neck for a well-deserved morning nap. She left Shannon in my hands because Tina needed to be seen at the inn to cement her presence.

I had breakfast with Shannon in her room. This was in the plan. We were to go over the electronics.

"How are we doing this morning, Shannon," I said after waiting an eternity it seemed for her to answer my knock on her door at 10 a.m.

She ignored my question and said, "Hi Hank. I wonder if Tina got enough rest after we waded through an indeterminate time of crying and consoling each other. But after crying out the shock, we stopped and …."

She lost it again. She ran to the bathroom for tissue.

"Take your time, Shannon. I believe in your sister one thousand percent and if she is going to go through with this, she will need you and me."

She returned, "We finally did agree on the plan by 3 a.m., Hank."

But, Shannon was still in no shape to reason as we sipped coffee and ate microwaved eggs and sausage I'd picked up in a 7-eleven store, which gave me an early morning flash back to that quiet July morning on my cabin porch when I was shocked by those bastard bulldozers that indirectly changed my writing plans for the worse and then changed my life for the better with Tina.

Shannon found herself. She assured me that she understood Tina's dilemma and why Tina suspected foul play in the reported "accident" four years earlier that killed their parents at Pine Gulch. She at one point finally looked me in the eye and said, "I want to get those fuckers too. Excuse me, Hank."

Yep, she was Tina's sister alright. I tried but could not stop myself chuckling a bit. It seemed to lighten Shannon's mood and cement our resolve, though.

Tina's promotion interview was scheduled for 10 a.m. with a panel of Vacation Inn managers from Boston, Oakland, Galveston, and Lake Charles, La. along with Goodbred, and Levine. Of course, Tina, not Shannon, was doing the interview herself. But it was a good learning opportunity for Shannon to watch and listen.

Gutsy Tina wore the fish pin with the camera for us to see the interview. More importantly, the trick would allow Shannon to know the players she would meet, while posing as Tina, at the reception that very evening.

The plan called for Shannon to play Tina at the reception dinner and corporate cocktail party after dinner. The charade might give Tina time for her espionage into the corporate files.

I put a video receiving monitor and headsets in the back of my Avis rental car, which was a Toyota Camry with tinted windows, where Shannon and I could monitor Tina's interview. For best reception, I parked in a residential neighborhood just off Old King's Highway about a mile from Vacation Inn, Cape Cod.

Tina was flawless. And I became convinced sitting there with Shannon that she was every bit as strong willed as Tina. She and I studied Tina and her review board well and became familiar with the faces Shannon would meet later posing as Tina. Luckily, there was Goodbred, along with two senior board members.

Chapter 65

Later in the day, the three of us huddled again in the motel room.

Tina revealed for the first time that her plan was to burglarize Levine's office for membership records. I pleaded with Tina one more time to let me do the break in. She adamantly refused, saying she knew the firm and what needed to be stolen and hopefully copied before she left the headquarters building and while everyone was at the reception. She said von Kindel had recently spoken with Pauline and got her to talk about the office in a sentimental way. He had loved that job, that office, when he worked for Vacation. Pauline sounded as if the office was still the same, Max told Tina.

I asked if we should rely on the woman closest to Levine for such information.

Tina said it didn't matter; a risk worth taking.

I resisted arguing. She was determined.

"I want the real membership records," she said, not surprisingly. Now, you know. But, don't worry too much. I have been here before, remember? Worked here for a year before they got the Trout Heaven brain storm and assigned me there. I know where the files are. Don't worry; you will be with me every step on the audio feed in my ear," she explained to calm my fears.

She reminded Shannon that while impersonating her, Shannon was to wear the fish pin camera and an audio receiver behind her ear, under her hair to hear Tina's comments and instructions through the proceedings of the corporation banquet. I would be parked nearby in the Camry and listen only with Tina. Tina didn't want me on the feed, so he only could talk instruct her sister. Tina knew I would interrupt.

Later, I would be in two-way audio communication with Tina during her burglary and Shannon would be on her own. We could not stay plugged to Shannon while Tina and I were focusing on the audio linked for the burglary, too confusing, we all agreed. We kept the monitor on Shannon without audio, just in case something appeared to go wrong and we'd have to rescue her.

If I were religious man, I would have been praying my brains out. As it was, because I had nothing to do physically at either location, I was the most nervous I could remember and tried to hide my jitters. The twins were on a family mission and focused.

That evening all was going according to plan, at first at least. Tina and I watched the monitor in the Camry. The room was full of over-dressed cheeky women, each with a drink in hand and anxious looking men who had one eye on Shannon and one on their own women. Shannon wore Tina's black evening dress with a pearl necklace and black high heels, the same outfit Tina had worn at every official evening reception at the company for two years. Tina talked Shannon along, telling her what to say to the execs at the dinner party.

Part of the deceit was that during the speeches by Goodbred and others following the reception, Shannon, as Tina, was to begin acting intoxicated and to distance herself somewhat among the 80 people gathered at dining tables. We worried that Goodie might announce Tina's promotion. The twins prayed he didn't, with the dreaded possibility that Tina (Shannon) would be asked to come to a podium to address the audience. He didn't.

Once the party would move out of the dinner reception hall to a cocktail party, Shannon would be tested, playing her twin sister and having never before met any of the other 'characters' in the room.

After Shannon entered the cocktail party without a hitch, Tina was to leave me alone in the Camry and drive her rental in the shadows to the corporate offices to burglarize their files. We had wired Tina with an ear piece and small mic. She stood outside of the Camry to test the system. I heard her clearly and her me. Thank God for John Hancock's handy electronics.

Chapter 66

Tina was dressed in black sweats and driving gloves with her hair tucked neatly and invisibly under a black Baltimore Oriole baseball cap. The image of the bird on the hat was the only visible bit of color on her body, besides a dark green backpack she wore to carry away copies of the membership files.

I parked at my off-road spot among the houses off Old Kings Highway and waited in the dark Camry.

I still didn't know how she planned to break in until she exited the car for her mission impossible. This was just killing me, but I loved her determination. I sat in silence far too long for comfort. I heard nothing on my headset. She surely had failed. What can I do, bust in there to rescue her?

And then, there was static, she turned on her transmitter and was already talking mid-sentence to explain her 'in.' "...it was Max. He still had kept his office key when they fired him. He gave me a copy. I didn't want you to worry, Mr. Ford. I'm sorry."

That irritated me. I felt distrusted because she had conceived the plan with von Kindel over coffee after meeting at Rev. Sugarman's church. A meeting I could not schedule. I suppressed my irritation at this critical point in the break in, but she admitted later that Von Kindel told Tina the key would open Simon Levine's office on the third floor of the executive suites at Vacation Inn headquarters. She took him at his word because she said he seemed like a changed man and, yes, she admitted he was still smitten with her. If the key didn't work, she would ditch the plan and find another way in. "It is a crummy building that any idiot could break into," she explained.

Listening helplessly, it would have been nice to know the background. She still was not solid with our relationship at that point perhaps. But the truth was that she hadn't invited jealous Mr. Ford to meet with von Kindel at the church because she knew that, as a newspaper sleuth, I would never have bought Max's shtick because he once served with Goodbred.

Back to the break-in.

Vacation's 'Cape Cod' location with its official Boston headquarters was in a converted high school that had been abandoned by the public school system 20 years earlier. Obviously, it was not actually in Boston or near the beautiful, wind-swept sandy beaches of elegant Provincetown. It was in step with the Vacation strategy, near but not in the tourist spot. The view from this location was over the swamp on the north side of the peninsula of Cape Cod, instead of on the sunny ocean side of quaint Falmouth or out further on the sandy peninsula.

The old school on the north swampy side was a cheap purchase for Goodie's gang. It was set on an inlet and pond. Some fancy promoting and good shuttles to attractions fit the bill.

The resort was in the renovated original, yet huge wooden school house with a new three-story executive building attached. The school's auditorium was retrofitted as a lecture hall and theater for local acting troupes. And, the school's cafeteria and spacious lobby were outfitted rather nicely as reception room and banquet hall where, on this night, the execs and a certain redheaded imposter-candidate for corporate vice president for public relations were gathered.

Down a hill behind those buildings were two rows of 40 cabins billed as having "beautiful views," of the ocean, across acres of swamps in reality. The lawn around the cabins was of crabgrass mostly, a pool usually of greenish tinged water, and far below was Hazard Pond, which looked quite nice from a distance. It was named a century earlier for its high population of snakes.

Mosquitoes menaced anyone renting a boat for that pond. Sixteen hundred feet of swamps and waterlogged woods separated the inn from the ocean to the north. But two converted fishing boats took guests out for ocean tours for a fee. Shuttling to the ocean beach owned by Vacation was available too—one time every hour for a fee if Mr. Outie, the shuttle bus driver, wasn't drunk. Yeah, that was his name.

Tina took several deep breaths. I heard her pray for her family. Ready at last, she climbed out of her rental on the dark end of a parking lot next to the old school.

She sprinted into the back of the office building. The audio intercom clamped tight to her head offered audio only in one ear with a stick microphone that was linked to me and an audio recorder in the car too. As I said before, thank you Hancock. After all my apprehension about him, Hancock was indeed an electronics wizard and a good guy wasting his time babysitting part of a sinking endeavor.

Chapter 67

"HCF?"

"Gotcha TOL," I said to confirm the connection after her entry.

"I'm in. I am surprised to see the executive suites completely deserted. All the lights are out, except for security bulbs. Even the watchman must be on duty at the ballroom."

"Don't get comfortable," I said.

She was thinking that the night of the banquet was the best, maybe the only, opportunity to find the real records in Simon Levine's desk, if they were still kept in that desk, the same one used by von Kindel before he was fired. It was a risk she thought worth taking. The possible reward was hard evidence that the corporation was falsifying membership numbers and revenues—clear and simple. This was no longer just fishing for data on a string, but a massive catch with a seine net.

"I'm going up the stair case now directly to Levine's suite overlooking the pool and pond where he and Goodie smoke Havana's with the ocean in the distance. God, I hate this man, HCF," she bristled.

"Please stay calm," I said.

"I should have brought Joe's pistol."

"Not in your state, my dear."

"I found his office. The key worked. No alarm. Whew."

I heard her flick on her flashlight when she sat in Levine's desk chair.

"I tried all the drawers. They are locked." She then mumbled, "Damn, Max said if the desk is locked, use a thin piece of sheet metal to slide over the center drawer. It will open and unlock the entire desk, he said. But, I forgot to bring a piece of metal."

"See if his secretary or somebody has a metal fingernail file or a letter opener on a desk," I said.

"I'll just pry the drawer open," she said faintly.

"No, god no!" I yelled, without thinking. "That would leave evidence, forced entry into the wooden drawer? No!"

She then said in a panic, "Someone is coming down the hall." She ducked behind the desk and peered through the glass door of Levine's office suite and past his receptionist's desk. She heard heavy footsteps moving casually, closer and closer. Soon, I could even hear pounding shoes on cheap carpeting over a wood floor of the old school.

"It's a thick body of a short man and he is standing just outside of Levine's suite," she whispered to me. "I can see his pants, tuxedo. He reached into his pocket," Tina whispered.

We both heard keys rattle. As he pulled out keys he turned his face toward Levine's office door. "It's Mays," she squeaked ever so low.

Silence. I strained to hear anything at all.

Silence. I could hear only my heart pounding. I was ready to dash over there.

Then … "There he goes," she whispered. Mays continued walking down the hall with keys rattling in his hand. He must have stopped to see his keys in some dim pool of light in the hallway.

Tina crawled back out to Levine's office door and saw Mays open another office at the far end of the hall, some 80 feet from Levine's and turn on bright lights that spilled out into the hallway where she would have to make her escape. She waited 15 minutes and heard nothing.

She was killing me. The whole thing was killing me. I was sweating profusely.

"I'm standing now over the receptionist's desk, Mr. Ford."

"Don't say my name. Remember?"

"I see an old fashioned letter opener in a big sheaf. I heard her crawl back behind Levine's desk and slip the letter opener over the drawer."

Even I heard it pop open.

"Ah, just as Max predicted," she whispered.

"What?"

"There are brown file folders dated and labeled with just 'M' and the year in the bottom drawer. I'm grabbing all ten folders, ten years of the real records, I hope."

In case those ten were not the treasure, she put tape on the lock hole on the door's edge, Watergate-burglary style, for her quick reentry to return files or if it would be necessary to steal more folders.

As she ran down the hall, she said she could see her shadow on the floor ahead of her from the light of Mays office. He was likely still in there.

Tina was stellar, knew the risk and accepted it.

On the first floor in the copying room, just where Max said it would be, she put her pen flash light in her mouth while she rifled through packs of paper into and out of the fast feed Xerox machine, putting each pack back neatly into its appropriate yearly folder. It took a long 15 minutes and five seconds, by my watch. I felt sweat dripping under my arms and my legs getting soggy. I imagine her with one eye continually looking back for Mays.

Tina's theft was perfect, the first thing she could ever remember stealing from another person. She put the copies into her back pack. Only after slipping the originals back in place into Levine's desk and quietly closing the locked suite behind her, did she spot Mays emerging, his back to her while locking his own office back up.

She freaked out and ran. Probably shouldn't have.

"Oh God, he sees me Mr. … ah, HCF."

She turned and saw him retrieve into his office then emerge again with something long and shiny in his hand.

"Hey you, halt. What are you doing here? Jack Mays shouted. He had a serrated fishing knife, the kind they sell at the bait store in Trout Heaven.

She reached the ground level and ran toward the slimy swimming pool and row of cabins by Hazard Pond trying to lose him by ducking between and around the cabins. But, she said she didn't think Mays was behind her anymore.

Mays had not seen her face. But her Oriole hat flew off as she ran across the lawn, exposing her well-known red hair in the breeze.

Feeling safer, she walked out past the pool to get back over to the back parking lot and her car. All was black and she moved cautiously.

In a flash though, bright flood lights came on from every direction exposing the pool, tennis courts, lawns, and the cabins and Tina.

I could hear him through Tina's mic, screaming, "It's you O'Leary. You broke into our building, you dumb broad. How'd you get over here so fast from the banquet?" [pause] He continued, "Well, well, well. I don't know, but I am very glad you did. Come here, you hussy. Let's talk," Mays said calmly approaching her with his hands locked behind him, she said later.

She stood still at first, trapped. Then she ran as fast as she could, with Mays just steps behind her. He tripped and she gained some ground as he threw off his tuxedo jacket. "I can outrun him HCF," she said huffing. "Stay there and listen please. I'll drive over to you."

Tina fumbled into her pocket for her cell phone.

She dialed 911 on the run. But the phone didn't work. She was too far from civilization and a tower. "Goddamn cheap company. Located in a no-signal gap this close to the real Cape Cod resort!!"

She reached a boardwalk across swamp land. I could hear her shoes tapping on the wooden surface. Mays' heavy steps followed on the planks.

"He's closer. How is that possible, HCF?" she panted. "Oh there, I see some men on the lawn. Thank God. Hey, hey there, you men."

But they were not men, not real men, but life-size silhouettes of bronze sculptures of the poets Keats and Byron, left over from the high school, against dim parking lot lamps.

It sounded like she picked up her pace, running faster.

As she almost reached her car, she said she could hear Mays breathing hard, still jogging toward her.

I heard Mays cry out, "I'm not going to hurt you O'Leary. Just want to know why you broke into headquarters. You have no right. No right."

He was shaking his hands in front of him, maybe forgetting that he was wielding his favorite fishing knife with a pearl handle and serrated blade.

Tina tripped over a concrete parking bumper at one of the spaces and tumbled to the asphalt. She scraped her face and hands falling. She looked back and was momentarily frozen by the sight of the huge blade in Mays hand waving at her.

"I'm here. At the car. Still there, HCF? I'm getting away. The car. Keys."

She had reached her rental car when she was only about 50 feet ahead of Mays. She tried the door and the car was locked. "Oh fuck!" she shouted without thinking. She'd forgotten to take them out of the ignition.

Mays laughed and say, "Okay, I accept. Let's fuck, yes! Won't go to the cops if we do it." As he reached Tina, Mays was out of breath. He tried to grab her around the neck and chest while wielding the knife over his head. "See this girl. Now behave yourself and your pretty face won't become acquainted with my little surgical friend here." He apparently put his knife up to her face.

That was enough for me. I put the Camry in overdrive and raced to rescue Tina. It would be a good 10- to 12-minute dash to get to her. My headset dropped to the floor mats. I could not reach it. As I drove I pictured her dead. I couldn't stop to find the headset.

* * *

My drive was sheer panic. But, I now know what happened because I had left my audio recorder run when I left the room. It is good that I hadn't heard it live. Tina managed to slip down out of his one-handed hold and roll under the car.

Mays screamed at her, "You can't get away O'Leary. You are trapped, just like your libelous daddy do-gooder was on Pine Gulch. Except dear mommy and daddy were in the car not under it."

"You murdered them you bastard, didn't you? Didn't you? I need to know. You've got me okay. But I've got to know."

"Yeah, and old man Smythe too. We're taking over his side of the lake real soon, baby girl. Your folks? I killed them, sure. Stubborn people who won't step aside for progress. Your father was blocking us from Trout Heaven, publishing lies. They were pushing us to the edge. People were saying bad things about us. So, me and my pals pushed first. How do you know? See the last paper in the car, did ya?"

Tina was likely puzzled because her parents' car burnt up. What was Mays talking about? Last paper?

He said, "Okay you know now. I've gotta kill you now, don't I? God, what a stupid broad you are. Shoulda fucked me in Boston, you slut. You'd be better off."

He unscrewed the car's gas cap and lit a match. She stalled him, "I wouldn't have taken a job had I known, dumb shit," Just then, Tina felt a sharp pain on her leg. Pinned like a trapped rat, she managed to twist her body enough to feel the point of the pain. It was the sharp letter opener from Levine's office. She had forgotten to put it back on the receptionist's desk.

Mays was acting like he enjoyed having the upper hand. Confidently, he laughed and said on one knee, "I want to see you sweating before I toast your ass and high-tail it back to the building.

He knelt down closer, at pavement level, she said, to look under the car, perhaps to get a final glimpse of the terror in her face; like a rapist exercising his power over a victim.

Tina in the shadow of the car saw his face before he could see hers. She aimed at his eyes. Wiggling a bit closer, she thrust out her arm and stabbed the letter opener deep into and through his left eye, the one highest off the ground. The letter opener must have passed through his eye and into his brain.

"Aaaaaaah. You bitch."

She rolled out as Mays rolled away. She grabbed his knife as he writhed in agony. Without another thought, a thoroughly enraged Miss Tina O'Leary proceeded to kill her parents' murderer—fast and purposefully. With both hands on she pounded the blade into his chest like she was beating on a door. Once he lay still, she straddled his hips and pounded the knife blade into his chess again and again, uttering obscenities.

Breathless, she screamed, "HCF? Are you still there?" expecting me on the listening line. She looked up to see saw me climbing out of my car with its lights off.

"No. I'm here, behind you," I shouted as I closed in on her.

I was running fast toward her, then no more than 20 feet away. I could now see her over Mays. "Is he dead?"

She just looked up at me with horrible pain on her face. "I had stupidly locked the keys in the car, Mr. Ford. He nearly killed me, did you hear?"

"No. When he was closing in on you, I jumped into the car and streaked over here. You weren't the only one forgetting something. I forgot my brain; should have stationed myself closer to you. Dumb, dumb. Let's get you out of here. There is my car. Come quick. You have prints on that knife?"

Still stunned, Tina couldn't talk.

"What about the knife, Tina and fingerprints? Were you wearing the golf gloves the whole time?"

She got on one knee and shook her head 'yes.' She stood up and reached for me. I stepped back away from her because she had May's blood all over her. I kissed her lips quickly without touching her anywhere else. "Come on, Tina. I'm here now."

She took off the backpack and shook it in front of me. She said, "I've got it Mr. Ford. All of it. I've got it, damn it. Look. Here too." She pulled two zip drives out of her pocket.

"The dumbshit left his computer on."

"Levine or Mays?"

"Scrapper Levine, man!" Right before Mays showed up. I moved the mouse and it lit up. I clicked on membership allocations. There it was, all of it. Where he was putting the fake money from each sign up whether a member, potential member or a ghost for all I know, was registered at some time or another, listed by month and year. Damn!"

"How'd you know to take zips?"

"I was a girl scout. I was prepared for any eventuality. Let's blow?"

Chapter 68

We ran to my car. I booked it back to my hotel room, helped get her clothes off. She was scratched here and there but no serious injuries. She quickly put on a blouse and slacks from Shannon's room. I raced her back to Vacation Inn headquarters in the Camry.

Amazingly when we got to Tina's rental, no one had discovered Mays bloody body next to her rental car. At the start of her burglary task, she had hidden her rental car in the shadows as far away from the Inn as possible.

I placed a blanket from the Marriott by the driver side door and smashed the window with the fire extinguisher from the hotel room, gathered the broken glass in the blanket, threw it in the car, and Tina drove it back to the Marriott.

I drove her rental around the Inn. Tina took the Camry to contact Shannon. She called to Shannon from the intercom video linked to her sister's ear bud. But, the video monitor from the fish pin was showing trash, maybe rubbish.

"Shannon, Shannon. You there, Shannon?" Tina listened then called me from her cell phone to mine, "She's back at the Marriott, got a cab. I just hope no one suspected her."

"What? Oh," she said to Shannon. "Stay there."

Shannon said before the party ended, she had walked out to a line of cabs at the inn's entrance and got in one. No one was there at the time by the cabs.

"While Tina cleaned up, I drove her rental car to Falmouth and to an all-night "You Wash" car wash for quarters I had spotted when we had arrived.

Meanwhile, Tina called Shannon's room at the Marriott. "Sis, let me in on four knocks."

I drove quickly back through the inn's back parking lot. I could see the dark lump of Mays body silhouetted on the inns lights and was satisfied that he was not alive and had not been discovered yet.

Tina told Shannon about Mays attacking her and that he confessed to killing their parents. She told Shannon that she killed him in a rage.

The O'Leary sisters never spoke of it again. Neither did I. We made a solemn pact.

When I returned to the Marriott, the sisters had passed out holding each other in the motel bed. The pillows were wet, likely from a flood of tears.

They looked terrible. They looked beautiful.

Chapter 69

Three days after Boston, Tina called me to invite me to an O'Leary family council meeting at Smokey Joe's. I was worried sick over her emotional state. I could not clear my mind of the frightening images of that night.

She had gathered her frazzled nerves after a day or two I assumed because I heard her steely resolve return to her voice to expose her bosses as crooks. She also said, "I love you, Mr. Ford. You and I were an incredible team up there. I never felt this way before about any man. I mean it. Now, let me be. Come to the family council, please," and quickly hung up. That was worth the three day wait.

She was back, and closer to me than I had yet known.

She asked me to come a half hour later than everyone else. They needed some hugs, she said.

When Lane and Shirley were alive, the O'Leary's used to get together occasionally to hash out any serious problems.

I was honored that she invited me to attend.

I arrived on a Sunday evening when the café normally was dark. In the shade of the mountains I thought I saw her with a dog outside. It was Shannon with Shirley's dog Mencken. She said hi and as I approached she made no effort to come any closer.

I hugged her and asked, "Is this Mencken?" And, then, "Oh, I'm sorry. You are Shannon; my mistake."

I've heard that identical twins expose separate identities only through motion, muscle tone and habits after the years of separate environments.

Shannon was gracious, "Tina's inside, Hank. And this is indeed Mencken, mother's best friend. And hey, don't be sorry. I needed a hug too."

"How have you been holding up/" I asked Shannon.

"I can't stop crying. But, I'll be okay. Tina is the strong one and she will see me through." She looked away, knelt to pet the dog and then looked up at me. "It is one of the most beautiful things in the world."

"What?"

"The love an animal can have for a human being. Let's go inside."

Just inside the door, Tina announced, "Everyone, this is Mr. Ford, Henry Clyde Ford." Tina must have told them about our little joke names: Mr. Ford and Miss O'Leary, because no one laughed. Along with the twin sisters, there were their older brother Thomas and his wife, Joe and Eloise, and me. Her younger brother Colin was not in the café.

"I know this is just family," Tina continued, "but Mr. Ford and I are more than friends and he is a ..."

Joe cut in, "Tee, that mean Hank is your man? Hey that's ..."

"Shut up Uncle Joe. I'm sorry, didn't mean that. But please wait if you want to talk about the friendship of Mr. Ford and me. It is not important."

I felt that! But, I understood the context.

She continued, "Mr. Ford, you know my Uncle and Aunt Eloise. You know my twin sister Shannon there. This big guy in the suit, fresh from his work, is my brother Tom and he is here with his wife Madeline. He's a realtor in Wheeling. And my younger brother ... where is Colin?"

Joe said, "He went up into the press room."

Tina said, "Yeah, well Colin is a mechanic here in Patrick. The best auto mechanic in the state and can fix anything that runs on gas or electric, or maybe steam, anywhere. Right, folks?"

They all nodded in agreement.

We all sat around a large corner table at the end of the café in a circular red vinyl booth. I sat to Tina's side, who was on the end of the seating facing patriarch Joe positioned at the other end.

"Uncle Joe, please, before you get us started, let's ask Mr. Ford if he has anything to say?" asked Tina.

"Yes," I said, "and I'll be brief. Vacation, the corporation we are dealing with here, has now purchased the entire east side of Green Tree Mountain along Route 6 and overlooking Crater Lake, the Garrett property, and own more than that sliver they first had. I just learned that the county has pushed a rezoning petition from Vacation to the top of its Planning and Zoning Board of Appeals agenda. The petition requests a change from agricultural to commercial zoning. I for one would like to know if this is unorthodox. The hearing is in just three weeks from now rather than two months forward as usual."

Tina's brother Tom, the realtor, answered briefly, "Yes. I would say so. It is unorthodox. But we can go into the logistics of that later; if that is okay, Hank. If by miracle, the rezoning is not approved, the purchase can be rescinded in some cases too."

The O'Learys grumbled and rustled, and then Joe said, "Okay, let's get started then. We all know what Tina found out that these bastards are so degenerate, that they resort to murder, that they were probably behind the death of my brother Lane and Shirley, Mr. Manny and God knows who else in other parts of the country that may be unfortunate to be infested with these vermin."

Everyone talked at once:

Tina, "I'm sure of it now."

Shannon, "Tina, how can you keep working for them?"

Tina, "I won't for long. First I want to expose those bastards as frauds and criminals for cheating their guests, investors and communities they've infested."

Joe, "Okay, what are we going to do to stop them?"

Tom, "I can think of ways."

I jumped in to slow things down, "Folks, I think a good start is to stop the rezoning. There is enough evidence to show they are crooks, but the federal Security and Exchange Commission has yet to catch them doing anything illegal. They will, but it might take time."

Again, all at once:

Tina, "There is plenty of evidence."

Shannon, "Then, let's go to the police."

Tom, "Sheriff Deeds? You're kidding. He's lazy; can't find Manny's killer."

Tina, "Mays did it ... ah ... I heard he did it."

Joe, "This is no local matter, right Hank?"

I stood and started to pace. Before I opened my mouth again to no avail, I felt I should try to rouse them up because they knew so little. But, I wasn't that familiar with the family and thought better of it. *This is their family and they should move at their pace,* I thought.

Instead of trying to stir them into some kind of action, I said, "Let's start with a broad perspective. If what you say is true, that they will stop at nothing, even murder, how is your family going to go up against a mob like this?"

I was prepared to answer my own question as I told Tina on the cell phone earlier in the day driving up to the meeting. I said, "Well, there is evidence of fraud in this company and we have excellent witnesses to it. For example, the former CFO, Mr. von Kindel, is willing to show that the company is inflating its guest membership numbers and its revenues. We now have access to copies of their fake membership records that contrast to their real membership records, thanks to Mr. von Kindel.

"Also, a guest at Trout Heaven, a Mr. Robert McGarrell and his family were cheated out of their so-called guaranteed free first vacation. He looked into the finances because he is a former employee of Vacation's financial consulting firm. Tina has met with him.

"Then there is the manager of the Trout Heaven Vacation Inn, Mr. Hancock. He is local and you may know him. Hancock has evidence of their crooked dealings that went on within the Inn, gathered from his secret video recordings. He has video of the top executives threatening the lives of the last surviving member of one of the Crater Lake shoreline properties, the Smythes. It's on tape. I saw it. Tina said I can tell you."

Joe was outraged, "Not Donnie. Oh my. I was hoping he'd marry and settle down by now. Raise some children to take their land over. My heavens, Tina. Are you saying they want the Smythe land and only Donnie is in their way? Did they threaten your life too? Get out now, Tina, like Shannon said."

"I can't," Tina replied quickly. "I'm okay as long as I finish my last month at Trout Heaven. I don't intend to start my promotion in Boston. Being here, I'm too visible for them to mess with. Don't worry."

Joe said, "Why not turn the recordings over to the sheriff? I know Roger would know what to do with them. And, he'd have to follow up, if for no other reason than all the free meals I serve up to him and his deputies."

Tom responded, asking his wife Madeline, "What about that Maddie? She works for the state police, Hank."

Madeline O'Leary shook her head, "Can't risk it, no. Sheriff Deeds might blow it and tape recordings are no good in court testimonies."

Joe thanked her and added, "Well, something has to be done. They are bullies and buying off our county, folks."

I added, "Madeline is right. And, about Donald, no one knows where he is. We only know that he and the Macintyre boys went fishing after the big rain storm we had that Thursday night and Friday morning. That was the last time anyone has seen him. Johnny and Jeb say they don't know where he is or if he is alive or not. The worst clue comes from Hancock. The following Tuesday afternoon, Goodbred asked him to set up a conference call to their Boston headquarters. Hancock of course listened to the conference call and watched on his secret set up. It was about Donald. Mays indeed had sent a couple of heavy weight thugs into the lake with a high-powered cigar boat after Donald and Jeb launched Friday. If Donnie doesn't sell to them and dies the property could go to auction."

Tina was crying and ran away from the table, "Damn Mays, for the love of God?"

One side of my heart wanted to go after her as she leaned on the lunch counter to gather herself. The other had to reach out to the family. They needed the full story right away.

I said, "On Hancock's video, Goodbred asked Mays on the conference call to Boston if the 'speed boat' recovered Sunday morning belonged to him. Mays admitted it, though he had an alibi, his trip to Boston earlier. When Goodbred told them Donald Smythe was still missing, Hancock could distinctly hear Levine scream in the background, and I quote, 'Goddamn it Mays, I told you to scare the kid not kill him.'"

The room filled with a collective gasp.

I added, "They say Levine is not a violent man, just a greedy cheat, right Tina?"

She returned to standing at her place, "Yeah, I guess so."

I waited a moment and then said, "You might have heard there were three large gun blast holes in the cigar boat hull which had capsized."

Tina returned to the table with a napkin to dry tears, "Maybe Donnie's alright. We can't worry about that now. Mr. Ford, the evidence against the Vacation Inn boys you've mentioned is good, but tell them about the icing on the cake, about the New York attorney we have."

"Okay. Valarie Moore says Goodbred and Levine physically and verbally abused her daughter, who was injured and almost died on a Christian fellowship trip to Luray Caverns. Counselor Moore is a top corporate expert on merger and acquisition law. She is suing Vacation for personal injury. That may keep them from escaping to their Swiss bank accounts before they are nailed by the law."

"Whoa!" said Tom, "Gotcha."

"Yeah, maybe the best thing yet, Tom," I said. "She met with me and the Washington Inquirer business editor Devin Shay. We compared notes and she has confirmed what Shay has unearthed, signs from Vacation's own accounting records of criminal intent to fraud stockholders, investors and their own guests. Much of what he spotted was confirmed by data from Tina's friend in the accounting department at Vacation. Moore and Devin have found enough SEC reporting tricks the corporation uses to hide law suits and inflate the values of companies they have bought or merged with in order to put them out of business.

"And again, it will take some time for the SEC to digest what we have and act."

"Write it up, Hank, don't wait another day," said Joe. "Do it now, boy. You can tear them down."

I held up my right hand, "Wait a minute. That is possible. However, we don't know how to make all this public without a lot of people, including possibly Tina, getting hurt."

Joe pursued his point, "You go put it in the Washington Inquirer, Hank. Just like you always do. Why else are you here, sir? Why stay in Trout Heaven?"

"I'm afraid to put it into the Inquirer just yet."

Shannon said, "Henry Clyde Ford, one of the most feared journalists in America, afraid? Of what Hank?"

"In my business, it is not viewed as solid reporting if you are in love with your principle source," I said anxiously.

I was not real comfortable confessing my feelings in front of Tina's entire family, but this was indeed my dilemma professionally. I sat and ran my fingers through my hair nervously. "I had to say that. Shannon, I do love your sister. Tina may not love me like I do her, [Tina's eyes said yes, before she looked down at her hands folded on the table.] but she is 100 percent the reason I am doing this. I am fortunate to have met such an outstanding woman.

"Thank you for the compliment, Shannon; perhaps you are right. I am a well-known writer. I don't need this story professionally. There are many other white collar scandals out there to stir my reporter juices. But consider this: if my relationship with your sister becomes public, the story loses credibility. Vacation Inns, Goodbred, and the rest of the gang could get away scot-free to Switzerland. I think I've been blinded to that reality until lately."

I looked at Tina for some help, but she still wore a blank expression.

I got back on track with, "I do have another bit of news. It is news that would release me from this fight in another way, my cabin property. This morning I purchased another piece of land on the western branch of the Sassafras River from Mr. Hancock; you know, the inn manager?

"I agreed to sell my 29 acres to Vacation Corp. as they wanted, with what is now a God-awful view of tacky Trout Heaven. The view that once drew me here—the river, the forest, the virgin hills—became the new town's clear-cut development, stripped naked of all the mature forest to the top of Charity Mountain.

"I gave the money back to Hancock in exchange for him selling me a nice property with a good view. It is not like I lost or sold out to them. They would get it somehow. It was my way of bonding with Mr. Hancock who has huge medical expenses in his family. He will now be set for many years with the cash I turned over to him and his ailing wife, and I'll get my view back."

Joe stood and took on an air of the wise patriarch, perhaps sensing my discomfort as an outsider. He said, "Well, if you can't, or just won't, expose these folks in your Washington Inquirer as we had expected until now, who will? We can't do it by ourselves. But, if I know this family, we will find a way, Hank. Thank you. Anyone?"

Tina's younger brother Colin—hands, arms and white t-shirt covered with grease—appeared on the top step of the staircase coming from the second story newsroom, "Yes we can. I got the press started."

Tom shouted, "At a boy! Colin means we can revive the Weekly!"

Colin said, "Yeah, you guys. That's what I said to Tom this morning, if I could only get it squeaking' and pumping' again. Listen to it, guys."

The slow-cranking machine sounded strong and well oiled.

Tina finally spoke up. She put both palms flat on the table and pushed herself to her feet warily, as if she were a rheumatoid senior with a painful back. She slowly raised her eyes, took my hand and squeezed while scanning the eager faces. She said, "I do. I do have the time because I will make the time. While we were away last week, Colin and Tom found that last edition of the Weekly on Daddy's computer. Jack Mays, Goodbred's strong arm security man, tried to intimidate me when I was at their headquarters in Boston. He told me my parents were publishing scandalous lies in their latest edition. I told Tom.

"It was on Daddy's computer. Daddy had trusted Tom with the password, right Thomas? I think daddy and mother were delivering bundles in the car when they were killed. What was the lead header on the opinion page, Thomas?"

"Vacation Inn: Recipe for Fraud," said Tom.

Tina quickly, "Mother wrote a highly critical op-ed. In it, she references criminal activities of the corporation that were reported from other regions in newspapers across the country. The collection of allegations came before I was hired. I do remember daddy talking about the Vacation group, but that was that. Our parents still wanted me to take that job, despite what they knew. Makes you think, doesn't it?"

Tom added, "I have the time too, Hank. I can handle real estate ads for The Weekly from here several days a week. I worked with Dad and Mom before Tina and Shannon were grown. And the zoning questions are right up my alley."

Shannon said, "Don't forget me. Let me be copy editor. I can do that remotely from my nursing office at the hospital in Charleston. I'll just hope no one gets sick next month."

I asked, "Are you all sure of this?"

Colin yelled, "Damn sight yes, we are sure. I work right here in Patrick. The Patrick Weekly printing press will be my hobby hot rod. Love to bring her up to speed. When do we publish the first edition? There is newsprint in the storage room wrapped in plastic."

"You need a big splashy headline to launch it," I suggested. "Let's have a town hall meeting of citizens. We can also form a citizen's group to organize it and to oppose the rezoning, which, if unfortunately approved, will put Vacation all the way to the shores of Crater Lake. If that happens, the Macintyers could be priced out of their livelihood, the charter business. I like them."

"Me too. You know though, I think they would like to do it," Joe said.

"Do what?" I asked.

"Lead the citizen's group from their business right on the lake there. Don't you think? They have the most to lose at this stage."

Young brother Colin jumped in, "Jeb and Johnny hate those Vacation guys now."

I asked, "Now?"

Colin said, "Yeah, they did this big promotion with the Inn, discounts on charter fishing. The Vacation excecutives went, right Tina?"

Tina, "I was there. They broke everything on the boat. Johnny relaxed his ban on drinking. Just to get the promotion off right he compromised his principles. The Macintyers, we all know, are devout church goers."

I added, "Except for one time when the boys skipped out and took to fishing with Jesus."

Everyone laughed and Tina continued. "I was last off the boat and Jeb was fuming. It seems Goodbred himself threatened him and said he would get his land. Jeb said he just played dumb Yocum so well that Goodie would take him lightly and lay off. Also, I've heard rumblings in the company, fear of the locals. They are spreading rumors of the locals forming armed gangs. Does this sound like Sassafras County, you guys, or a paranoid flock of Northeastern city slickers out of their element?"

Tom said, "Hank, get back to this town hall thing. Would we need to put an edition out to announce a protest meeting?"

"No, my friend and one of my heroes Lois Gibbs—you know, the Love Canal lady? Well, she now runs the Center for Health, Environment and Justice Clearing House Against Hazardous Waste. She advocates that town halls can back–fire if they are publicized as protests, rages against the machine, if you will. Lois told me that a town hall designed to fuel opposition to big corporate injustice should be monitored by an independent yet non-political officer, who has invited the population to the party to air out the issues. Is there a volunteer fire department?"

Colin, who was still sitting on the second floor steps, shouted, "Fire Chief Barnes. He listens to me. I keep their trucks running. Would the fire hall in the county seat of Mt. Beacon be a good place for this?"

Tina laughed, "God, Colin. I swear you've got all the brains in the family. Can you ask John Barnes if we, I mean the citizens can book his hall?"

Tom added, "And Colin. Do it soon. The hearing is in only three weeks. Don't forget now."

Colin, as the exasperated little brother, replied as he stepped down the stairs, cell phone in hand, "Yeah, yeah. Tone it down will you, Tom? I already dialed Chief Barnes' house. "Hello, Chief? Colin O'Leary. 'member you said if I ever ..."

Colin had Barnes on his cell and walked outside for better signal strength.'

As the O'Learys watched their clever Colin go outside, I said, "Folks, I've got to go to the newspaper. They are expecting this story, which I don't intend to write yet. I am stringing them along and have some explaining to do. I think your plan for reviving the Weekly and asking the Mac family to help is fantastic. I'm with you 1,000 percent. I can't write copy. I can't edit copy. But I can be your managing editor." I looked at Tina, who appeared sheepish.

I was ready to give my parting speech, which I had mulled it over and over, "I just want to leave you with the bottom line as I would report this story. There are major accounting irregularities that are being delayed and covered up by the corporation until a planned merger with Princess Resorts and Spas of Europe is completed. That merger plan by Vacation is a hoax, right Tina? We know the truth. Instead, they are plotting to sell the corporation lock, stock and barrel to those same Europeans. Most of the Vacation Inn executives plan to flee with their millions and, in some cases, billions in cash before Vacation folds. Vacation has to report the irregularities this year. This deal will come down right after the annual report is published in January. We are in a race to slay the giant before then. Good luck. See you all soon."

I was almost out the door when I heard Tina, "Wait, wait Mr. Ford. Wait." She was running after me.

I walked halfway back into the café to meet her. Instead of talking to me, she turned back to the others and said the most brilliant thing yet, "Let *me* organize the town hall meeting."

No one said anything. Everyone just sat with their mouths open, in shock, until Joe broke the silence, "Yes! I get it. Tee's in a perfect position to make them appear to be the victims first, just like the best of Hank's investigative series, right?"

I was intrigued.

Tina explained, "Yes, here is what I see us doing: Start the paper. Raise hell. Excite the citizens. Then I will try to convince Goodbred that he thought up the idea of a town hall meeting. I think he will take the bait, that is, after I offer him a report on how the community is uprising. I will convince him that the community is in need of full explanations from the out-of-town corporation. I will tell him that only I can arrange for Vacation Inns to run the town hall meeting because I know the people here. I will say this will be his opportunity to sell the community on the benefits of the expanding resort—jobs, tourist dollars, you know the script, Mr. Ford. Meanwhile, we can plant our experts in the audience, those people Hank mentioned tonight and maybe more.

"Each of the critics Mr. Ford mentioned will come prepared with a script to tear them down—Bob McGarrell, Valarie Moore, somebody from the Inquirer, Max von Kindle and local property owners they've harassed, not the least of which is Johnny or Jeb Macintyre. Does anyone think this is a good plan?"

The entire assembled group stood and cheered.

Tina, beaming and energized, asked, "Shannon, please ask Colin to call me at my office at the inn in the morning."

I was bowled over. I said, "I get it completely. So, you will be in charge as public relations of the speakers, the agenda, who to invite and what Goodie and the boys plan to say. We will have the revolt in our hands waiting in the public audience and the press to ambush them."

Tina was ecstatic, "Yes, yes, yes. We can do it. We can bait and switch. They will think it is their day to crow and face the community complaints. Can the outside media attend the town hall?"

"If they hear a fight brewing out here, yes," I said.

Everyone cheered again and joined me and Tina in the middle of the café. The family hugged us both and I said my goodbyes.

Colin came in from outside wondering about the cheers, "Hey, what did I miss? What's happened?"

Chapter 70

Tina began spreading her cover story as soon as she returned to work at the inn. She told people that her family was blessed because a prominent publishing group in Virginia has purchased rights to her parent's former newspaper the Patrick Weekly for a 'handsome sum'. She told everyone why she wore such a self-satisfying smile, which many people had noticed.   Mary thought Tina's performance was spectacular, complete with hand wringing, moaning and even tears as she said the money would finally allow her elderly aunts and uncles, many former coal mining workers, to retire in comfort.

She called me to brag about how everyone bought her initial foray, the cover story. I told her I couldn't have invented such a great cover and congratulated her.

* * *

The first thing I did back at my desk at the Inquirer was to ring up Devin Shay in his upstairs office with a surprise that was sure to annoy and piss off my friend. It couldn't be helped. I asked him to meet me at Starbucks ASAP.

When he found me in a back corner of the coffee shop, Devin was already upset. "Whatever this is, it better be good news on your Vacation Inns story because I am totally underwater today, Ford." He then seemed to notice my worried face. "Hey, you look terrible. What is it?"

"Devin, I can't report the story after all," I said. "Please do me a favor and assign someone in your section to cover the scandal at Vacation." I foolishly tried to convince Devin that a town hall meeting pitting the Vacation execs against protesting citizens was a golden opportunity to corner the Vacation top dogs. "An eager young writer would eat it up," I pitched, leaving out the venue, a dinky fire hall in a remote county.

"Are you nuts? No way," he said as he spit out a little of his first sip of coffee.

"Listen, Kevin. It is a broader business story than at some little town hall. The citizens are protesting new zoning favors from the county. I think Levine bartered free memberships or something to the zoning board chair. They are going to hold the town hall meeting in the open, at … ah, at ah, a fire station to convince the community of their good intentions." I was showing my anxiety.

"Hank, stop!" Devin put down his coffee cup and stared right through me.

I faked ignorance of his concern, "What?"

"You know that I know that this is not you, Hank. Stop this bullshit. What's the problem? You are not really talking about an official zoning and planning committee meeting way up there. It's local news, buddy."

"It won't be only local and you know it. This thing is going to explode. Listen, I will buy you coffee, dinner, ice cream, anything for the rest of our careers if you help me clear this with Mrs. Grayson. I hear she is expecting a big expose of these creeps."

Jennie Grayson was the Inquirer's savvy publisher.

"Yeah, I'm getting pressure to deliver it."

"I can't do it. I can't … ah, God," I looked off to nowhere in particular for courage. I was not aware that I was pleading.

Devin leaned back, sipped more coffee calmly knowing he had me pinned, though he still didn't know why. "So, what's the problem?" he asked. "You are the corporate assassin, Hank. I'm just a drone on the business beat."

"Okay. I need to come clean. I can trust you with the truth. I'm in love with my primary source. That's the problem, Devin. I can't do the story. It is not ethical. Besides that, the thugs in this group would kill her if they knew she was talking with an investigative reporter."

He looked like he didn't believe me. His mordant expression screamed, 'Another middle age fool, clinging to his youth, lost in lust with a young piece of ass.' He asked instead, "The red head our intern spotted with you? [I nodded.] Nice Hank. Congratulations. But, let me ask you something?" He leaned into my face and tilted his head down to look at me over his glasses.

It crossed my mind that Devin was too decent to ask about the sex.

He didn't. He gave me his typical clean shot, hitting the bull's eye. He said, "What the fuck are you doing?"

I didn't flinch, "I need you to meet some people, especially the red head, the reason I can't report the story. We need to talk this out. And I am hoping we can come up with some explanation to [managing editor] Ben Tucker and Mrs. Grayson."

"No, Hank."

"Okay, please then."

"No, Hank."

"Why not? Do you know something I don't? Does Monroe have more than we think at the Times?"

Devin then admitted, "That's partly why I've been reticent. I think he is going to beat us if you can't get your dick off the redhead long enough to put the story together. You got me into this."

"Shut up Devin. Fuck you. I don't care." I stormed out and threw a $20 bill at him for the coffee. It hit him in the nose. I was sorry about that.

When I got to my desk, I had an email from Mrs. Grayson: *Hank, need to see you immediately, signed Jennie Grayson, publisher Washington Inquirer.*

Chapter 71

I was the last of several people to enter Jennie Grayson's top floor suite.

Devin was sitting down on a pleated leather bench. But, the others with Mrs. Grayson, managing editor Benson Tucker, assistant managing editor Hanna Quincy, and Devin's top young reporter Erich Lindstrom, were settled in and cordial, leaning on bookcases and chair backs as if they had been there a while.

Jennie Grayson was 76, gray, that is, her hair, her skin and her eyes—a very bland look of granite—with well-defined worry wrinkles. But she always wore smart, bright colored skirt suits seen more on much younger women.

"Come on in, Hank. Sit there," Grayson said with a smile while summoning me to a fine, white upholstered stuffed chair of splashes of red roses in the middle of her office. Not only was it the best chair there, but I was the only one facing Grayson dead on who sat behind a huge oak desk and surrounded by my colleagues. She wore tortoise shell shaped Eyebobs, which are oversized, designer glasses that looked ridiculous on the old gal. Besides that, Jennie had bad eyesight of a seasoned editor, which made her eyeballs half the size of the Eyebob frames. It was intimidating by being the focus of those huge peepers, which seem primed to explode at any second.

Instead of sitting as ordered, I chose to stand behind the big chair and lean, fearing I was about to be interrogated. Figured I had earned such a privilege.

Jennie said, "Thanks for coming Hank. Ben, you want to take it from here?"

My managing editor Tucker, rotund, short, wrinkled shirt tail half out, asked me, "Can you clear something up for us Hank? Jennie has seen a futures note on Devin's story budget in the business section for more than a month about a scandal at a motel chain. The slugs are always vague. She wants to know why the story hasn't run."

"If you mean Vacation Inns—they don't call themselves motels, actually …

"Yes, yes, Hank. Where's the story?" demanded Tucker. He was not a happy camper to be summoned into the publisher's office.

"I don't have a story on Vacation Inns," I said as I faked a cool composure.

I was about to get blasted.

"Well somebody does have that story. And, we seem to think you do," Tucker said, face flushing red, as he wheeled his right arm in a gesture to include the others.

Devin rescued me, "Hank, it's my fault. I thought something was coming, that is what you told me. So, I've been adding it to the bottom of Erich's story budget. Sorry if I overstepped." Devin was a better liar than I expected.

Tucker cut in quickly, "Will somebody tell me if we have a story on Vacation Inns or we don't have a story on Vacation Inns?"

Jennie Grayson remained deafeningly silent. I felt her growing impatience. Her eyes opened even wider. Her head tilted in wonder.

"Mrs. Grayson," said Devin, in his most respectful tone, "Hank came to me with some SEC notes on Vacation Inns and Resorts. He thought it would be in my basket. I believe we will have a story on corruption, a sort of Ponzi scheme by the executives who are running up false revenues and phony acquisitions. Right, Hank?"

"That is right, sorta. I've been tied up; thought Devin's staff could jump on it right away. Not much was there for weeks, right Devin?"

Devin started to answer, but Tucker cut in again, "Yeah, Hank's been under a lot of pressure with other leads, Jennie." He seemed to sense an escape route and buy in. Tucker's face lightened up. "So, if that is all, we will take our leave and look forward to the story soon."

She nodded, "Good afternoon, gentlemen. Thank you."

The four of us were silent in the elevator down to the newsroom until the door opened and Tucker was suddenly showed his angry again and demanded, "Ford! Shay! In my office, now"

I was glad Hanna and Erich were not invited because I needed to come clean on my entanglement with the beautiful young redhead—the description of gorgeous being the only identification the men would likely remember, not smart, dynamic, or humane.

"Close the door," Ben said, crashing into his desk chair and lifting his feet onto the desk. He folded his hands behind his head and looked at me, saying, "So, what's been tying you up Hank? I'm sure you realize I covered for you in front of Jennie. Your stuff has sucked for a month, man. Now tell me, guys: what the hell is going on?"

* * *

Affable Ben Tucker had always had my back, always given me freedom and time to get the story. I could not lie to him. I told the two men of my affair. I told them the unlikely coincidence that the much younger woman had studied my reporting in graduate school and that her father, a local journalist, had also admired my work. She had wanted to meet me and brought a proposal from Vacation to purchase my land. It was in their way. They want a ski lodge there.

And, I told Tucker and Devin that the most unlikely timing of all was that we had a love affair going on before I knew anything about the trouble that Vacation Inns was in. I swore to that. I also told Ben and Devin the truth that I had agreed to look into it to protect her, not take advantage of a vulnerable source.

"When I also said she was the PR vice president for that very corporation, Ben put his head on his desk, then sat up and pounded his fists on it. He said calmly, "You expect me to believe such a cock and bull story?"

"It is the truth," I pleaded.

"Even if you said you bedded down your source while investigating Vacation Inns …"

"I didn't," I said.

"Well, even if you did, I could maybe just let that go and forgive you, especially if she seduced you to get you to sign off your property to her. You said you once considered that possibility."

"It occurred to me, yes. But, I didn't look at the proposal when I met her, no." This was getting too private, but I had to say, "I somehow seduced her after maybe the most enjoyable day of my life. I don't even know how I did it. It seemed mutual. We clicked and she was very consenting. It was a huge surprise to me as you can imagine. Can you keep this to yourselves, please?"

Tucker seemed to calm down a little, "Well, if you are thinking this looks bad, you are right. It would not look good for me to allow you to do this story either." He looked at Devin who just nodded in some kind of agreement, his head circling up, down, right and left. He looked worn out, exasperated.

I was pleased to be anticipating Tucker's plan going forward. He seemed to have come around. I sat down with great relief and said, "Thank you Ben. I was hoping for just that. I have too much respect for the paper, for the …"

"Get the hell out of here, both of you," Tucker screamed. "I want to see something on this mess soon, Devin. Hank, stay out of it."

My body snuck out of Tucker's office as my brain reminded me that I could not 'stay out of it' completely. What they don't know won't hurt anyone, I rationalized.

Chapter: 72

Relief!!!

I was free of that itch, my temptation to write a corporate corruption story while sleeping with the enemy, so to speak. Yes, I admit it. I still wanted to do it; couldn't help thinking how my story would run, even after the O'Leary family council when I declared that I definitely would not write it.

Devin assigned Erich to cover Vacation Inn's odd financials. Erich was young, about 28, but a sharp, serious minded reporter who was one of the few of us not yet divorced. He was fit, with dark brown hair, mustache and goatee. Erich never smiled and he liked to stick with local business stories, I was told. I didn't expect him to want the Vacation story.

My deal with Ben Tucker was to answer Erich's questions, but not to volunteer any information on the personalities, which meant the good, the bad, and the ugly behavior of Vacation's weirdo execs. I didn't even know if the Town Hall meeting would be on Erich's agenda. I already told Devin there would be one. Erich didn't have to ask me.

I also then had a clear conscience about helping Tina with her dilemma. I was so in love with this incredible woman, I would do anything for her, and anything to keep and protect her.

Chapter 73

Four days later, McGarrell returned to Sassafras County. We met him at Joe's.

Before Bob arrived, Tina's brother Colin met me at the door and told me the exciting news that the O'Leary's were laying out a first edition.

"Great," I said. "Now, remember what I said about using me; I can help as a sort of hobby in the eyes of anyone who might recognize me, and not as an Inquirer employee. As long as my name or byline does not appear I'm in like Flint," I said.

"Who?"

"It was a spy movie with James Coburn. Oh, long before your time. He plays a detective Flint who was fully committed to his cases. So, let me know when I can look it over before publishing, please."

"Okay. You are our secret agent." Colin quickly ran back upstairs to the press. He had only come down to greet me, for which I felt an extra dose of warmth and welcome from the family.

McGarrell settled into a booth. He shook Tina's and my hands firmly and got right into it, no coffee, water, food, just the facts, pouring out of this man's mouth in succinct order. He confirmed some of what we knew, but we played opossum and let him run on.

McGarrell said, "They give Wall Street exactly what they want all the time. After the main Vacation accounting department gets reports from its regional accounting departments, it uses a complicated formula to deceive regulators in their quarterly and annual charts and figures, and Wall Street sees only growth and buys in.

"You probably know that in the past two years, shares of Vacation have increased 400 percent. That's fool-hardy, folks. As you know, Tina, memberships are sold under different payment plans of one to three years. Revenues are recorded but the expenses are delayed for months, even years."

McGarrell's report confirmed Devin Shay's instincts of what Vacation was up to.

Said Tina, "Miss Rapshire, our membership and quasi-finance officer, mentioned that exponential expanding makes no sense to her because memberships are lagging recently."

The bitter, ex-G&M accountant continued, "Several years ago, they began to acquire more supply and distribution companies."

I asked, "Those would be the allieds?"

"Yes, many are allieds, some completely phony," he said. "More recently their acquisition of more and more real estate properties shows investors they will soon expand. It is a very clever deception. No longer could the bookkeeping sustain that level of growth in properties from their income. Tricky folks, these fellows. Wouldn't you say?"

I said, "Do you think this adds evidence of them planning their escape sooner rather than later."

"I think so," said McGarrell. "Friends at G&M told me they had thought of blowing the whistle when they saw receipts of purchases of Swiss chalets in Geneva and Zurich initialed by Mr. Levine. He may be nervous while Goodbred is just too arrogant to think he might get caught. Never has. He's Teflon."

"What else, Bob," I asked.

"The company's 'independent' auditors, Granson & Granson, are really part of the corporation," he said. "G&G reported potential irregularities to G&M in the last quarter of last year but the annual report only mentioned that the report was "under review" by the accounting department. They were delaying bad news to investors. "Your Mary Marinaro sent to me confirmation that Vacation purchased Granson & Granson LLC. G&G hired a team that specialized in travel and hotel firms. That team was headed by my firm G&M. We danced to their tune, I've learned."

I jumped in, "At the paper, we traced the Granson team, a husband and wife team of Harry and Harriet Wiggin, back to Florida A&M, Coral Gables. Goodbred attended A&M for one semester before flunking out and getting into the Smith Business School in Maryland where he didn't finish a degree their either. He stayed at the Wiggin's home."

Tina added, "Yes, he lists a phony B.S. degree from Florida A&M on all his biographical information and another from Smith."

McGarrell continued, "That fits his rep." McGarrell wondered, "Also, someone said to me that the accounting problems began to surface after an acquisition of a minor part of that European company?"

"Princess Resorts and Spas of Europe, or PRSE?" I asked. "What is that? Can you tell us?"

"Vacation's imminent purchase of the European company is said to be the beginning of the larger worldwide chain of cheap vacation resorts for lower income people," he said.

"Suckers you mean," said Tina.

McGarrell laughed and said, "Check out this double talk from Vacation's CEO letter in the footnote of its 8K report to the SEC."

He read from notes: *After consulting with our independent public accountants, our auditors, we have concluded that internal control, which we have relied upon for the life of our company, are inadequate to provide a basis for its independent public accountants to complete reviews of the quarterly data for the last three quarters.*

The auditors saw evidence of improper accounting, but decided not to push our independent accounting client too hard ...

"Nice cover, right? That is G&G, their company" said McGarrell, leaning back into the vinyl booth bench, nearly exhausted.

He agreed to give us those notes.

I think we both wanted to hug Robert McGarrell at that point. But there was more.

He sat up straight and then told us he could "prove" that Levine and Goodbred, maybe other officers, were investing in Swiss banking.

I said, "Wow, here is my cell number, Bob. Call me when you have proof." I felt my 'job' fishing for evidence of fraud, was nearly completed, except one supremely important thing: Tina was still vulnerable to their methods, deceit and vengeance, as an employee.

Tina made a signal to the kitchen for Joe. And then, she said to Robert McGarrell, "Bob, I think we can bring them down, with your help."

He said to both of us, "Are you willing to help get this stuff into the newspaper?"

I said, "Let's first see what strategy is best." I felt a bit guilty that McGarrell would expect me to report it.

McGarrell concurred, "Let's bust this thing wide open."

Smokey Joe arrived with his best plates. He was out of breath, but managed to say, "Mr. McGarrell, my niece said you deserve the best meal you ever had."

Tina jumped up to help Joe unload the serving tray.

Joe said, "Your choice, Porterhouse steak with wild mushrooms, mash potatoes from my garden and green beans and corn; or turkey with my special sausage dressing, mashed potatoes and gravy with kale and ham bits; or rainbow trout—not from Crater Lake, God forbid—but from Foster's Creek, with rice and creamed spinach, again from my own garden."

McGarrell was overwhelmed with joy, "I'll take the steak."

I also chose the steak and Tina took the trout, actually her favorite meal since childhood I learned. Joe joined us with liver and onions.

I was first to push away from the cuisine, "Miss O'Leary, can you start issuing press releases in coordination with your friend Mary?"

"Heavens, no."

"Let me finish. If Mary gets the okay to release word of particular uncertainties, there are ways of couching the words to tip off regulators. Trust me on this. It can be safe for you. Let's start with trade-off deals with other companies, called boomerang deals, right Bob? Have there been any complex deals lately that you can publicize?"

McGarrell, between bites of medium rare steak said, "Pro forma earnings reported in a press release can obfuscate the truth." He chewed and said, "Oooh, this is good. Excuse me." Then continued, "Pro forma earnings used to be a tool used by companies legitimately to signal investors what earnings of a company's new business would look like from a merger."

Tina thanked McGarrell and offered, "You brought some red meat on Vacation's shenanigans. And, confirming our research on the membership numbers? You needn't bother. I think I can take care of that part of the puzzle."

Chapter 74

Judging by emails to the paper, the revived Patrick Weekly was getting rave reviews. It was again available in groceries, barber shops, schools, and in all the old street boxes. Shannon hired young men and women in maintenance at her hospital to place missing boxes back where they had been. She prohibited family members participating in fear of being recognized.

The first edition wasted no time. A bold headline screamed, "Vacation Inn Grabs Land at Lake." At column right over the article was a sub head: "Fed behind them; execs 'turn over new leaf for county."

Also, below the fold was a box with smaller typeface introducing the citizen's group:

Citizens oppose rezoning Vacation Inn and Resort's purchase of Garrett property. The group claims county officials are being unduly pressured by big money to rush proposed rezoning into its next meeting agenda on October 3, according to Jeb Macintyre, spokesman for the newly formed Save Our County Citizen's Movement (SOCC'M).

Macintyre said Vacation's CEO Trevor Goodbred, "is not to be trusted." The Vacation Inns' top official took a drunken party out on Macintyre's fishing boat recently resulting in $65,000 in damaged equipment, he said.

"This man then threatened to bully his way into owning our charter service and harming those who would get in their way," said the SOCC'M spokesman.

At the bottom of a left-hand column on page two was the following identifying note:

The Patrick Weekly is the latest local newspaper owned and operated by Henderson Publishing, 705 Pennsylvania Ave., Charlestown, Virginia. (304) 388-6669. Editor-in-chief S. O. Henderson. (Shannon's maiden name served to anchor the paper legitimately, she said.)

I think she wanted to own a prominent role in the fight. The number was linked to a phone bought by a fellow nurse living in an apartment near Charlestown Children's Hospital, their employer.

The address on the notice however was for an unmarked warehouse of the hospital, which sets back from Penn. Ave.

Shannon and her friend set up an elaborate voice menu of publishing departments: dial one for, dial two for, etc. And, the final choice of "For any other questions, stay on the line" eventually rang to a new, unlisted cell phone Shannon kept with her at all times.

In two consecutive weekly editions, the O'Leary's cranked out vitriol news reports and op-eds under fake names, suggesting ulterior motives for Vacation Inn's "land grab" of the Garrett property on Crater Lake. One quote, from a Sierra Club official I knew, was the first reference to the Vacation Corporation "trashing" the environment around Trout Heaven, ignoring federal and state regulations.

Chapter 75
Trevor Goodbred's suite at the inn, 9:30 p.m.

"Oh yes, Tina. Come in," said Trevor Goodbred. He wore a green robe over bright green pajama pants and slippers. "May I call you Tina?"

"I've worked with you Trevor for a few years now. Of course," she said as she reminded herself not to tussle about or lean forward because she took the precaution again to carry her tiny digital recorder in her bra.

He said, "Well, you know I'm a supporter of your work. I am concerned that we treated you pretty roughly at that full board meeting in late July. I understand that Jack Mays was rough on you following the meeting, according to my nephew Bradley Armstrong." He paused and poured himself a drink. "May I offer you a drink, Tina?"

"No thank you, Trevor. It is rather late."

He didn't acknowledge her comment. "I hate to drink alone. Are you sure? Well, okay. To continue, we have all been so upset by the death of Jack, our extraordinary chief of security, I have not been able to get back to you. I guess the man made his enemies. Caught up with him, eh?"

"I wouldn't know."

Anyway, sorry we ganged up on you at that meeting. It was all in fun, okay?"

"Forget it. I should have focused more on marketing, not on those lake fish so much," Tina said, faking a modest attitude. "What was it you wanted to see me about? As I said, it is rather late, you know."

"Oh, it is? Sorry. The weasel Hancock left this under my door this afternoon with a note. It says, 'Sir, is this a concern?' Have you seen it Tina? It's a petition for citizens to fight our rezoning of the Garrett purchase."

"No sir, Trevor, I have not. May I see?" She acted as if she was reading the flyer for the first time. She told me later that she felt an anxiety attack coming on, feeling trapped in his private quarters. And, she wondered why Goodbred mentioned the Mays murder right away? Why was careful Trevor Goodbred in his pajamas offering up whiskey to her? Was he calculating a deal? Did sex enter his equation?

She wished bellboy Donald Smythe was around to stand outside Goodbred's door for her. But Donnie was still missing.

She jumped when Goodbred moved close and touched her on the shoulder.

"Oh, I'm sorry Tina," he said, removing is hand. "Are you nervous?"

"Not at all. Just didn't see you approach me. I suppose you want me to respond to this, perhaps form a strategy?"

"Absolutely. This can't wait until tomorrow. This group of trouble makers also took out an ad in this paper." He pushed a copy of the New Patrick Weekly into her midriff. "I'm told your father's paper has somehow been resurrected. It reminded me to speak to you and apologize again. I was told after the board meeting I had insulted your father. He ran a fine newspaper, Tina."

"Trevor, I'm sure your intent is not to make me uncomfortable in the shank of a long day. It just seems that way. Let's stick to the point, please. I can help you with public relations to counter the protests. In fact, I would like to get a plan on your desk by noon tomorrow. I am very grateful to be able to tell you that, as far as the Patrick Weekly is concerned, my family sold rights to it to a large publishing firm up state for a handsome sum. It will help our family elders get along in their silver years. It confirms to me that folks respected its journalistic reputation.

"And, I don't have any information on the ads or the content, if that is what you are implying by all this," she said, getting a bit too exasperated, I thought, while masking her emotions over his continuing comments about her parents. "The Weekly, as you surely must know, is the only local newspaper in the immediate region, so we need to counter this."

Backing up a step or two, Goodbred replied coldly, "Fine. Have that report on my desk by noon. It is top priority. Good night, Tina. Thanks for coming up." He turned and chugged down his drink.

Tina said she was hiding a grin as she closed Goodbred's door behind her. He had been trying to play her for inside information and, likely got frustrated and agreed to give her the reins in countering the activist group's opposition to the resort, the same opposition that Tina and I created. The awkward meeting with the boss had met Tina's goal easier than she had expected. She nearly walked off whistling a tune, and then caught herself.

Chapter 76

Tina told me Mary turned pale when they met in the accounting office after Tina told her about her late night meeting with the boss, when he seemed desperate and at times incoherent. "I asked her if perhaps he intended to act out a sexual fantasy."

"Not that guy," I suggested. "What did she say?"

"Mary said no, that Trevor would never take such a risk, but the rest of his behavior fits. They are not going to be derailed by a bunch of rowdy nobodies, Mary said. Mr. Ford, Mary knows about at least five deals at other Vacation Inn regions nationwide that just popped up suddenly and similar to the rezoning of the Garrett purchase to get to the lake. In all her years with the company, she's never seen six paradigm shifts at once"

I asked, "So, does she think that clinches it?"

"You mean that they are pushing perceptions of the corporation's value to the limits before selling off? Yes, Mary is sure of it, now. But get this: she advised me that because Goodbred would have no patience with a local uprising here in Trout Heaven, he needs me here because I know the local politics."

The two women agreed that it is unprecedented in the county that Vacation got the zoning commission to push aside all other county business to focus on its expansion. Tina showed me notes she took after meeting with Mary:

Just this week, Mary recorded major land deals on the road near to, but not actually at a small town near Hilton Head, on an abandoned lumber yard near a ski lodge near Glacier National Park, on Suwannee River marshes near the Everglades, and in the Santa Fe foothills near a casino--all potential stockholder candy.

"Mary said if they aren't learning Swiss Alps yodeling now, she is not an astute accountant. They are getting big time bold, Mr. Ford."

"Indeed," I said, "I sense it too."

Finally Tina said she ended her meeting with Mary by sharing her counteracting strategy of getting Goodbred and Levine host a town hall meeting to make their case for the Garrett property rezoning. Tina said, "You should have seen her, Mr. Food. Mary jump up and clapped her hands, then invited me to take a walk with her outside to get all the details from me."

Chapter 77

John Hancock was quite the snoop. When Tina also shared her thoughts with him on her weird Goodbred meeting, he bugged Simon Levine's usual room at the inn. Levine was returning to Trout Heaven, Tina informed Hancock, likely to help Goodbred deal with the local uprising. Hancock calculated that he had a fifty-fifty chance to eavesdrop on a likely private discussion: Levine's room or Goodbred's and Goodbred's room was off limits to even housekeeping when he was in town. Tina agreed it was worth the chance.

It worked. Goodbred came to Levine's guest room to discuss strategy for convincing locals at the town hall meeting of their altruistic and kind intentions for the new resort's expansion, but not before Hancock bugged the room with a sticky button transmitter under the mini-bar door handle. The spot guaranteed good reception because Si loved beer.

The bug picked up Goodbred and Levine clearly:

"She says the best way to beat the protesters is to do it publicly," Goodie told Simon. "Our resort is good for the community, lots of jobs, boost in the economy, and all that."

Levine was quick to warn, "It's a trap Trev. Somebody is running her daddy's news rag again and promoting these scumbags."

"No, Si. She said the family sold the paper. It checks out. Rights to the name, the style, and journalistic content were all protected. It was purchased by Henderson Publishing in Charlestown. O'Leary said her relatives needed the money for assisted living or something. She got pretty hot though when I tried to apologize for belittling the paper at the board meeting. I guess I shouldn't have made fun of that little paper. She's real sensitive about it, with her parents' accident, you know."

Levine said, "Yeah, yeah, that was so weird, just when they were giving us some bad press. Strange. Anyway, what the hell happened to the plan you had to fire her in Boston?" Levine asked superficially.

"That was Jack's idea and I agreed. I couldn't believe he made so much sense; like he read the books or something. Jack suggested that we get rid of O'Leary and all public relations people right away before we sell. They are great when we are growing. In a crisis or in this case when we want to dump the whole damn house of cards, any stupid PR moves could set us back."

"Mays said that?" Levine was astounded. "Well, we were invaluable to him, you know. Had built up millions in stock options from all the bonuses we gave him for protecting our properties. He was good I hear, but creepy sometimes, you have to admit."

Goodbred said, "I won't admit to such a thing. Jack was invaluable to me. Well anyway, he knew we are close and didn't want to be left with useless paper shares, I bet. He had been seen in accounting recently. He was asking about O'Leary's sudden interest in our books too. We do need to fire her soon. The fool had the biggest fucking hard on for Tina O'Leary. My nephew Bradley said almost all of Mays time when he was in Trout Heaven was focused on her whereabouts and activities."

"He was definitely distracted by her big time, Trev, even before Bradley came aboard. Maybe she found out Mays wanted to fire her and killed him," Levine said in all seriousness.

Goodbred laughed, "Get real, Si; she is a highly educated, refined woman. She'd have to be out of her mind."

"Guess so."

"No, it was clearly a robbery murder. He was still wearing his $1,000 tux and his body was found near the highway without his wallet or watch. Besides, she was with us when Mays was murdered. Remember? At the reception?"

"Maybe she hired someone to kill Mays. She acted like she hated the bastard," said Levine still stern and expressionless.

"Motive, Si. Motive."

"I could think of one."

"What then?"

Levine cowered away and changed his mind, "No. You are right. Wouldn't make sense. You say she has a plan?"

"Plan? Oh, yes. She says we can take the high road by inviting the community to hear us outline our support and interests in Trout Heaven, the regional headquarters here, and the amenities and jobs we will offer by expanding. She will reserve the fire hall in a nearby town called Mt. Beacon, she said, because it is a central location in the region, and set our agenda for a town hall meeting. Should work."

"Why not do it here? I still don't trust her."

"That's the best part. She advised me to do it here. That way it looks like we are making people come to us on our terms, she said. And, she said many locals are already mad about our intrusion into their world, as she put it. So instead, we do the proper PR thing and go to the people. Mt. Beacon is the county seat.

"And, with her promotion and a 60 percent increase in salary, plus hefty stock options—never mind that the notes will be worthless soon—she is surely on board with us by doing this. I think she will be a team player and help her hometown region. We had drinks in my room the other evening. She is aboard, Si. Hey, we have the best investment on this side of the Mississippi. We appear to be here to stay."

Levine said defiantly, "You had her in your room, with drinks?"

"Well, ah … "

"Stupid idea, Trev. You are trusting her and I'm not going to any town hall meeting. It is foolish."

"Oh, yes you are."

* * *

Goodbred left Levine's guest room. Simon then called his assistant in Boston and told Pauline that he did not intend to attend "any town hall circus O'Leary might cook up." He told her to reserve a return plane ticket to Boston.

Meanwhile, Goodbred composed the following email to Tina O'Leary, which she received the next day:

Tina dear,

Simon Levine and I talked over your idea. Go ahead with your announcement of our Town Hall Meeting to inform the community of our plans and benefits of their new resort in Trout Heaven. Make sure to ingratiate people to the huge success of the corporation in our 35 locations across the country. Mention that the membership benefits extend beyond the region to other Vacation Inns and Resorts, that membership privileges are to all of our exotic and glamorous resorts.

Levine's schedule makes him doubtful for the meeting, but I will moderate it and bring other board members. Email the announcement to Si's girl Pauline in Boston. Say she is to distribute it for a formal clearance procedure to the entire board. I will call you to discuss.

Genuinely yours, Trevor

Chapter 78

Two days later Simon Levine was sitting contently at his desk at corporate headquarters, according to Pauline, with the controversies at Trout Heaven a safe distance 400 miles away.

At Trout Heaven, word circulated that Levine had skipped town. Tina would have none of it. She wanted Levine's head. She hoped Levine would be forced to come back to Trout Heaven when he read his mail.

She said she could see their office in her mind and imagined the scene. Through the glass wall between their spaces, he would be watching Pauline wiggle herself out of her tiny desk chair in a tight white skirt and puffy pink blouse. She'd make eye contact with her boss. According to Mary Marinaro, the mere presence, the very scent, of sexy administrative assistant Pauline Hahn excited Simon Levine each time she brought in a visitor, made coffee for him, or just brought in the mail.

Pauline might be also wearing a worrisome frown when she implored him to open one particular letter first.

It featured a disturbing letterhead: *Save Our County Citizen's Movement (SOCC'M), Somewhere in Sassafras, County, Our Precious Community.* It was addressed to Mr. Simon Levine Vacation Inns Corp., 1000 Barnstown, MA.

A handwritten note, signed by just SOCC'M, was attached to only one piece of white paper, a flyer. The note read: This invitation is for you to attend a special zoning hearing and was sent to each resident of Sassafras County and surroundings. Hope to see you there.

It was Levine's personal copy of the public invitation. Tina and Jeb Macintyre had worked hard on composing and printing the flyer as a shocking diversion from their actual purpose for the town hall meeting. Tina wanted the executives to be prepared to answer environmental concerns of citizens as they had skillfully in many of their sloppy development sites in different parts of the country. Many of the points in the invitation were entirely bogus and exaggerated, just to agitate sly Si and clever Trevor.

Save Our County Citizen's Movement

Dear Citizen,

Help stop Vacation Inns and Resorts Corp. (VIRC) from ruining our County.

Offer your voice to oppose rezoning of 102 acres formerly owned by the Garrett Family on Charity Mountain. With this ill-advised rezoning, VIRC will have access to Crater Lake for the first time, breaking the private property lock on the shores of this cherished recreational waterway.

The corporation's purchase of the Garrett property is just the latest move to jam an unwanted massive resort onto our quiet communities. As the "hospitality" chain launched and expanded its Trout Heaven Vacation Inn during the past several years, **its leaders in Massachusetts have side stepped and ignored every environmental protection provision our state has imposed on the region during the past 20 years.**

Citizens need to know that county officials have not asked for any environmental impact assessments from these outsiders and have turned their heads as the VIRC made a mockery of our citizens by bullying their way through planning committees and our laws.

Apparently, the County officials' verbal acquiescence in closed door meetings was all the seduction VIRC needed with its promises of a tourism bonanza in economic development. But it was a lie, folks.

SOCC'M has learned that VIRC has also made an offer to purchase 29 acres ACROSS the Sassafras River to build ski slopes. The corporation now has a lock on our river resources too!!!

Please attend a special and hastily scheduled meeting of the Sassafras County Board of Zoning Appeals on November 17 to oppose VIRC's illegal and improper imposition on your life here in this once pristine and lovely countryside.

Points to make at the hearing:
- VIRC received **no runoff permits** to block and destroy streams that run into the Sassafras River.
- Forest clearing and excavation for their Trout Heaven Inn, the corporation's newest "resort," poured **millions of tons**

of unfiltered silt into our river. The same will happen to Crater Lake if the rezoning is authorized.

- **The development ignored federal laws for waste sediment ponds**.
- *In 1991, the state government declared the Sassafras River a Wild and Scenic River to protect its shores with proper buffer zones and wildlife habitat. VIRC has ignored recommended protections accorded.*
- *A rare habitat of the bucktooth, spotted lizard,* **an endangered species, was destroyed** *with illegal construction of the "resort's" golf course. Native son Hap Nickles, a PGA tournament champion called the course a design disgrace.*
- *Roads in and around the "resort" run straight downhill in many cases,* **against Mountain State erosion laws.**
- *SOCC'M has gained access to a secret VIRC plan for a Crater Lake waterways pier and entertainment center. The plan calls for fresh water wells to pump 450,000 gallons a week from our underground aquifer. Such a volume has caused* **surrounding residential and farm wells to dry up.**

Help stop the devastation of our region by a greedy gang of outsiders.

Attend the hearing, citizens!

Pauline told Tina that Levine screamed at the top of his lungs after reading the flyer. And then he screamed for her to call Goodbred to talk about it.

With Goodbred on a fund-raising luncheon with Wall Street Bankers in New York, Pauline located Tina first. Pauline was whispering and laughing on the phone all at once. She said Levine had immediately stood up like he had gotten a hot seat shock. He was waving the flyer as if it was on fire. The woman seemed completely disrespectful of her boss, Tina said.

Delighted, yet playing it cool, Tina told Pauline to email the flyer down to Tina. She asked Pauline to tell Levine that Public Relations' Tina O'Leary was shocked by it and that she would develop a counter strategy for the corporation's Town Hall Meeting next week. Tina meanwhile, still on the line, got an earful when

Levine walked to Pauline's desk ranting over the environmental points of SOCC'M.

Tina had to get off the phone quickly to conceal her outburst of laughter.

Tina called me in Washington next, "Mr. Ford, they took the bait. Pauline said Levine wants to address these "hooligans" and their "outrageous lies" at the Town Hall, just as we hoped. He wants to, and I quote him, 'head off these liars before our rezoning hearing.' I could hear him on the phone. The best part is that the flyer enraged Levine enough to make him come back here to Trout Heaven. Zing! They think the community's beef is about environmental destruction by the resort. Yes!"

I was not surprised by Tina's steely conviction to her fake "kiss up" relationship with her bosses. They had given their "PR girl" the generous raise. They evidently felt sure the raise held her loyalty in check and kept her fast within the fold of the corporation—she hoped so anyway. I was surprised by Levine, however. I told Tina, "Why go after Levine? I didn't think he liked you at all, Miss O'Leary. Is Goodbred fine with this?"

"Yes, right now Sly Si is booked on a private jet to New York to share my strategy with Tricky Trevor," she giggled with delight. "Have to go now, Mr. Ford. I need to write up responses to my, I mean those, hooligans' environmental complaints against our fair and generous firm. Bye!"

The next day, Vacation Inns and Resorts, Corp. released the following press release, which Tina had composed for Goodbred's signature:

Vacation Inns and Resorts, Corp.
Affordable memberships to nationwide pleasure

Recent environmental concerns raised by a few residents of Sassafras County on rezoning our recent property purchases are false.

Vacation Inns and Resorts, Corp. will present details of its environmental impact statement at our previously announced Town

Hall Meeting at the Mt. Beacon Fire and Rescue Co. No. 48 on Sunday Nov. 10 at 7 p.m.

    The allegation that we don't follow strict environmental standards is incorrect. Our corporation has abided by all county, state and federal regulations needed to legally and properly build and expand the Trout Heaven Vacation Inn and Resort so that we may serve you and visiting guests.

    Citizens attending our town hall will receive a Frequently Asked Question sheet of answers to untrue concerns about new roads, water and other utilities, excavation, fire prevention, and pollution control. In a show of faith in the community, our executive officers of the Vacation Inns and Resorts, Corp. will be prepared to address these and other questions.

    We are conducting the Town Hall Meeting in a spirit of community cooperation to keep residents informed of our progress and plans and invest all the citizens of our region. Thank you,

    Most graciously yours,
    Trevor Goodbred, president and CEO
    Vacation Inns and Resorts, Corp.
    Boston, MA.

Chapter 79

The erudite Trevor Goodbred would surely not recognize the Mt. Beacon Fire and Rescue Co. #48 as a firehouse. It was not an architectural marvel like those he might have seen in San Francisco, Boston, Chicago, nor even Hilton Head—locations he'd previously visited this year to scout out new spots for near-resort Vacation Inns.

By contrast, the Mt. Beacon's firehouse was just a firehouse, nothing more. No office space or dance hall, no state-of-the technology equipment.

Tina had hoped that the modest #48 firehouse of gray cinderblock with a stone facade might turn out to be a difficult PR venue for slick corporate players. She anticipated that Goodie, Si and company would find themselves nervously close to a tough audience of doubters and hecklers. She hoped so, although she told me not to underestimate the charm and persuasion of Trevor Goodbred at a podium.

There was that chance, she warned our group, that our trap could backfire and the Vacation Inn gang could hold serve and win over the crowd. They had money, the slick talk, and promised jobs and a world-class resort.

She warned, "Even with all of our good intentions, it is possible that we could lose this thing, big time, by risking a town hall as an opportunity to expose their cheating and deceptive methods."

The one-story stone firehouse structure was only 65 feet long with three garage doors and only one other entrance, on the side behind the restrooms. I thought how that ironically would not meet fire safety codes elsewhere.

We assumed correctly that the arrogant executives at Vacation would not feel the need to check out the venue, which their new vice president for public relations chose as "the best gathering place in all of the county and so ideal for our meeting where people who will hear and appreciate our plans to their benefit," Tina told me she said to them. Damn she was good.

Simon Levine may have had some doubts about their pretty PR lady lately but maybe not Trevor Goodbred, who, she told me, was becoming "a bit falsely smitten" with her. He had seen her outstanding work and was impressed. He likely felt they were in competent hands. After all, she knew the territory and they didn't. She told them repeatedly that the Vacation's Town Hall Meeting she planned would assure citizens of the good intentions of their extensive vision for a resort on the mighty Sassafras. She told him not to expect a big crowd. "This is a local issue, Trevor" she proposed, while she actually hoped to see a Little Big Horn-like massacre by great numbers of angry people.

Logistically, Tina chose Mt. Beacon for the meeting, despite the tiny fire department, because the town bordered on two other counties bordering Sassafras County.

Her sister Shannon sent the flyer from her apartment in to hundreds of stores, schools and libraries in those counties as well.

On any other day, #48's single fire truck would be parked just inside of the largest of the three garage doors in a section of the small building that was two feet higher than the remainder of the structure. Smaller trucks were normally stored inside the other two doors.

Tina told her bosses that there would be plenty of parking spaces for their big limos right out front because the fire vehicles will be parked behind the building. That part was true. It was Tina's brilliant, well-conceived trap, having additional audience chairs and then to get the newly arriving cars to park behind the limos for as long as it takes to keep the Vacation execs at the meeting.

We would work the small building-size to our advantage. The garage bays opened to a concrete apron outside that the fire department used for staging and cleaning the trucks. Moving farther out was an adjoining parking lot, all visible from the inside garage bays where we set up a podium and microphone at the far back. The Macintyers, Joe, Colin and Tom O'Leary and I set the meeting up on Saturday night beforehand, all on Tina's logistical instructions. I sprung for 200 folding chairs, extra hand-held mics, and a hidden video recording system.

The fire department owned another 85 chairs, which we set up as the official, visible chairs inside the empty garage bay, while we hid my 200 chairs behind the building. We planned to keep the garage doors closed until Goodie and his entourage arrives. The plan was that they would only see the inside chairs. The concrete apron and lot outside would be empty. She told them to park there. We would ask about a dozen early arriving citizens to be patient and wait outside until we opened for the meeting. Hopefully we could recruit teenagers from arriving guests to monitor the parking lot to keep it clear at first. Once Goodie's entourage was in the building, we'd put up the 200 chairs up on the apron and beyond and thus further block the Vacation Inn's limos from leaving early. The teenagers could then park additional cars behind the chairs. We would give them some cash.

All we had to do Saturday night and Sunday was hope and pray Tina's plan would expose the executives and the Vacation firm for what we knew they were.

Chapter 80

I didn't sleep at all that night before the town hall meeting for worrying about what could go wrong. It also would be one of the last nights I spent in the cabin before the property settlement.

Tina slept at the Inn. My mind and my body were numb with tension, knowing that she will now do anything, take any risk, to inflict just revenge on the Vacation creeps.

After all of our plotting and counter plotting, all the highs and lows with Tina and her family, all my covering up at the Inquirer, I suddenly felt helpless to control anything. The gamble at the little firehouse would have to play itself out without my hand.

We had amassed countless data and inconsistencies in their books and financial reports, all now shared with the Inquirer staff. We had audio recorded them conspiring to hurt locals, minus our recordings from Boston which we destroyed for obvious reasons, plus Hancock's recording of Levine and Goodbred discussing parachuting out with the cash. And, we had created a perception of the Trout Heaven Inn in violation of state and federal environmental laws and regulations. I liked the research as a reporter, a trifecta of threats—financial fraud, criminal acts, destruction of the environment.

As I tossed and turned, I wondered which, if any, of the three would be enough to take them down?

Again, I had never felt so helpless. For this critical moment, I was not the Pulitzer Prize writer any more, not a protesting citizen, not an employee of the inn, not a state official or businessman affected by the foul incursion of Trout Heaven Vacation Inn and Resort. My usual boundless imagination was betraying me. Instead of the pleasure of engaging my brain to contrive a plan of attack or even retreat from an unfolding story if we failed, my mind was spinning with the worst kind of thoughts and images.

And my worst image was reading day-after news of Vacation's triumph over the agitators. Suppose the media we invited, local TV and print reporters, even D.C. media on a prayer, ran stories supporting the grand promise of Vacation Inns for fantastic golf and skiing resort attractions? My worry was that they clearly had the fun story to tell, you see. It might weigh better than people trying to tear down nice men from Vacation, who were only just offering people a good time cheaply.

As I dozed off I was imagining the phony charm of Trevor Goodbred Tina talked about. In my dream, he was capturing the crowd's favor with offers of free vacations or jobs or even worthless shares of stock. I pictured a devastated Miss O'Leary sitting up there with him and getting exposed as the hometown girl turncoat or worse, the principle agitator of an angry crowd.

Helpless and alone with my head rolling about my pillow, I tossed in and out of horrible dreams. I then dreamed a bloody Jack Mays dragging a tied-up Tina in ragged clothes into the board room to face judgment for her crimes, while board members jeered and ridiculed her as a traitor. It was similar to the underground trials before the King of Thieves in the classic "The Hunchback of Notre Dame," with Tina the helpless gypsy girl pleading mercy for her people.

I screamed and sat up, only to drift off again.

And then, I dreamed of a column trail of massive green bulldozers rolling across the new state bridge toward my cabin but in silence. The door flung open and there was Goodie dressed in a green tux of rhinestones telling me, "Well now, if it isn't too much trouble my learned Mr. Ford, you will have exactly five seconds to get out. We've come to watch my angry friends outside knock you and your little spy house right off my mountain."

By 3 a.m., I was on the porch staring at the glimmering new town of Trout Heaven, which in the dark misty night actually looked quite harmless, even pretty. There was no escaping my horrible anxiety until Tina sent me a text, "All systems go. Lv ya." I texted back "Lv ya 2." She must have had insomnia too.

I went back to bed and rested well until mid-morning.

Chapter 81

The last of the fall tree colors, oaks and beech, painted streaks of dark red and yellow on the hills beyond the quint town of St. Beacon. The air was cool and fresh with a cloudless azure blue sky. It was the kind of autumn day in the mountains that Norman Rockwell might have enjoyed setting up his easel on the town square. He would perhaps sit in the bright warmth of the sun and capture freckle face boys carrying homemade fishing poles and a tin can of worms down to the river in the background. Or, perhaps he'd capture mom showing off her young daughter's new Sunday dress to the ladies on the church steps. Such idyllic scenes one could only wish to see that day. We had a far, far uglier prospect dead ahead.

Tina rode with Goodbred, of course, in the first of four shiny lime green limousines, which arrived early at 6:40 p.m. as she requested. He brought his entire board of directors and John Hancock and several managers from other Vacation sites in the trailing limos.

She said Goodie was speechless when he saw such an unpretentious stone building, the Mt. Beacon Fire and Rescue Co. #48 in black plastic letters spread evenly over the three garage doors and a few dozen people milling about, who appeared to be locked out. She said Goodbred's reaction was to suggest that 'Well, this shouldn't take too awful long.' He thanked her for arranging the meeting and 'looks like you are earning your promotion already, Tina'.

We could not take any chance that Goodie and his band of thieves might skip out of the meeting early. The four limo drivers parked in the VIP parking spaces right in the middle of the firehouse apron pad as she had instructed, "And please park facing the firehouse garage doors," she insisted.

The plan worked. As soon as the limos were parked per Tina's instructions, and the Vacation gang entered the fire hall by the side door, we jumped into action outside. We set up most of the 200 rented chairs around and behind the limos. There would be no early escaping for them. Three teenage boys we hired to monitor the parking lot began to let arriving people to park their cars behind the chairs.

The limos were soon entombed.

Also, despite the O'Leary's flattering of my investigative reporting skills, I stuck to my resolve that my byline should never appear in the Patrick Weekly. Instead, I would generate copy for Shannon and Colin to publish under pseudonyms. I sat behind a tiny window in Fire Chief Barnes office overlooking the hall. I could see the audience but the panel of speakers could not see me. John Hancock—God bless him, *again*—set up a television monitor where I could see the speakers though.

The fire chief told me with a sort of forgiving smile, "I only have two conditions. First, you can use my office here, but stay here. Don't be seen; you are famous and I don't want these folks knowing I'm helping you."

"And, second?" I asked, knowing the answer.

"Keep yourself out of the papers?"

"You got it buddy!" I said. "Good luck with all this confusion today. I just hope there's no three-county alarm this evening or a mining collapse."

"There won't be."

"Huh?"

"Everybody will be here," he joked.

About 50 citizens found seats inside facing the podium and people kept coming. On Tina's signal, which was simply tying her hair back, the Macintyre twins opened the firehouse garage doors, revealing more than 100 more people in the seats around the limos.

Tina said Goodbred muttered as he walked passed Levine to take his seat behind the podium, "Golly be. Hey Si, turn around. Look at all the new vacationers." Levine, camouflaged in jeans and flannel shirt with a wide brimmed floppy hat in the front row, sunk lower in his seat and sheepishly looked about.

Jeb and Johnny Macintyre stood on opposite sides of the fire hall, emptied of fire trucks but full of people, an audience by 7:15 swelling to more than 200 in folding chairs, and another 140 standing. The Macintyre brothers held portable microphones for people with questions.

Chief Barnes stepped up to a microphone, which teetered on a thin silver stand. "Folks, we all have heard of Vacation Inn and the Resorts expanding here," Barnes voice was then drowned out by ruckus booing. "Folks, folks, please. You'll get your chances. On your chairs, you will find, if you haven't already, an agenda that reads like this:

"Opening remarks from Vacation Inn CEO Trevor Goodbred ..." Boos again and louder. The crowd was angry.

"Folks, it is only courteous to give our new neighbors a chance to ...." Again boos. "Then we will hear from our former state Senator Jimmie P. Jenkins, who is a board member at Vacation Inns, and other officials. There is a sign-up sheet for your questions and comments circulating. Please keep your remarks in the public portion of our agenda to two or three minutes each. Thank you. Rev. Gideon Sugarman will give the benediction now."

The audience applauded politely for the popular, yet generally considered wacky, reverend. His prayer settled the hall down. Folks remained respectful for a while.

Barnes continued after the prayer, "Also sitting up here is their chief financial officer Reverend Anita Rapshire, the motel manager John Hancock, Sen. Jenkins, Public Relations Director Tina O'Leary and other members of the corporation. Mr. Bobby Macintyre, spokesperson for Save Our County Citizen's Movement, or SOCC'M, is in the first row and will speak after Mr. Goodbred for the citizens' group."

The hall cheered Bobby as if the high school football team just won the state championship.

Barnes finally restored order, "Okay enough of the crowd participation. We'll be here all night. I will introduce the other names on the agenda as we get to them. Mr. Goodbred? If you will, sir.

Trevor Goodbred nearly leaped out of his seat and bounded to the mic with high energy.

I had never heard Goodbred speak in public before. I will never forget that first time. To call his speech inspirational would not do justice to his remarkable Messianic persuasion, which, in my mind, put Sugarman and Rapshire into the preacher minor leagues. No kidding. He seemed to walk on air. His face became angelic and innocent in expression.

He began with soft, surprisingly calm, soothing tones of a young man in love with his betroth, "The river is quiet this lovely evening. (pause) The forests and meadow flora are retreating to winter. We are enjoying the last days of the sweet summer air of Appalachia. It is a season of reflection. My friends this is a wonderful place in the world and nothing I can say about our hospitality chain will dampen your spirits one drop.

"The other sites around the country where we have established low-cost, high-quality recreation and relaxation for busy lives are one and all the same. We have more than 50 resorts either operating or under development. They are all established in cooperation with local ordinances and environmental restrictions under state and federal laws. Nothing can be truer than the adherence to such rules, regulations and citizen considerations than at your inn at Trout Heaven, [Slowly, majestically, he raised both his hands over his head palms out to the audience.] My heavens, what a lake, huh?"

I knew right off this was a calculated move. Right on cue then, some people applauded and a few answered in measured voice with 'yeah' or even 'yes, sir'."

He was winning them over and I was getting sick to my stomach. Tina, sitting motionless next to Goodie's chair, turned pale it seemed on my TV monitor and she appeared to be hiding her face in her lap. I was worried.

Goodbred continued, but seemed to sense he had done his job and would likely then be brief, "This is about the lake, isn't it? It is about the river, isn't it? It is about the mature and diverse forests all around us, isn't it? I believe you. We need to protect the environment, number one, before my people at the inn make one more zoning request, add one more amenity, like skiing, boating, nature walks, or our Olympic-size pool in our futures case of blueprints, at our fantastic resort, make one more garden or plant one more tree. Thank you for welcoming us so graciously to the community and I want to make sure you enjoy our facilities here and around the country whenever you wish.

"Now, here is my friend and mentor, your own former Senator Jimmie B. Jenkins, brother of the vice president of these God loving United States of America, and, as a native, is a supporter of our work at Trout Heaven."

As Jimmie creaked to the mic, I realized that Goodbred had strategically skipped Bobby, who was scheduled to speak on the agenda next and was already standing.

I saw Bobby shrug and tilt his head looking toward Tina. He didn't seem to mind and sat back down.

Slowly, gracefully, Goodbred padded lightly back to his seat, with head up and shoulders back, as would a proud and feared despot having reassured his peasant populace.

Again, applause, polite, but most of the audience was clapping and seemed supportive of Goodie. Oh my, was I ever sick. He was winning!

Distinguished 87-year-old Sen. Jenkins wore a baggy three-piece gray suit with a wide pin striping. His white mustache matched his thick shock of hair. He meandered to the microphone help by a black cane with a big glass knob resembling a giant diamond. He spoke in a manner of a beloved elder offering his pearls of wisdom to wide-eyed adoring youngsters. He said, "What you are hearing is correct. The Vacation Inn folks want to buy and rezone property so that they can expand down to Crater Lake."

A squeaky voice of an elderly lady interrupted Sen. Jenkins abruptly, "You mean WE can expand to the lake, not THEY can expand to the lake, don't ya Jimmie. You ain't foolin' anybody here. You'z one of 'em." A restless crowd responded with uproarious laughter.

Sen. Jenkins just laughed along with everyone and replied, "Sure, I'm on their board of directors. I was flattered they asked as a retired official of these here hills, one of you folks, to help 'em. Sure, I wanted to give these fellows a native perspective. I met Trevor Goodbred who happened to knock on my door one day three years ago to introduce himself. I'm here to tell you he is a fine gentleman.

"Now my good friends and neighbors, there are two issues. The second issue as a former state senator I cannot or would rather not address. However, the first issue is the question of the process of rezoning I can address. It is entirely legal to make a request to rezone once Vacation Inns' has purchased a property, in this case Mr. Garrett's land. The company can file to rezone from residential farmland to commercial. We don't want industrial zoning, just commercial. We see it all the time and too much with the coal industry."

Another voice from the crowd, louder and angrier than the previous lady, shouted, "Yeah like Mr. Peabody's coal trains stole paradise down in Muhlenberg County? Never again, Henry."

The crowd murmured.

I sensed Goodbred's momentum waning. Goodie was shifting in his chair with a worried expression.

The former Senator replied, "Come now. Is that you, Georgie Yancy? You know this is not the same as that story in the song. That was your daddy's issue. Pay attention is all I'm saying. In addition to the land rezoning hearing at the Planning Commission this week, watch for any industrial rezoning. Mr. Goodbred has assured me there will be no intent to put heavy industry into his park. Make yourselves known at the hearings. Get your voices heard. Show up or send a letter to the commission. It will get there with just three lines. Those lines on the envelope would be Planning Commission on the first line and then under that write court house addressed to our county seat. Easy, see?"

I noticed Goodbred writing something on a pocket notebook and, with his mind absent for just those few seconds, he had lost control of the faltering old colleague on his board. He looked up in considerable concern for the first time as old Jimmie kept chugging along.

"The second issue is environment. I cannot speak to that. Is there an expert here who can? Trevor, sir?"

I noticed Goodbred cringe as Sen. Jenkins was overstepping his bounds and opening up the floor. And then, Goodbred nearly fainted, I think, when the State Fire Marshal Billy Mitchell raised his hand from the front row.

Jenkins, unaware that he had disturbed Goodie, said, "Oh hi, Billy. Come on up here boy to the mic. Hey everybody, it's Fire Marshal Billy. Ya'll know him."

Trevor Goodbred sprung out of his seat to head off Billy Mitchell only two steps from the audience. I could not hear, but it looked like Goodbred was whispering instructions to Mitchell as he speared an aggressive handshake toward Mitchell's midsection and held his hand tightly as he dropped his other arm over Mitchells shoulder. He walked the fire marshal in step to the mic and spoke first as he shouldered Mitchel off momentarily.

Goodbred offered, "If I may, Fire Marshal Mitchell has met with our board over the well and septic systems at the Trout Heaven Vacation Inn and plans to implement the latest, most environmentally sound infrastructures at each and every new building. I think, if I may sir, Mr. Mitchell could brief you on our plans. Thank you for coming, sir."

With that said, Goodbred began vigorously applauding as Mitchell grabbed the microphone stand and continued to shake his head in positive affirmation.

Was that enough Goodbred charm to control the fire marshal? I wondered.

Mitchell pulled out one of the *Save Our County Citizen's Movement* flyers from his orange and blue fireman's jacket peppered with sewed on patches of various civic groups. He ticked off general comments on each environmental complaint on the paper, beginning with the water question. "The wells on the high elevation of the mountain will not be sufficient to contain a fire at this time. Only at lower levels at the river will we be able to handle things if a forest fire breaks out from one of the camp sites, the restaurant, or along the golf course as presently planned. [He looked at Goodie.] We discussed that. Isn't that right Mr. Goodbred?"

"It is being addressed with your department," Goodie cupped his hands and said loudly with a smile.

"Yes, I know. I should have said that, sir. Thank you," added Mitchell.

Goodbred's head sunk into his shoulders as Mitchell then continued and revealed potential problems, "Their plan for a Crater

Lake waterways pier and entertainment center does call for fresh water wells to pump 450,000 gallons a week from our underground aquifer. Such a volume in neighboring counties where there is industry has caused surrounding residential and farm wells to dry up. We will monitor the plan. It might have to be delayed or cut back."

Goodbred shrugged with his shoulders as if to say 'whatever.'

Mitchell then told the crowd that he has heard that wastewater permits are being processed, silt control is being inspected and straight downhill roads were a mistake by the corporate developer and that Vacation Inns has agreed to recut those roads.

He said he didn't know anything about an endangered species called a bucktooth lizard but "I've heard its bite is harmless. Can't chomp down on ya."

The crowd roared with laughter as Mitchell laughed at his ridiculous comment.

Trevor Goodbred leaned over to whisper something to Tina, who immediately stood and walked to the microphone, "Thank you, Chief Mitchell. Very informative. We have one or two more panelists to meet with you, John Hancock, from Sassafras County, and manager of the Trout Heaven Vacation Inns and Resorts, and the dynamic Reverend Anita Rapshire, whom Mr. Goodbred and Mr. Levine recruited from Lynchburg, Virginia to manage memberships and finances. First, we give you your very own John Hancock."

I didn't know John was to speak and was concerned.

Without sharing with me, Tina had thought Handcock could be a more trustworthy advocate for the positive side of Vacations, the amenities and promises of the Trout Heaven location, than any other director could. And she thought that, for showing balance to the other presentations, Hancock was the only Crater Lake shore resident on the panel. She deliberately complied to pass by Bobby and to evidently get on with our special 'plants' in the audience as soon as she could. But Hancock would be worrisome.

John was smiling broadly, proudly. Just like in our meeting, the goofy guy hit the audience with his oddball brand of humor, "Hi Folks. You will be the first to know. I'm thinking of upgrading our entertainment at the Inn. How about another 3-day Woodstock-style concert right on Charity Mountain folks from the Inn to the river?"

A few teens and 20 somethings cheered like they were just freed from chains of zombie high school. Everyone else grumbled in shock.

"Nawh. Not gonna do that," Hancock said with a straight face.

"Well then, how 'bout this, folks: we'll have live entertainment in our new casinos to rival Reno or certainly do better than Charles Town Races and Casinos. We can invite Sinatra ... ah Nancy that is, or Wayne Newton maybe."

People started heckling rudely. One man threw a Coke bottle at him. He ducked. It whizzed past Goodbred, who looked as if he had begun to stand and give Hancock the hook.

"Nawh. Can't do that," John said. "No gambling license yet. But we could carve out a horse track for racing in the meantime, maybe circling the mountain. [The heckling reached a high volume.] Just kidding folks. Sure, there will be some famous singers or bands from time to time right here in your neck of the woods at Trout Heaven. But what we really intend to continue to offer is great vacations."

He began laughing at himself. He shrugged and flapped both hands at the audience in jest and landed them on his hips and began again, "Okay, I'm sorry. What I mean is this place is not drastic, not doing any of such crazy ideas. It's family vacationing. At Vacation Inns you stay where you love to play, we like to say.

"We have vacation packages for every one of every age. We have a Spa Package with an overnight room and a back, neck & shoulder massage, and a dinner. There is a Bed & Breakfast Package consisting of a room, buffet breakfast and free access to our many amenities—the pool, saunas, gym, nature trails and more. And, there is the Golf Package including a room, a round of golf, and dinner. We also offer a Spa and Golf Package.

"Rev. Rapshire will tell you about the membership deals. Just to preview, we offer guests lifetime memberships with any stay of three or more nights at any location. Memberships offer families heavily discounted vacation packages for return visits to any other nationwide location. How about that folks? Better than Woodstock or Reno, right?"

Tina stepped up after chatting briefly with Anita. Anita shook her head.

Tina said at the mic, "I think we can start with a few questions now before Mrs. Rapshire on membership opportunities. But before we start down the sign-up sheet, are there any questions for Mr. Mitchell or for Mr. Jenkins?" She was really pushing for chaos.

She gave John Hancock a pass on questions; likely on purpose. I thought his purpose may have been to set up an ambush as the night regressed. I hoped.

Tina pointed to the crowd, "I see a hand up in the back. Sir, wait for the hand-held microphone to reach you. We have gentlemen on each side there. Okay, what is your question?"

I was watching a master at work. Tina planned this. The evening's audience participation would begin with some pre-arranged softball questions from our plants, friends of the cause you might say.

As Jeb held the mic, the man with the first question began asking, "I'd like to ask Jimmy about that eight-hole golf course. Do you intend ..."

The audience burst into laughing and drowned him out for a minute.

"No, no," he said, "I've really got a question. Do you intend to continue to allow all the sediment to keep running off the hillside fairways and bunkers, because grass won't grow with people tramplin' up and down the inclines playing golf or riding in the carts? It all washes into our river. Did you know?"

Former Senator Jimmy Jenkins took forever it seemed to get his legs to lift him up again from his seat. He seemed to be spent.

As the audience murmured in a state of restless anticipation, they watched the old man awake from a daze, meander over to consult with Goodbred, then Hancock, and begin to speak to Tina. She accommodated him, holding his elbow. She led the old man to the microphone, reaching it perhaps six to eight minutes later. Finally, he asked, "What was that question again sir?" The audience again roared with laughter.

The man repeated the question and Jenkins said he hadn't seen the Trout Heaven Vacation Inn golf course, but would look into the problem.

As he turned to walk back to his seat, Jenkins nearly stumbled. Tina ran the few steps to help him. He whispered to her. She escorted him into the back of the hall and out of sight.

On the opposite side in the front, a lady then asked "Mr. Goodbar" if he or any of his "friends from Boston" had ever heard of the endangered species called the bucktooth, spotted lizard, "because I've lived here all my life and I haven't."

Tina acted like she didn't hear the question. She introduced Anita instead, who gave a brief outline of membership privileges and sat down quickly, seeming to be spooked by the proceedings. No personality at all. Odd, I thought too, she made no references to God, Jesus, or the divine Crater Lake.

Chapter 82

Goodbred glided confidently to the mic and reassured the lady that indeed he had heard of the bucktooth, spotted lizard. "My company is working diligently with the state department of environment."

He hadn't finished his lie when Tina seized the chance to trap him standing naked, so to speak, before his accusers. She interrupted, "Perhaps you can take the first question on the sign-up sheet now, Mr. Goodbred."

Bob McGarrell was already standing and taking the mic from Johnny Macintyre. The wiry frame of McGarrell appeared taller and more upright, transformed from the rather meek fellow we met at Joe's. He spoke directly with a cocky, macho tone that might intimidate Charlton Heston in Ben Hur.

I saw his demeanor and hoped that perhaps the dam was about to break that was holding back Vacation's dishonest doings from the public.

He said, "I'm Robert McGarrell, Cincinnati, Ohio. For the past five years your corporation grew faster than any hospitality firm in history, but ..."

Goodbred interjected, "Thank you kindly. That's right." He seemed bolstered and smiled broadly.

McGarrell stared bullets back at Goodie. Before Trevor could move another jaw muscle, McGarrell raised his voice and spoke rapidly, "but, your accelerating profits are a sham and a deceit to a vulnerable public and to your stock holders. How do you account for revenues skyrocketing as your company ages? It is unnatural, unless you are planning to skip out and leave us with a half-baked mess up on Charity Mountain?"

Even then, Trevor Goodbred just smiled and cocked his head in a pleasant pose. He said, "Wow, quite a falsely based indictment from this gentleman from Cincinnati, wouldn't you say, folks? Well, it is flattering to have such an out-of-state fan of Trout Heaven. If I may, sir, and I think I can speak for our panel, that you may be someone who indeed needs a vacation, Miss O'Leary would be pleased to offer a tour of our facilities. There are no grounds for your insinuations. Thank you, just the same."

Bob was just getting started, "No grounds? Ha! The grounds for my comments are solid. I know the time-tested trend in this category of business is when companies get older their income slows. And yes, my family did need a vacation. Our Trout Heaven trip was a sham. Now sir, I'm angry, yes sir. Your corporation, Mr. Goodbred, is still growing almost exponentially, *on paper*. I repeat, on paper only.

"The cash flow from its operations lagged behind its net income by 20 percent for the past three years. That does not make sense. Regulators are sure to start noticing and I think you know that better than anyone. And you are planning to vanish when they do, leaving these folks and stakeholders in your company nationwide holding and empty bag, sir."

I saw Trevor's bearing shaken. Again, ignorant of McGarrell's power, Goodie made another costly miscue, a cover up, "Folks, this fellow from Cincinnati has no way of knowing those things, They are …"

McGarrell sensed his prey was wounded and jumped in, continuing, "Vacation's long-term receivables, those of more than a year ahead, ballooned last quarter. That is a corporate a neon sign of aggressive or fraudulent accounting methods."

Goodbred leaned into Tina's ear. I later learned it was to ask her to cut off the rude man. Tina refused saying it was a free forum. Goodbred again smiled and condescended to the rude man, "How do you know, sir? Let's move on, shall we?" He again glanced at Tina who shrugged.

The crowd got angry. Someone shouted, "Let the man from Cinci talk!"

McGarrell replied, "How do I know?" I was fired last year by your former accounting firm G & M. I knew what was going on inside your fraudulent cesspool of deceit, sir."

The audience seemed to gasp collectively.

Trevor now wore an angry scowl and offered to shut him up, "I think that is enough, mister. This is our meeting to address any environmental issues for our rezoning proposals that are well and reasonable, not this finance jumbo mumbo."

McGarrell shook his fist in the air. He took two steps forward and continued, "This *is* environmental, a rotten economic environment for your supporters. It was your screwy pension assets that sent up a red flag for me last year and got me fired. Your shadow money man hiding down there in the front row in the green floppy hat, Mr. Simon Levine, reported an average of a 10 percent return on employee pension asset investments for nearly two years now. It is a lie. As a bookkeeper, I had never seen a company report pension assets rising so rapidly. You've got employees thinking they are earning time on pension. But it is a pension they will never see."

You could hear a pin drop as the crowd seemed mesmerized, not from the complicated finances Bob was spouting out, which few understood or cared to, but from his passion and anger.

He jumped on a chair and pointed to the first row, saying, "And on inventory, Mr. Levine. Sir, please stand and be seen. Tell us why Vacation Inns' receivable goods and inventories were growing faster than sales, while also reporting big-time inventory reserves piling up. You report supplies for Vacation Inn's sites—bed linens to hot dog buns to beach chairs—from companies that do not exist. I checked. You and your cronies are up to something, buddy boy."

The crowd applauded briefly and peacefully, as if expecting to hear more.

I took a peek out the window to see that Bob had spoken with no notes, just off the cuff. What a salvo. He seemed poised to storm the podium, but people nearby spoke to him and pulled him back into his seat. McGarrell's threatening tone was getting fanatic and I was glad he stopped before damaging his credibility.

I credit Tina with then maintaining order. She edged Goodbred to the side and asked for the next question. She covered her familiarity with Bob by saying, "Mr. McGrandall, we will look into your ideas. Thanks. I see the next name is a Miss Moore. Please stick to environmental topics if you will please Miss Moore."

The dark-skin lady in a gray business suit stood and said, "I am Valarie Smith Moore, senior partner in the New York office of

Braunstein, Gibson & Crockett and Columbia University professor of business mergers and acquisitions practices.'

Goodbred's voice cracked, "Nice to meet you Miss Moore."

"We've met previously, Mr. Goodbred."

Si Levine began coughing violently. He covered his face and exited quickly to the restroom behind the speakers. We learned later that he then slipped out the side door to the street.

Valarie addressed the panel, "As I said, we met at Luray Caverns, me and my little daughter. So, I decided to look into Vacation Inns. Not because it was desirable, but I think you know why.

"I have also discovered that you've cooked the books, as the previous speaker asserted, with your M&A's. That's mergers and acquisitions, for folks not familiar with corporate finances. Many of your acquisitions of unprofitable allied companies you reported to the SEC are phony. Others were accounted for by you as 2-way transactions of stock swaps that you fraudulently reported as assets and/or revenues. You have rolled up dozens of meaningless or non-existing partnering companies. Unlike growth acquisitions that were consistent with your products and services, when your firm was young, such as food, transportation, decorating, tour guides, and such, many of the recent acquisitions had nothing to do with what you do."

"Look here, miss," Goodie was flustered.

Rather than pause for his comment, she oh-so-gently blasted him, "These violations of the Securities and Exchange Commission's regulations are criminal and makes you and your executives liable for long vacations in federal prison. I intend to alert them."

Many in the audience cheer rowdily.

It was then possible that Trevor Goodbred seemed to recall meeting the lady. He slithered back to his seat and held his hand in his head to one side, leaving Tina to deal with Miss Moore.

Tina's performance was flawless. She said in all innocence, "Do you have an environment question, Miss Moore?"

I watched Tina carefully. I believe I alone could detect a slight smirk rising on one side of her mouth.

"No, I do not," snapped Valarie in a fake harsh tone. "Let me finish and don't try to shut me up again, please lady." She had met Tina and was fully aware, of course, that Tina was a co-conspirator. Valarie, as composed as always, then offered, "The company's so-called independent auditors, Granson & Granson, are really part of the corporation. Here is a cover story they slipped into their latest SEC report and I quote 'We have discovered some potential irregularities in the last quarter of last year' but then the annual report only mentioned that the report was "under review" by the accounting department'.

"Citizens, hear me. What this commonly means is that the company is delaying bad news to investors. I'm saying, by all the waving financial red flags, it looks like these guys are about to split! Take the money and run. Company accountants reported all the mergers and acquisitions, land purchases, and loans to a parent entity in the group called, Greater Ability Corp. And, that company does not exist."

As the crowd became angry with grunts, oh no's, and shouting obscenities, a sickened Rev. Sugarman walked out of sight to a backroom of the firehouse. That left only Goodie, Tina, Anita, and Hancock facing an increasingly restless crowd.

"Next?" Tina demanded. A question on the environment please. Yes, Mr. Macintyre? Oh, there you are in the audience and you were on the agenda. I apologize."

Bobby stood and asked for an explanation for company's expansion plans. I had to assume that he intended to clear the air before losing his exclusive commercial access to trout fishing on Crater Lake.

Goodbred pointed to his attorney, Mr. Turner in the front row next to Levine's vacated seat. Turner took the mic and proceeded confidently to provide a nonsensical legalistic answer that I took to mean that the company may expand or not, may want shoreline property or not, may petition the county for more rezoning or not. He didn't return to his seat either but exited in the back.

"Well that clears that up," Tina said, perhaps feeling a bit too good. I worried that it was showing. "Next on the sign-up sheet, let's see here, oh, it is of all people. There is Mr. von Kindel. Nice to see you, sir. We thought you returned to Europe when you left the firm."

Max, looking tanned and fit in a white silk suit, blue shirt and tieless, rose from his chair just outside the garage door opening holding two rolls of old fashion fax paper. "Always a pleasure to see you Miss O'Leary and you, Trevor. Congratulations on your new resort here. It is really something," he said with a trace of sarcasm not escaping the crowd.

I could hear snickering and shifting chairs.

"And yes, I now live in Europe but would not have missed this for the world. I saw the announcement in the Blue Hills Gazette on line." He lied. Tina had invited him.

"As the former CFO for this illustrious firm, I am impressed that you called this public meeting to address environmental issues of your resort. Need to do that nationwide Trev." [Sharper sarcasm was evident in his voice as he gained volume.] My question is about the brilliant membership environment of Vacation Inns. When we founded the chain, I suggested keeping two membership lists—those active, I mean wanting to remain members for frequent visits and visitor discount points, and those potentially signing up after one visit. Well, there are still two lists but the purpose has changed. I don't see your finance genius Simon Levine in the room now. He may be the only person familiar with the new purpose. In my two hands I hold the two lists of memberships. I received them on my old fax machine in my apartment."

He held out a roll of fax paper in his left hand and let the end drop. It unraveled to about three feet. "That is the real list of current memberships. And in my right hand …" He threw out the second roll of paper from his right hand that extended about 15 feet and fell over several rows of people who just laughed about it. "… is the so-called official list. This is the fake one that the corporation reports in the SEC statements to inflate revenues and impress investors. It is a fraud, Trevor Goodbred, and you…"

Goodbred ran to the mic, as Anita Rapshire slipped off to exit in the back and away from Goodie's view. Despite all the turmoil erupting in the crowd, Goodie still presented a calm demeanor, "My good man Max von Kindel. I am surprised and somewhat amused to see you here at a town meeting over a simple rezoning issue. Yes, I hired you in the beginning. But you no longer work for Vacation Inns because of your sloppy methods. I am pleased to announce here and now that no one in the corporation still calls you Max von Swindle, though that was a fitting moniker. We don't have a membership issue. We have a rezoning issue. If there are environmental concerns before we receive approval for that rezoning, let's hear them. Therefore, I beg the pardon of the citizens here when I must say bluntly sit down Mr. Max von Swindle."

There was laughter and I thought maybe some resurging support for Goodbred.

Max sat down without further protest. I wondered for a brief moment whether Goodbred may have something on him I didn't know about. I didn't have to wait long. Goodbred was showing confidence again, "Sheriff, if you would be so kind to remove those papers from Mr. von Swindle, ah, I mean Kindel?"

The sheriff didn't budge. During the entire proceedings, Sassafras County Sheriff Roger Deeds had been standing, arms folded, looking intimidating, at the side of the panel, at Tina's invitation. I hadn't notice how close he was.

Soon, he was flanked by two men at his sides wearing dark gray three piece pinstripe suits with short cropped haircuts and sunglasses.

Goodbred, still pointing to Deeds, then tried, "A few weeks ago at our annual banquet at Boston headquarters, as we celebrated well-deserved promotions of several senior staff, including our lovely vice president for public relations Miss Tina O'Leary here, someone broke into our financial records office. That I would surmise is our membership roll that you stole, von Kindel. You may still have a set of keys. Yes, that is it. That theatrical streamer you threw at our citizens is NOT a fake membership list. Please seize that man, Sheriff."

"Not my district, sir," said Deeds with a half grin that likely meant 'not on your life. sucker.'

Goodbred pleaded, "But it was Max who asked me to use a duplicate list and we fired him for it. Our membership list is real and legitimate."

"I'll take them Max," said Valarie Moore, who was still holding a mic and making her way across to take the two lists from Max.

Chapter 83

The performance to that point in the Town Hall meeting was all that Tina had hoped for. The crowd had turned on Goodbred, Levine had bolted in shame, Anita left embarrassed at the membership revelations, Turner and Rev. Sugarman were gone too, likely ashamed to be part of such criminal insinuating. I looked again and Hancock too was missing. Slick fellow.

She was left alone with Goodbred behind the microphone and several empty chairs from the departed former panelists. She rose to the mic, and to my great surprise, after recognizing the next, and as it turned out, the last questioner, she would also walk off after reading the name. She stared at the card with a frown, "The next question will be from D.D. Smith. I don't know if it is Mr. or Miss …"

She glanced up to see Donald Smythe walking right up to the front with one of the hand-held mics and stood near the sheriff.

Tina said, "Oh, Donald. My God. We've missed you." She removed the speaker's mic from the silver stand and meant to hand it to Goodbred. It fell hard on his crotch. She exited swiftly, out the back door.

"Oahff," Goodbred grunted audibly.

I had to chuckle, but was riveted to the scene unfolding on the monitor. Sheriff Deeds moved closer to Donald at the front of the audience facing Goodbred, now standing. Hefty Roger Deeds actually put his arm around Donald's boney shoulders, an obvious protective gesture. The two men in suits accompanying Deeds were close by and riveted on Trevor Goodbred.

"Well young man," Goodbred managed, "what is it? Do *you* have an environmental question?"

"It is me. Donald Smythe, alive and well. The name is Scottish for Smith, I think. Sorry for the deception. And I am sorry I have not been at work for the past several weeks as the Trout Heaven Vacation Inn and Resort bellboy, sir."

"That is quite alright." Goodbred smiled and seemed to regain some composure.

Donald pointed at him and said, "We have evidence that you arranged for your security chief, ex-convict Jack Mays to kill my grandfather, Manny Smythe, at our produce stand."

The crowd gave out a collective angry furor, temporarily overtaking Donnie's momentum.

He continued, "Mays thought I was the sole benefactor of the Smythe land on Crater Lake. I'm not. Uncle Roger was secretly married to my mother Elsie Smythe who passed many years ago. We, and I emphasize we, also have solid evidence that Mays also killed the publishers of the Patrick Weekly, Lane O'Leary and Shirley Fox."

The crowd was standing and in shock, some shouting obscenities at Goodie, who was backing his way toward the exit slowly.

Donald stepped closer, as his tenor drifted farther from his kind-hearted character, "You son of a bitch, you killed them. We have proof you basta…."

Deeds pulled him back by the shoulder, "I'll take it from here Donnie. Officers, if you will, please?"

The sheriff took the mic from Donald and stuffed it in his back pocket, while he took handcuffs from his belt. Cops in suits appeared. I don't know from where. On Deeds' order they held Goodbred by the arms. They led him out the side door and clicked handcuffs on him.

The mic was still live in Deeds back pocket.

Goodie said, "No, sir. I'm going. No need for that little side show. You will be hearing from my attorneys."

I went to the window and was stunned by what I saw. Dozens of cops on both sides of the firehouse began ushering out the audience swiftly and efficiently, as if rehearsed. They must have been recruited from all three counties. When they had the hall half empty, I heard voices again coming out of my TV monitor from the mic in Deeds pocket, I assumed.

I sat back down quickly to listen. There were no people on the screen just voices. A cop was reading the Miranda rights, "Trevor Goodbred, you are under arrest for the suspicion of planning and complicity in the murders of John Joseph Mays,

Emmanuel Smythe, Lane O'Leary, and Shirley Fox. You have the right to an attorney."

Goodbred replied angrily, "That is nonsense. Who says? Yes, that's right; I do. I want to call my attorney, you damn fools."

"You will have more than enough time for that at the station, sir," said a second voice, a familiar voice I concluded was Sheriff Deeds.

Who was the first cop? I wondered.

Goodie said, "Deeds, you've overstepped your authority. I don't care about the Smythe land. You and that kid, your stepson, can have it. I just want a resort motel here."

"Thought it was an inn?" the sheriff quipped.

"Of course, it's an inn. It is all over our publicity, our PR newsletter, this damn agenda for this stupid town hall meeting in a rat hole. Hey, where is Tina O'Leary?"

I wondered that too.

I climbed out of the cramped fire chief office and hid myself walking behind people exiting. I wanted a peak at Goodbred's encounter and to find Tina.

I managed to maneuver around several citizens to catch sight of Sheriff Deeds, Goodbred and two men in plain clothes, likely cops, walking toward a circle of policemen who had surrounded the four Vacation Inn limos, which were still blocked in by chairs.

I didn't want to be seen, but I heard someone shout, "Hey Hank, over here, over here." Beyond the crowd, there was Erich Lindstrom. I ran to him.

He spoke first, "What the hell happened here? Somebody get arrested for murder?"

I asked, "Accessory to, is what I heard. Man, am I glad to see you, Erich. And surprised. I didn't think Devin would ..."

"Devin doesn't know. I don't have a Monday deadline. Remember, the business section starts on Tuesdays. I came up on my own. So, you don't know why this guy is being charged?" Devin asked.

"No. I was not expecting anything like this. I've been counting on the financial frauds to take them down. The cops never told us Goodbred was under their radar too. The kid might have tripped this whole turn of events into action. As I told you at the paper, the town hall was about a rezoning request by Vacation Inns to get them to Crater Lake. That's the one the space ball hit."

Erich said, "Heard about it. Say, I was here on time but could not get in, amazing crowd, huh? I was in the back and couldn't see the questioners' faces. Do you know them? The sharp dressed black woman attorney, the hysterical young man shouting 'you bastard' and stuff? What a show this was. Not your typical small town meeting."

"Listen Erich. I know them all. My advice is to let me get them to you. First, go over to that country cop over there with some other cops. They are holding Goodbred, the CEO they arrested. I don't see him anymore."

Erich just nodded at this point to every suggestion.

I said, "That is Sheriff Deeds, Roger Deeds. If I were you, I'd start with him right away. He is the young man's stepfather, which no one knew until tonight. He didn't actually make the arrest. I think those plain clothes cops with him there did that. I don't know them. I would first ask why they are not going to the station yet and instead hanging around those ugly green limos. Call my cell later. I'll have the questioners for you. Go man, hurry. Don't let them get away. Just keep me out of it."

Erich waved his hand in approval as he ran toward the limos, now nearly free of exiting citizens. The cops were clearing the chairs to free the limos too. Curious, but I didn't want to know why. Not my story. Where was Tina?

After promising Erich his sources, I reached Donald Smythe first because he was still hanging around the side door of the firehouse and looked to be in a very sad state.

Donald had been staying in hiding with Sheriff Deeds, who did not raise Donald but had supported his education. Manny raised Donald after his mother, Deeds wife. Elsie died and a grieving Roger Deeds went to work in law enforcement in Pittsburgh. He returned home to run for Sheriff 15 years later.

As things turned out, Sheriff Deeds sheltered the boy after the shooting incident on the lake and the recovery of May's vehicle there. Donald and his estranged step-father Deeds were never before close, but in the past days they had bonded. I think Donald phrased it that way. Deeds told Donald that he never believed the rumors of killings associated with 'that Vacation gang' until they tried to harm Donald.

And then, Deeds began investigating background from other Vacation locations with the help of the FBI, Donald told me. That was the extent of Donald's explanation of his disappearance and bold re-appearance at the town hall.

He was trembling and anxious to leave with his step mother, Deeds second wife, Donna, who got to him as I did. She hugged him and they walked to her car.

I hoped to learn the rest of the details from the bizarre conclusion of the town hall meeting from Erich later that night at my cabin.

I tried to reach Tina via cell phones. I didn't leave a voice message when she failed to answer.

I got the firemen to take a half dozen of the folded chairs I'd rented for the weekend to the cabin. On my cell phone I quickly called Bob McGarrell, Anita Rapshire, John Hancock, Johnny Macintyre, his brother Jeb, Valarie Moore, and von Kindel to invite them to meet with me and Erich. McGarrell and Moore agreed, who were all still checked into the O'Leary Hotel in Patrick. Johnny also agreed to meet. Rapshire and Hancock didn't answer my call.

Chapter 84

"What a cool cabin in the woods, Hank," Erich said when he arrived around 10 p.m. "I had no idea."

"Good. It was supposed to be my hideaway from the Inquirer and my ex-wife. But I will soon give it up. Welcome and thanks for coming. I introduced him to the others. Before he listened to their thoughts and facts on Vacation, we listened to Erich, who somehow liked my coffee.

Erich explained, "They were all in the limos. A cop got into each one and once the crowd disappeared they were escorted by police cruisers to the cop station. I followed. Quite a parade."

He was thoroughly enjoying himself.

I felt vindicated of my guilty conscience over dropping the story.

I prompted him, "Who?"

"Who was in the limos?" Erich asked.

We all responded anxiously, 'Yes, who?'

"The Vacation execs. At the station, first to climb out was that amazing redhead Tina O'Leary. Then, Goodbred got out with a cop on his arm. What a stupid name, huh?"

"And?" I asked eagerly.

"I learned their names. Let's see." Erich pulled out the tiniest of notebooks, ala classic TV's Lt. Columbo. He felt around for a pencil. "Oh yes, here they are. John Hancock, the funny one. Anita Rapshire, who is really a church lady. And, there was a Mr. Turner, board member ..."

"That would be attorney James Whitfield Turner, the chief operations officer," I said. "I'd go light on Hancock. He is a local who was leaving Vacation anyway. And Rev. Rapshire. Well, what can I say? Please get a quote from her concerning when and how she has learned about the crooked membership scheme. She is a fine person who came in innocently to the company and has since expressed her regrets to Max von Kindle, the guy who threw the rolls of paper."

Erich continued, "And Jimmy Jenkins, that creaky old fellow, who told me immediately he was the vice president's brother. I hadn't asked him anything yet. There were two FBI agents too, those guys with the shades and three piece gray suits sweating up there with Deeds at the Town Hall. Didn't get to talk with them, damn it."

I wondered if he'd seen Simon Levine.

"No. There was no Simon Levine. Who's that?"

"The real comptroller, an ex-con who was up front in the floppy hat. See if anyone at all has seen him."

Erich stayed the night on my couch after taking copious notes from my sources, who graciously and patiently held no information back until after 1 p.m. and two pots of coffee.

I emailed a digital copy of the video recording we made of the town hall meeting to him at the paper.

His story, which Devin Shay got on A1 with a mug shot of Goodie, appeared on Tuesday under the headline:

Vacation Inn Chain CEO Linked to Multiple Killings.

His follow up piece on Thursday quoted sources on alleged financial frauds of the Vacation gang, but with little supporting facts or figures.

Chapter 85

Summer solstice, sunny early afternoon.

I invited friends to my new log home on the riverfront property I got from John Hancock. It was a tribute luncheon to remember Manny Smythe on the anniversary of his death.

Donald Smythe brought his new bride Elizabeth. She was a nurse he met at the hospital while waiting for injured Bradley Armstrong in the E.R. last summer.

John Hancock and his wife, Belle, came partly to see the house Bobby and sons built for me on my 20-acre slice of their land, which extended down to the Sassafras River, with no view of Crater Lake.

Clarence and Anita Rapshire came to stay overnight after their drive down from Lynchburg. She got her old job back at her church there.

Roger Deeds and wife Donna were also my special guests that day.

Bobby Machintyre and his sons promised to come but were booked solid with fishing charters and sent their regrets by email. I saw them frequently anyway when we fished local streams.

And, Valarie Moore also had a scheduling conflict.

Bob McGarrell called to say Alice would rather go to hell than go anywhere near Trout Heaven again. He thanked me for inviting them.

And Shannon, Colin and Tom O'Leary stayed away for fear of exposing their central roles in the behind-the-scenes publicity machinery that helped take down Vacation, though in the end we were clearly trumped by the homicide arrests.

(Oh, had we only known that Sheriff Deeds and Donnie had been working with the FBI and state police in several states for several weeks to nail Goodbred and Mays.)

The most surprising guest, but perhaps not so much though, considering the trout streams nearby, was Stan Monroe, who accepted my invitation to the celebration and some fly fishing to get away from his dreaded New York City confines.

Monroe's reporting on Vacation Inns and Resorts took on another direction, he told us, after the Inquirer exposed the financial fraud and covered the bizarre town hall meeting with Goodbred's arrest. Ironically, considering the fake environmental scare we promoted at the town hall meeting, The Times reported on newly uncovered evidence of a federal incinerator and medical waste facility, which had been destroyed by the meteorite that created Crater Lake. Scientists at the University of Maryland's Department of Marine Biotechnology in Baltimore theorized that residues of biological compounds from the destroyed plant may have caused rainbow trout trapped in the lake to grow faster and reproduce without migrating. No one knew for sure but the fish were not deemed to be toxic, yet perhaps not in the healthiest waters ecologically.

While overlooking the Sassafras River, we sat around before dinner in a semi-circle chatting when we heard …

"Anyone for drinks, appetizers? Tina asked as she sprang onto the porch with a tray of snacks. "They are from Smokey's Café."

In came Joe and Eloise, all smiles. Joe shouted, "Best Darn Cookin' East of Tennessee. Hey, Donnie. Good to see you."

"I'm glad to see anyone," Donald remarked, "especially you and Tina."

Tina asked again for drink orders going to each of us, while Eloise trailed and repeated them, memorizing them.

Everyone chatted pleasantly.

I still could not stop my eyes from following Tina's every move, every gesture. There she was happy and healthy after facing and surviving multiple layers of extreme danger dealing with the Vacation gang, especially her bosses.

The women wanted to see her diamond ring. The Monday after that fateful day of the amazing town hall meeting I asked her to marry me. I had to wait for her release after questioning that Sunday night by Deeds, law officers from Massachusetts and FBI agents, all of whom had been sniffing into the hijinks of Goodie and Si.

Oh yes, the house. It is and all log home with four bedrooms, two bathrooms, two stories with a stone foundation and fireplaces, wrap around porch, and large windows in the front triangle to the peak of the pitched roof. Cost? $400K. Nice, huh? Tina paid half, part of the stock options she cashed in two days before the town hall meeting. Mary Marinaro kept it off the books until the next week. Why not? Just another bookkeeping trick. Who will ever know, right?

Understandably, Mary had assumed a very private profile after Vacation's troubles became public and therefore we didn't expect her at the house the day of our tribute to Manny. Her secrets will stay with us. In addition to Tina cashing out the Thursday before the meeting, Mary also temporarily concealed the stock option take out by John Hancock, Anita, and Levine's assistant Pauline, in addition to Mary's own. None of the above had reported for work that Friday in November before the town hall meeting.

Tina handed Anita's husband Clarence a Budweiser just when he was asking the group, "So, you all didn't really need to use all that stuff against them about memberships and pensions anyway? We are grateful for that, my wife being part of that end."

"Nope, didn't need it," Tina said, "nor fake mergers and acquisitions, marketing, false revenues, incestuous board of directors, phony auditors, falsifying SEC reports (pause). What a burden it was, but I'm not thinking it was wasted. Did I forget anything, Hank?"

"Swiss bank accounts. But, we gave the feds plenty of ammunition," I said. "They have it all now."

Donald said, "Well, the government is getting them anyway, just as good, right?"

I agreed and said, "The Securities and Exchange Commission will have its turn after the murder trials. We provided a high profile to the finances. I'm sure we helped. My business editor even gave his SEC source a copy of the town hall meeting tape. There is a lot for the feds to chew on.

"But you folks might not know—I know Anita does after being cleared of charges—that they are really after Simon Levine, who is still a fugitive. Look over your shoulder Anita."

Anita was shocked, "What? Why me?"

"No, no. Just look over your shoulder now," I said, laughing and pointing to Tina, just off Anita's shoulder coming from behind. Tina handed her a glass of Chateau Francois Pinot Noir. I continued, "The former unofficial financial executive Levine was last seen in Toronto and has disappeared after being hit with nearly $120 million in civil charges and fines in cases filed by the SEC. So good luck Si!"

Retired Sheriff Roger Deeds reminded everyone that Trevor Goodbred was still being held for accessory to several additional murders or missing persons, which Goodie may have believed to be justified to keep his dream alive. "According to reporting by Erich in the Inquirer," Deeds said, "Goodbred was a sort of serial director of killings, starting even before his Vacation Inn scheming. Levine was evidently innocent of any involvement in the killings. I doubt if such a dedicated company man even knew. He is a shadow exec you can't see."

Tina handed a Yuengling to Donald, as he asked me, "Mr. Ford, did Mr. Goodbred then have Jack Mays killed?"

Tina left the room for more drinks.

"Maybe. There could have been a rift in their relationship, sure. For years, though, I think he owed favors to Mays. Many years ago, Goodbred hired Jack Mays, a recently released convicted murderer, to kill Trevor's father who had become a drunken bum in Boston. He always hated is dad for beating his mother, who remarried a business tycoon and was able to finance Trevor's college days. I think Erich reported that in his articles. Goodbred went to college in Florida for a while at least. Later he attended the University of Maryland Smith School of Business where he first met fellow student and future business conspirator Simon Levine. That about right, Sheriff?"

Deeds nodded while accepting a VO and water from Tina.

I told my guests about Trevor's first scheme, pretending to be the wealthy heir to the Chummy Chowda Cafes in Boston, when he lied that the chain was owned by his father, who by then was on skid row, living in the park, Boston Commons. "I guess he asked Mays to make his father vanish before anyone checked."

"Amazing. I still think all this is amazing. The man was so pleasant," said Anita. "I need to minister to him in prison. What a lost soul."

Clarence Rapshire dropped his beer. "Oh, please don't, dear. Sorry Hank." He got up. "I'll get a towel."

"It's treated deck wood. Don't bother," I said.

All agreed Trevor was charming. Anita was deep in thought, perhaps praying for him. She then said in a tranquil voice, "What fools so many were so betrayed by you, Mr. Goodbred. In the end, [as she recited by memory from the Bible] it was not an enemy that reproached me; then I could have borne it: neither was it he that hated me that did magnify himself against me; then I would have hidden myself from him. But it was thou, a man mine equal, my guide, and mine acquaintance. We took sweet counsel together, and walked unto the house of God in company."

Clarence stood and pulled his wife to her feet and they hugged. He said to her, "Psalms 55, right Sugar Babe? Just take it easy."

"Yes," she said, and they took their seats again. She said to everyone, "This man, this company, is what I, everyone there, believed in. And he betrayed us for his own greed and revenge. It is truly Trevor Goodbred's own self, really, who betrayed him to himself."

Everyone was nearly moved to tears, not for Goodie, but for all the damage he had inflicted on so many people in the region, not to mention in other Vacation Inns around the country.

I spoke up to revive the happy celebration, "A toast? Tomorrow's upon us friends; let's drink to our health and survival."

The toast was roundly approved, all standing except John Hancock. When all returned to the seats he said, "Not all will be forgiven. Trevor Goodbred was Hitler's worst dream. We all hated him. At least Hitler's leaders could fraternize with the devil. But, Goodbred's diabolical behavior didn't stop at his inner circle. You always looked around to see if he was coming. He fired people on whims. He berated us in private. Now, we know he hired to kill."

Donald asked Hancock, "Do YOU know if he had Mays killed?"

Tina entering the porch again made an about face. "Oh, I forgot napkins again."

"Probably," I said, "although blood never touched Trevor's hands. My guess? An educated one? Mays' string had run out."

Hancock had everyone's undivided attention. Even Tina hung by the porch door to listen. Hancock speculated what would later that year come out at Trevor Goodbred's trial, that he had a contract on Mays that night he was knifed to death on the parking lot on Cape Cod.

Roger Deeds also reminded us what had been published, "And, Massachusetts State Police knew Vacation was a sham and was also on Goodbred's trail. They called in the FBI, which was taping phones at Cape Cod Vacation Inn and Resort, which included the executive suites in the old school building."

"Tapping phones in that rat trap would be kids play," Hancock added. He described a scenario fit for Goodbred and again it played out later at his trial. Emails implied Goodbred was paying Mays for more than security. Mays salary also reflected his pay for hits. The FBI phone tap was the clincher. Agents broke code words linked with the names of people later found dead in conversations between Goodbred and Mays. Those likely hits by Mays were only those discovered by the agents. No one will ever know how many people Goodbred deemed as threats to his ambitious rise in wealth and power, as he spread his expansion formula nationwide in towns like ours."

Hancock was aware of the O'Leary's presence as he laid out his theory and he avoided mentioning Tina's parents and their murder. But we all knew they were the most egregious of all. We fell silent when John Hancock, in all seriousness for once, concluded his speculations on the lecherous Mr. Goodbred. Tina handed him a glass of Merlot and a straight Old Grand Dad to me.

The conversation turned to the Smythes and many, many colorful stories of the old farmer, Manny.

Chapter 86

Meanwhile a half world away in many ways, former Vacation Inn's executive chauffeur Gordo Jones dialed Tina's cell from a hallway just outside of a physician's office in a suburb of Zurich Switzerland:

"Gordo? Is that you?" she answered in our kitchen while fixing more trays of snacks for our luncheon on the deck.

At that very time, I had come into the kitchen to check whether I could help carry drinks and snack trays. She put her hand on the phone when I asked, "Who's that, Max? [my usual tease]"

Hand still on the phone, she whispered, "Gordo."

"Who?"

"The chauffeur Gordo Jones. Remember? He's still with Levine. Be quiet, Hank."

I pulled her into the living room where she put him on speaker to let me listen.

Tina said to Jones, "I thought we lost touch with you. We are having a luncheon to remember Manny Smythe. You should come; where are you?"

"I can't say. I just called to say they will probably never catch Simon."

"Levine? Why?"

"I know you'd disapprove, God knows I love ya girl. I would not want to disappoint you after all we went through with that Vacation Inn gang. But Simon hired me to drive for him after the company collapsed. He paid me a king's ransom. Couldn't walk away and besides, I still kinda like the guy."

Tina's eyes flared as she gave me a laughing smile and told Jones, "Tell me everything."

Jones, continued, "He's in there, getting plastic surgery. Wants to look like Trevor Goodbred. We found this doctor who does movies stars, they say.

"So, we got him all dressed up in black hat with brim and an all-black suit. He's got this long full black beard now too. We got to this doc he was closing his practice today."

"At 1:00 p.m.?" Tina asked. "Wow, he must be good. Better than the old banker's hours, eh?"

Jones slipped up and said, "No, it's like seven or something. Oh, no it's not. Must be jet lag. My watch stopped. Forget that. Wanna hear the story, or not?"

"Sorry."

I went in with him. He stares at the plastic surgeon like some lost soul on his last hope and says—you are not going to believe this—he says ... (pause)

"What? What? You are killing me, Gordo."

"He says, just as serious as can be, 'Just make me handsome, doctor. I can pay anything you like. And taller, okay?' The doctor says with this harsh German accent, 'Come back in two weeks after you shave and clean up,' says the doctor. He leans down into Simon's hairy face and adds, 'And don't wear that silly Rabbi outfit, will you? It is phony. I don't know what you have done, sir. But, you certainly stand out like that.'

"Simon stands and demands, 'I can't come back in two weeks. Do it now.' Doc says he can't, office will close soon.' Simon puts a roll a hundreds in the doc's hands, U.S. dollars, and says, 'Good. Do it then, I can pay ten times your normal rate. Please.'"

Tina was choking down laughter, holding down the phone between her knees. She recovered as I waved my hands toward her, implored her to continue. "That is amazing, Gordo."

"That's not all. The doctor takes him aside and counts the money. He says, 'It will take me a little while to prep for measurements, x-rays and such. Wait out there.' Our notorious Simon Levine then thanked the reluctant doctor," Jones said.

Jones was laughing as he added, "As the doctor walked back to his little O.R., Simon shouted from the empty waiting room to him, 'Remember? Handsome.' I got out of the room before I burst out laughing and called you. I had to tell somebody. Thought of my old gossip buddy, Tina O'Leary back home. So Tina dear, I don't think the cops will ever find my drinking buddy Simon Levine any time soon."

He said as he left the room he had handed Levine the waiting room copy of the International Herald Tribune and could hear Levine mutter, "Well, I'll be."

A little Googling on my smart phone revealed a headline from yesterday's International Herald-Tribune:

Infamous Trout Heaven Inn at Crater Lake Up for Auction
Giant Fish in Lake Freed to Migrate "At Last," say Feds, via New River Outlet
by Stephen Monroe, courtesy of the New York Times

* * *

After our guests left on that very pleasant afternoon, Tina and I sat on our porch with brandy avoiding the obvious.

"I finally breached the subject on both our minds, "Tina, your friend Gordo said our favorite fugitive Simon Levine was reading the International Herald Tribune at the surgeon's office. That is sold in Europe."

"Right. I think he said it was about 7 o'clock there," Tina said, staring into her brandy. "That puts him somewhere in mid Europe. From the number on my screen, he was in Zurich, Switzerland. I looked it up."

"Right. Seems so."

"Well?"

"Well, what?"

"Well then, we know where Simon Levine is. So?"

"So, what?"

"So ... are you going to ...?"

I quickly cut her off, "Not on your life. Let's go fishing."

Epilogue
Current late afternoon, near Patrick.

The day is perfect for fly fishing in a swift trout stream in an eastern mountain forest.

A woman is leading a man carefully downhill on a narrow, rocky trail. Relaxed and alert, they listen and enjoy the sound of Foster's Creek. Without saying a word, they each 'feel' the sound getting louder.

"I can hear it running full now," he says at the top of a small ridge.

The sound dominates the valley surroundings as they arrive. It is a sound not easily described. As the shallow water of Foster's Creek rushes sharply over the stream bed of smooth rocks and gravel, it is not a burbling sound. It is not trickling, babbling, tumbling or a bubbling, or even a grumbling and growling sound. It is all of it, a fly fishing allegro dominating the woods as they arrive at the stream.

This, their favorite creek, flows west into the Madison River toward Kentucky, not east to the Sassafras, serving them as another comfort after too many anxious days near that river and freaky Crater Lake. The change was simply psychological.

They stand and admire the gray green cool water splashing up in frothy white patches and swirling arches of the flowing current that reflects flashes of the warm afternoon sun. For a few moments, they peer into the streaming water's uneven surface to adjust their vision underneath hoping to spot trout on the prey for bugs or moving from spot to spot.

They separate to start fishing. Free of worries, souls at peace, they will play in the stream until dark before walking back up the trail to Smokey Joe's Café for supper.

They wear no traditional fishing waders. They carry no heavy gear. They each carry an insulated catch basket across the shoulder, fly fishing poles and flies in satchels. They plan to get wet and enjoy it, wearing only tennis shoes, tee shirts, khakis and baseball caps, his New York Mets, hers Pittsburgh Pirates. This is not a planned fishing trip.

"Spontaneous is always best," she says.

"I agree. But will the trout like it?" he asks. He cups his hands to give her a tempered shout as they separate. He tries to annoy her with, "But will you spook the rainbows with your orange sneaks? And, hey girl, "Better tuck in your hair. They know you with that red flag waving behind you. Don't want to give me more advantage than I already have."

They laugh quietly.

"They will more likely be spooked by you, stranger, not me," she teases.

There is clear purpose to her movements as she treads from boulder to boulder along the stream bank to reacquaint herself with her favorite fishing hole since her childhood, about 150 feet downstream. She whispers to still-hidden trout, "Let's show him the state teen champ still has it, ladies."

He watches her and guesses as much. She is out to out fish him. But, he'd rather admire her ways.

She points the 9-foot flexible fishing rod up and away from her body. And, with the grace of a ballerina and strength of a gymnast, she then whips it straight overhead five times before throwing it out, each time extending more line. The relatively small backward and forward motion of the fly rod sends the line streaking through the air. With a small plop her feather-light fly and hook drops 50 feet downstream exactly where she intended.

It is a narrow section of the creek where trout are more confined and, as her theory goes, will more likely be hooked. But, the winding stream though is bordered with overhanging swamp birch, maples and scrubby willows and service berry. She has told him time and again to cast high to avoid snagging the branches.

Still, his first cast upstream is not arched straight and it hits light-pink rhododendron flowers hanging low over the stream. He whispers to himself, "Hope she didn't see that ... oh, damn."

She did.

She laughs at him until her line tugs tight against her wrist. Her spinning reel whizzes. She's got the first hit where she tossed the fly by a whirling pool of water beside a large boulder. She tugs, lets out line, tugs again, spins, tugs, spinning out less line each time as a rainbow trout fights, splashing and flipping about on the surface. She nets it, unhooks its jaw and gently lowers it into her basket and closes the lid.

Tina catches three more at her favorite 'hole' before Hank lands his first trout. No matter. He has been continually watching her, thoroughly entertained and totally unconcerned with her competitive prodding and joking. He is truly contented, having already landed the best catch of his life, Miss O'Leary.

#

Made in the USA
Middletown, DE
20 November 2018